the THOMASITE

THE THOMASITE

Victoria A. Grageda-Smith

ORANGE BLOSSOM PUBLISHING

Maitland, Florida

Orange Blossom Publishing
Maitland, Florida
www.orangeblossombooks.com
info@orangeblossombooks.com

First Edition: May 2023

Library of Congress Control Number: 2023907223

Edited by: Arielle Haughee
Formatted by: Autumn Skye
Cover design: Sanja Mosic

Print ISBN: 978-1-949935-62-2
eBook ISBN: 978-1-949935-63-9

Printed in the U.S.A.

For Steve, my *Americano,* who paused the world,
enabling me to hop off the carousel and write this book.

Those who cannot remember the past are condemned to repeat it.

Santayana, *The Life of Reason*

CONTENTS

CHAPTER 1

Voyage to the Unknown

Eleanor Karsten heaved a sigh as she stood on Dock 12 of the Frisco port. Like a mother leaving her young child in school on the first day of classes, she cast an anxious last glance at her steamer trunk and crate of books. Especially the books. Her eyes followed the derrick as it lifted her precious cargo onto the ship, where they'd be kept in the storage hull for the month-long voyage across the Pacific.

She examined the ticket the steward had given her—checking her name, freight details, and port of destination. Assured all was in order, she closed her eyes and, in deep, slow breaths, willed a blanket of quietude against the churning chaos and chatter around her. Sensing a shadow passing over her, she glanced up.

An albatross circled like a carousel in the pale blue sky—gliding, dipping, rising—until it caught an air current and rode it to the open sea. A westerly wind fluttered the brim of her hat and blew a few curly tendrils off her golden chignon. Bayside, the breeze traced soft, concentric rings on the silvery-ceil waters and swept toward the hills, chasing away the fog's last specters. Eleanor decided all these augured well for her new adventure on this fine morning of July 23rd, 1901. And she smiled.

She turned her gaze toward the vessel, a colossal white knight on the water. Painted in crisp, black, bold script near the bow on the starboard side was her name: *U.S. Army Transport Thomas*. All of 467 feet long, with a carrying capacity of more than 7,000 gross tons, she was, according to the briefing packet from the Office of the Secretary of War, the newest, biggest transport ship in the service of the United States. Eleanor smiled and saluted the vessel by tapping the right side of her hat with her index finger.

She felt for her reticule hanging on the crook of her left arm. It held her identification and appointment papers and a few banknotes. Reassured the items were secure, she pulled her day gloves higher on her wrists, picked up her Gladstone travel bag, gripped her umbrella, and marched toward her fellow teachers boarding the ship.

The newspapers said there were an astounding 509 of them. Some appeared to have even brought along their spouses and children. Lugging grips, sacks, portmanteaus, parapluies, and a menagerie of caprice, such as victrolas, easels, and bird cages—with the poor screeching birds inside—the throng of teachers looked like a veritable twentieth century Noah's ark parade. Or an army of worker ants hauling provisions to their nest. Yes, an army. For what else would an army transport vessel transport? Eleanor preferred, however, to think they were a different kind of army: an army bearing benevolence—just as President McKinley said they were.

A little more than a year ago, the Division of Insular Affairs of the Office of the Secretary of the Interior had put out a call for teachers to help establish a public school system in the new U.S. territory in the Far East: the Philippine Islands. Eleanor knew little of that part of the world, except that her country had paid Spain $20 million for it under the Treaty of Paris, which officially ended the Spanish-American War. After five years of teaching at a one-room school in the heart of Iowa farm country, she was sure that was where she wanted to go.

With no expectations, she mailed her application to Washington, D.C. Three months ago, she received her appointment—much to her shock and delight. It gave her just enough time to close her affairs in Iowa and arrange for her train passage to San Francisco.

Seeing herself amid the chosen pedagogues now, a warm feeling unfurled in her chest. The nation's leaders and newspapers had lauded them as "America's best and brightest"—bestowed with a noble mission: to uplift their little brown brothers and sisters from the dark age of feudalism to which Spain had abandoned them and bring them into the light of industrial-era American democracy. The President described their goal as "winning hearts and minds" under a policy he called "the benevolent assimilation of the Filipino." Eleanor was partial to the notion.

The teachers trudged up the gangplank, pushing Eleanor along with them. Short-winded and choked by the congested group ascent, she turned her face upward to suck in the fresher air above the mass of sweaty, musky bodies pressing against her. When she reached the main deck and came within sight of the grim-looking quartermaster, Captain Coulling, she observed how the officer processed the passengers. As her turn with him came, she stated her name and presented her credentials. A subtle smile on Captain Coulling's face registered in the raised tips of his handlebar mustache before he handed Eleanor a key labeled with her deck and cabin number. She smiled back at him.

The *Thomas* had other names in prior lives—the most recent of which was the *Minnewaska*, which served the cattle trade between New York and London. The U.S. Army christened her with her current name when, on the eve of the Spanish-American War, it purchased, refitted, and commissioned her to transport troops, horses, and commissary supplies to Cuba and Puerto Rico.

Eleanor grinned to herself, amused that a vessel that once transported cattle now practically served the same purpose, for there was no better way to view the corralling of people out of their frenzied confusion into the pens of their assigned cabins. Other spectacles ensued as the passengers—composed not only of teachers and officials of the Office of Public Instruction, but also soldiers and army officers— spilled onto the various decks looking for their quarters. Adding to the ruckus was the discovery of a stowaway whom a couple of the crew had collared and thrown back to the wharf to much cussing by the expelled. Many of the teachers returned to the quartermaster to argue about their accommodations.

It appeared there weren't enough staterooms—particularly for the ladies. Thus, a series of rooms designated as the "Women's Quarters" had been improvised under the dining saloon. The gentlemen were appointed to the troop decks along with the soldiers enroute to reinforce the army of invasion still subduing pockets of insurrection on the islands.

Eleanor sighed in relief when she found her cabin on the regular passenger deck, glad it wasn't in the Women's Quarters. She could just imagine what rackets would likely be heard under the dining saloon.

Her name appeared on a sheet stuck on the door that listed the room's designated occupants.

Miss Ida Covell, Michigan; University of Michigan 1875

Miss Eleanor Karsten, Iowa; Iowa Normal School 1895

Miss Maude Bancroft, New York; Radcliffe College 1899

Miss Arabella Palmer, Connecticut; Radcliffe College 1899

She knocked. Hearing no answer, she unlocked the door and entered. A mere sliver of floor space separated a pair of bunk beds consisting of stacked double berths. At the foot of each lower berth sat a steamer trunk. It was the kind that opened on one side into a hanging compartment for ladies' frocks and, on the other, compartments and drawers for folded clothes, shoes, and travel accessories. Eleanor thanked herself for having packed minimally, for there was no way the room could accommodate another trunk. To supplement what she was wearing, she had packed her Gladstone with an extra blouse and skirt with matching waistcoat, a corset, two sets of stockings, three pairs of underpants, and basic toiletries: bar of soap, towel, and two sets of rags for her menses. The bulk of her clothes and other personal effects were inside her steamer trunk in the cargo hull.

One of her cabin mates appeared to have had the good sense to pack the way she did. A travel bag and umbrella lay on one of the two lower berths. On the two upper berths, hat boxes and sundry personal items were strewn about as though their owners couldn't wait to return outside. Eleanor likewise tossed her Gladstone and umbrella on the remaining lower berth and proceeded to the main deck. Many of her fellow passengers were already gathered there, waiting for the departure fanfare to begin.

She surveyed her fellow passengers, curious if she'd recognize anyone. She didn't. *How silly of me to think otherwise!* It wasn't as if she met other teachers enough to make friends, although she did manage to attend one teachers' congress, the one held in Chicago last year. That was where she learned of the call for volunteer teachers to teach Filipino boys and girls.

She estimated the male teachers outnumbered their female counterparts by twice. Moreover, the men did not appear limited to the Anglo-Saxon race. Eleanor spotted Italians, Turks, Africans, Indians, and Chinese from their fezzes, caps, and silken robes. Apart from such cultural markers, the men were almost indistinguishable from each other, for they had dutifully donned the universal gentleman's uniform: starched white collar, three-piece lounge suit, and frock coat—topped by a Homburg, bowler, or summer boater straw hat.

To designate seniority, they seemed to distinguish themselves based on whether they were bearded, mustachioed, or clean-shaven, such that more facial hair suggested greater seniority. Eleanor considered, however, that higher social status often corresponded with older age, which explained the inverse ratio of men's scalp to facial hair. As head mops receded, facial hair flourished! Eleanor tittered, inviting curious and disapproving glances. She fished a handkerchief from her reticule and covered her mouth to suppress her laughter.

The ladies looked regal and confident in their high-collared blouses, waist jackets, and skirts that hugged hips before flaring down into hems that hinted at Balmoral ankle boots. The women also appeared professional yet feminine through the softening of the vestiges of Victorian style. They wore wide belts that cinched waistlines, thus creating the illusion of small waists and curvy hips. Flowers, feathers, and lace embellished their hats into millinery masterpieces that framed their brimmed Gibson Girl hairstyle, a look made popular by the eponymous male illustrator whose drawings of the ideal woman had graced many magazines and newspapers.

Eleanor smiled to herself. If she squinted, she could almost imagine the ladies as a flock of birds, not because of their feathered hats and stoles, but due to the new corset that molded their bodies into a uniform pouter-pigeon shape. Women literally bent over to wear it because fashion mavens, who happened to be all men again, extolled the new undergarment as most conducive to producing the perfect female shape for the new millennium. Eleanor tugged at a spot where her corset chafed against her rib bone, realizing with shame she wasn't immune to the illicit persuasion.

A singing of "My Country 'Tis of Thee" spontaneously erupted from the people on both deck and dock. Soon, there were hardly a set of dry eyes except for Eleanor's. As she gazed at the sea of waving hands and fluttering handkerchiefs, she realized she had no one to say goodbye to among the well-wishers. But she waved anyway, for it seemed the proper thing to do when departing the only country one had ever known to journey into the unknown.

Just before the singing ended, Eleanor caught sight of a rowboat hurrying toward the *Thomas*. The crowd cheered as sailors threw a rope at the man in the boat and hoisted him to the ship until he managed to climb over the railing, swing himself onto the deck, and land within inches from Eleanor's feet. The young man glanced up at Eleanor with bright eyes and smiled. "Pardon my entry, ma'am!"

Onlookers jockeyed to get a closer look and chat with him, pushing Eleanor out. She walked away smiling, knowing how nothing fascinated Americans more than one who'd triumphed against great odds to achieve a goal. It was the same spirit that compelled the passengers of the *Thomas* to leave the comforts of home and partake in America's bold, new experiment in the tropics.

At noon, the ship left the dock and anchored in the bay. The luncheon bell rang and turned the throng of teachers into a hungry pack of wayfarers who streamed down the hatches into the dining saloon. The men forewent with removing hats and overcoats, crowded the tables, grabbed whatever they could snatch from the trays carried by passing waiters, and hollered for more food. The women hung onto civilized decorum, glaring at what, only a few minutes earlier, appeared to be gentlemen—now reduced to the manner of newsboys and bootblacks. It was perhaps this show of unequal talent for aggressiveness that prompted the quartermaster to appoint separate dining areas for the genders, allocating the dining saloon to women and the hurricane deck forward to men.

The sun was an hour and a half past meridian when the *Thomas* set out for the open sea. The ship passed through the Golden Gate strait that led from the grayish-blue waters of San Francisco Bay to the aquamarine depths of the Pacific Ocean. Neptune appeared to bless the voyage through three gentle giants. Whales of the blackfish kind, about fifteen to forty feet in length, breached the surface and spouted, as though toasting the voyagers. Eleanor spotted the sea mammals off the bow and cheered along with her fellow passengers.

It wasn't long after the *Thomas* left San Francisco Bay before many of the passengers rushed out to the deck rails, expelling what they'd just had for lunch. Eleanor grinned at the sight of grown men making a contest of who could shoot their projectiles farthest. The malady of retchings appeared to prompt a following of fish that, in turn, instigated jokes among the pedagogues about which type of schoolmaster was best for certain schools of fish, especially the incorrigible sharks.

The quartermaster divided the teachers into companies, each led by its own captain—whose role, it seemed, was mainly gathering complaints. The residents of the ladies' staterooms elected Miss Ida Covell, who immediately embarked on procuring buckets to contain the ejecta that, she declared, was sure to plague many a cabin hold. By anticipating this need before other group captains did, Miss Covell secured enough pails for her constituents before it became clear there weren't enough for everyone else.

For the next two days, many fell seasick. Eleanor was pleasantly surprised to discover that, despite being the landlocked Midwesterner she was, her stomach proved stronger than those of her East Coast cabin mates whom she assumed were better acquainted with the ocean's rhythms. The Radcliffe girls—brunette Miss Maude Bancroft and blonde Miss Arabella Palmer—hardly kept in whatever they ate and thus stopped eating altogether. Bespectacled, stern-looking Miss Covell turned out not to be stern at all. With Eleanor's help, the older teacher patiently nursed the Radcliffe girls through their bout of what she called *mal de mer*. Miss Bancroft and Miss Palmer, despite earlier rejoicing over getting the upper berths for themselves, immediately acquiesced to Miss Covell's urgings to transfer to the lower berths for ready access to the bucket on the floor between them.

"Thank you, Miss Karsten," Miss Covell said upon Eleanor's return from washing the bucket in the shared bathrooms. She had the tender voice of a matronly schoolmistress. "Let's hope these girls' constitutions prove equal to the challenge," the older teacher added, wiping Miss Palmer's young, pretty face with a damp towel.

Eleanor nodded and sat on the edge of the mattress where Miss Bancroft lay, seemingly as comatose as Miss Palmer was. She was aware that more soldiers died from tropical diseases than from war. Although pox vaccinations were available to Americans in recent years, there were still no inoculations for the lung disease called tuberculosis and the malarial and yellow fevers from which most soldiers and engineers perished in the Panama Canal, Cuba, and Puerto Rico. The fevers were simply managed with quinine tablets and anti-toxins after they'd already attacked their victims. Often, such medications were not sufficient to save the afflicted.

Eleanor took it as a good sign, however, that the Radcliffe girls were now sleeping after a whole night of moaning and burying their faces in the pail. They appeared to be no more than twenty-one or twenty-two years old and, judging from their alma mater and finery, likely came from pedigreed families. It was to the girls' credit that they didn't settle for the sheltered lives of debutante socialites. Eleanor smiled at Miss Covell. "I'm sure they're tougher than they look, ma'am. Let's hope, though, they don't put them on too many boats."

The older teacher grinned softly. The gray strands in her salt-and-pepper hair picked up the morning light streaming through the porthole. Eleanor wondered why a teacher of Miss Covell's age and experience chose the risks of a foreign post over peaceful retirement at home. "Miss Covell, what's bringing you to the Philippine Islands? I mean, aside from teaching."

Her colleague smiled back. "I don't mind at all. Before I became a teacher and for almost a decade, I was in various academic programs in Europe and the U.S. The latest was Michigan, as you know. My father teased me. Called me a professional student." She shook her head and chuckled softly, as did Eleanor. "Then, it struck me: I did not have to stop learning just because I was no longer the student. Thus,

I decided to be a teacher. Allowed me to brag to my father I was in a real profession!"

Eleanor grinned along with Miss Covell, who added, "I've been a teacher now for sixteen years. Missed traveling. Hence, when the call for teachers to the Philippine Islands came, I knew I just had to do it. Had to see the world again before I kick the bucket, so to speak." She glanced at the empty pail with a poignant smile.

"But you mustn't say that, Miss Covell!" Eleanor exclaimed. "You may outlive us all."

Miss Covell scoffed. "God forbid! I would rather have quality than quantity of life. You young ladies, however, still have your whole lives before you." Melancholy seemed to set in with the older teacher, whose eyes looked misty under their wire-rimmed glasses. She appeared to force a smile as she glanced back at Eleanor and asked, "And how about you, Miss Karsten? What made you leave the constancy of the Midwest for the vagaries of the Orient? Were the men in your home-town so blind that none of them had stayed you with a ring?"

Eleanor sighed. "It wasn't that the men were blind. It is, rather, I was never blinded by dreams of that ring. When my parents died in the tornado of 1898..."

"Oh, my dear Miss Karsten," Miss Covell interjected, reaching out to pat Eleanor's hand. "I am so sorry."

Not usually given to sentimentality, a stinging behind Eleanor's eyes surprised her. She cleared her throat. "Thank you, ma'am. That same tornado, well, it also wasted our farm. The only way I could keep our land was to marry the old widower who owned the adjacent farm. And, boy—did he make sure I understood that when he pro-posed!" Eleanor grinned before her tone turned grave. "But I believed my father hadn't sent me to school to become a teacher only to sell myself short by settling for a life of keeping house and making babies for old Farmer Borg. Thus, I sold the farm to the miser at thirty cents on the dollar, convinced I was making the better bargain. For the alter-native was unthinkable."

"That was good—what your father did," Miss Covell said. "Equipped you with an education that gave you the freedom to live your life the way you choose. Can't think of a better display of love by a father for his daughter."

The stinging behind Eleanor's eyes developed into tears. She blinked and smiled them away. She recalled how rural folk shook their heads and clucked their tongues, declaring her father had spoiled her by schooling her beyond the basics of learning how to be a good wife and mother. Now, she wanted to help little girls in the Philippine Islands to get an education so they, too, might wield some power, no matter how picayune, over their indentured lives as women. She glanced up at her colleague. "Isn't it funny, Miss Covell, that it takes a man to ensure a woman's independence?"

Miss Covell grinned and nodded.

Eleanor added, "I'm not averse to marrying and raising a family. Like most women, I imagined myself married. Yet, unlike most women perhaps, I never viewed it as my life's goal. While I've had my share of male attention, not one of them appeared to be worth the trouble of losing my liberty." At that moment, an albatross flew within view of the porthole and turned its head toward Eleanor before it disappeared. *Is it the same albatross I saw at the port?*

Miss Covell smiled wistfully. "I quite understand, my dear. I, too, have hoped my vocation would be enough to fill my heart if… if I never met a… a… I mean, s-someone who could. Now, I'm content with the student who occasionally tells me that I, at least, made a difference in his or her life." She gazed at Eleanor. "But you, my dear… you're much younger than me. Everything is still possible for you."

Eleanor burst into soft laughter, careful not to rouse their cabin mates from precious sleep. "Oh, ma'am, you wouldn't believe how many have already dismissed me as an old maid at my twenty-six years!"

"Believe me, I do!" Miss Covell exclaimed under her breath. "In my time, the cut-off was even earlier—at twenty!"

Eleanor grinned before turning pensive. "You know, an odd thing happened after my parents' funeral. I felt this… this strange stirring… the same one that urged me to sell the farm and apply for the Philippine Islands post. But it's more than a need for a change of scene. I think… I wanted… to belong to something bigger. Something that mattered."

Miss Covell arched an eyebrow. "But didn't you think teaching your hometown's children mattered?"

"Yes, of course. But to be honest, I never felt I truly belonged there, especially after my parents passed." Eleanor marveled at herself for saying this. It was the first time she'd confided such intimate thoughts and sentiments with someone other than her parents.

She added, "When my parents died, I discovered the advantage of being an only child: I didn't have to consult anyone to decide what to do. I told myself farming was simply my family's way of planting themselves in America after leaving Scandinavia. For that was all they knew. But I also believe there was a bigger dream behind all the uprooting they'd done—the ultimate dream of freeing future generations to dream their own dreams. Therefore, when I found myself the sole heir to my family's dreams, I was keen on not wasting the privilege."

Eleanor heard herself say the words with confidence. Yet, she wasn't always sure she did the right thing—selling the farm that had been in her family for three generations. *And for what? For a tropical escapade?*

"My dear, don't burden your heart with useless guilt for your choices," Miss Covell declared. "I'm sure if your parents were alive, they would be proud of what you are doing. The best way to honor their memory is by being the best teacher you can be to the least of those little ones where we are headed."

Eleanor was amazed at how Miss Covell perceived her self-doubt. *Am I that transparent?* She caressed the golden locket resting on her breastbone. It opened into a pair of hinged medallions that held a photograph of each of her father and mother. When she folded them closed, she imagined her parents kissing. "True, Miss Covell. Beyond that, I intend to dedicate to them a book I plan to write about this adventure when it's all over."

Miss Covell smiled a knowing smile. "That's all good, Miss Karsten. But I doubt this adventure would ever be over for us. I rather think it will stay with us for the rest of our lives."

Mal de mer, helped by a calmer sea, only succeeded in temporarily halting the merry bunch of college graduates, teachers, soldiers, and other adventurers from seeking amusements beyond their pint-sized quarters. Consistently fine weather, moreover, made promenading and fraternizing on the various outdoor decks supremely satisfying.

An optical illusion on the main deck, in particular, became an object of novel curiosity. Once the Radcliffe girls felt good enough to be left alone, Eleanor and Miss Covell went to see it for themselves. As they gazed toward the horizon, they experienced the strange sensation of being in the center of a crater—with the ocean's horizon as the peak. The depression's depth appeared proportionate to the height of wherever they stood. Eleanor and Miss Covell glanced at each other in disbelief, smiling in awe at the wonder that seemed capable of only being grasped by direct experience. Having previously contented herself with the second-hand knowledge afforded by books, Eleanor felt that this, alone, had vindicated her decision to travel to the other side of the Pacific.

The sea provided additional entertainment by way of marine life that came to the surface and interacted with the ship's passengers or displayed their talents. Eleanor watched, mesmerized, as a school of flying fish, ranging from about one to fifteen inches long, rode the silver crests of the lazulin waves until momentum propelled them up as high as a hundred feet into the air, where they appeared to be more creatures of sky than of sea as they spread their iridescent wing-like fins.

Seemingly intent not to be outdone, a flock of waterbirds likewise showed off their peculiar skill—which wasn't flying but diving. The "divers," as the sailors called them, had brown bodies no bigger than turtle doves, ebony heads, white-ringed eyes, and red-and-white beaks. Like quails, they rapidly flapped their wings to fly before they dove, head first, into the center of a wave. Just before one feared the ocean had claimed them, they reappeared some thirty or forty feet away where they soared to the sky, shook themselves dry, and repeated their stunt to the thrill of their audience.

In between entertainments provided by the marine life, when the interregnum seemed endless in a similarly endless sea, the pedagogues appeased their boredom by devising their own amusements and refining how the sociable found kindred spirits. They organized themselves according to their special interests.

Miss Covell and Eleanor joined the Mad About History Club which held meetings about the histories and cultures of the Hawaiian and

Philippine Islands. The religious gathered for Bible study and prayer in the Young Men's and Young Women's Christian Associations, which also supplied the choir for Commander Buford's Episcopalian Sunday service.

Others sought out their fellow enthusiasts in particular pursuits: scientists and engineers; physicians and nurses; writers and poets; playwrights and actors; sports fans and athletes; and the unbearably grave political and military strategists. The musically talented formed an a cappella choir and a string quartet. There was a lonely guitar player who played the Intermezzo from Cavalleria Rusticana so well, it made the ladies swoon and follow him around. Eleanor thus doubted that he was lonely at all.

One afternoon, as Eleanor, Miss Covell, and the Radcliffe girls were promenading on the main deck, they heard bawdy whistling and cheering from the ship's section frequented by the volunteer regiment soldiers, who were replacing the militias in the islands being called back to their home states. The ladies went to see what was happening.

A sailor was singing "Ma' Filipino Babe," a song that became popular on the mainland with the return of the first batch of soldiers who served in the army of invasion.

> *On a war boat from Manila,*
>
> *Steaming proudly o'er the foam, ….*
>
> *… up spoke a colored sailor lad,*
>
> *With bright eyes all aglow,*
>
> *"Just take a look at ma gal's photograph."*
>
> *How the white crew laughed and chaffed him,*
>
> *When her shiny face they saw,*
>
> *But he said: "I love ma Filipino baby."*

…

There's no yaller gal that's dearer,

Though her face is black as jet;

For her lips are sweet as honey,

…

She's ma black-faced Filipino baby….

The soldiers erupted into ribald hoots. Despite the song's suggestiveness, Arabella, Maude, and Eleanor couldn't resist giggling along with the infectious laughter of the uniformed young men, many of whom looked barely out of high school.

Miss Covell, however, smirked. "Hmph! Now we know what our boys think of Filipinos. Ladies, I have news for you: The Civil War did not end. It just moved to a new battleground!"

The Radcliffe girls blossomed from all the reinvigorating new activities on deck and recovered their youthful energy seemingly as quickly as it had succumbed to seasickness. No sooner were they on their feet did they join a group called The Greek Social Club. It had nothing to do with being Greek, they explained, but one which consisted of college graduates who were members of sororities and fraternities.

"Our club has a party at the dining saloon tonight!" Miss Bancroft declared with bright eyes. "Why don't you join us?"

"Yes, yes!" Miss Palmer exclaimed—giggling and clapping her hands as though she were a little girl. "Won't you please come, dear Miss Karsten, Miss Covell? The Harvard boys are going, too. And dare I say how awfully handsome they are?"

Miss Covell grinned. "Ah! I'm afraid these bones are no longer equipped for the diversions of the young. You all go and enjoy the party, my dears. I'm quite content to read."

Eleanor had noticed Miss Covell reading Worcester's *The Philippine Islands and Their People*. It was published a few years earlier, but Macmillan recently reprinted it to take advantage, no doubt, of the current interest in America's new territory. "I had hoped to get a copy of that book, Miss Covell, but it was sold out. Might I borrow it when you're finished?"

"Why, of course, my dear!" Miss Covell replied, smiling.

"Well, if you're happy to stay in tonight, ma'am," Miss Bancroft interjected, "please feel free to take back your old bed. I assure you I'm more than well now to climb the upper berth—many thanks to you and Miss Karsten."

Miss Covell grinned. "Don't mind if I do! Can't say these bones welcome all the climbing you like to do. Thank you, dear."

"Same here, Miss Karsten!" Arabella exclaimed in her sing-song voice. "You may have your bunk back, too. That is, only if you want. I mean, just in case…"

Eleanor interjected, grinning, "Thought you'd never ask, Miss Palmer!"

The mess hall was decorated with colorful buntings and balloons, which was pleasantly surprising. For a ship charged with the grave mission of delivering an army of teachers and soldiers to an ongoing war and likewise carrying a cargo of whimsical accoutrements seemed strange yet uplifting. "How'd you all get these party favors?" she asked her companions.

Miss Bancroft chuckled and replied, "We raided the dry pantry! Found them and begged the steward to share some with us."

Arabella giggled. "We told him it's for a party to celebrate the resurrection of America's best and brightest from their dark nights of the gut and soul! And he couldn't resist our charms!"

Eleanor and Maude chuckled along with her.

Someone had brought a Berliner gramophone, now playing the latest hit by the Sousa Band. The attendees were mostly a younger crowd. They milled around a cut-glass punch bowl on a buffet table that also served tuna fish sandwiches, fruit, and cheese.

The men looked dapper with their dinner jackets and clean-shaven faces or freshly-trimmed mustaches and beards. The women bared their heads, showing off their Gibson-Girl hairstyle and long, slim necks. The more daring young ladies, like Miss Palmer and Miss Bancroft, chucked the day's Victorian outfits for evening frocks with low necklines that flaunted their ample décolletages.

Eleanor had no choice but to wear the simple clothes she'd packed for the sea passage: her tailored woolen skirt and high-collared blouse—which, tonight, she'd adorned with her mother's cameo brooch. It never occurred to her she would need more than a schoolmarm's attire for the voyage.

Miss Bancroft and Miss Palmer found their Harvard boys and introduced them to Eleanor. After the usual niceties, the young circle devolved into the insular talk usual to those with shared experiences. Thus, Eleanor wandered discreetly toward the buffet table.

She served herself a cup of punch. As she sipped, she grimaced. The cocktail was stronger on the alcohol than she liked. There appeared nothing else to drink except even stronger liquor: brandy and whiskey. She helped herself to a tuna sandwich and some fruit and cheese. And she continued to sip the awful punch for, otherwise, she'd feel silly standing alone with nothing to occupy her hands, pretending she harbored no hunger other than for food and drink.

"Ma Blushin' Rosie" was playing. She smiled upon spying the Radcliffe girls dancing with their Harvard beaus. She was happy for them. It wasn't long ago when she was their age. Now, keenly aware her youth was almost gone, she remembered what her mother had once said. She was a teenager then, and her mother suggested that she join their church youth choir's excursion to the Iowa State Fair. She refused, preferring to stay home to read the new book she'd borrowed from the library: *Little Women*.

"Oh, my dear Eleanor, there's an old soul in you," her mother declared—sighing, hands on hips, head shaking. "Careful not to let it steal your youth."

She wondered whether her mother's warning had finally come to pass. Here, where everyone seemed to be having a good time, she was struck with unbearable loneliness and by a sense of missing something—or someone. Of course, she missed her parents, she told herself.

But this felt like something else. She was consumed by this riddle that when the young man who'd been hoisted up by rope to the ship on departure day asked her to dance, she declined. He walked away, palpably disappointed, yet had no trouble succeeding in asking another girl to dance with him. When she realized what she did, she wanted to kick herself.

Eleanor fidgeted with her collar and downed the rest of her punch. The accumulated body heat in the saloon and the liquor were starting to feel suffocating, as though she were being strangled. *I need to get out for fresh air.* Without notifying Maude and Arabella, she left. *No use dampening their fun.*

Out on the deck, just as in the dining saloon, love appeared to be very much in the air—spiced with wafting scents of meerschaum pipes and perfume. Eleanor smiled in amusement. The *Thomas* had been rife with rumors of spontaneous honeymoons erupting overnight between acquaintances or strangers—a novelty to many that, to the quartermaster, appeared the usual. His familiarity with the phenomenon demonstrated itself when he separated the wives from their husbands in the designation of sleeping quarters: He assigned the husbands to where the soldiers slept and their wives and children to the staterooms.

Eleanor realized this allowed the men to visit their wives and children by day while protecting them from their wives' suspicions by night—thereby minimizing domestic disputes on board. The quartermaster certainly wasn't just thinking of the merits of the wives in mind, for unfaithfulness, if the gossips were to be believed, appeared not confined to males. Eleanor tittered, unwittingly scaring off a couple canoodling in the shadows.

She walked to the deck's edge and draped her arms over the railing. The ocean mist felt invigorating. Perhaps she wasn't lonely more than melancholic. She assured herself it was perfectly normal to be especially nostalgic on a voyage like this, where everything felt new and strange, thus making one lonesome for the familiarity of home. *But I no longer have a home.* Out here, on the high seas, the reality of what she'd done—selling the family farm, embarking on a journey into what, she wasn't quite sure now—hit her like a blast of cold, ocean spray. *What have I done?* The stinging sensation behind her eyes returned.

Blinking back tears, she reminded herself of what Miss Covell said. *It was time to let go of self-doubt.*

The moderate winds that blew earlier in the day continued, helping to cool off the liquor's effect on her. She breathed in deeply and gazed at the stars. They seemed to shine more brightly in the open sea than she'd observed from land. She tried to pick out the Southern Cross that astronomers and other star-gazers had been raving about — describing it as a blazing cross in the southern hemisphere. Yet, Eleanor could see no less than eight different star formations that resembled crosses. When, finally, she'd spotted it, she was nonplussed to discover it was far from blazing and not so much a cross as it was an irregular diamond.

A cool breeze chilled her, prompting her to return to her cabin. As she turned to leave, she thought she heard a whale song echo from the depths behind her. She swung around to see if the magnificent beast would breach the water. It didn't. Yet, she noticed a faint glow where the leaden sea met the indigo sky. Something urged her to press the image of that feeble yet certain light in the dark horizon between the pages of her memory. And she did.

CHAPTER 2

All the Queen's Men

Eleanor awoke to excited whisperings and someone shaking her arm. "Eleanor, get up! Look!" It was Arabella. After a week of sharing the intimacy of a tiny cabin, the younger ladies spontaneously progressed into addressing each other by their first names.

Eleanor turned her head to Arabella's smiling, pretty face. "Why? What is it?" she asked with a voice forced out of still-sleeping chords. "What's happening?"

Maude stood by the porthole window, grinning. "Well, don't just lie there, sleepyhead! Come and see!"

Eleanor groaned and rose from her berth. Both Radcliffe girls stepped aside to make room for her at the porthole. It was still dark. Eleanor rubbed the remaining film of sleep from her eyes. She peered out again. Along a stretch of what could be the Honolulu coastline, electric lights shone as though twinkling with the rise and fall of the *Thomas* on the undulating sea.

They roused Miss Covell from slumber. As soon as everyone was dressed, they rushed out to the foredeck where they hoped for a glorious sunrise to give them their first glimpse of a tropical paradise. And they were not disappointed. The rising sun illuminated the azure shades of the sky and sea. The colors began, up close, with aquamarine that, farther out, turned into brilliant topaz. Near the horizon, the hues deepened into dark sapphire. The sun's rays flashed silver on the crests of waves that fell and burst into frothy, snowy scallops upon the shore.

The famous Diamond Head lay on the starboard side: a deeply-ridged crater wall of pinkish-brown volcanic tuff that peaked, seaward, into a cone. An old gentleman who stood on the deck alongside Eleanor and her friends volunteered that the mountain's name in the native Hawaiian language connoted the tuna's dorsal fin. The ladies agreed it was most appropriate. On the port side, they glimpsed a hill called the Punchbowl, which embraced a shallow crater. Between these iconic Oahu landmarks lay a beach that glowed ochre in the morning light, sometimes sparkling as if there were diamonds in the sand.

Clasping the shallow, coral-fringed harbor was the wharf. It sheltered sundry sea vessels with white masts that looked like lances charging at the young, periwinkle sky. Honolulu's modest steeples and rooftops peeked at the new arrivals between swaying palms and glossy vegetation. Behind the town, crop terraces in chartreuse climbed halfway on the slopes until the bulkhead of emerald forests began.

The *Thomas* anchored a few miles from the harbor for a quarantine check, and the ship's engines ground down to a hum. As the doctor's launch approached the vessel, Captain Coulling directed everyone to return to their quarters for the duration of the inspection. It took two and a half hours before the *Thomas* was permitted to dock and disembark.

Eleanor, Miss Covell, Maude, and Arabella waited on the main deck with most of the passengers while the gangway was set. Meanwhile, a group of shockingly naked little boys entertained them with their diving skills. An anthropologist, eager to show off his knowledge of the Hawaiian Islands, said the boys were from the Kanaka tribe.

The teachers watched as the boys dove for pennies shipside in the crystalline waters, meandered among the dancing kelp, and zigzagged with colorful fish between similarly colorful coral until the youngsters seemingly disappeared into the dark depths. Silence ensued, followed by an increasing buzz from the audience, who expressed worries about the boys drowning. As if to reassure their patrons, the urchins resurfaced almost simultaneously—throwing back their wet, black hair from their brown faces. Thereupon, they cheered their fellow diver, who announced himself the winner by holding up his prize of a shiny coin.

The champion slipped his treasure into his mouth, rolled it around with his tongue, and pressed it against his dumpling cheeks.

He clambered up one of the volcanic boulders, raised his trophy for everyone again to see, and gleefully rolled upon his craggy perch as if it were a mere bed of hay. The boys gesticulated for more coins to be tossed into the waters—and thus began another round of treasure diving to the cheers of the captive audience.

The routine continued until the gangway was finally in place, announcing to the week-long weary, wide-eyed residents of the *Thomas* that other marvelous amusements and curiosities awaited them on shore—thus diverting their attention away from the now crestfallen divers. The boys, nonetheless, appeared to instantly recover their happiness by diving back into the sea in search of unclaimed, sunken treasure. Eleanor smiled. *What children of joy!*

The ladies stepped down the gangway and paused on the wharf to take their bearings. The explosion of activity, sound, and color that greeted them seemed almost too much for the senses. Eleanor marveled at the babble of languages that littered the short stretch of road from the dock to the town. She picked out what could be Hawaiian, Japanese, Chinese, Portuguese, Dutch, and German and noted the lilt of the British and the brogue of the Irish and Scot.

The ladies spotted a newspaper and magazine kiosk, around which many of their fellow passengers were already gathered, noses buried in newsprint. "My dears," Miss Covell said, "shall we find out what the world has been up to?" Her younger colleagues eagerly nodded.

Eleanor and Miss Covell shared a copy of the *Island Times*, while the Radcliffe girls pored over copies of *Vogue* and *McCall's*.

The older teacher chuckled as she perused the headline story, and Eleanor grinned.

Maude glanced up from her magazine. "What's so funny?"

"It appears there's now a name for us teachers going to the Philippine Islands!" Miss Covell replied.

"And what's that?" Maude asked, eyebrows arched.

"The Thomasites!" Eleanor declared.

"How splendid!" Arabella cried. "We're famous!"

Their fellow teachers glanced up from their copies of the paper and chuckled along with them.

The ladies sauntered toward the harbor market. Eleanor tried not to stare, but it was difficult to look away from the native Hawaiians and the Japanese and Chinese hawking their wares or going about their shopping. It was one thing to have seen pictures of such peoples in magazines and books, quite another for her to see them now in person.

Hawaiian women wore flower wreaths around their heads and necks, which added color and gaiety to their otherwise grim and shapeless Mother Hubbards that covered them from neck to ankle. Huge, bare-chested Hawaiian men with the physiognomy of the Comanche adorned themselves with flowers around their necks instead of warrior insignias. Japanese women shuffled about in their platform wooden sandals, dressed in kimonos, their babies tied to their backs. Chinese women wore silk Mandarin tunics over black trousers, grasping the hands of children wearing similar, yet more colorful attire in hues of cerulean, malachite, saffron, and rose.

As the heat began to feel oppressive, the ladies paused to take off their day gloves. Nearby, some Hawaiian women sat on the sidewalk, stringing fragrant flowers into necklaces. They rose to their feet, greeting Eleanor and her friends with cheerful alohas, and hung what they called a *lei* around each of the ladies' necks.

"Goshamighty, aren't these heavenly?" Arabella exclaimed as her head emerged from the perfumed ring.

Eleanor felt the island itself embrace her. "What do you call these flowers?" she asked the Hawaiian woman draping the wreath on her.

"Frangipani," she replied.

"Fran… gee… pahnee," repeated Eleanor. "A name as sweet as the flowers!" A penny per lei seemed a pithy exchange for the pleasure.

At the fish market, it was the foul scents that greeted the ladies. Eleanor and her companions retrieved handkerchiefs from their reticules to protect themselves from the olfactory assault. The fishmongers likewise assaulted their ears as they screamed, while alternately waving away flies and splashing seawater on the panoply of seafood: "Buy! Buy! Try! Try!" But the offensive odors faded as the curious forms and vibrant colors of the marine produce captivated the ladies: the astonishing crimson flesh of the *aku'* or "skipjack tuna;" the glistening, pink bodies of tiny prawns; and the rainbow colors under the glassy skin of the horrific hydra that was the octopus.

On the opposite side of the street were vendors selling heaps of strange-looking fruits just as colorful as the seafood. There were green, yellow, and red bananas and citruses, big and small, in shades not only of yellow and orange, but also coral, peach, and tangerine. Crates full of the fruit of the palm tree called the coconut lined another stall. Elsewhere, there were fruits that looked like big tomatoes—only rounder, with purple, waxy, woody skins. Most intriguing were the spiky, little red balls that looked like anemones.

Miss Covell pointed to some oblong jade fruits she called alligator pears that Maude insisted were paw-paws, but which the locals referred to as papayas. A merchant cut one in half to show off its glistening, red-orange flesh and the hundreds of tiny, glossy, black seeds nestled at its hollow center.

Further out, they spotted stacked stalks of sugarcane. A boy chopped off about a foot from a five-foot cane, stripped it of its greenish-purple skin, and showed them how to eat the peeled ivory stick. It appeared one "ate" it by biting off one piece at a time, chewing it to both press and suck the saccharine juice, and then spitting out the masticated fibers.

They continued strolling, and Eleanor spied the oddest-looking fruit. She was about to go to it when Miss Covell distracted her and the Radcliffe girls with offerings of palm-sized, heart-shaped yellow fruits she said were called mangoes.

As the ladies bit off a piece of the fruit, they instantly pushed it onto their hands and tossed it with the remainder of their mango into a nearby garbage bin. After wiping their hands with their handkerchiefs, they were dismayed to discover yellow stains remained on their skin.

"Thunderation!" Arabella cried. "First, that horrid taste; now, this handkerchief is ruined!" She glanced at Miss Covell. "Oh. Sorry, ma'am. Didn't mean to sound ungrateful."

"No need for apologies, my dear!" Miss Covell exclaimed. "I quite agree with you!"

"Actually," Eleanor interjected, "the combination of peach, pear, apple, and apricot flavors wasn't bad. Except for the turpentine aftertaste."

"That dastardly man over there assured me his mangoes would be exquisite!" Miss Covell declared, pointing to the vendor.

The ladies glanced at the Chinese-looking vendor, who was laughing mockingly at them, brazenly displaying his incomplete, yellow, and rotten teeth.

"I suspect we should have peeled off the skin before we ate it, and he should have said so," Eleanor declared, shaking her head at the mango merchant.

Chagrined, the ladies walked away.

Eleanor then remembered the strangest-looking fruit and led her friends toward the stall that sold it. Its outlandishness, up close, appeared more bizarre. It looked like a green-orange pinecone the size of a human head, and the head had a hundred eyes, each banded with spiky eyelashes, and on top of the head was a crown of stiff, leafy blades.

The young Hawaiian lady selling them wore a single scarlet hibiscus blossom behind an ear and a continuous loop of bright-green cotton fabric gathered above her bosom and firmly tucked between her breasts—from where it fell into graceful folds to her knees. Her thick, dark, glossy hair draped her bare, golden-brown shoulders like a mantle that cascaded in luxurious waves down to her buttocks. Eleanor, mesmerized by her beauty, smiled at her.

The Hawaiian woman smiled back at Eleanor. "You like have taste this pineapple?"

"Is that what you call it—a pine… apple?" Eleanor said. "Yes, I do!"

"You like very much. I promise," the seller said, smiling brightly. She offered a sample of peeled, bite-size chunks to Eleanor and her companions who, perhaps, because of the episode with the mango, declined.

As Eleanor placed a piece of the pineapple in her mouth, it was its slightly slimy and fibrous texture that initially struck her. But when she bit and chewed it, it burst into a tangy-sweet piece of sunshine. "Goodness!" she exclaimed. "Ladies, you must have some of this!" Her reaction persuaded her friends to taste it, and they all agreed it was most delightful.

As they continued on their walkabout, two men on the other side of the street grabbed their attention with their wild gesticulations as they talked loudly at each other. They were short, had dark-brown skin and button-like noses with flaring nostrils, and wore long-sleeved tunics with standup collars over loose trousers.

"I wonder who they are," Eleanor remarked. "Can't place their language."

"Ah! If I'm not mistaken, they could be Filipinos!" Miss Covell replied. "And they are speaking, I believe, in Tagal—the language of the Tagalogs, who, as I recall, are the inhabitants of the capital, Manila."

The older teacher shared her encounter in Ann Arbor with a Filipino student whom she described as a *mestizo*, which, she explained, was the miscegenation of a Spaniard and Filipino. She'd tutored him in English, and he returned the favor by teaching her some Tagal. She soon got the gist of the language because since she was fairly fluent in Spanish, she noted that much of Tagal sounded either a derivation of Spanish or a distortion of it. "'Twas my encounter with that Filipino that motivated me to apply for the Philippine post. He was a warm and friendly young man. I expect most Filipinos would be the same."

"Well, these Filipinos don't seem friendly," Maude said. "They appear to be quarreling!"

The ladies stopped talking as they passed the men. Eleanor turned around to take another look at them. They caught her looking and ogled back at her with lecherous smiles. One hollered, "Comusta, señorita?" The other snickered. Eleanor felt a red heat spread upon her face like an ink blot. She instantly faced forward and hurried to catch up with her friends, scolding herself for her poor etiquette that may have invited the men's prurient interest.

The ladies followed the crowd of sightseers who, as could be expected of a tribe of educators, headed straight for the sole museum on the island. Eleanor and Miss Covell waved and smiled at their fellow Mad About History Club members who appeared to be first in line to enter the building.

"How impressive!" Maude exclaimed, pausing to examine the museum's façade. "Done in Richardson Romanesque Revival! I see elements of the Boston Trinity Church."

The other ladies stopped with Maude as the latter pointed to the Romanesque arches and Gothic pediments that she said were the hallmarks of the architectural style.

"Do I note an interest in architecture, dear Maude?" Miss Covell asked.

"Indeed, ma'am," Maude replied. "I'd once dreamed of becoming like Sophia Hayden—the first female graduate of MIT's architecture program. She designed that gorgeous beaux-arts Women's Building at the Columbian Exposition. I was a young girl when Father took me to Chicago to see it."

"What happened?" Eleanor asked.

"What do you mean?" Maude glanced sideways at Eleanor.

"Well, you said you dreamed of being like Hayden," Eleanor said.

Maude smiled wistfully. "Yes, I did. But Father learned that the training required apprenticeship in ateliers filled with men. Allowing me to attend Radcliffe was the most I could get out of him." Maude shook her head, grinning.

"But If you couldn't persuade your father to send you to architecture school, how did you convince him to allow you to go to the Far East?" Miss Covell asked, eyebrows arched.

Maude grinned. "Simple. He didn't have a choice! When I turned twenty-one, I came into my late mother's inheritance. Told Father—my money, my choice."

"And you were so brave and steadfast, dear chum," Arabella said. "Made me proud!"

Maude grinned. "Oh, but the credit is yours, darling! Father only calmed down when I told him you were coming with me!"

Everyone chuckled.

"It isn't as if you can't do it, anymore," Eleanor interjected. "That is, if you still want to."

"What? Me? An architect?" Maude scoffed. "It's too late."

"It's never too late to pursue your dreams," Miss Covell remarked.

"You think so?" Maude asked, a faint smile on her lips. "I suppose." She turned her gaze back to the building. "I might do just that after our Philippines stint." She turned around to face her companions and exclaimed, "Then—I'll design my own school *and* teach in it! Wouldn't that be something?"

"Oh, that would be marvelous, dear chum!" exclaimed Arabella, nodding vigorously, eyes wide and sparkling, hands clasped in prayer.

"And if you hire us as your fellow schoolmistresses, we could call it, The Thomasite School for Girls!" She thrust her forefinger at the sky.

The Radcliffe girls pealed into laughter. Maude put her arm around her best friend and walked hand in hand with her toward the Bishop Museum. Eleanor and Miss Covell followed behind them, smiling.

They each took a slim brochure from the receptionist after donating a nickel. An American businessman and philanthropist, Charles Reed Bishop, had built the museum to house the heirlooms passed on to him by his late wife, Princess Bernice Pauahi Pākī Bishop, who was the sister of Queen Lydia Liliʻu Loloku Walania Kamakaʻeha—the last Hawaiian monarch. The collection included artifacts from various tribes in the Pacific region, particularly the ancient Polynesians from whom indigenous Hawaiians believed themselves to have originated.

They proceeded briskly toward the Hawaiian and Polynesian halls, greatly anticipating the treasures there displayed. They found finely woven baskets, mats, fabrics, huge masks, shell and wooden household implements, and animistic deities carved in stone, wood, and bone. Most spectacular were the vibrant, colorful feathered cloaks, head-dresses, and helmets of Hawaiian royalty. Certain birds were valued for their gold and scarlet feathers, of which the magnificent royal robes were made.

The collection struck Eleanor as contradicting the view that such a civilization was primitive. What impressed her most was the culture's reverence for the sacredness of the land—the creation and destruction of which the Hawaiians attributed to a female deity called Pele, goddess of fire and volcanoes.

After an hour in the museum, the ladies went to Iolani Palace, the monarchy's former residence. The empty niches that had held the busts of the islands' great *aliʻi* conveyed the sad story of the Hawaiian royalty. Eleanor sensed it, especially in the empty throne room. It had only been eight years since the last queen sat on the same baronial chair Eleanor was now admiring. A sign on the seat stated it was carved of a native tree considered sacred to the islands. *Everything seems to be sacred to these people.*

Eleanor recalled from the Mad About History Club's lectures on Hawaiian history that the ill-fated monarch was summarily ousted in a coup that resulted in the islands' annexation as U.S. territory.

A Citizen's Committee of Public Safety composed of foreign businessmen demurred from the queen's allegedly restrictive economic policies.

Eleanor imagined what the queen must have felt—being thrown out of her palace and stripped of her heritage and legacy—because those men, who weren't even Hawaiian, happened not to agree with her. The public exhibition of the royal rooms suddenly struck her as brazenly irreverent, despite her government's claim of the legitimacy of the American takeover. She couldn't bear to stay a minute longer.

She told her companions she wanted to see the Administration Building. Maude and Arabella expressed a preference to return to town and browse the stores, while Miss Covell said she'd join Eleanor. They all agreed to meet back in town in an hour.

In the Administration Building, Eleanor and Miss Covell found members of their history club pondering on a life-sized bronze statue of King Kamehameha, the first king of the united islands. Eleanor blurted, "Was he really *that* tall?"

Their club leader chuckled. He was an elderly professor from Princeton sporting a full, white beard. "As a matter of fact, he was," he replied. "He's said to have been seven feet tall and three hundred pounds. Add the height of his feathered helmet, and he must have appeared to be a giant to his enemies, who must have been struck with terror by the mere sight of him. Lavishly cloaked in his feathered robes, he must have looked no less a god to his people."

"Indeed," Eleanor said, visualizing the feathers' brilliant colors, such as those they'd just seen at the museum, draped upon the man represented by the statue.

"Yet, a tragic king," remarked Miss Covell.

"True," the Princeton professor replied.

"Why?" Eleanor asked, shifting her glance between the two older teachers. "Wasn't he known as Kamehameha the Great? That doesn't sound very tragic to me."

Miss Covell and Professor Lawson exchanged knowing smiles. "Go ahead, Miss Covell," Professor Lawson said. "Please do us the honor."

Eleanor and the other members leaned in to listen as Miss Covell, in her teacherly tone, stated, "It was the king's acceptance of his European backers' military aid that ultimately led to the monarchy's downfall.

In return for such aid, he allowed Europeans and, later, Americans, to buy land and establish businesses on the islands. This allowed them to accumulate enough economic and political power later to topple his descendant—the last Hawaiian queen."

"But how do we know this is true?" a woman asked.

"The queen herself wrote a book on these facts," Miss Covell replied. "To the skeptical, there are plenty of independent sources supporting her version of history. I think it's time we study, not just the history of the conqueror, but also the story of the conquered. I place my bet on the queen's version." Miss Covell grinned.

"But didn't our government say it had to intervene to protect American investments threatened by the queen's anti-business policies?" a man asked.

"Threatening perhaps to foreigners, but reasonable to her people," Professor Lawson replied. "One could say that her policy that disallowed non-Hawaiians from further buying land was necessary to protect her people, who were tricked, manipulated, and harassed into selling their land to shrewd foreign businessmen, often for a pittance."

Eleanor mulled over what was said. Though not especially politically minded, she understood there were always two sides to a story. She marveled at the insights and learning of her colleagues, who'd mastered the art of reading between the lines of history to get to the probable truth. She now wondered whether the Thomasites' assignment in the Philippine Islands was what her government claimed it was—a benevolent mission. It never occurred to her, until now, to question it, for she believed with all her heart she'd only be doing good by serving Filipino boys and girls as their teacher.

Miss Covell excused herself to find a lavatory, and Eleanor wandered into a churchyard. There, she found a pair of algaroba trees, a type of mesquite with drooping foliage. A sign underneath one of them stated it wasn't native to the Hawaiian Islands but was brought there by Catholic missionaries. It thrived and flourished, eventually dominating Honolulu's landscape, particularly along its mountain slopes.

Back in town, Eleanor and Miss Covell met with Maude and Arabella, who were excited to report that they happened upon a demonstration of the Marconi system of wireless telegraphy.

"Can you imagine?" Arabella cried. "We would soon be able to send telegrams across the ocean!"

"And, eventually, around the world!" Maude interjected.

"Indeed, I can," Miss Covell replied. "What I could not have imagined, dear girls, is you choosing a wireless telegraphy demonstration over shopping!"

Eleanor snorted into laughter, inciting everyone into chortling.

The ladies boarded a small, shabby streetcar drawn by mules to join their fellow Thomasites who were already frolicking on the yellow coral sands of Waikiki Beach. Eleanor, Maude, and Arabella ditched their shoes and stockings on the beach, gathered their skirts to their knees, and raced to the water. The Radcliffe girls shrieked as they splashed seawater at each other and chased Eleanor with similar threats. Eleanor glanced back at Miss Covell, who was sitting on a folding lounge chair on the beach, grinning as she watched them. She couldn't remember a more carefree time of unbridled childlike joy. Thus, she recorded it in her mind's diary, ready to be accessed when she needed it.

The next morning, a military band came to play an hour's concert on the *Thomas's* promenade deck—an apropos rousing for the ladies' Pali adventure that day. They wanted to see the infamous site where King Kamehameha forced 1,500 enemy warriors to jump to their deaths from a rock precipice that was also famous for its panoramic view of Oahu Island.

Eleanor, Miss Covell, and the Radcliffe girls packed themselves with a few other female Thomasites and an army nurse into a wagonette. Their driver was an old Yankee who bragged about being a veteran of the Civil War. He was pleasant enough at the beginning until Miss Covell suggested in her teacherly tone that he might let down the checkreins on his horses. Having lived with horses most of her life, Eleanor understood Miss Covell's concern. If the checkreins were pulled too tightly, they placed a great strain on the horses' neck muscles and ligaments, thus causing great pain to the poor beasts.

"Ma' 'orses are just fine, ma'am," the driver retorted. "An' ah need no 'elp from any'un ta look aftuh they comfuht!" He extended his irascibility to the non-Caucasian-looking people crossing the streets—refusing to slow down for them, cursing them as he passed them, and calling them n***ahs and ye**ars.

Miss Covell declared, "Sir, if you continue with this despicable conduct, I'd be obliged if you drop me off at the next corner so I could report your outrageous behavior to the city administrator!"

The driver cocked an ear. "Wha… whaaat? What that? Can't 'ear nothin,' ma'am! Damn bushwhacker got me good in ma' ears in them damn sedition! And ya upsettin' ma' horses with ya yackin' if ye ask me! So, I be sure 'bliged if ya shut ya trap, ma'am!"

"Well! I never!" Miss Covell cried. She attempted to stand and would have surely fallen off the wagonette if Eleanor hadn't grabbed her arm and pulled her back to her seat.

"Sir," Eleanor intervened, "I suggest you stop talking back this instant and focus on completing this trip for which we've hired you! Or you'll not get a cent out of us, I promise you that."

"Yeah, that's right!" Arabella exclaimed, harrumphing. The rest of the passengers echoed their agreement.

Eleanor was relieved when the driver refrained from replying, for it helped deescalate the contest of wills between him and Miss Covell, thus allowing the group to better enjoy the beauty of Nuuanu Avenue and its neatly trimmed lawns, majestic trees, and stately houses.

"If I'm not mistaken, ladies," Maude said, "this is where we would be feted tonight!"

The other passengers, except Miss Covell, hummed with awe and excitement. One of the city's wealthiest men, Mr. Waterhouse, had invited the Thomasites to a reception in his home. Judging from the type of houses in the area, they anticipated his home would be more of a mansion.

The wagonette wound up to a steep valley, amid terraced mountain slopes. Intermittent showers and sunshine alternately drenched and dried the passengers as they climbed up the Pali. It was a wonder no one remembered to bring an umbrella. Miss Covell constantly took off her eyeglasses to wipe them. When they arrived at a gorge between a sharp peak on their right and a mountain on their left, the driver stopped the wagonette and announced he could go no farther.

The group continued on foot. As they trekked up the mountain path, a deluge poured on them again. Laughing at their predicament, they ran toward the bare rock wall up there, hoping it would provide them with cover. As they approached it, a strong wind blasted against them, sending them shrieking, their skirts flying. The gale persisted in pushing and tearing at them until they found themselves dangerously close to the precipice at the gorge's end. It occurred then to Eleanor that this must have been the spot where Kamehameha's enemies had perished.

The place would have posed a logistical nightmare for a retreating army, for there was no escape from the funnel within which the warriors would have found themselves trapped. This enabled Kamehameha's soldiers to push their enemies toward the ravine and fall hundreds of feet to the gorge below. The wind was a natural accomplice to the ruthless deed. Here, the trade winds that arose from the windward coast of Oahu—beneficial to masted ships—became a danger to the unwitting tourist. It whipped up suddenly from nowhere and struck with such strength and velocity capable of shoving the uninformed off the rock precipice to where the bleached bones of those who'd defied Kamehameha hundreds of years ago were said to still lie.

Eleanor noticed a fence probably meant to protect tourists from falling. Yet, it appeared to be damaged and, thus, provided no such protection. *This was why the driver said he could go no farther!* Eleanor's eyes searched for him down the road and saw him laughing at the women's dilemma. *Oh, I could wring his neck!* He wasn't just a crude, ignorant fellow. His failure to forewarn the ladies about the area's propensity for dangerous squalls evinced a treacherous nature. And his shocking display of prejudice against the natives made her wonder about how he could have fought on the side of the abolition of slavery. Yet, she recalled that, unlike her father, a Union soldier who was also a staunch abolitionist, many bluebacks had fought the Confederates simply against the South's treasonous secession, not necessarily against slavery.

Another gale compelled the ladies to crouch and crawl cliffside. Their hats were either long gone or held down by nervous hands, and their hair hung loosely from lost combs and hairpins. The path narrowed sharply as it turned around a curved rock wall. Fortunately, a group of men from the *Thomas* arrived and helped them to their feet. Together, they navigated the slim, tricky footpath toward the leeward side of the mountain. It was then that Mother Nature relented to allow the Pali to reveal its glory.

The wind wound down, and the sun's rays shone in clefts between the clouds to illumine the view of the great valley below. The land rolled in emerald patches, slid up to verdigris woodlands and peaks, and poked through the mist until it spilled and snuggled against the splendid, azure embrace of the Pacific Ocean. Serpentine ribbons of fog wove around spires of scattered peaks and the linen-fold cliffs of the Koolau Range evoked the formidable wall of a lofty castle fortress. Smoky clouds billowed in the trade winds, bestowing gentle rain on crop terraces in separate yet concurrent showers.

The effect of it all, in Eleanor's mind's eye, was that of a mystical portrait of Mother Earth remaking herself in light and shadow. None of the other Thomasites likewise appeared to escape the goddess's spell.

It was mid-afternoon when the ladies returned to the *Thomas*, affording them enough time to eat a tiffin, freshen up, and change out of their much-abused clothes in preparation for the evening's festivities. While they dressed, the Radcliffe girls chatted excitedly about their Harvard beaus' plan to introduce themselves to Mr. Waterhouse in hopes of gaining his patronage and expanding their career opportunities after their teaching stints in the Philippines.

Maude and Arabella opened their cosmetics chests to share the latest accoutrements to a lady's toilette. There was zinc oxide powder mixed with crushed pearls for radiant faces, a cream tinted with carmine for blushing cheeks, and a lip salve with beet stain for desirable lips. Miss Covell declined to partake, while Eleanor consented to the full treatment—minus the eyelash enhancement that consisted of applying beeswax to lashes and tapping powdered charcoal on them. She feared the nightmarish possibility of the beeswax melting in the heat and running down her face in dark streaks.

"The trick is to paint the face without looking painted," Arabella chirped as she applied the rouge on Eleanor's face.

From a hand-held mirror that Maude held up for them, Eleanor observed how Arabella blended and spread the tinted cream on her cheeks so the color faded toward the contours. Next, Arabella dipped the tip of her pinky finger in the lip salve canister and spread the reddish balm on Eleanor's lips. "Now, press your lips together," Arabella said.

Eleanor was pleased that she could still recognize herself under the cosmetic layers when Arabella was done with her.

The Radcliffe girls insisted on Eleanor trying one of their gowns, instead of wearing what they called her spinster outfits.

"No offense to you, dear Miss Covell!" Arabella added, giggling.

"None taken, my dear," replied Miss Covell, grinning.

Arabella offered Eleanor a silk, coral gown, but it proved short on Eleanor and big in the bosom area. Maude persuaded Eleanor to try one of her summer evening frocks—a pale blue muslin that complemented Eleanor's flaxen hair. It featured billowing gigot sleeves that ended at the elbows, a scooped passementerie-banded neckline, and a broad ribbon sash that emphasized Eleanor's small waist.

"I think it's just a little long," Maude said, "but you can still walk without tripping—can't you?"

"I think so," Eleanor replied, turning around to check that she was right.

"It's perfect!" Arabella cried.

Maude and Miss Covell nodded, smiling.

The Radcliffe girls put up Eleanor's hair in the Gibson style—gathering up sections of Eleanor's long, curly locks into one voluminous mass and pinning it into a bun on the crown of her head.

"You're lucky," Arabella said, as she delivered the finishing touches to Eleanor's hairdo—strategically pulling out strands of hair to create a wispy look.

"Why is that?" Eleanor asked.

"Because you have naturally curly hair that makes it easy to achieve this volume. It's the foundation for the brim shape," Arabella replied. "I, on the other hand, have wavy hair I still have to tease before I could create this mass. Girls with straight, fine hair have it worse. They have to pin a wig on top of their heads and cover it with their real hair."

"I knew this was complicated, but not like this!" Eleanor remarked, grinning. "But thanks to you both, I know now how to achieve what used to be a total puzzle to me. That is—if I ever need to do this again on my own."

"Oh, believe me, darling, you will!" Arabella exclaimed, chuckling.

"Ah, the cares and travails of young women in the name of beauty!" Miss Covell declared, shaking her head. She'd been long ready for the party and was sitting on her berth, reading her book. "I'm so glad I am beyond such concerns!"

The young ladies chuckled.

Eleanor finished up by wearing her gold necklace with the locket that held her parents' photographs. The medallion lay on her breastbone, just above the hint of cleavage suggested by the scooped neckline.

"Dad-sizzle, Eleanor!" Arabella cried. "There's the real woman hiding behind those spinster clothes!"

CHAPTER 3

Pearl of the Orient Sea

Inside the Waterhouse mansion, native servants in colorful shirts and Mother Hubbards greeted the Thomasites with leis and served trays of champagne and bite-sized foods. Four Hawaiian women, dressed like the pineapple lady from the other day, sang beautiful yet melancholic songs in their language, accompanied by a small band playing diminutive guitars called ukuleles.

To Eleanor, it didn't matter she couldn't understand the lyrics, for it was easy to feel what the songs were about: loss and yearning.

Miss Covell whispered into Eleanor's ear, "Ironic, don't you think?"

"What do you mean, ma'am?" Eleanor asked, glancing at her older colleague.

"These Hawaiians performing their people's songs and dances for a man who is reputed to be one of the Gang of Thirteen," Miss Covell replied.

Eleanor raised an eyebrow and searched the crowded reception hall, in vain, for Mr. Waterhouse. She glimpsed some gentlemen, who never seemed to notice her before, now glancing at her appreciatively. They smiled at her, but she was bothered by what Miss Covell said and looked away.

She learned from their history club discussions about the thirteen members of the Annexation Club who'd conspired with U.S. Minister Stevens to overthrow Queen Liliuokalani. The Gang of Thirteen had initially called themselves the "Citizen's Committee of Public Safety"—a misnomer—for, far from being citizens of the Hawaiian Kingdom, they were foreign nationals and missionaries who happened to own large landholdings and businesses in the islands. When the queen restricted their right to buy more land to protect her people from further usurpation of their lands, they undermined her power and appealed to the U.S. government through Minister Stevens to send them soldiers, allegedly to protect their economic interests. The U.S. eagerly obliged them. And this, in the end, was what made the American takeover of the Hawaiian Islands a *fait accompli*.

Eleanor observed the conspicuous wealth on display in the palatial home. Huge Hudson-style paintings of the islands' iconic landscapes and seascapes adorned the exotic wood-paneled walls. Palace-size Ming dynasty porcelain jars and other Oriental and South Pacific antiquuities commingled with the Victorian proclivity for an abundance of ornate European *objets d'art*.

Her breath shuddered, and a sour sensation shot up from her gut, turned into bile in her throat, and threatened to eject itself into her mouth. A vertiginous spell gripped her, causing everything to seemingly spin around her. She clutched onto Miss Covell's arm.

"Oh! Miss Karsten! Are you all right?" the older teacher exclaimed.

"I just need a minute," Eleanor replied, breathing heavily as she continued grasping her cabin-mate's forearm.

Miss Covell grabbed a glass of water from a passing waiter's tray. "Here, dear, take a sip."

Eleanor washed down the bitter taste in her mouth and cleared her throat. "M-miss Covell, I… I'm sorry, but… I may have overestimated my capacity for socializing tonight. I'm returning to the *Thomas*."

"Great idea! I, too, am exhausted!" Miss Covell exclaimed. "Would you mind sharing a coach?"

"Not at all," Eleanor replied.

She searched the room for Maude and Arabella. When she found them, she signaled that she and Miss Covell were leaving. The Radcliffe girls nodded, gesturing their intent to remain with their Harvard beaus, who appeared to be engaged in a fascinating conversation with an older gentleman dressed in coattails. The distinguished-looking man's back was turned to Eleanor. *Could he be Mr. Waterhouse?* The Harvard boys seemed completely captivated by him—alternately leaning in to listen to and chuckling over whatever the man was stating.

Eleanor turned around, but before she and Miss Covell stepped out of the mansion, she glanced back at the partying crowd. She was amazed at how those many excellent minds gathered in that august home—intellects which, in their academic settings, would have otherwise been critical of how men like Mr. Waterhouse had amassed their wealth and power, appeared quite at home in the luxury of his mansion, as if oblivious to the history that made it possible for their host to entertain them in such a grand manner.

Fortunately, she and Miss Covell experienced no difficulty hiring a carriage to take them away. Many of the coachmen who'd brought the Thomasites to Mr. Waterhouse's home remained on the street, anticipating the same patrons' need for a ride back to the ship.

Not long after the carriage rocked to the horse's trot, whistling breaths told Eleanor that Miss Covell was already sleeping. She glanced at the older woman seated beside her. Her head hung forward, neck limp. Laying Miss Covell's head gently on her shoulder, she wished she could nap as easily. Yet, something was rocking her apart from the jouncing carriage.

A distinct yet amorphous unease was growing inside her, one that was calling into question the *raison d'être* of the Thomasites themselves. How could men like the Harvard boys, for instance, understand what common people needed, let alone indigenous peoples—of whom hardly any of them, including herself, knew anything? And if they didn't understand this, why had they assumed they'd be qualified to be their teachers? This hit her in the gut. Wasn't this precisely why she was going to the Philippine Islands—to help save their little brown brothers and sisters from ignorance and deprivation? *But what if I am the ignorant one?*

She sensed something askew, something possibly pointing to the origin of things. Of how people, nations, and history developed. The history of inequity. Injustice. Untruth. *Don't they say history is written by the victors?* And the victors now appeared to be America's elite, who were not only men but white men who came from families who possessed the clout and wealth to send their sons to the ivy-covered towers of the nation. White men, who then became captains of industry and government. And of women. That they happened to be exclusively male and white did not appear to be accidental nor circumstantial. It shouldn't have been a wonder to her why many Thomasites seemed at home in the luxury of Mr. Waterhouse's mansion. Many of them had come from similarly gilded backgrounds.

She now suspected a link between the ruling elite and the educated elite that spawned an unholy alliance. Their combined power couldn't be ignored, for it was such captains of industry and government who ousted women like the last Hawaiian queen from their thrones and indigenous peoples from their lands—all in the name of progress. Yet, progress for whom? In Hawaii, this was, clearly, for people like Mr. Waterhouse.

She had previously ignored the debates between the imperialists and anti-imperialists in connection with America's acquisition of Hawaii, Puerto Rico, Guam, and the Philippine Islands. She'd turned a blind eye to accusations that she and her fellow Thomasites were serving the imperialist agenda and dismissed them as the politics of cynicism.

Yet, now she heard the dissonant notes of Kipling's call to take up the white man's burden to civilize the colored peoples of the world. Wasn't this the Pied Piper calling? The treacherous Pali? Shouldn't she perhaps retreat now, while it wasn't too late to escape the trap?

Eleanor heaved a heavy sigh, and Miss Covell stirred.

Knowledge is power, she'd written on the top portion of her Iowa classroom blackboard. She'd meant it to inspire her students, especially the girls, to stay in school and not surrender entirely to farm and family life—to leave something for themselves, which was essential, she'd stressed, for anyone's soul. She reminded them that man and woman did not live by bread alone. Now, she was beginning to see that life outside the classroom could be more complex than that.

If knowledge was power, and men held the keys to knowledge, then power was reserved for men. Was it any wonder, then, that only male Americans possessed the right to vote in their so-called democracy? Yet, how could she—a woman and, clearly, a second-class citizen in her own country—hope to instruct little brown girls in faraway islands to pluck off, and eat the fruit of the Tree of Knowledge?

On the other hand, what harm could she do if she only meant to do right? *Hell is paved with good intentions.* Was it now when this saying applied? Was it possible that she, who believed herself motivated only by good intentions—be serving, unwittingly, as a puppet for nefarious schemes? If so, how could she ensure she wasn't complicit in illegitimate ends like the Gang of Thirteen?

Should she stay the course, stick with the mission? She wished Miss Covell was awake to guide her out of her mire of doubt. She wished her father were alive to advise her confounded mind, assuage her restless heart. The stinging behind her eyes became tears. This time, she didn't blink them back but allowed them to fall.

At about nine o'clock on the evening of Wednesday, the 7th of August, the *Thomas* crossed the International Date Line at the 180th parallel and stole twenty-four hours of her passengers' lives. Wednesday became Thursday without so much as alarm bells ringing. The otherwise science-educated became disoriented, glad when midnight arrived, for it allowed them to reset their watches and lives.

Ship life resumed its course—with a tropical twist that pushed social and dress etiquette to the back seat. Dispensing with jackets and suits, both men and women bared their arms. Some set up hammocks over the hatches, while others lounged at the spar deck in near negligée fashion to the shock of the prim and proper who persevered in their civilized attire in the saloon's sweltering heat. Many of the ladies, including Eleanor and the Radcliffe girls, freed themselves of the corset's oppression. They also dispensed with their stockings until they started to itch around the ankles where little red spots had appeared.

"Pulex irritans!" exclaimed Miss Covell.

"Goshamighty!" Arabella cried. "What's that?"

"Fleas," the older teacher stated matter-of-factly. "Rightly named, don't you think?"

"Irritating, indeed!" Arabella wailed.

"My Lord!" Maude groaned. "It's one thing to be badgered by flies and disgusted by cockroaches, but this—this!—is unforgivable! Miss Covell, won't you please speak with the quartermaster?"

"I will do my best, dear, but I doubt anything would come of it," Miss Covell replied. "I reckon all Captain Coulling would advise is to wear your stockings again. These insects are a perennial nuisance on ships. Like the cockroach that will survive humanity, the flea will persist!"

Miss Covell's younger colleagues moaned in protest, yet promptly returned to wearing stockings.

On the high seas and bereft of mail which, in the mainland, arrived thrice a day, and, absent the morning dailies, the Thomasites lost their sense of time. Thus, they succumbed to the pleasure or vice, depending on one's perspective, shared by most human beings when boredom set in. Gossip. Deprived of news from home and the world, they amused themselves with speculations on what could be happening on the ship. A few marital altercations, nourished by rumors, exploded into full-blown scandals. Given the disproportionate ratio between males and females, some plain Janes bloomed into popular Juliets who inspired jealous Romeos into reviving the gentlemen's duel—thankfully resolved by the commoner's fistfight.

The Mad About History Club held lectures and discussions on the history and culture of the Philippine Islands, which attracted many new members. Miss Covell gave a presentation on what she learned about Filipino culture and history from Worcester's book. Some shared personal accounts gathered from letters sent by soldiers, doctors, nurses, and clerks serving in various parts of the archipelago. They assumed that Filipinos spoke the language of their former colonial masters, and, thus, Professor Lawson persuaded Miss Covell to teach a Spanish class. Eleanor attended the lessons daily, while the Radcliffe girls dropped in exactly twice.

During one of the many balmy evenings, while the Radcliffe girls were out promenading—this time, not with the Harvard boys but with the gentlemen from Yale—Eleanor and Miss Covell likewise strolled to take in the fresh air. At the forward deck, they happened upon a group milled around what appeared to be a robust discussion among some academic and non-academic personalities sitting on the lounge chairs. They noticed Professor Lawson among the discussants and a few other members of their history club in the audience. They couldn't resist listening in.

Professor Lawson addressed a paunchy, slightly younger-looking gentleman. "Listen to what Mark Twain wrote in the Northern American Review on the Philippine issue," he said, holding up a copy of the journal. "'Shall we… go on conferring our civilization upon the peoples that sit in darkness, or shall we give those poor things a rest?' I say, Carter—Twain hit the nail on its head!"

"Nonsense!" cried the man called Carter, standing. The curled and waxed ends of his handlebar mustache lifted with the arching of his eyebrows. "As our president says," he began, pausing to look the crowd in the eye as though they were there solely for him, "'it's our duty to educate the Filipinos, and uplift and civilize and Christianize them, and, by God's grace, to do the very best we could by them!'" He punched the air for emphasis, mimicking President McKinley's voice and oratory style. "Could anyone think of more righteous reasons?"

Some of the audience clapped and murmured approvals, while others chuckled. Eleanor clenched her teeth.

"Who's this clown?" asked a man's voice not far behind Eleanor and Miss Covell. She turned around and recognized him as the one who'd been hoisted by rope onto the ship—the same young man she regretted declining to dance with during the Greek Social Club's party. She smiled at him, and he smiled back at her.

"A pencil pusher from the Office of the Interior," an older man replied. "Tasked to oversee the Taft Commission."

"Damn pencil pusher!" exclaimed the young man.

"Oh, Carter!" Professor Lawson interjected, laughing as he sat in his chair. "That sounds too much like Kipling! White Man's Burden and all that hogwash!"

"Why hogwash?" Carter retorted, his head jerking toward Professor Lawson. Turning around, he addressed the crowd again as though it was his congregation. "Does not the Good Book say, 'To whom much is given, much is expected?' We Americans have been blessed with progress not heretofore seen in the modern world. And to what do we owe this? To our Christianity, capitalism, and democracy—in that order, I dare say! Is it the Christian way to be selfish? Are we not obliged by our faith, precisely because we are divinely favored, to share the blessings of our democracy with the rest of the world? How could anyone not see this is our manifest destiny as a nation?"

The young man behind Eleanor yelled, "You're just mouthing discredited clichés, mister! A self-serving argument is no argument!"

"Yes!" Some of the crowd nodded and clapped, including Eleanor and Miss Covell.

Carter chuckled. "Oh, but clichés are clichés for a reason, young man! Certain statements are repeated over a long period of time, which, by the way, is what makes them clichés—not their lack of merit—for no other reason than they state the absolute truth."

Eleanor scoffed. "Absolute truth? Is there truly such a thing?" she blurted, surprising herself. She clasped her hands to prevent them from shaking.

Carter shot her an equally surprised look. "Why, young lady—I'm stunned you even question it! I didn't know that was even up for discussion."

Eleanor's breath shuddered, and her fingernails dug into her palms. Having dropped the glass, she now felt challenged to gather the shards of her reasoning. "Uh… what I… I m-mean, s-sir, is… who is to s-say what… what's the absolute truth? Do you really think… a civilization could simply be planted by one people to another… and expect… the same result? I mean…"

"Forgive my French, but that's bullshit!" Carter interjected, waving his hand in dismissal as he returned to his lounge chair.

"Hey, wait a minute, Carter!" Professor Lawson cried. "Give the young lady a chance to finish! Isn't this supposed to be a scholarly debate, like you said earlier? So, be scholarly! And let others argue their point!"

"Oh, if we must!" Carter scoffed, rolling his eyes as he sank into his seat. He glanced back at Eleanor and stroked his beard. "Well? What did you mean, Miss…?"

Eleanor bit her lower lip to prevent it from trembling. "K-Karsten," she replied.

"All right, then, Miss Karsten—speak!" Carter said, grinning and glancing around at the audience.

Eleanor gulped, shifting her glance between Carter and Professor Lawson, who nodded and sent her an encouraging smile. Miss Covell placed a reassuring palm on her back.

Eleanor flexed her hands and cleared her throat. "W-well, s-sirs," she began, "the way I see it… we, um, Americans… have arrived at where we are through certain developments in our history. F-firstly, we… we won our independence from the British by revolution. We had to fight for it."

"Yeah!" much of the crowd yelled almost in unison, with a few following with scattered yesses.

Eleanor glanced timorously at the audience, whose eyes were all trained on her, and she continued, "N-no one… handed our freedom to us like… like some of us appear to be promising the Filipinos, which, one must stress, sounds downright disingenuous! Because, apparently, such granting of independence depends on Filipinos proving themselves… worthy of it. But doesn't our Constitution say, 'all men are created equal'? Who, then, are we to judge them worthy or not?"

"True! True!" many cried, nodding and applauding.

"Bravo, Miss Karsten!" the young man nearby declared.

Miss Covell squeezed Eleanor's arm.

Carter appeared about to say something, but Professor Lawson intervened with, "Ladies and gentlemen, may I just say that Miss Karsten is a member of our history club?" People grinned and clapped, and he glanced back at Eleanor with a smile. "I believe you have a second point to make, Miss Karsten?"

Eleanor smiled back at him. "Yes, thank you, Professor. It appears to me that our industrial economy… may have arisen out of particular inventions necessitated by our capitalist economy—while the economic system of the Philippine Islands, I understand, remains feudal. Why do we assume we could just plant our system of government and economy on them, and expect it all to work as well for them? How… how do we know we're not planting seeds that are not appropriate for the clime and soil of that land, those people?"

An approving buzz arose from the crowd, and a couple of people yelled, "Bravo! Good point!"

Carter sneered. "I'm curious, Miss Karsten: Where are you from?" He smiled at her as though it were a trick question, which made Eleanor feel nervous again.

"Uh… um… what do you mean, sir?" she asked.

"What do you mean what do I mean?" Carter exclaimed, chuckling. "It's it an easy enough question? From where did you graduate?"

"Oh, Mr. Carter, how is that relevant to this discussion?" retorted a gray-haired lady professor sitting on one of the lounge chairs. She sent a rueful glance at Eleanor.

"Just asking!" Carter cried, smiling an alligator's smile. "Unless I'm not allowed to ask certain questions in this otherwise scholarly forum?"

Addressing the lady professor, Eleanor said, "Um, it… it's fine, ma'am. Thank you."

She turned back to Carter, replying, "Iowa, sir. Iowa Normal College." Eleanor glanced around and caught a couple of people snickering and whispering.

Carter guffawed. "Oh, Iowa! My, my! Aren't you a little green there behind the ears, young lady? Just like the corn in your fields, perhaps?"

A few chuckled, while Professor Lawson, the lady professor, Miss Covell, and a good number of the crowd groaned and shook their heads.

"What?" Carter asked the audience with raised eyebrows, smiling. "Can't I make a joke either?"

Eleanor pressed her lips, took a deep breath, and, in a matter-of-fact tone, declared, "Actually, sir, the corn is just ripe and right for harvesting this time of year. Having been born and raised on a farm taught me a lot about planting. This is how I know seeds are mighty picky where they grow, and that most, if not all seeds from our hemisphere are absolutely not suitable for the tropics!"

Much of the crowd roared, hooted, and applauded, while many of the seated professors arose from their lounge chairs to clap. Some history club members yelled, "Bravo! Bravo, Eleanor!" Miss Covell patted her on the back.

Carter smiled a crooked smile. "Well, then, Miss Karsten, there's only one way to find out, isn't there? If democracy and capitalism are right for Filipinos? Using your metaphor, just plant the damn things and see if they'll grow!"

"Oh, c'mon, Carter!" Professor Lawson interjected. "You're ignoring the issues rightfully raised by Miss Karsten—issues we should have more carefully studied before we even set out on this so-called mission of benevolence! As Bryant said, this business of acquiring new territories in the name of democracy is contradictory to the very principles of *our* democracy!"

Carter waved his hand as if shooing a fly. "Oh, damn Bryant! If he had his way, we'd all be union people and Marxists. The people have spoken: He lost the election and McKinley won! Isn't it clear enough what Americans want?"

"Pardon me, Mr. Carter!" Miss Covell declared in her commanding, teacherly voice—forcing the man to swing around and face her. Miss Covell continued, "How do we know that is what the Filipinos want? Seems to me, the simple fact they're still waging a war against us should tell us they do not want us there! Whatever happened to government 'by the people, of the people, and for the people'?"

Carter pealed in laughter. "Oh, ma'am, do you seriously think those coloreds are capable of knowing what's best for them?" His eyebrows and whiskers rose in sync. "Take the negroes, for example. They wanted freedom—so you abolitionists shed our blood to give it to them. But look at them now! They're languishing in poverty. They still can't speak correct English. They're drunks and criminals. And their neighborhoods are a blight upon our towns and cities. Why, they're worse off now than when they had a sure job, sure meal, and sure place on which to lay their heads at night!"

The crowd arose in an uproar. Professor Lawson exclaimed, "My God, Carter! Don't tell us we have to debate slavery all over again! Now, it's my turn to remind you: We won that war and you lost!"

The gathering broke into a free-for-all, shouting match. Eleanor and Miss Covell looked at each other and agreed they'd both heard enough.

In bed later that night, Eleanor reflected upon the debate. Far from the overwhelming sense of doubt and despair that she experienced on leaving the Waterhouse mansion in Honolulu, a sense of hope and peace now suffused her. She wasn't alone. Many other Thomasites and Americans shared her thoughts and feelings about their mission. They, too, appeared to believe in the goodness of their good intentions.

Because of this, making a positive difference in the lives of Filipino boys and girls was possible.

Although there were those among them whose main goal was conquest and control, Thomasites like her would be the countervailing force. She needn't be complicit with an imperialist conspiracy; she could make her own way. Her heart would guide her. And her heart could be trusted. That much she knew.

The ship's laundry service was overtaxed, forcing Eleanor and her cabin mates to wash their own clothes. None of them felt comfortable about a crew of men handling their intimate wear, anyway. They tied ropes between their bunks to hang up their washings to dry, which made their tiny cabin feel even tinier. To relieve crowding, they agreed on taking turns on their laundry.

The cabin, however, became a curtained den suffused with the rancid odor of inadequately-dried fabric. To maximize the ventilation, they kept their door open during daytime, as did other women. Hence, passing by the women's cabins lent one the sense of trespassing into a veiled harem that exposed the scandalous secret lives of women.

They had two more weeks at sea. To mitigate boredom, a Mr. Gleason organized a committee chaired by Miss Adelle Clendenin of Illinois to produce shows and other modes of entertainment. In this new universe, punctilious pedagogues became vivacious vaudeville stars. During their first production, Mr. Grossman performed a clever imitation of the famous New York stage actor, Dave Warfield, while a Miss Chase inspired nostalgia for their Honolulu stop-over by a rendition of Hawaiian songs, and a Mr. Sullivan brought down the house with his parody of the popular song, "Just Because She Made Dem Goo-Goo Eyes."

During the sailor's festival on August 9th, the entertainment committee presented a comedy. It was a mock trial of the *Thomas's* officers by Neptune, god of the sea, played by a rather boisterous, robust, dark-bearded coach of college athletics, and his beautiful, golden-haired queen, played by Arabella. They recruited Captains Coulling, Buford, and Garrard to play themselves.

Neptune accused the officers of trespassing and theft by steering the *Thomas* into his kingdom without permission and robbing Neptune's cousin, Father Time, of a whole day by crossing the 180th meridian. The sea god also charged the officers with kidnapping a multitude of youths in the persons of the Thomasites—whose beauty had stirred jealousy among his subject mermen and mermaids that further disrupted the peace in his underwater kingdom. But most egregious of all, Neptune declared, were the officers' acts of polluting the sea air with smoke and heating the ocean waters through the coal-powered ship. The sea god then pronounced the officers guilty and penalized them with a fine consisting of sandwiches and pink lemonade for the audience, plus a box of cigars and bottles of grog meant for the sea god himself.

The play was followed by the green seamen's initiation, a ritual lathering of the initiates with flour paste and broken eggs—which soon included the Thomasites and other passengers. The riotous fun swept over everyone with contagious silliness and laughter. Even Miss Covell tossed flour and eggs at Professor Lawson, who reciprocated likewise. Some sailors succeeded in enticing the Radcliffe girls' attention away from their Harvard and Yale beaus—spurring on a playful ruckus of egg-hurling between the collegiate and non-collegiate young men.

Eleanor now understood why the steward had an astounding 60,000 eggs in the refrigerated pantry.

The Greek Social Club spearheaded other modes of entertainment: by day, football scrimmages, tugs of war, boxing bouts, and games of whist and chess; by night, dances in the mess hall and duels on the saloon piano. Maude and Arabella metamorphosed into the ultimate social butterflies, flitting constantly between events—to the amusement of Eleanor and Miss Covell.

The *joie vivre* on the *Thomas* seemed to infect even the sea life. To the delight of the ship's passengers, a school of dolphins with a light slate color and pearly undersides presented a water ballet—with their sleek bodies leaping in twos and threes to a precise choreography.

Recalling the whales' send-off for the *Thomas* at San Francisco, Eleanor viewed the smaller sea mammals' appearance as an advance welcome party for the Thomasites' imminent arrival in the Philippine Islands.

Mealtimes continued to be stellar—deliciously shattering Eleanor's expectations of drab, bland meals on an army transport vessel. The steward's department impressed her with restaurant-quality meals—served three times a day. The culinary feasts consisted of three to four-course meals. For breakfast, the Thomasites enjoyed rump steaks or omelets; for luncheon—bean salad, onion soup, mutton, cold roast, and sausages; for dinner—soup ala Reine, pickled cabbage and gherkins, roast beef, chicken, and salted salmon bellies. Desserts included college pudding with sweet sauce, apple pie, orange jelly, and canned nectarines with cheese and crackers—with the customary tea and coffee service.

One morning, as the ladies were dressing up for the day, Arabella shrieked, "Consarn!"

"Goodness, dear girl!" Miss Covell cried. "You do have a talent for colorful language!"

"What's the matter, Arabella?" asked Eleanor.

"I think I'll skip breakfast today," Arabella said glumly, slumping onto Eleanor's bunk with pouting lips and a furrowed brow.

"Why?" Maude asked as she was buttoning her shirtwaist. She glanced at Arabella, smiling, as though unperturbed by her chum's distress. "What's the problem now?"

"Everything!" Arabella wailed. "I swear—if I eat one more pancake, I won't be able to fasten this damned skirt! Oh, woe is me! I'm fat as a cow!"

Miss Covell cracked into chortling, while Maude and Eleanor fell over laughing on the mattress on either side of Arabella, who protested, "What's so funny? There's nothing funny about this. I assure you!" Yet, she also burst into squealing laughter when Maude and Eleanor started tickling her.

On the afternoon of August the 10th, Miss Clenendin and her ladies' circle gave the Thomasites a rare treat: a high tea service at the dining saloon. It was an event that called for restoration of the social and dress etiquette abandoned as the *Thomas* drew close to the equator.

The ladies attended in their most charming, feminine attire—marked by floral prints, lace, and matching hats. The gentlemen wore light-colored three-piece linen suits and boater straw hats, shaved off their stubbles or trimmed their beards, and, quite possibly, even bathed.

The Radcliffe girls gasped in admiration of the spread, which featured an English heirloom silver tea set, brazier-heated kettle, bone china, and sterling silverware—all laid upon a white linen-covered buffet table. Arrayed upon various tiers of plates and platters were frosted cookies, cakes, and diminutive sardine and cucumber sandwiches.

"Great horn spoon!" Arabella cried upon seeing the center floral piece. "Roses! How on earth did they get fresh roses in the middle of the Pacific?"

Eleanor grinned. "Honolulu, perhaps? Then, the refrigerated pantry, surely!"

At about six-thirty in the evening of August the 15th, a buzz arose from the outer decks. Eleanor and her friends went to see the cause of the excitement. They hadn't seen anything but water for weeks, except for the occasional marine life led to the surface by its curiosity about the *Thomas* and its passengers.

In the early evening hours near the equator, it was still light, allowing them to see the irregular-shaped island. It appeared to be green with vegetation up to its tallest mountain, which was dappled with white patches, indicative of limestone.

"Is it the Philippines?" someone yelled.

"No!" another yelled back. "Saipan!"

"That mountain—isn't that a volcano?"

"Yes!"

"Alive?"

"No!" replied one.

"Yes!" replied another.

The geologist on board announced that the *Thomas* had now entered a geological bed of extinct and non-extinct volcanoes. Hence, rumors of volcano sightings circulated daily among the highly imaginative passengers who were often thinking they'd spotted a live one.

One evening, after word spread they might see the lights off the southeast coast of Luzon Island, the volcano enthusiasts stayed up all night. In the morning, a roar erupted from the group that had kept outside vigil—waking Eleanor and her cabin mates. The ladies peered out of their porthole, and their breath caught, for what greeted them was a sight as breathtaking as the Pali's. Throwing modesty aside, they rushed out to the starboard deck wrapped in their night robes.

They'd been sailing overnight along the coast of Albay province in the Philippine Sea. Now, there, standing before them—a surreal teal tower against a topaz sky—was a perfectly cone-shaped volcano: Mayon Volcano. A volcanologist volunteered that the Mayon, soaring more than 8,000 feet above sea level, was the largest and tallest volcano in the Philippine Islands. From its narrow crater, a trail of white smoke streamed continuously, which, to the delight and vindication of the non-extinct volcano watchers, meant the volcano was very much alive. A geologist mentioned that the last time the Mayon erupted was a mere four years ago, which was just one of its many regular eruptions throughout the centuries that were often cataclysmic.

How the geological wonder managed to keep its perfect conical shape, despite its constant destructive eruptions, struck Eleanor as short of miraculous. She looked upon the majestic earthly pyramid and a strange feeling came over her—as though the Mayon was calling out to her, enticing her with a power beyond its mesmerizing beauty. Those who brought photographic equipment were now busy trying to capture its almost otherworldly presence. Possessing no camera, Eleanor did the next best thing: She seared Mayon Volcano's image on another page of her memory bank.

The Philippine Islands appeared to be an exquisite, exotic land beyond Eleanor's wildest imagination. Her heart raced as she imagined the possibilities of where she might be assigned. She gazed at Mayon Volcano and whispered a wish.

On the morning of the Thomasites' entry into Philippine waters, Eleanor and her friends awoke early to secure choice spots on the main deck from which they expected to enjoy an unencumbered view of the islands as the *Thomas* navigated around them. Eleanor's heart hammered against her breast, and Arabella and Maude hopped like little girls expecting a treat, but Miss Covell assumed the sage's brow: tranquil yet somber.

The formidable mountains of Southern Luzon rose above the clouds like a huddled tribe of hunchbacked giants. On the port side, the sun peeked through the parting clouds and shone upon the shimmering shores of Samar Island. On the starboard side, the San Bernardino Strait lighthouse stood guard—a cylindrical tower of granite with a double balcony.

Neptune sent emissaries again—this time, in the form of giant porpoises that peeked above the purplish-blue waters. They escorted the *Thomas* as it wound around the viridian islands foreshored by white, pink, coral, and black volcanic sand beaches. Thatched huts and canoes gathered around coves, where the glistening, brown bodies of little girls and boys dove into the water and played with no shame of their nakedness, reminiscent of the Kanaka boys of Honolulu.

Capping the mountains were forests of interwoven bamboo, coconut, and hardwood trees, which created an illusion of the islands as floating emeralds on a sapphire sea. Rocky promontories, mangroves, and grassy hillsides ran abreast of the surf. The earth hugged the ocean as the waves kissed its shores. Eleanor recalled there were possibly more than seven thousand islands in the archipelago. How easy it was to get lost in such preponderance of beauty!

She remembered that, during one of their history club meetings, someone mentioned that a Filipino author martyred during the Filipino revolution against Spain wrote a poem on the eve of his execution, which he dedicated to the country he called, *Perla del Mar de Oriente* or "Pearl of the Orient Sea." This, Eleanor could see. This, she grasped as they passed the various islands. *Linked pearls they are.* To her, there was no better name for a land that, unfortunately, Ferdinand Magellan christened after Spain's King Felipe II. She frowned. *How unseemly of foreigners to exercise naming rights to another people's land!*

Suddenly, a thought dampened her excitement with foreboding. Behind every paradise lie hellish truths. As if to validate this, the winds picked up and clouds appeared—dark and pregnant with rain. The rain fell and continued pouring for the next two days.

Eleanor reassured herself by what her orientation packet stated. The archipelago had only two seasons: dry and wet. They happened to arrive during the season when one could expect daily rain. The voyage had earlier enjoyed exceptionally fine weather. Now, the downpour served to moderate the heat that had steadily arisen since the *Thomas* journeyed closer to the equator. Rain was a good thing.

On the third straight day of showers, they sighted the island of Corregidor. It emerged from the curtain of rain as a behemoth rock jutting out of the sea, impeding the entrance to Manila Bay. The conqueror of Manila, U.S. Commodore George Dewey, was said to have entered from the left side of Corregidor through the strait of *Boca Chica* or "Little Mouth," not from the island's right side—the *Boca Grande* or "Big Mouth."

Judging from where the *Thomas* appeared to be heading, Eleanor concluded that the captain may have decided to mark the Thomasites' historic arrival in the Philippine Islands by steering his ship toward Manila Bay—following Dewey's route. The significance of his act wasn't lost on his passengers. The captain was giving a victor's welcome to the Thomasites, who cheered and applauded his gesture. It was the *21st of* August, 1901—a date Eleanor etched in her memory.

CHAPTER 4

Distinguished and Ever-Loyal City

The *Thomas* passed the rooftops, towers, docks, and armory of the town of Cavite, including the eerie sight of the Spanish fleet's ghostly remains still scattered on the water, reminding the Thomasites it had only been three years since Dewey defeated the Spanish navy at what now appeared was Sangley Point. The ship followed a curve of about eight more miles of shore before the red, ivory, and verdigris skyline of Manila appeared.

The rain had finally stopped. Church domes, towers, and roofs made of clay tiles, painted metal, and patinated copper still glistened wet between the glossy foliage of coconut palms and West Indian rain trees. Someone admired the impressive canopy of one of the West Indian rain trees, and an arborist seized that moment to remark that Filipinos wrongly referred to them as acacias. Eleanor recalled that, in Honolulu, the locals called them monkey pod trees. She understood scientists' rigidity regarding their labels for the subjects of their study, but she preferred to call the native flora and fauna whatever the natives called them.

Manila was a riot of both vibrant and soft, pastel colors. Golden-yellow and pinkish-white spicular blossoms dotted the umbrella-like canopies of Philippine acacias. The mature trees towered over buildings, except the churches, whose domes and bell towers dominated the skyline, simultaneously piercing and cupping the sky. Bougainvillea vines, which seemed to have more flowers than leaves, copiously climbed fences, trellises, and houses—splashing the landscape with clouds of scarlet, magenta, and gold. Above all this were the lavender-blue peaks of the Sierra Madre mountain range, which provided a romantic backdrop to the city that the Spanish king and the Vatican baptized as *Insigne y Siempre Leal Ciudad* or "Distinguished and Ever-Loyal City."

The *Thomas* dropped anchor a few miles from the port of Manila for quarantine inspection. It was a humming beehive as it awaited the doctor's launch. An hour after the medical team arrived, Miss Covell announced to her constituents, "Ladies, we are advised to remain in our quarters for the next twenty-four hours, while the doctors perform a comprehensive check."

Her audience let out a collective groan of disappointment.

"I'm sorry," Miss Covell said, "but it looks like not everyone has had his or her required shots. The doctors want to make sure everyone is protected. So, please, I suggest you make good use of the time by ensuring you've got everything packed and ready to go when we receive the go signal. By the way, I've been informed we can only bring hand-carried bags to our dormitory. All steamer trunks and cargo crates will be loaded separately on lighters headed directly to customs for inspection and storage. Therefore, those of you who have trunks in your cabins, please pack only what can be contained in your Gladstones."

"What!" Maude and Arabella protested in unison.

A wistful serenity settled among Eleanor and her friends as they repacked their belongings. They had grown fond of each other in the tiny cabin they called home during the nearly four weeks of voyage. Now, it was hard to believe they were leaving the *Thomas* and even harder to accept that this, possibly, was the last time they would be together. They promised to write each other and hoped to meet again.

Next day, their melancholy turned back to excitement as the *Thomas* finally docked at the harbor. Representatives of the Superintendent of Public Instruction came on board to brief everyone. The more than five hundred Thomasites and their families would be transferred to steam lighters upon their disembarkation from the *Thomas,* for the most efficient route of transporting their number to their temporary city quarters was through a river called Pasig, and only vessels of limited tonnage could navigate the waterway due to its silt bars.

With the sun's return after days of rain came the unendurable heat and humidity—exacerbated by jackets and suits called for by the momentous occasion, yet unsuitable for the tropical location. Miss Covell's eyeglasses fogged up, and Eleanor felt suffocated, as did the Radcliffe girls who complained of being smothered by the very air they breathed.

"Thunderation!" hissed Arabella. "I wish we had the good sense to buy ourselves some of those fans at that Chinese emporium in Honolulu! Remember?" she said, turning to Maude.

"Only hindsight provides perfect vision, dear chum," Maude retorted. "Now, please, stop aggravating what's already an exasperating situation!"

After what seemed an eternity on the sweltering deck, an efficient movement of people and cargo began. The derricks screeched and groaned from the weight of trunks and crates being transferred onto lighters bound for the customs building. The soldiers who, not many nights ago, were young men indistinguishable in youthful deportment from their pedagogue peers, were now a solemn army in khakis, carrying knapsacks and canteens. They descended the gangplank in martial cadence and lined up on the harbor to board lighters that would deliver them to their new barracks.

"Goodness knows what awaits those boys!" Miss Covell sighed. "If tropical diseases don't get them, I fear heat stroke would. I don't know how they're bearing this heat in those woolen uniforms!"

"Indeed!" Maude replied. "Just shows how our army hasn't quite caught up with the realities of the Far East. In contrast, I hear, Spanish and British soldiers wear canvas uniforms specially made for the tropics."

"Well, they do have the benefit of a few more hundred years of imperial hegemony," Miss Covell remarked.

"True," Maude said. "But I'm going to write Father about this. There's no excuse for this lack of logistical foresight. I'll suggest he advise his friends in Washington accordingly."

Arabella sighed. "God bless and protect those boys. It'll be a shame to waste such Adonises! "

"Amen!" everyone chorused, grinning.

After the ladies boarded their launch, Eleanor claimed a spot on the forward deck to avail of unobstructed views of the city as their lighter approached it. She always found it comforting to watch people and places from a distance. It just now occurred to her that this was also how she'd lived her life thus far, as though she were merely a spectator of it. She watched it unfold after introducing a few simple stimuli: applying for teaching school, to teach at the elementary school, and for the teaching post in the Philippine Islands. It all happened easily to her. She didn't have to risk anything precious—proceeding only with the next logical step, viewing obstacles as mere hurdles to jump over to move on to the next goal she fancied.

By the same token had she instructed her students, according to what she'd learned almost exclusively from books and journals, contented with vicarious experience, sheltered from the realities of the bigger world. Then, the tornado came and blew away the luxury of living that way. It forced her to examine her life when almost none of it remained. Tragedy compelled her to stop being her life's voyeur—to see it so she could reimagine it.

Now, as she surveyed the landscape of her new life—seeing it from a strange vessel on a strange river, with strange people and still stranger things ahead, a voice inside her screamed, *I did this! I risked everything for this! I am here of my own will. Therefore, I am.*

As the steamboat continued to chug along on the river, Eleanor closed her eyes, felt the breeze on her face, and breathed in the strange scents of the splendidly bizarre city.

From Manila Bay, the lighters carrying the Thomasites swept up the Pasig River toward the old walled city of Intramuros. For more than three hundred years, the citadel had been the Spaniards' bulwark against foreign invasion, such as against the Dutch and British, who had displayed their own ambitions for the archipelago. Although the British succeeded in occupying Manila sometime in the mid-eighteenth century, their hold lasted no more than two years.

Now, another army was penetrating the city, armed only with brains and books. Eleanor wondered how the Thomasites would hold up to their own battles. While it took U.S. naval supremacy to bring them to this moment, her country now relied on her and her fellow teachers to win young minds and hearts—to help secure the American occupation.

Yet, how to win minds and hearts while blood was still being spilled? There were reports of continued guerrilla attacks by *insurrectos* in the northern biggest island of Luzon and the central islands of the Visayas. In the second-biggest island of Mindanao in the south, the Muslim Moro people continued to wage a fierce, full-scale war against the Americans.

Eleanor returned her thoughts to the more pleasant scenes before her. Although she was familiar with magazine illustrations of the views along the Pasig, she was stunned by how much more charming the same now appeared in living color. Along the river's edge, bamboo trees drooped gracefully to caress the water as canoes and rafts floated by. The bustling riverbanks spoke of a city well-versed in maritime trade and a syncretic culture both oriental and occidental.

The superintendent's representative on their launch, a portly man named Mr. McCauley, provided them with informative and amusing commentaries on the passing views. He pointed to the Chinese junks from Hong Kong, steamers of light tonnage called *vapors*, big canoes called *paraws* carved out of a single tree and balanced with bamboo rigs, and the small, ubiquitous dug-out canoes called *bancas*. Most remarkable were the *cascos*—lumbering hulls partly covered with nipa palm leaves that made for a cave-like dwelling of floating bamboo rafts. They appeared to be most vulnerable to the vicissitudes of water and weather, yet Mr. McCauley described them as generations-old family homes. "Inside those decrepit-looking covered barges," he said, "children are born, grow up, get engaged and married, and have children of their own. These people spend their whole lives on the water—along with a goat, dog, a couple of chickens, and a gamecock for food, entertainment, and company. Now, how's that for a life?"

The teachers hummed in awe.

Having now crossed an ocean, Eleanor marveled at how people could live their whole lives in the place they were born and raised, as though nothing else existed outside the confines of their insular world. It was even more amazing to her when she considered this was exactly how she'd lived before. Subscribing to the notion that life was how one imagined it, she relied on her imagination to create a self-sufficient world isolated from the universe. Yet, the terms of her old life fundamentally changed and threatened the freedom of her imagination. Thus, everything had to change. A creative life dictated what it needed, and Eleanor was certain that one ignored it at the risk of great personal suffering. If there was anything that books taught her, it was that human misery, at its core, was the product of one's resistance to this mandate. And she didn't want to become another miserable human being.

She craned her neck to peek into the interior of one of the cascos. A native woman, who strangely appeared instantaneously both younger and older than Eleanor, was shockingly naked to the waist, breast-feeding her baby, while a bare-bottomed little girl played with miniature clay pots by the mother's side. A dog leaped from inside the cabin to the casco's edge, barking at the passing launch. The woman glanced up and locked eyes with Eleanor. The Thomasite gasped, unsure of what to make of the native's gaze, except that it unnerved her. She didn't know why when she was a safe distance away.

Mr. McCauley cut through her musing. "Now, ladies and gentlemen, may I have your attention, please? One thing I suggest you familiarize yourselves with is the Spanish coinage still in use in the islands." He held up a couple of coins. "This here, for example, is media-peseta, which is half of a peseta—the equivalent of our ten cents. And this one is what we Americans call the 'silver Dobie' or Mexican coin. While these would all be replaced shortly by U.S. currency, you'll have an easier transition if you understand the current coinage, in the meantime. You don't want wily merchants getting one over you. And believe me, they will try!" he chuckled.

"Now, may I direct your attention to the streets, please?" Mr. McCauley suggested that the Thomasites likewise acquaint themselves with the different means of public transportation. "Because unless you're going to the Escolta business district, accessible through one of two public streetcars by way of horse-drawn tramways, city travel is mostly limited to foot traffic or equipage for hire." He pointed to the various victorias and other carriages and described the differences among what he called the *calesin, carromata, quiles,* and *caruaje,* according to how many passengers they carried. "The two-horse, four-wheeled carriage is called a quiles or caruaje and carries about six passengers. The one-horse calesin and carromata are limited to two and four passengers, respectively. Oh—and there's a calesin now!" he exclaimed, pointing at it.

It appeared odd and comical to Eleanor. It was a two-wheeled, iron-tired, covered carriage with a square trap, pulled by a single ratty-looking horse that looked more like a pony than a proper horse. The calesin rattled along with surprising speed and agility, but because it was top-heavy, it threatened to turn bottom-up at any moment. Its *cochero* or "driver" was perched up front in the tightly packed cab, so that he seemed to be sitting on his passengers' laps.

"Goodness, me! Oh, my!" a rotund lady cried and chuckled. "I hope I'm never mistaken for a chair—especially not by a man!"

Eleanor and everyone else laughed with her.

Commerce was not confined to store buildings but expanded to the boisterous streets and waterways. Traveling stores in the form of cattle-drawn rattan carriages—from which hung basketry, pottery, tinwork, and other household tools and utensils—lumbered at snail's speed and stopped to transact business wherever anyone hailed them. Domesticated water buffalos, which Mr. McCauley called *carabaos*, pulled bamboo carts carrying hay and other produce to wet markets. Steam-powered vapors shared the river with tiny bancas, whose operators called out to the teachers, offering all kinds of goods and vegetables.

Among the kaleidoscope of pedestrians, notable were the native *señoras* and *señoritas*. Their dresses impressed Eleanor as adaptations of European frocks that accounted for the tropical heat. Their blouses were made of surprisingly sheer yet beautifully-embroidered fabrics. A delicate chemise secured the women's modesty under their transparent tops. Whether dark or fair, they seemed obsessed with shading themselves from the sun, for they were seldom without parasols or umbrellas that either they or their servants held up over their heads.

Eleanor saw no Japanese women, unlike in Honolulu. But there were plenty of Chinese women, recognizable by their Mandarin tunics and black trousers, who minded storefronts, shopped, or held the hands of young children. She also saw veiled Hindu women dressed in vibrant saris and Muslim women covered from head to toe except for their dark, charcoaled eyes.

The gentlemen, both Filipino and Caucasian, walked about like Englishmen with their perennial walking canes or umbrellas. They strutted about like peacocks in their European three-piece suits or the native man's shirt, which was a long-sleeved tunic with a standup collar—similar to what the Filipino men in Honolulu wore. Eleanor flushed again on remembering them. The material for the native man's shirt appeared to consist of a wide array of materials that included cotton, linen, and the same sheer fabric of which the women's blouses were made, likewise paired with a simple white shirt underneath. She also spotted many Chinese men with their caps, pigtails, and blue silk robes; Sikhs with their turbans and tunics; and Arabs with their caps or fezzes and cloaks or dhotis.

As the teachers' lighter approached the golden-domed customs building, *bodegas* or "warehouses" with painted metal or terracotta tile roofs dominated the views. Ferns and other plants swayed in the breezes and grew in the cracks and crevices of walls painted in pastels, lending the industrial district a charm of its own.

The Thomasites disembarked from the Pasig River at the Anda monument that stood on a road that a sign stated was Malecon Drive. There, army ambulances and Doherty wagons were already waiting to transport them to their dormitories that Mr. McCauley said were located at the Exposition grounds.

It was about half past ten in the morning when the women teachers arrived at the Exposition Building. It was there where they'd stay until they received their respective school area assignments. The men, including husbands who came with their spouses and children, were directed to the huts at the old artillery barracks nearby.

Eleanor was impressed by the resourcefulness demonstrated by the Office of Public Instruction in converting the Exposition Building into a temporary hostel capable of housing the 141 lady teachers. The three-story building, according to Maude, was built in the California Mission style—characterized by its red tile roof, white stuccoed walls, and arched windows. The interior consisted of an assembly hall, now set up as a reception area, and more than two dozen rooms fitted with military cots and mosquito nets. There were separate latrines and shower stalls outside the building.

"Regarding laundry," Mr. McCauley said, "you'd be happy to know there are many Chinese laundries in the area offering fast and efficient washing and ironing services."

The men's and women's dormitories were again given their respective group captains, chosen from among the teachers who had arrived weeks earlier in smaller ships such as the *Sheridan* and *Buford*. Miss Covell expressed surprise and delight on learning that the matron of the Women's Quarters was a Miss Bertha Thompson, who had sailed on the *Buford*, and was, the older teacher stressed, not only her fellow Michigan alumna but a friend.

As Miss Thompson registered the name of each of the ladies under a room and cot number, Miss Covell, urged by Eleanor and the Radcliffe girls, requested her friend if she could arrange for them to be room-mates again. Miss Thompson agreed on the condition they volunteered to serve under a plan wherein three different groups of women—four each in the morning, afternoon, and evening—performed daily duty whereby a pair of them served as clerk-receptionists while the other two acted as couriers delivering messages or summoning residents to the reception area. Eleanor and her friends agreed to sign up for the afternoon slot so they could take advantage of the cooler mornings and evenings to explore the city.

By five o'clock in the afternoon of the same day the Thomasites arrived, the atmosphere in the Exposition became one akin to a presidential nomination convention, teeming with the drone of delegates negotiating and trading alliances, gossiping, or discussing sightseeing plans. The crowding, confusion, and noise were magnified by the male teachers who lounged in the reception hall to catch up with the women, seemingly intent on pursuing the party lifestyle on the *Thomas*. Compounding the condition was the sociable nature of the lady Thomasites, who seemed somehow to know someone somewhere in the city, whether it be from the military or civilian population. Thus, it looked like opera opening night at the Exposition Building as its entranceway became congested with carruajes converging to drop off their passengers and parking to wait for their patrons.

Soldiers came calling in their gold-buttoned white uniforms, along with civilian men in European-style suits or the Filipino gentleman's sheer dress shirt that Eleanor learned was called, *Barong Tagalog*. While some of the male visitors had legitimate reasons to be there, many were only hoping for a chance to meet some lovely, single, American female teachers.

Ladies likewise came visiting in the persons of military wives and local society señoras and señoritas eager to see and take their measure of *las maestras Americanas* with whom the dailies, like *The Manila Sun*, were reportedly agog. The señoras and señoritas came elegantly dressed in exquisitely embroidered, pastel-dyed frocks, about which they were happy to educate the lady Thomasites. They called their dresses, *camisa at saya*, which appeared to consist of no less than four layers of clothing: first, the *camisa*, which was a sheer blouse with large butterfly or bell-like sleeves paired with a light chemise underneath; second, the *panuelo*, a stiff kerchief draped over their shoulders with its ends crossed and pinned at the breast; third, the *saya*, which was a long, flaring skirt that sometimes culminated in a train; and, finally, the *tapis*, an overskirt wrapped around the saya and drawn tightly around the waist and hips, down to just above the knees—from where the main skirt or saya re-emerged, flaring to the floor in a shape suggestive of a mermaid's tail.

Eleanor observed that the long skirts and tapises were usually made of silk or fine linen, paired with solid pastels or coordinating bold stripes and other geometrical patterns. Most astonishing to her was learning that the gossamer fabric that shone almost like silk or satin, of which the ladies' camisas and panuelos and the men's Barong Tagalogs were made, was woven from the refined fibers of the leaves of the *piña* or "pineapple" plant—thus, the name, piña cloth.

In jewelry, the native ladies appeared to favor lustrous pearls and brilliant, yellow gold. They flaunted their affluence by the size and intricacy of their pearl or gold hoop earrings and their opera-length, filigreed, gold necklaces—from which hung large, golden starburst medallions they called *tambourine*. The tambourines often had center glass lockets that contained religious icons in the image of the wearer's favorite saint—usually, the Madonna. One society matron bragged that her tambourine held a piece of Christ's cross that her husband had brought from the Holy Land.

Eleanor learned to spot the married señoras and unmarried señoritas mainly by the way they wore their hair—apart from the gold wedding bands the señoras wore Continental style on their right-hand fourth finger. The señoras gathered their hair into severely pulled buns pinned to the back of their heads. They called it a *pusod*, which was the same word for navel, Miss Covell said, and so apropos, because the hair bun was coiled into what, indeed, looked like a navel.

Although some señoritas also sported the pusod, many of them proudly wore their thick, glossy black hair loose, made glossier through the application of coconut oil, down to their waists or buttocks. On one occasion, Eleanor was shocked to see a señorita's mane reach her heels, which, for most of the native women, were not shoes but wooden sandals with straps of leather or fabric across the toes.

Eleanor reflected on how Anglo-Saxon culture, as did some other cultures, especially religious ones, viewed uncovered women's hair suspect, particularly when worn loose and long. A Jezebel's mantle. Here, however, unmarried girls unabashedly flaunted their luxuriously long, shiny locks. Was this a temporary privilege granted young women to enable them to entice prospective husbands? A brief moment of permissible wanton beauty—before the bonds of husbands and homes confined them to their lives as wives and mothers?

The locals who came visiting constituted a melting pot of races, and none of them looked like the natives Eleanor observed elsewhere in the city—those who performed the menial tasks of street sweepers, vendors, stevedores, and servants, who were short and had dark complexions and flat faces and noses. Thus, Eleanor gleaned, the Exposition visitors were likely the elite, who seemed to observe a hierarchy among themselves based on the degree of Spanish or European lineage they possessed or could claim to possess.

Eleanor was bemused by the tendency of members of the various rungs of such hierarchy to be eager to expound on what distinguished them from the others by undermining their rivals' social status. She ignored her usual instinct not to entertain gossip whenever they whispered into her ear, for she considered them as doing her a favor by educating her about the culture's realities that neither books nor history club lectures had availed her. This was how she learned of the way the different groups ranked each other.

The Spaniards residing in the islands were called *Kastilyas* and were apparently divided into the *peninsulares*, full-blooded Spaniards born in Spain, and the *insulares,* full-blooded Kastilyas born in the islands. Beneath the Kastilyas were the mestizos and mestizas, the miscegenations of Spaniards or other Europeans and the indigenous Indo-Malay stock—who were called *indios*, if one meant to disparage them. Underneath the Spanish or Caucasian mestizos and mestizas was another group of mestizos and mestizas who were the combination of indigenous natives and the Chinese. The elevated status of Chinese mestizos and mestizas appeared to be derived mainly from the wealth and corresponding influence they'd amassed through their acumen for business enterprise. For the same reason were wealthy, pure-blooded natives considered their equal. Beneath them all was the indigenous servant and working class and, lower still, the pure-blooded Chinese, unless the latter were rich merchants such that their economic clout couldn't be ignored.

The Spanish or European mestizos and mestizas were a stunning combination of the fair complexion, high-bridged nose, and tall stature associated with Caucasians and the native's brown skin, button nose, and black hair and eyes. The Chinese mestizos and mestizas were characterized by the slanted, hooded eyes and round faces of their Chinese ancestry mixed with the features of the Indo-Malay. Sometimes, the mestizos and mestizas were a mix of all the races, and they were whom Eleanor found most interesting.

Filipino society struck Eleanor as so highly stratified, it operated almost like a caste system that kept everyone in their place and condemned a large number of the population to a servant class. From one of Professor Lawson's lectures, she recalled, this may be attributed to a heritage of slavery in pre-Hispanic indigenous society as reflected in the language, such as the Tagal word for "slave:" *alipin*.

Much to the excitement of Arabella and Maude, another pair of Radcliffe alumnae—Miss Eliza Cummings and Miss Mabel Foster—also came to visit at the Exposition. They had traveled with Miss Thompson on the *Buford* and were staying with her in a dormitory at the *Escuela Municipal* inside the walled city of Intramuros. Much to the dismay of Miss Thompson, however, the *Thomas* Radcliffe girls' discovery of the *Buford* Radcliffe girls presented serious challenges to her role as matron of the Women's Quarters.

Miss Covell's friend called the four Radcliffe girls, Miss Covell and Eleanor to a meeting at her office. She said she looked upon her duties to include protecting the reputation and safety of all the women — especially the younger, unmarried female teachers. She pointed out that a pair of Radcliffe girls may have been enough, perhaps even too much for some of the more prudish schoolmarms on the *Thomas*. Now, a double pair of them — together — posed a threat of crisis proportions on her ability to keep out the men from sneaking into the Women's Quarters.

The four lovely, lively, and popular Radcliffe girls attracted such a great number of avid admirers, including local Lotharios who, being miffed about their failure to secure their time with the girls, resorted to creative means of seeking them out. "I assure you, ladies," Miss Thompson declared, "that I don't look forward to having to check the broom closets, nooks and crannies, and all possible hideouts in this building before I close for the night with the peace of mind I need to finally enjoy a good night's rest!"

Miss Thompson announced that her only option was to resort to the teacher's disciplinary tool: detention. She ordered all the Radcliffe girls confined to their rooms.

After two days, Miss Thompson continued to be sour with the Radcliffe girls, relentless regarding their detentions. Miss Covell assured Maude and Arabella she would do her best to try to placate her friend.

One late afternoon, just before the turnover from the afternoon to evening shift, Eleanor went to the supply room to get a replacement notepad for the reception desk. She was in the poorly-lit backside of the room when the two older teachers entered and shut the door.

"No, no, no!" Miss Thompson cried. "I won't have those girls gallivanting about again, wreaking havoc on our ladies' reputation — and complicating my job!" She was a tall, hefty, and rather bosomy woman. Next to her, Miss Covell looked like a waif. She'd gathered her long, graying hair into her usual pair of braids, looped them in opposite directions up and over the crown of her head like a wreath, and pinned their ends into pleats above her nape. Her brows squeezed into two deep grooves, and vertical lines marred the symmetry of her slim lips. Yet, Eleanor imagined she could have been an attractive woman in her youth, for she had stunning green eyes that possessed the power to hypnotize or terrorize.

"But, my dear Bertha," Miss Covell said in a pleading yet unyielding tone, "consider the fact that these girls might have been among New York's reigning debutantes—if they weren't smarter and more sensible than their peers! They did not just sit around like many rich girls do, merely waiting for the season of silly balls to begin and for marriage proposals from men as dreary as tea time with gilded society's match-makers. Surely, you cannot overlook such virtues, which, I hope, could persuade you to accord my girls some clemency! After all, it isn't their fault they are pretty and popular."

Eleanor smiled to herself, seized with the urge to rush to and hug Miss Covell. But before she could make her presence known, Miss Covell reached up and pulled Miss Thompson's face to hers and pressed her mouth on her friend's lips. Eleanor muffled a gasp, stepped back, and crouched behind the crates. She took a deep breath before she peeked again.

"Ida—please! Don't!" Miss Thompson cried, pushing Miss Covell away. She covered her face and whimpered.

Miss Covell staggered back, but regained her balance. After straightening herself, she declared in a steady, solemn voice, "Bertha, we were once young, beautiful, and spirited girls, too. Remember? I do, and I shall never forget. But you and I chose to miss our chance at happiness. Because we were cowards. Don't let my girls miss theirs by default." She opened the door and closed it behind her.

Miss Thompson sniffled, fished out a handkerchief from her skirt pocket, unfurled it, wiped her eyes and blew her nose, folded it back into a neat square, and returned it to her pocket. She tucked her blouse into her skirt, smoothened her hair, raised her chin, and left.

Eleanor remained frozen where she hid. She wasn't sure what to think or feel about what she witnessed. Yet, now, she understood Miss Covell's occasional retreats into wistfulness.

Eleanor was sleepless that night and felt as though she were sleep-walking all of next day. She avoided both Miss Covell and Miss Thompson, afraid of giving herself away and embarrassing them. On the second night, she lay awake again in her cot as Miss Covell read in bed. The older teacher's eyeglasses reflected the light of the oil lamp sitting on a stool outside her mosquito net. Maude and Arabella were, as usual, already sleeping off the frustration of their unjust incarceration, as if by so doing the day of their liberation would come sooner.

The questions that had been nagging Eleanor since the supply room incident demanded answers: Did she feel any less affection, respect, or admiration for Miss Covell because of whom she loved? Would she also choose to miss her chance at happiness if it didn't conform to society's norms?

Eleanor glanced at the older teacher, whose head was now poking out of her mosquito net blowing out her lamp. "Goodnight, dear Miss Covell," she said. "Sweet dreams."

Miss Covell smiled. "And a good night to you, too, dear," she replied.

On the morning after the third straight day since the Radcliffe girls' seclusion, Miss Thompson finally acceded to Miss Covell's plea to free the young ladies. They celebrated the Radcliffe girls' coming out of isolation by visiting the second pair of Radcliffe girls, Eliza and Mabel, in Intramuros. The matron of the Women's Quarters had likewise kept them detained, until now, in their dormitory at the Escuela Municipal.

They set out early to avoid the sweltering heat of the afternoon, which they learned the locals whiled and willed away through a siesta nap. Since there were four of them, they hired a carromata. It was Eleanor's first ride in one, and she was soon alarmed by what sounded like a half grunt, half moan. She assumed it came from the poor horse struggling to pull the weight of five passengers, inclusive of the cochero. But when the same noise started again a minute later, she discovered it was the driver producing the sound.

"What's that about?" Eleanor whispered to the Radcliffe girls, who giggled.

"That's the driver's way to direct his horse," replied Maude, grinning.

"Odd, isn't it?" Arabella said under her breath. "When I first heard a coachman make that sound, I feared he was afflicted with a respiratory disease I might catch. I wanted to climb out of that calesa! But, then,

I thought: Arabella, you're a fool. It's harder to catch a carriage here than it's likely you'll catch tuberculosis! So, I stayed."

"Oh, dear girl," Miss Covell said. "Your mind does work in mysterious ways!"

Eleanor and Maude burst into laughter, while Arabella replied, "Why, thank you, ma'am! I'll take that as a compliment."

They rattled onto a street named the San Fernando. The area looked similar to San Francisco's Chinatown—only bigger, noisier, and more chaotic and cluttered. They crossed a quaint stone bridge over a canal and passed a church near a district sign that stated, *Binondo*.

"Oh, look at that church!" Maude exclaimed. "Wonderful interpretation of High Italian Renaissance! Doesn't the octagonal bell tower remind you of a pagoda?"

"And appropriate for the area," Eleanor said.

"This must be where the Spaniards sequestered the Chinese," Miss Covell remarked. "The *Parian*, I think, they called it. The Chinese ghetto. Same thing we did to the Orientals back home."

The younger ladies glanced at each other and fell silent.

They approached the *Puente de España* or "Bridge of Spain" to cross the Pasig River. It was a beautiful stone bridge with graceful arches and elegant though massive piers—as commanding as any similar structure Eleanor had seen in Chicago or San Francisco.

They entered the bridge from the Binondo side by a steep grade. Miss Covell expressed worry their combined weight would be too much for the horse. "Should we get off until it reaches the top?" she suggested.

"Yes, perhaps we should," Eleanor replied.

"Don't worry," Maude interjected. "I've seen these hardy horses carry bigger men in our number. Just wait and watch."

The horse struggled to pull them, coaxed on by its owner, who launched into a level of grunts and groans that reached plague intensity. Eleanor worried not so much for the horse but for Miss Covell, who began hyperventilating. "Miss Covell, there are no checkreins, at least," she said to comfort the older teacher. In addition to his coaxing, the cochero flicked his whip in the air—the mere sound of which seemed enough to prompt the steed to do its master's bidding. In the end, the poor horse managed to successfully carry them all to the other side of the bridge.

They passed under a pedimented neoclassical gate called the *Puerta de Parian*—one of several entrances to the walled city, according to Miss Covell. The carromata jounced upon the cobbled streets until it reached a low, square structure with the sign, Escuela Municipal, carved and painted above its portal. Almost as soon as it pulled up to the building, the front door opened, and out came Eliza and Mabel.

The ladies from the Exposition stepped down the carriage, and Miss Covell paid and thanked the cochero, who left with his little horse neighing, as though glad to be rid of its load of women.

"You've arrived!" cried both Eliza and Mabel. "Welcome to the Walled City!"

CHAPTER 5

The Walled City

Eleanor smiled. The second pair of Radcliffe girls looked like sisters. Although Eliza was taller than Mabel, both had brown hair, brown eyes, and porcelain white skin. They could even be mistaken as twins from afar.

"Come in and see where we live!" Mabel said, leading the way. "Did you know this was a girls' training school during the Spanish period?"

"Was it, really?" exclaimed Arabella. "How interesting!"

The Exposition ladies surveyed the interior of the colonial structure as they followed Mabel and Eliza. Eleanor noted the dark, rustic wooden beams on the ceilings and unevenly plastered stone walls. Some plaster had fallen off, while other parts of the walls showed powdery rings around bloated spots that were crumbling around the edges—due to the humidity, she suspected. Yet, these only enhanced the charm of the place for her, while attesting to its age.

Miss Covell glanced around as though she was searching for something or somebody. "Is Miss Thompson around?" she finally asked.

Eleanor watched her older colleague's countenance, noting some anxiety there.

Eliza replied, "Oh, she's just stepped out for errands. She said she'd meet us for luncheon at eleven-thirty at the cantina nearby."

"That is kind of her," Miss Covell said, with a smile that nonetheless failed to mask her disappointment.

Mabel and Eliza led them across a loggia that banded a rectangular courtyard garden lush with ferns, palms, and birds of paradise flowering plants. They entered a room furnished with three four-poster beds overhung with mosquito nets. Eleanor had learned the critical value of the nets on their first night in Manila. As soon as the evening shadows set in, mosquitoes attacked them.

Although the tropical mosquito looked puny, it was deadly. Malaria was reportedly prevalent in the islands, including the cities. The Thomasites suffered itchy red welts not only on parts of their skin that may have been exposed during the night but also on covered areas of their bodies. This suggested that the insects could pierce through clothing if the material was thin enough. Yet how to wear thick fabric in the heat? The ladies considered themselves fortunate that none of them had yet caught the malarial and yellow fevers common to the soldiers, who were also said to be dealing with other kinds of tropical maladies, not the least irksome of which was persistent feet fungus bred by woolen socks soaked in sweat all the time.

In the *Buford* Radcliffe girls' bedroom were three handsomely carved four-poster mahogany beds. They were reminiscent of plantation beds in the American South, except they had a caned board instead of a feather mattress to lie on. There was a pillow and bolster near the headboard and a rolled woven mat and folded bedsheets at the footboard. Maude asked about the sleeping accessories, and Mabel explained that they covered the caned surface with the *banig* or "woven mat" and laid a bedsheet over it. The second bed sheet served as their blanket.

"Practical for a warm climate," Maude remarked. "But not very comfortable, I imagine. I miss my feather bed."

"Well, I think they're lovely!" Arabella declared. "Beats the army cots we sleep in!"

"Now, now, Arabella," said Eliza. "Don't forget—these pretty beds also come with Miss Thompson as a roommate!" She glanced at Miss Covell and added, "Oops, sorry, ma'am! I know you're chums and all."

The young ladies chuckled, including Miss Covell, who replied, "Miss Thompson may be strict but has a soft spot hidden inside her. Don't forget it was this soft spot that released you girls from detention."

Eleanor smiled and touched Miss Covell's arm. "And we are all grateful to you, dear Miss Covell, for it was surely you who appealed to Miss Thompson's soft side."

"Yes, indeed we are!" cried all the Radcliffe girls. "Thank you, Miss Covell!"

Miss Covell smiled shyly before abruptly looking downward, appearing almost flushed.

"What curious material!" Maude exclaimed, touching the opaque little square inserts within the wooden window grids. "I've seen them on windows all over the city."

"Why, they're like jewelry for windows!" Arabella said. "Like mother-of-pearl!"

"That's because they are," replied Eliza. "Our landlord said they're made from capiz shells—a kind of oyster. And they're surprisingly durable and functional. They let the light in, but afford privacy and protection from mosquitoes, rain, and wind."

"Shells!" Maude exclaimed. "Who would have thought?"

"Amazing even more when we consider these islands get a beating during typhoon season," Miss Covell remarked.

"Typhoons?" Arabella said. "What are those?"

"They're like our hurricanes," Eleanor volunteered. "Only they call them that here."

"When do they come?" Arabella asked.

"As I recall from our orientation packet," Eleanor said, "they could strike any time during the rainy season, which runs from June to September."

"And so... officially, we're still in typhoon season?" Eliza said, concern flooding her eyes.

"Yes," Miss Covell replied.

"Goshamighty!" cried Arabella. "I hope they don't send me to some island where I have to get on a boat again, especially not during a typhoon! We all know what happened on the *Thomas*!"

"How could we forget?" Eleanor exclaimed, chuckling.

The other ladies, including Arabella, joined in the laughter.

Eliza and Mabel suggested a stroll at Fort Santiago. "It's a citadel, a fortress inside a walled city," Mabel explained. "Makes for quite a lovely walk. You feel as if you were walking back in time, back to when this place was a Spanish fort."

"True," Eliza agreed. "It's amazing to think most everything you'll see—the houses, churches, convents, schools, and other buildings—could be two hundred years older than the United States."

"That's a good point," Maude said. "Yet, here we are, aiming to educate a people with a history older than ours."

"You have got that right, dear Maude," Miss Covell said, nodding and smiling.

The ladies wandered among the surprisingly wide, cobbled streets, noting the unusual architecture of the structures that featured cantilevered second floors overhanging sidewalks. "Smart way to gain interior space!" Maude remarked. The upper floors featured wooden walls with parapets fended with wood-turned balusters under the window sills. In contrast, the first floor was made of stone walls with windows secured by wrought iron grills.

"Look at those massive iron bars!" Arabella pointed to a window. "One would think thievery was rampant here."

"Yes, interesting," Miss Covell said. "Either that, or it's the people they want to keep in."

"Well, we certainly know how that feels!" Arabella exclaimed.

Everyone chuckled.

"See how the panels behind those balusters seem capable of being opened?" Maude said, pointing to the parapets below the windows. The prospective lady architect was in her element, enjoying the unique architecture around them. "That's probably meant to let in the breeze."

"You may be right," Eleanor replied. "And have you all noticed how they hardly use glass for windows and doors here?"

"I believe that's because of the earthquakes," Miss Covell replied. "Which is also why many of the roofs here are made of galvanized metal—lighter than clay tiles."

"Earthquakes!" Arabella exclaimed. "I can't imagine what that's like."

"I imagine quite scary," said Miss Covell, grinning. "The islands, I understand from our geologists, lie in an earthquake zone."

"Oh, could everyone please stop scaring me?" Arabella exclaimed with knitted brows. "Typhoons and earthquakes and malaria! Oy! I'm starting to question why I came here."

Maude chuckled. "Oh, don't be a wimp, old chum. Remember—it's all part of our adventure!"

"Yes, but I could do with less scary and more adventure," Arabella groaned.

"All right. Let's all agree to speak of more pleasant things now," Eliza said.

"Agreed!" everyone cried.

Maude placed an arm around Arabella, and the latter looked cheerful again.

They passed two pretty, young maidens within a block of each other, leaning out of their second-floor windows. Dressed in finery, they appeared to be engaging with suitors standing on the street below them with what sounded like flirtatious repartee.

"Dad-sizzle! I should take lessons from them!" Arabella said under her breath, snickering. "Have you all noticed what natural flirts the girls here are?"

"Arabella, dear, I don't think you need any lessons in that department," teased Eleanor.

Everyone burst into laughter, including Arabella.

"Well, at least we now know who the iron bars were meant to keep inside!" exclaimed Miss Covell.

Everyone laughed again.

"Right you are, Miss Covell," Mabel remarked. "But I'm not sure they're women as much as they're merely girls. Look at them! Why, they couldn't be more than thirteen or fourteen. Fifteen, at most, I reckon."

Eliza grinned. "You should hear them in the evenings when their amorous callers serenade them with maudlin love songs. It's either a man alone with his guitar or a whole band of them."

"Yes, that's true," Mabel interjected. "I'm told that it's called a harana. And if a girl opens her window to acknowledge her harana, that means she accepts the boy's courtship. If not, then he only needs to be more persistent!"

Everyone chuckled.

Just then, uniformed students from a boys' school, escorted by shovel-hatted priests, exited a building. The young men appeared to be going out for a walk. Then, as if on cue, coy *colegialas* in white dresses stepped out of a convent and walked in pairs on the other side of the street, under the watchful eyes of nuns in black habits, who ensured their wards refrained from talking with or even glancing at the boys. The religious guardians promptly pinched and scolded any offending maiden.

"Goshamighty! What's this?" Arabella chuckled. "Recess time? Let's follow them!"

Both sets of boys and girls appeared to be headed in the same direction. The ladies exchanged glances and grinned when they saw where the two groups went: inside a church.

"Looks like confession time for their naughty little thoughts and deeds," Eliza remarked.

The ladies chuckled and moved on. There seemed to be a church at every turn and a great variety of the religious present everywhere: *madres* in black habits, novices in white; *frailes* in brown robes with hoods; and *padres* wearing black or white cassocks, sometimes accompanied by a sacristan or two.

"My goodness, religion is everywhere here, isn't it?" Maude declared.

"Eleven churches in the citadel alone, plus a cathedral!" Mabel volunteered.

"This is why it's imperative to teach our students our democratic principle of separation of church and state," Miss Covell stated. "Remember the Spanish Inquisition."

"I shudder at the mere thought!" Eleanor exclaimed. "But, Miss Covell, do you think they're ready for democracy?"

"That, indeed, remains to be seen," Miss Covell replied. "The Spaniards left the Filipinos in a state of feudal theocracy. During their rule, they also denied the natives meaningful roles in government. This is why we'll be educating the children in civics."

As they approached the ramparts of Fort Santiago, they noticed an increase in road traffic. Carriage drivers shouted, "Ta-beh! Ta-beh!"

"What on earth are they screaming about?" Arabella exclaimed as she hopped to the side of the street just in time to avoid being hit by a horse.

"I think they're asking us to get out of their way," Eleanor suggested.

"Zounds!" Arabella cried. "That's a feat, considering there are no sidewalks!"

Eliza and Mabel led them up a flight of moss-grown stone steps. When they reached the top, they discovered they were on a rampart overlooking a moat. The ladies paused to gaze across it at an avenue lined with elegant European-style street lamps and a charming parkland with verdant lawns dotted with mature acacias.

"Oh, what a pretty park!" exclaimed Arabella. "What's it called?"

"It's the Paseo de las Aguadas," Eliza replied. "But it's referred to here as Bagumbayan."

Fort Santiago revealed itself to be a cavalier inside the walled city, fortified by a second wall separated by the moat and an exterior wall. The ladies found themselves standing on an eight-foot-wide terreplein above the curtain of the second wall. The cavalier walls were higher than those of the first wall. Some of its battlements still had cannons pointed at Manila Bay and the Pasig River.

"I could see how this fort might have held off pirates and other attacks from the water," Eleanor remarked. "But Dewey's victory suggests the Spaniards should have anticipated that the fight for Manila was going to be decided by battleships before anyone even got close enough to bombard the city."

"True," Maude replied. "Naval superiority was key."

"I agree," Miss Covell said. "Despite the fortunes amassed by the Spanish empire from its colonies, its antiquated bureaucracy failed to modernize its ships. Therefore, it failed to keep up with the latest technologies of war. The singular advantage of our empire is that it is still young. It is not yet hampered by lumbering, old bureaucracies quagmired in incompetence like those of the Spanish."

"Empire, Miss Covell?" Maude retorted, looking and sounding offended. "Do you really think one could equate our policy of benevolent assimilation with the imperialistic greed of merry old England, France, and Germany? Let alone the corrupt colonial empires of the Spaniards, Portuguese, and Dutch?"

Miss Covell smiled somberly. "I have no doubt, my dear Maude, that each of us here came with pure and noble intentions." She took a deep breath before adding in a grave tone, "But we cannot assume such is the same for all our fellow Americans here or on the mainland. Have you seen the postcards sent home by our soldiers, the ones flaunting what fun they had in administering the water torture on their Filipino prisoner? And how about those pictures of trenches stacked with the corpses not only of native men and women but also children?"

Maude winced and shook her head. "Yes, but what has that to do with our mission? I've no mind for torture, but I'm also not an expert in war. Our soldiers must have done only what they needed to do to defend themselves. Sure, maybe those postcards suggest they were having a little fun doing unpleasant things. But those pictures also appear to be staged! Simply for amusement, I reckon. And I'd like to think that if some of our soldiers truly did such horrible things, they're the exceptions, not examples of American policy."

Eleanor braced herself as her glance shifted between Miss Covell and Maude. She realized that neither she nor the elder teacher had discussed politics with the younger ladies.

A couple of seconds passed before Miss Covell replied, "Think all you like, dear, but those images have much to do with our mission as Thomasites. The face of the American here is the face of a soldier with a gun pointed at a people whom we patronize as our "little brown brothers and sisters." Does benevolent assimilation require us to kill and frighten Filipinos into submission to educate them? Make no mistake about it, dear ladies: We are here on an empire-building mission."

Maude scoffed and interjected, "Well, then, Miss Covell, the question begs to be asked: Why are you here?" Maude's face turned red; her chest rapidly rose and fell with her breathing.

Miss Covell sighed, clasped her hands behind her back, and looked downward. When she glanced up at Maude again, she replied, "To present a different face of the American to the youth of this land." Turning to each of the ladies, she added, "To soften the blow of this so-called benevolent assimilation. Because, believe you me, my dears, we haven't seen the last of it."

A long, thoughtful silence settled upon them. Everyone, except Eleanor, looked away from Miss Covell toward varied directions.

Something about the citadel walls seemed to have grabbed Miss Covell's attention. The older teacher adjusted her eyeglasses on her nose as she bent down and straightened up to touch and examine various spots on the stone surface.

Mabel broke the uncomfortable silence by announcing, "Well, ladies, I'm afraid we have to go if we're to meet Miss Thompson on time. You all know how she hates anyone being late." She sputtered a nervous grin. "And if I'm not mistaken, she scheduled an early lunch so you all could make it back in time for your afternoon shift at the Exposition."

"You're absolutely right, Mabel!" Eleanor exclaimed. "Thanks for the reminder. Let's go, my friends!" She exchanged thankful smiles with Mabel.

At that moment, all twelve churches inside the walled city rang their bells, tolling the eleventh hour. To Eleanor, it sounded both auspicious and ominous. She was struck with a sense of something having shifted, pushing the women toward their separate journeys. Despite the heat, she shivered, anticipating what lay ahead.

Mabel said Miss Thompson was waiting for them at a canteen across the Escuela Municipal. They ascended the two-story structure through a set of broad, wooden stairs from a stone-flagged hall where, judging by the smell that greeted them and the sight of two shrouded, unhitched carriages, suggested it used to be the stable and carriage house. When they reached the second floor, they entered a long room with a high ceiling and capiz shell windows. Eleanor smiled on seeing the balustered panels of the parapets below the windows open, which confirmed their cooling function.

An outdoor courtyard garden with a tiled floor bordered one side of the deep room. On the other side, facing the street, was a covered terrace that served as a solarium, lush with hanging ferns and tropical plants. Apart from a piano in a corner, on which a young Filipino sporting a pompadour was hammering a ragtime melody, the furniture consisted of several mismatched dining tables and chairs. Eleanor surmised the cantina must have served as the drawing-room or sala of what used to be a grand house.

"Ah, there you all are!" cried Miss Thompson, who was seated at a table already set for seven. She waved the ladies over.

Eleanor noted how the glassware and plates were set upside down on the tables, a preemptive practice, she guessed, against dust and flies, which were perennial in the city, apart from the heat, mosquitoes, churches, and capiz shell windows.

"Bertha, thank you for arranging this lunch for us," Miss Covell said as she sat beside her friend, smiling.

"Don't thank me yet!" Miss Thompson smirked. "I'm afraid the meals here haven't been up to par. Our landlord owns this place, too, you see, and he certainly found a way to make more money out of us by forcing us to eat here, since our rent includes meals. And he seems to think canned food is what Americans want!" she sniggered. "Yet, this was the most practical place to have lunch before you all have to return to the Exposition. I'm hoping the food is better today. I asked him to prepare something different. A native dish, I said—as long as it's not too adventurous or spicy and is prepared from fresh ingredients!"

"I am sure it will be fine," Miss Covell replied, grinning.

Eleanor was glad to see that the pair of friends were behaving as though they'd already forgotten their row the other day. Was it possible for old lovers to settle for friendship?

She was surprised to see the waiter was an American negro. He brought them a pitcher of iced *limonada*. She'd learned the lemonade was made from the juice of tiny, native, green citruses called *calamondin* when someone prepared it at the Exposition during a particularly warm afternoon. The cool, tangy beverage sweetened with sugar proved refreshing.

"Thank you!" Eleanor said, smiling at the waiter. He nodded yet seemingly avoided eye contact with her and everyone else at their table. He picked and turned up her glass and poured her a serving of the juice. It struck her that, even here, an ocean away from the mainland, the negro remained measured in his conduct toward the white ladies. It had been about forty years since their country fought a civil war over slavery. Yet, it was clear to her the war hadn't yet been fully won, as Miss Covell once said on the *Thomas*.

An inhuman screeching coming from the terrace startled everyone. "Thunderation!" Arabella exclaimed. "What's that?"

Mabel chuckled. "Oh, that must be George!"

"Who's George?" Arabella asked, eyes wide.

"Why don't you go to the azotea and see?" Miss Thompson suggested, smiling a knowing smile.

"You mean the terrace, ma'am?" Maude asked.

"Yes. Go on, you two," Miss Thompson urged.

Arabella and Maude went as told. Soon, Arabella shrieked, followed by Maude laughing. When the pair returned to the table, chuckling, Eleanor asked, "What?"

Arabella, still in stitches, replied, "Apparently, George is a monkey!"

"A monkey!" Eleanor exclaimed, grinning. "This, I too, have to see!"

George was a small, light-brown simian. He was secured by a chain around his chest to a perch in a corner of the azotea. He glanced at her indifferently as he peeled and ate one of those diminutive bananas that appeared to be a staple offering of fruit street vendors, who also sold a myriad variety of tropical fruits, many of which resembled the fruits in Honolulu. Eleanor returned, smiling with amusement. "I guess George beat us to lunch."

Everyone chuckled.

The entrée consisted of boiled rice and a viand the waiter called *asado*. It appeared to be chicken braised in tomato sauce with potatoes and sweet peppers. There was also a side dish of thin, greasy noodles sautéed with a variety of vegetables and pork cutlets. Eleanor had seen similar noodles stirred into deep frying pans at Chinese chow-chows in San Francisco's Chinatown. Dessert was the diminutive bananas, peeled and topped with some kind of fruit jelly.

"Well, I'm sorry that was unpleasant," Miss Thompson said, wincing. "Didn't care for all that garlic, onion, and pepper. And can you believe the lard on those noodles?" She shook her head, adding, "And I've always detested those acidic little bananas with that gross guava jelly! But this seems to be the only dessert our landlord provides!"

"Oh, but I rather thought it was all good, Bertha!" Miss Covell exclaimed, smiling.

"It's certainly an improvement on the canned green beans and corned beef we usually get here!" Eliza said, grinning.

The negro soon served coffee—a dark, robust roast called *barako*. Miss Thompson declared it was the only item that came close to decent among the cantina's offerings. She said it was grown in the adjacent Batangas province, cultivated from Arabica beans brought over by the Spaniards from Morocco.

Their first sip of the barako elicited approval from Miss Thompson, Mabel, and Eleanor; aversion from Miss Covell, Maude, Arabella, and Eliza, who tried to neutralize its strong flavor with generous dollops of canned condensed milk the waiter provided at their request.

Miss Thompson took another sip of her unsweetened cup of black brew before she assumed her usual grave expression and announced, "Ladies, I have news."

"What news, ma'am?" asked Arabella with wide-eyed anticipation, pushing away her barely consumed cup of overly sweetened and creamed coffee.

The ladies sat up, their eyes on Miss Thompson, who pulled out several letter envelopes from her tote and distributed them according to the names typed on them. "We finally have our assignments!"

On the night after they received their designated school territories, the ladies decided to mark the occasion through a stroll at the *Paseo de la Luneta*, a park near Manila Bay known to be especially beautiful at sunset. It was said to have charming promenades, park benches, and lawns from where they could enjoy the newly-formed Constabulary Band play its evening concert.

Before they left the Exposition, Maude and Arabella treated Miss Covell and Eleanor to a surprise. "We have presents for you!" Maude announced, handing them what looked like ladies' Spanish fans. The spines were made of varnished wood, and the fabric between them was silk painted with romantic Continental scenes, trimmed with lace.

"They call them abanico here," Arabella said, smiling brightly.

"Why, thank you!" Eleanor exclaimed, smiling.

"Oh, how lovely and useful!" Miss Covell said.

"Ah, but they are more than fans!" Arabella declared. "Want me to show you?"

"Please!" Eleanor replied, enthused by Arabella's excitement alone.

Maude grinned as though she already knew what was about to transpire.

With mirthful, naughty eyes, Arabella began with, "The fan seller said that if you want to scrutinize someone without betraying your interest, just hide the lower half of your face with the fan, avoiding eye contact, yet stealing glances at him. Like this—see?" The younger ladies giggled, while Miss Covell smiled in amusement. Arabella continued, "And if someone is boring you, simply wave your fan in a slow, lazy manner like this, without saying anything, and you can be sure he'll soon stop pestering you. But if an attractive man approaches or, better yet, addresses you, and you really, really like him, you can convey your interest by rapidly beating your chest as you fan yourself—like this!"

They all roared into laughter.

They hired a quiles so they could also include Mabel and Eliza in the ride. Although the sun was lower now, the concrete streets still radiated the day's heat. The ladies grinned at each other as they produced their abanicos. They tried to mimic how the local ladies employed their fans: spreading their fans open with a single flick of the wrist; fanning themselves with a few gentle staccato thumps on their chests; and, finally, closing the fans with another flick of the wrist. They chuckled over their sorry attempts and laughed even more at Arabella's mimicry of the way the local girls flirted through their fans.

Their cochero answered yes when they asked him if he could take them to the Luneta. He drove the quiles through Malecon Drive and emerged at a charming seaside avenue lined with street lamps. People strolled in pairs or groups along the promenade beside the ocean, while others rode in open victorias on the carriage road that circled the lawns. The waters of Manila Bay splashed against the adjoining sea wall.

"This reminds me of Chicago's Lake Shore Drive," Miss Covell remarked, "but this view, in my opinion, is superior!"

Eleanor smiled and nodded, admiring the graceful curve of the beach. On the southern end, she could make out the shapes of Cavite's skyline and the purple plateau that preceded the town. Dotting the water were all manner of sea craft, and on the horizon stood a mountain that appeared to have risen from the sea like one of the giants in Homer's *Odyssey*.

"What's that mountain called?" Maude asked.

The cochero volunteered, "Mariveles Mountain, madam."

"Mar—what?" Arabella cried.

"Mari-ve-les," Maude repeated.

"Sounds like the Italian meravigliosa—which, if I'm not mistaken, means marvelous!" Eliza said, smiling with self-satisfaction.

"Or, simply, the Spanish maravillosa!" Miss Covell interjected.

Mabel sighed. "We do have to learn Spanish if we're to have an easier time here—don't we?"

"Yes," Maude replied and turned to Miss Covell. "Now, I wish, dear Miss Covell, that we'd paid more attention to your Spanish classes on the *Thomas*."

"Ah, indeed, that would have been good," Miss Covell said. "But it's never too late to start, my dear." She exchanged knowing smiles with Eleanor, who was happy to see that Maude and Miss Covell appeared to have overcome their differences.

Suddenly, all sound seemed to cease. The ladies glanced around and saw everyone turning to face west. The sun had begun the final arc of its descent. The cochero stopped the quiles, as if acknowledging the sacred moment. Even the relentless clacking of ladies' fans stopped in reverence. Except for the collective hush and sighs of the crowd paying homage to the setting sun, silence fell upon everything like the soft shawl of the evening. Apart from the gentle breezes caressing the face of the ocean and swaying the palms, blowing the sea's salty kisses toward the land, the whole world stood still. And, for a moment, the sun hovered over the Mariveles like a giant, pulsating egg yolk. When it finally touched the peak, it dropped behind the mountain and exploded into streaks of color, staining the sky with all the crimsons, golds, pinks, and purples that recalled all the sunsets in Eleanor's memory.

When the shadows took over, the street lamps all lit up simultaneously, to Eleanor's surprise. She hadn't earlier noticed the electric wires between the timber poles spread across the park. Except for the arc-lights along the Pasig River, she'd come to expect street lights to be powered by kerosene or, to her greater surprise when she first learned of it—dishes of coconut oil from which wicks were lit like candles.

The orbs shone their yellow light upon the scene, enhancing the already festive atmosphere that anticipated the Constabulary Band concert.

The ladies' quiles proceeded toward the Paseo de la Luneta alongside the rectangular, raised turf with lunette-shaped ends, which, Eleanor surmised, was probably how the park got its name. The cochero let off the ladies at one of two bandstands that stood on opposite ends of the lawn at the half-moon terminals. Chairs sat in neat rows before the bandstand. Miss Covell claimed a row for them, while the younger ladies expressed desire to stroll around the park until the show started.

Eleanor wandered a short distance from the four Radcliffe girls to survey the scene by herself. An increasing number of people from various stations in life continued to arrive. Groups of more modest-looking folk kept to the park's fringes, watching elite society parade in all its finery as though this was what they'd come to see.

The most prominent figures were the police and soldiers. The Manila police, in particular, appeared to be of the most capable sort, easily spotted by their distinctive gray-green khakis with tan caps, shoes, and spats. Said to have been selected from honorably discharged soldiers of the army of invasion, they still had to pass certain size and height requirements. Their manner was that of the disciplined soldier: alert and ready for action, yet reserved and polite toward the law-abiding civilian.

Likewise notable were the army and navy officers who looked most handsome in their pristine white hats and uniforms accented by shiny, brass buttons that transformed even plain-looking men into princes. Some officers presented a greater regal sight seated on their huge, tall steeds shipped from the mainland.

Many young ladies congregated wherever army and navy officers could be found. There were hatless American women with large, brimmed hairstyles and easy smiles; Spanish beauties with big, proud eyes, wearing lace *mantillas* and *peineta* combs; and demure, doe-eyed Filipinas with long, graceful necks above stiff panuelos.

The two latter sets of women that represented the former ruler and the ruled presented an amusing study of contrast and commonalities. They seemed to set themselves apart not only by the distance they stood from each other but also by their manner of dress and appearance. If there was anything they shared in common, it was their expertise in wielding their fans as instruments of seduction as Arabella had demonstrated. Eleanor grinned to herself when she glanced back at the Radcliffe ladies. They appeared to have finally mastered the flirtatious fanning techniques, as evident from the number of officers now surrounding them.

Most delightful was the sight of American and mestizo children enjoying pony rides around the park. The little boys and girls looked adorable in their sailor suits and dresses with their pudgy little legs dangling and bouncing off the ponies' sides. The girls daintily rode sidesaddle, showing off their pastel stockings and white patent leather shoes.

When the Constabulary Band arrived, Eleanor and the Radcliffe ladies rejoined Miss Covell. After the band members occupied their chairs on the bandstand, they played "Stars and Stripes Forever." Eleanor glanced at Miss Covell and her Radcliffe friends, catching them misty-eyed. But when she touched her cheeks, she found that it was she who'd shed tears.

There was much haranguing and negotiating by the teachers with the superintendent about their designated school districts. Many wished to remain in the nation's capital. Ultimately, however, they obeyed like soldiers. They were an army of teachers, after all.

There was hardly time for goodbyes as the ladies proceeded to arrange for their respective passages to their provincial territories and claimed their trunks and crates from the customs building. Arabella and Maude were devastated to learn that their assigned areas couldn't be farther from each other: Maude in the northern Luzon province of Benguet; Arabella in the southern island of Mindanao. Miss Covell was enviably asked to remain in Manila to help set up the new Manila Normal School. Miss Thompson was going to Capiz Island, in the central Visayas islands. The other pair of Radcliffe girls, Eliza and Mabel, were assigned to different towns in the broad, central plains of Luzon.

Eleanor was cautiously elated to know she'd been appointed to Legazpi, which was the capital of the Albay province in the southern Vicol region of Luzon—elated, because it was the home of the great Mayon Volcano; cautious, for in addition to the location being an active volcano area, its people were also known to be among the fiercest fighters in the revolution against the Spaniards. They also continued to pursue an insurrection against the Americans.

"I can't believe I'm off to the boondocks of Ifugao!" cried Maude as she finished packing.

"Boondocks?" Eleanor asked, grinning. "Is that even a word?" She pulled out the Spanish-English dictionary she'd recently purchased at the Escolta district.

"Sure, it is," replied Arabella. "We learned it from the soldiers." She was holding up one of her infinite number of frocks and sniffing it, as if determining whether she needed to make another run to the Chinese laundry.

"But what does it mean?" Eleanor insisted, leafing through the dictionary. "It's not Spanish, is it?"

"I suspect it's an adulteration of the Tagal word for mountain," Miss Covell volunteered. "Bundok."

"Yes—that makes sense!" Maude exclaimed.

"Huh," Eleanor mumbled. Here, it seemed, even the English language was changing. As she tucked her dictionary back into her Gladstone, she mused about how their new world might transform each of them.

"Consarn!" cried Arabella. "I need to return to the laundry service!"

"I'll go with you," Maude said. "To make sure you don't get into trouble before our departure!"

"Pfft!" Arabella scoffed. "Don't know beans about that!"

Everyone laughed, including Arabella.

Later, while the Radcliffe girls were in the reception area saying tearful goodbyes to their Harvard and Yale beaus, Eleanor expressed a worry to Miss Covell for Arabella, who was being sent to the land of the Moro people, stronghold of the Muslim insurgency. She was especially concerned about the local *datus* or "chieftains" reputed for kidnapping women they fancied and claiming them as second wives or concubines.

"Try not to worry," Miss Covell urged. "As we said during the girls' bout with mal de mer, they are tougher than they look. Arabella may seem naïve, but she's far more clever than she lets on."

Eleanor smiled. "You're right, Miss Covell. Thank you."

Miss Covell handed her Worcester's book. "A little parting gift to wish you good luck, my dear."

"Oh, but Miss Covell!" Eleanor's eyes widened in disbelief. "This is too generous. I only meant to borrow it."

"No. I insist, dear. I've already enjoyed it. And, while I may be getting old, I do retain some of the photographic memory of my youth." She grinned. "Besides, I think this was meant to be yours."

"Why do you say that, Miss Covell?"

"Open to the frontispiece and see." Miss Covell smiled.

Eleanor did as instructed and was thrilled to find a picture of Mayon Volcano opposite the title page.

"Do you see what I mean?" Miss Covell said.

Eleanor smiled, nodded, and hugged the woman she now considered both her mentor and friend.

CHAPTER 6

White Devil Woman

The easiest way to reach Legazpi, Eleanor learned, was by sea, again. Otherwise, it was a fortnight's journey, at least, if not a whole month—through rough roads, water, and uncharted mountain trails, with no dependable inns or other lodgings along the way. Mr. McCauley helped her arrange passage on the *Daragang Magayon*. She was an old steamboat whose ambition appeared greater than her capacity. Newly painted in glossy marine paint in red, white, and blue, she was only about fourteen feet in length. She was like a little old lady who tried to compensate for her lost youth and beauty through cheap, flashy clothes and fake jewelry.

"But Mr. McCauley," Eleanor protested, "isn't this boat too small for the voyage I'm taking?"

"I regret to say, Miss Karsten, this is the only inter-island vessel going to Albay province at this time. And even if there were others, they can't be bigger than thirteen or fourteen feet to be able to load on the Pasig. The silt bars—you know?"

Eleanor thus resigned herself to fate as she boarded the vapor near the Bridge of Spain. She endured a tortuous wait under the tropical sun along the banks of the river, where all kinds of human and animal feces and garbage washed up among the aquatic plants. Having been fore-warned by Miss Thompson that time didn't mean much for the Filipino, she was prepared for delays. Yet, she was still shocked when it took almost three hours from the scheduled departure before the steamer left.

From the Pasig, the *Daragang Magayon* swept out to Manila Bay, backward on the route the *Thomas* sailed toward Manila. It passed Corregidor Island on the Boca Chica and proceeded through the San Bernardino Strait. As she expected, the boat's facilities left much to be desired.

Only one shabby toilet served about twenty or more passengers, and the so-called staterooms were not stately at all. Two cabins in the hull served as separate sleeping quarters for men and women. When Eleanor went to check the women's cabin, what she found was a room that barely fit five rows of double-stacked bamboo berths. The sleeping shelves had no mattresses or pillows. Apparently, passengers were expected to bring sleeping mats, blankets, and pillows. Eleanor brought none. And, unlike Maude and Arabella, who'd preferred the upper berths, the native women, especially mothers with young children, favored the lower bunks, which appeared to have all been claimed.

The heat and humidity in the cabin were suffocating, and she imagined it would be warmer on the top berths where all the heat rose. Thus, instead of taking one of the upper berths still available, she returned to the deck upstairs. The captain and his assistant had monopoly of the Lilliputian deckhouse from where they operated the vapor and where they also ate and slept. The only other spot where she could put herself was on the five rows of benches under a canopy on the deck, to which the other passengers had already beaten her.

An ancient-looking native woman glanced up at her. To Eleanor's surprise, she made room next to her by lifting the little girl sitting beside her onto her bony lap, offering Eleanor the vacated spot. Eleanor guessed they must be grandmother and granddaughter.

Eager to practice some of the Spanish she'd learned, Eleanor thanked her, saying, "Gracias, señora." The old woman replied with an almost toothless smile, "De nada, señorita." Whatever remaining teeth she had were red-stained or blackened. Eleanor soon learned why. She'd seen the same ritual performed by many native women sitting on their haunches beside the baskets of fresh vegetables and fruits they sold on the sidewalks of Manila.

The old woman lifted her granddaughter from her lap and placed her on the floor. She reached down into the sack that lay at her feet and brought out a small brass box. Setting the box on her lap, she opened it—fishing out a paper sachet, unfolded one of its ends, and tapped out what appeared to be lime powder into a tiny tinplate saucer inside the box.

She pulled out a gourd from her sack, uncorked it, and, very carefully, added a couple of drops of water into the powder. With her crooked index finger, she stirred the mixture into a lime paste and smudged some of it onto a betel leaf. She added an areca nut to the paste and what appeared to be shredded dried tobacco leaves and folded the leaf into a neat, little envelope.

"Buyo, señorita?" the old woman said, offering the betel nut chew to Eleanor. Eleanor shook her head with a smile, but the old woman insisted. After a few more rounds of the old woman insisting and Eleanor declining, the old woman smiled, popped the snack into her mouth, returned everything in her sack, and lifted the child back onto her lap. She merrily chomped on the same chew for what seemed like hours and, to Eleanor's appallment, occasionally spit out red juice on the deck floor.

Miss Covell had been right to worry about the availability of safe food and drinking water during their passage. Although they were informed that meals could be purchased on board and from roadside canteens, the older teacher urged Eleanor and the Radcliffe ladies to pack some travel food. They went shopping at the army commissary where they procured tinned water, baked beans, corned beef, and sardines. In addition to the canned goods, they bought fresh bananas, bread, and *jamon*—a salted and aged Spanish ham they figured would withstand days of travel without spoiling. Miss Covell helped them prepare their little picnic bags despite her increasing busyness with the teachers' college.

Eleanor was grateful Miss Covell had insisted on such essentials, for she didn't trust the food on the vapor. A few enterprising vendors magically appeared during meal hours, peddling smelly food wrapped in banana leaves. On their first supper on board, the old woman offered Eleanor some of what she had, which looked like smoked fish on a bed of steamed rice. As the fermented fish odor filled Eleanor's nose, she declined—with a smile. This time, it took one less round of offerings and refusals before the old woman quit trying to share her food with her.

Eleanor watched, fascinated, as her seatmate dexterously deboned the fish with the fingers of one hand and scooped a dollop of rice with a sliver of fish with the same fingers to feed her granddaughter. In this manner, the old woman alternately fed herself and the girl until no grain of rice and edible part of the fish remained in the banana leaf wraps. The grandmother instructed the girl to toss out their trash boat side like the other passengers did.

When Eleanor opened her picnic packet, she took her cue from the old woman by offering half of her ham sandwich and banana to her seatmate who surprised her by immediately accepting and then halving her share with her granddaughter. This repeated in the next meal, emboldening Eleanor to try a piece of the old woman's smoked fish. She was delighted to discover it was good and savory and not rotten at all. In this way, Eleanor and the old woman and her granddaughter shared their meals, which established a quiet new friendship among them.

During lulls in the voyage, between meals, when there was nothing but seemingly endless water to view, Eleanor occupied herself with the book Miss Covell gifted her. Yet, in this passage through a now familiar sea, an acute melancholy besieged her, preventing her from digesting what she read. She dismissed it as simple sadness from being bereft of the company of her Thomasite friends. It surprised her to realize she now had friends to miss.

Back in her Iowa hometown, she never felt she had friends, apart from her parents. She'd always sensed some mild yet ever-present hostility from the other girls and their mothers. Perhaps they resented her for aspiring to a different life, as though by daring to be different, she'd portrayed herself as better than them. If she was honest, she would likewise confess to begrudge them their small minds and even smaller imaginations. They trusted her enough with the education of their children, yet not enough to include her in their social circles nor invite her to their parties, where many a hometown girl had found a hometown husband. Not that she wanted one.

Early in her teenage years, she'd dismissed the idea of romance as absurd. Though she was no great beauty, she wasn't unbecoming, either. Yet, every boy who'd shown interest in her soon appeared to be discouraged by her reputation as a bookworm. Not good farmer's wife material, it seemed to scream to potential suitors.

And despite small-town gossip to the contrary, she also had no ambition for grand living. She wasn't merely holding out for some rich farmer to claim her and combine their landholdings. She thought she proved this when she rejected Mr. Borg's proposal, but to the country folk, it appeared, her decision to let go of her family's farm merely confirmed their notion of her. She did not belong. And that was why she had to leave.

Of all the accusations against "that odd Karsten girl," which was what the townsfolk called her behind her back, one was truer than others: her unyielding independence of mind and spirit. She clung to this as the singular remarkable thing about herself. Whenever an idea challenged her thinking, she didn't skirt the opportunity to reexamine her beliefs. Her rigor for rational thought spilled into other aspects of her life, so that, early on, religion became suspect to her. Except for her father, this likewise made her suspect to just about everyone, including her mother, who'd wished for her to have been more conforming to community life.

Yet, by what one could almost attribute to divine intervention, if it weren't so ironic, Eleanor nipped religion in the bud before it had the chance to blossom in her. Among the few things she asked was why God punished the first woman and all women thereafter for simply desiring knowledge. Even as a young girl, Eleanor perceived the divine injustice done to Eve and her daughters.

"How could it be bad for Eve to want to eat the fruit of the Tree of Knowledge of Good and Evil?" she'd asked Pastor John, who was then preparing her for confirmation. "Shouldn't people want to know what was good and evil—so they can choose to be good?"

Pastor John replied, "Eve was punished, not because she wanted to know good and evil, but because she disobeyed God's command not to eat the forbidden fruit."

"But what kind of god would forbid his children to have knowledge?" she argued. "Did He not want his people to be good?"

"Good is nothing more than what God says is good!" the pastor retorted.

"And how do we know for sure what God says?" young Eleanor challenged.

"Why, that's easy, dear girl," Pastor John said with a self-assured smile. Eleanor remembered the way he leaned back in his chair, looking quite confident he'd won the debate. "It's all here in the Bible!" he declared, tapping the black leather-bound book he always carried around like some badge of authority.

"But... who wrote the Bible?" young Eleanor insisted.

"Holy men inspired by the Holy Spirit to discern God's will!" he exclaimed in half exasperation, half pompous piety.

"But... were there holy women, too, who wrote in God's book?" she pressed.

"Goodness gracious, girl!" Pastor John cried. "Can't you see that women were not entrusted with such wisdom by God? Or He would not have created Eve from Adam's rib!"

In the end, Eleanor decided that the pastor failed to give her convincing answers. She concluded that God, quite possibly, was simply a boy bully. Thus, she purposely flunked her confirmation test and refused to go to Sunday services—to her mother's frustration and embarrassment in the community.

On her mother's pleas, her father intervened. "Daughter," he said in that voice her childhood ears might have associated with a good and loving god, if she'd believed in one, "when you're of age and earning your keep, you could decline to accompany your mother and me to church. But not before. Is that clear, young lady?" He scolded her— with a wink. She relented and feigned her answers to her next confirmation examination, which she passed with a perfect score. Seven years later, her father sent her to the Iowa Normal School, as she asked, so she could earn her keep.

The first two days of the voyage to Legazpi were marked by capricious sun, clouds, and rain. It didn't rain on the first night, thus most passengers slept on the deck to avoid the heat and humidity down in the hull. Eleanor followed their example—sleeping seated on the deck benches, while some men lay on woven mats that shared the floor with crates and baskets of live fowl. Her book crate and steamer trunk were marked by the black oilcloth with which she'd wrapped them, on advice by Mr. McCauley, to protect them from moisture.

She was the worse for the wear. The breezes that blew with the trade winds thankfully provided relief when the sun shone, but also caused Eleanor's lips to chap. Moreover, the sun's rays reflected off the vessel's white-painted surfaces and caused sunburn on the skin of her face, neck, and forearms. She coped with the heat and humidity by returning to the island style of dressing on the *Thomas*: doing away with her waist jacket and folding her sleeves to her elbows. Because of the lack of privacy even in the women's cabin, she couldn't take off her corset, which chafed at her skin.

Among the inconveniences, what she found most trying were the stench and filth of the latrine. Whoever was charged with cleaning it, if there was anyone in charge at all, was utterly remiss in duty. She was also shocked to discover that, instead of the tissue or brown paper to wipe with, merely torn-off pages of newsprint were provided—hung on a wire. As the voyage progressed, so did the stench and filth worsen and the strips of newspaper soon disappeared. The soap on the sink outside the toilet also vanished. Eleanor ached for a long, warm bath.

As if the situation couldn't get worse, a typhoon developed on the afternoon of the third day. Gusty winds blew non-stop rain at a horizontal angle and stirred up waves twice the height of the *Daragang Magayon*, tossing the steamer like a paper boat in a drainage canal during a storm. The captain banished all passengers to the hull, forbidding anyone from staying on the deck. Most became seasick—including, this time, Eleanor.

Since there was only one bucket shared by all in the women's cabin, accidents became inevitable. The cabin floor became slick with vomit, and the stench filled the room, along with the wailing of children and the groaning or praying of the adults. No one stayed on the upper berths for fear of being thrown off by the vessel's heavings. The old woman crouched in a corner, holding her granddaughter with one hand while fingering her rosary beads with the other. Eleanor offered to take the girl, but the urchin turned her head from her, burying her face in her grandmother's chest.

Eleanor couldn't understand why her cabin mates were glaring or glancing at her with fear in their eyes, until a woman pointed at her, screaming, "Demonia blanca!" White devil woman. Two other women aggressively gesticulated at her, yelling what could only mean one thing: They wanted her out of their cabin. Perhaps even off the boat!

The woman who called her a demon or witch started pushing her out of the room. To allay the children's fears, Eleanor refrained from resisting and retreated into the corridor just outside the cabin. Her accuser slammed the door on her.

Eleanor was glad to discover that the air quality outside the cabin was much better. However, she soon realized there were a few men in the hallway who were also staring at her ferociously. It appeared she'd become a universal pariah. Her fear of being thrown overboard grew. Fortunately, the men's stares ultimately proved benign, compared to the women's glares.

To everyone's great relief, the typhoon only lasted a day. By the second half of the fourth day, the sun peeked between the clouds, and the wind wound down enough for the captain to allow passengers back on deck. Eleanor was surprised that the *Daragang Mayon* had held up to the storm and her precious cargo remained secure on board. The man who owned the live fowl, however, lamented his loss.

The old woman and her granddaughter returned to the deck benches, along with other passengers who were now mostly smiling at her, if not timidly glancing her way. The grandmother invited her to sit by her side again, and Eleanor happily obliged. The girl surprisingly crawled onto Eleanor's lap. Everyone must have concluded she wasn't a witch who'd cursed the sea passage, but an angel who'd saved them from sinking. Eleanor sighed in relief and smiled back at them, including the woman who'd accused her of being a demonia blanca and now declared her a *santa* or "saint."

The sea stilled and the temperature cooled enough for Eleanor to enjoy the scenic journey around familiar-looking islands. The pulchritude of the passage remained, especially as the steamer rounded the southeastern tip of Luzon toward Albay Gulf, for there, the regal majesty and beauty of Mayon Volcano filled her eyes again. She was struck with the sense of being reunited with a long-lost lover, which was strange because she'd never had one. It was as if the volcano was waiting for her all that time.

At noon on Friday, the 6th of September, the *Daragang Magayon* docked at the Port of Legazpi—five days after its Manila departure and a day late of its scheduled arrival. Eleanor wasn't sure what to expect when she stepped down the gangplank. The Superintendent's instructions were for her to meet with the former teacher when she arrived, but she wasn't sure whether such a person would be waiting for her at the harbor, considering the vapor's late arrival.

A glance around the crowd greeting the newly-arrived passengers revealed no one seeking her out. A pair of *cargadores* or "stevedores" carried her cargo on their glistening, toasted backs and stood in a stupor, waiting for her instructions. She gestured for them to simply set down her things on the harbor platform and paid each of them a media-peseta.

She sat on her steamer trunk, placed her Gladstone at her feet, and leaned her umbrella against her crate of books. The crowd was gone now. Apart from a few stevedores who continued to transfer cargo to a warehouse, she was alone.

Northeast of the dock, Mayon Volcano was a calm, cyan giant smoking a cigar. The occasional breeze swayed the palms of the now omnipresent coconut trees, tempering the sun's searing stare. Eleanor unfurled and hoisted her umbrella to mitigate her sunburn. She understood now why Manila women obsessively shaded themselves.

Her stomach grumbled. She had partaken of a meager breakfast on the vapor consisting of what remained of the last of her overripe bananas and three boiled eggs that the enterprising deckhand sold her, which she then shared with the old woman and her grandchild. She bet she couldn't go wrong with the eggs: if they were fresh, they appeased hunger; if they were rotten, she'd know instantly. The eggs proved fresh and, sprinkled with just a little sea salt that the old woman kept in her sack, they were excellent.

The deckhand must have kept some hens in the deckhouse for the eggs to be that fresh. Eleanor wondered, however, whether the chickens were his or part of the live fowl that were believed to have been blown away by the typhoon. The man who'd lost the hens kept glancing suspiciously at her and her seatmates as they ate their eggs with relish.

Her eyes presently roamed the wharf, wondering where she might procure lunch. She checked the food in her Gladstone. She still had a tin of water and canned baked beans. Pulling out the water can, she used a bottle opener to punch a hole into it. While sipping, she heard a girl's voice crying out, "Pan de sal! Pan de sal!" Eleanor turned around to where the voice was coming from and saw a girl balancing a basket tray on her head at the entrance to the port.

She smiled, put down her parapluie, and jumped to her feet. "Yoo-hoo! ¡Niña, ven aquí!" she hollered, waving the girl to come to her. In Manila, she'd become acquainted with the salted bread bun and loved it. It was no bigger than her fist, and when one bit into its crusty exterior, it gave way to a soft, moist center. Street vendors peddled the freshly-baked pan de sal outside the Exposition Building in time for breakfast and the afternoon *merienda* or "snack." The Thomasites rushed outside whenever they heard the pan de sal vendors' call before the warm bread had sold out. Eleanor discovered then that, filled with a native sweet coconut preserve or strawberry jam procured from the U.S. commissary, the pan de sal made for an excellent pastry that went well with coffee or tea.

Eleanor presently bought three pieces of the bread from the girl, who handed them to her in a small brown paper bag. Eleanor stuck her nose inside the bag, relishing the delicious sweet-sour scent of the still-warm bread. It occurred to her that the buns would be excellent with baked beans. She reached for the canned food from her Gladstone, including a can opener and a spoon. At the end of her humble meal, she felt quite sated.

While sipping the last of her water, she scanned her surroundings for a garbage can. There didn't appear to be any. She'd noted the natives' habit of tossing their trash seemingly wherever they wished, yet blamed this on a lack of public sanitation facilities, such as municipal garbage bins. Averse to simply throwing out her trash on the harbor, Eleanor gathered it all in the paper bag and stuffed it in her Gladstone for proper disposal later.

It had been about thirty minutes since the stevedores left her with her cargo. She hoisted her umbrella over herself again. She started to worry no one was coming to fetch her, contrary to what the super-intendent stated in his letter of instructions. She noted the seashells embedded in the tuff stones of which the seawall was constructed. Looking up at the Mayon, she wondered if the goddess Pele also held residence inside the volcano.

She decided to wait an hour and not worry until then. To while away the time, she reached for Worcester's book from inside her Gladstone. Deep into the pages about Luzon, she sensed she was no longer alone. When she glanced up, she was startled by several pairs of black, spar-kling orbs trained upon her, watching her every move.

"Oh, hello! How are you?" she asked, smiling, and they giggled.

Eleanor folded her parapluie to get a better look at her audience. Little children had begun gathering around her, standing or sitting on their haunches. Behind them, balancing toddlers on their hips or cra-dling infants in their arms were, she assumed, the children's nannies, who didn't appear much older or taller than their charges. More chil-dren arrived, until she was completely surrounded.

Eleanor recalled it wasn't long ago when she was the one who'd ogled like this at the natives of Honolulu. Now, she was the object of curiosity—the *extranjera* or "foreigner." The children observed her with the curious amusement of one watching a monkey in a zoo. They occasionally grinned and whispered to each other, probably com-menting on her appearance or venturing guesses about who she was and why she was there on the port, alone, sitting on a trunk, reading a book.

She smiled at them again and said, "Nice day to play outside, isn't it?"

They covered their mouths as they burst into giggling again— another seeming habit of the natives. Eleanor supposed they did this out of shyness, modesty, or, to hide bad or missing teeth.

She noted how her attentive yet mute audience wore simple but clean clothing: the babies—low-necked cassocks draped over their slim or chubby shoulders; the older children—miniature, simple ver-sions of traditional adult clothes. Their faces were clear of soot and grime, apart from a few toddlers whose snotty noses were occasionally pinched and wiped by their nannies' fingers.

The girls wore their hair like many of Manila's señoritas: loose and long. Some of the young nannies wore theirs in a pusod, Eleanor supposed, out of practical necessity. The boys didn't seem to favor a particular haircut. Some had their hair cropped close to their skulls; others wore bowl cuts or chin-length bobs that framed their cheeks; and the rest grew their thick, wavy, raven-black hair in lengths down to their shoulders—appearing to be girls themselves were it not for their short pantaloons. Many of the boys wore straw hats with the front brims curled up, as though to free up their sightline, which seemed to Eleanor to defeat the purpose of shading their eyes. The girls wore no hats at all, as though to show off their coconut-oiled cascades.

Suddenly, a small girl brashly pushed her way from the back toward the first row and plopped herself on the ground, sitting cross-legged in front of Eleanor, who was stunned to realize the girl was smoking a cigar. The girl sat, observing Eleanor—just as Eleanor sat, observing her, and they stayed that way for a few minutes before the girl stood and reached out with her little, brown fingers to pick a curly tendril off Eleanor's chignon and examine it against the sun.

"Ay! ¡Oro!" the girl exclaimed. Gold.

"¿Oro? ¡Oro!" the other children cried before they rushed toward Eleanor, likewise reaching out to touch and tug at her hair.

"No, please don't!" Eleanor pleaded, holding onto her hat. But the children's curiosity couldn't be contained. She would have been completely overpowered and her hair would have become a jumbled, knotty mess had not a man's commanding voice boomed, "Hoy! ¡Vete! Esa es tu maestra Americana! ¡Vete! ¡Vete!"

"Ha? ¿La maestra?" the children exclaimed. "¿La maestra Americana?" Jumping and clapping with excitement, they pulled back to make way for the man, yet remained as close as they could around Eleanor, ogling her with new interest—mouths agape, eyes wide with awe.

Eleanor stood to see who had rescued her from the urchin mob.

A tall, large, mustachioed man wearing the standard dark-blue sack coat with white chevrons of a State Volunteer Sergeant walked with a limp toward her. When he reached her, he took off his campaign hat, revealing thinning, gray hair. He smiled, and the lines on his tanned, leathery face deepened. In a baritone voice that spoke with a distinct southern mainland accent, he said, "Pardon me, ma'am. Yer Miss Karsten, I pershume?"

She smiled back at him. "Yes. I'm Eleanor Karsten."

He shook her hand. "Sergeant Samuel Munro at yer service, ma'am. Welcome to Legazpi!"

"Thank you, sergeant," she replied. "But I don't understand. I was told to expect the former teacher."

"Oh, but I am, Miss Karsten. I am the former teacher. An' I've come to get ya an' bring ya to yer new home!"

Sergeant Munro fetched Eleanor in a *carretela*, a bamboo cart pulled by a single horse. He and his manservant loaded her steamer trunk and crate of books onto its flatbed, and the soldier helped Eleanor to the seat beside him on the driver's perch.

"I'm sorry for not bein' at the harbor to greet ya when ya docked, Miss Karsten! T'was no way of knowin' when yer boat would've come. That *Daragang Magayon* is always infernally late. And with the typhoon, ya see—"

"I understand, sergeant," Eleanor interjected, smiling. "No need to apologize."

"Thank ya kin'ly, ma'am. Made use a waitin' time to visit with ma' old buddies at the Regan Barracks in town." He pointed at his manservant. "By the way, this here be my muchacho, Pedro. Sent 'im checkin' on you vapor's arrival every now an' then."

Pedro smiled timidly and nodded at Eleanor when he heard his name. Eleanor smiled back at him.

"Am sure glad ye arrived in one piece, ma'am!" Sam said. "The slightest wind could a' whipped up giant waves."

Eleanor smiled. "Yes—it was indeed scary. But I'm grateful we survived it."

The sergeant grinned. "Yup! Those little vapors are a miracle on the water. No one in the states would believe what they're cap'ble."

She smiled and nodded. "Must say I'm impressed by your Spanish, sergeant. How'd you come to be good at it?"

He chuckled. "Well, ma'am, I'm from Texas. An' ya don't get 'round much in Texas without knowin' no Spanish. But truth be told, it only gets me by out 'ere. Folks 'ere mostly speak a mix of it an' Vicolano—the local language."

She noted that he said the "v" in Vicol as a "b"—reminding her this was how the letter was pronounced in Spanish.

"An' as if this ain't hard 'nuff," he continued, "there be many kinds of languages in the islands. Only folks who speak real Spanish 'ere are the ilustrados."

"Ilus… what?" she asked.

"Ilustrado. The schooled class. 'Round 'ere, they be the hacienderos—folks who own plantations. Or what they call cacique. They be the moneyed class. But don't ya worry, ma'am. Vicolano has plenty Spanish in it. An' I can talk some with ma' wife an' the barrio folk with the 'elp of lots of hand signals." He chuckled.

Eleanor grinned but was chagrined to learn their Mad About History Club was ill-informed about the language that Filipinos spoke. They had assumed it was mainly Spanish, sometimes perhaps Tagal, yet now it appeared it depended on the province and social class. She was relieved to hear, though, that Vicolano had a lot of Spanish in it like the Tagal language of the Manileños.

She glanced at him. "I gather you're married to a Filipina then?"

He smiled. "Yes, ma'am! But only before the church. Sadly, the army don't honor no union 'tween soldiers an' natives."

Eleanor's eyebrows arched. "Oh. Didn't know that. Sorry to hear."

"Nah, it's a'right. Don't matter to ma' wife, ya see. All she wanted, she says, is a marriage before God." He chuckled. "I told 'er God won't bring 'er no army ben'fits when I'm gone. She said she don't care. Her fam'ly got some rice an' coco land. Not like a proper hacienda, mind ya, but big 'nuff to feed us. Good thing, too, 'coz the little 'un's comin.'" He pushed his chest forward and beamed.

"Why, congratulations, sergeant!" Eleanor smiled.

"Thank ya kin'ly, ma'am," he replied, still beaming.

A sizable pothole came within sight and Sergeant Munro pulled on his reins to maneuver the carretela around the crater to prevent its wheels from dropping in it. However, one of the back wheels still slipped. Eleanor gripped the seat rail and her luggage lurched on the creaking bamboo flatbed. She turned around to check. Pedro was pushing the cargo away from the edge of the carriage bed.

"Don't ya worry 'bout yer things, ma'am!" Sergeant Munro said, grinning. "Pedro will make sure they arrive safe an' sound!"

When they settled into a smoother drive, she asked, "Sergeant, do I also gather you intend to stay here?"

"Yes, ma'am! Am bein' 'onor'bly discharged next week. There be nothin' for me back in Texas. I got 'ere all I want. So, if ya need any 'elp with the school an' all, don't be shy to ask."

"Thank you," Eleanor said, smiling. "I'm likely to take you up on that offer." It was then that she pursued her curiosity about something that had intrigued her from when he fetched her at the port. "Tell me, sergeant, how'd you come to be the teacher?" He guffawed, and she quickly added, "Oh, I'm sorry—I didn't mean it that way. I'm just surprised soldiers like you also served as teachers here. Isn't that a civilian's job?"

He was still chuckling when he answered, "Oh, fer sure, ma'am. But when we got 'ere an' beat the insurgency an' all, there was no U.S. civilian. Just us. When I got ma'self injured on ma' knee, ma' captain—he sign me up on this mission a winnin' hearts an' minds. Guess I got the hearts part with ma' wife, an' the minds part with the teachin.'" He roared into laughter again, and Eleanor chuckled along with him. "But am sure glad yer takin' over, miss. 'Coz these young 'uns 'ere? They be smarter than ya think. An' I got no more to give 'em b'yond the alphabet, numbers, an' basic English speakin.'"

She grinned. "I'm sure there's more service that could be squeezed out of you, sergeant. I'm grateful for what you've done. Now, I'll do my best—with your help."

They'd been riding a while, passing mostly thatched huts and a few two-story stone and wooden houses similar to those in Intramuros. She figured they were now heading toward the countryside. "Sergeant, excuse me, but are we still in Legazpi?"

He grinned. "Yer right to ask, ma'am. Yer school an' house are in the next town, Magayon."

"But I don't understand!" she exclaimed. "I was told I'd be teaching in the capital. Isn't that Legazpi?"

"Used to be, ma'am. No longer," he replied. "Legazpi got demoted from cap'tal city to a town. I guess 'twas 'coz of that darned insurgency it drag out." The sergeant spit over his left shoulder, roadside.

"Relocatin' the school to Magayon was meant to be a slap to Legazpi folks, ya see."

"Oh. So which one is the capital now?"

"Fer now, none," the soldier said. "Is a toss-up, I guess, 'tween Magayon an' another town." He added, "But to be honest, ma'am, I think ye'd like Magayon more than Legazpi. Has a purdier church an' view of the Mayon, if ye ask me!"

"I see," Eleanor said. "And is Mag... um,... is that where you also live?"

"No, ma'am. But not far from where ya'll be. Ma' wife an' me—we live near the border tween Legazpi an' Magayon. Maybe I come an' get ya some Sunday an' 'ave lunch with us? The missus said to ask." He grinned sheepishly.

"Oh, that's kind of you both," Eleanor said. "Would love to—once I get settled."

"Fer sure, ma'am. Fer sure."

Eleanor turned her attention to the bucolic scenery. Rice, corn, and sugarcane fields swept across the land on both sides of the dirt road. Ubiquitous views of the Mayon could be had—looming over village huts, glimpsed between trees, or framed by rice paddies in the foreground. The sun reflected on the water in irrigation ditches like stripes of silver between rows of jade. Clumps of bamboo, coconut, and what appeared to be banana and papaya trees marked where farmers' huts nestled behind the foliage. It all presented an idyllic backdrop to her new life. And she smiled. "Sergeant Munro, this town where you're taking me. Magayon? Sounds like the vapor's name I'd sailed in."

He smiled and nodded. "Ye be right, ma'am. Ya sailed with the *Daragang Magayon*, an' the town's called Magayon. Daraga means 'maiden' in Vicolano, an' magayon means beautiful. So, ya come in on the Beautiful Maiden!"

"How charming." Eleanor smiled.

"What ya may find intrestin' is the vapor's name is the volcano's original name. From a legend 'bout a beautiful maiden, Magayon. She fell in love with a brave an' 'andsome warrior. But she 'ad another suitor—the chief of a warrin' tribe who later killed 'er sweetheart by skullduggery. Instead of acceptin' bein' the wife of a cheatin' an' murderin' guy, she killed 'erself with 'er lover's sword. Story goes, after the lovers' bodies were buried together, the volcano grew from their graves. The beauty of the mountain remind folks of the lovely maiden an' the fire of 'er love. So, they name it Daragang Magayon. After long time, I guess, the name got short'end to Mayon."

"What a beautiful but tragic story!" Eleanor exclaimed, gazing up at the volcano.

"That it is, ma'am. Folks say the spirit of Magayon still roam the mountains an' foothills in the form of a lovely nymph. An' when the volcano 'rupts, that's 'er protestin' true love's loss. So, they keep the volcano peaceable by keepin' romance alive an' well!" He chuckled. "Mind ya, ma'am—people 'ere are as fiery as their volcano when it come to love an' war. For me, am just grateful to be the casualty of one an' not the other!" Sergeant Munro bellowed into infectious laughter.

"Let's hope it remains that way, sergeant!" Eleanor said, laughing with him.

"Oh, please, ma'am. It's Sam to ya!"

"Thank you, Sam. You may also call me Eleanor."

As the carretela progressed toward Magayon, Eleanor dwelled upon the story of the maiden who chose death instead of marrying someone she didn't love. She thought about how she, too, had to die in her old life because she couldn't accept old farmer Borg's proposal. Now, she would be living under the shadow of a beautiful volcano named after a beautiful maiden who gave up her life for love. Could anything be more Shakespearean? Eleanor fixed her gaze on an unencumbered view of the perfectly cone-shaped volcano, thanking the goddess who lived there.

CHAPTER 7

All the World's a Stage

They entered a town square in front of a church built on a low hill. At the foot of the hill was a whitewashed, concrete stage, behind which were stone stairs that led up the church. Sam said it was the Franciscan church of *Nuestra Señora de la Cosecha* or "Our Lady of the Harvest." Though small compared to many of the churches in Manila, it appeared to be uniquely built of volcanic rock, judging from its speckled charcoal stone walls.

It boasted a Baroque façade accentuated by two pairs of spiral Solomonic columns crowned by medallions carved with images of the four Evangelists. The front exterior also featured statues of other saints inside niches. A pedimented center niche held the figure of the Mother of God, framed with intricate carvings of tropical fruits and flowers, sheaves of rice, and ears of corn. On its left side stood an octagonal bell tower likewise decorated with carved figures of other saints. The church overlooked the plaza. Combined with the Mayon that loomed large over the town from the Northeast, it all made for a postcard-perfect vignette. A picturesque backdrop to a stage set. And the lines from Shakespeare's play whispered to Eleanor,

All the world's a stage,

and all the men and women merely players;

They have their exits and their entrances….

She wondered what kind of play was being staged now that she was here and how her role as la maestra Americana fit into its plot.

"Welcome to Magayon, Eleanor!" Sam said. "I hope ye be happy 'ere as I am."

"Thank you, Sam." She smiled. "I hope so, too. Most of all, I hope I can truly help the children here."

He turned the carretela to cross the plaza center, which was surrounded by some important-looking buildings in the colonial style she'd admired in Intramuros. Sam pointed to each of the structures as they passed them. "Now, this be yer typical Spanish town square, with the church facin' west. An' that be the ayuntamiento or 'town hall' facin' the church. An' that gran' ol' villa there beside the town hall be the home of el presidente, the mayor. An' over there be the former HQ of the guardia civil. The police. It's now our infantry station."

She smiled. The American flag flying high on a bamboo pole in front of the station greeted Eleanor like an old friend. Then, she noticed something odd. "But where's everybody, Sam?" Apart from a stray, runtish mongrel scuttling about, foraging in garbage piles—the town looked deserted.

Sam chuckled. "Siesta time, ya know."

"Oh." She'd forgotten about the custom of taking afternoon naps to escape the warmest hours of the day. Their arrival was timely, then, for she wasn't ready to face her new townmates. She felt tired and sticky and longed for a bath. Just then, it occurred to her to ask, "Oh, by the way, Sam—where's the school?" It was strange that such an important structure didn't appear among the notable buildings around the plaza square.

He smiled rather tentatively. "Oh, not far. I'll show ya on Monday."

She arched an eyebrow. "It's not in the plaza?"

"It is," he replied with a strange smile.

"But where?" Eleanor pressed, puzzled by his seeming evasiveness.

"It's somewhat there."

Eleanor raised both eyebrows and turned to him. "Sam, something is either here or there, but not somewhat somewhere. What's going on? Why are you dodging my question?"

He smiled ruefully. "Well, ma'am, it's behin' the church."

"Behind the church? Where, exactly?" She kept her gaze on him.

"Next to… the church."

"Next to the church?" Eleanor frowned. "What do you mean, Sam?"

He cleared his throat. "It… it's act'ally part of church property."

"Part of church… Oh, but Sam!" she exclaimed. "We're a public, secular school!"

"Yes, but," he interjected, "ya 'ave to understand, Eleanor, that for 350 years, the school 'ere been under the church's wing." He turned to glance at her sideways. "Now, don't ya worry. The padre 'as offered to lend ya his school buildin'… dependin' only on one condition."

Eleanor narrowed her eyes at him. "What condition?"

He smiled ruefully again. "Basic'ly… that he… get to… teach a religion class."

"Oh, but Sam! That's impossible!" Eleanor cried. The play had begun.

"Yes… an'… that's why…" Sam said slowly, as though inviting Eleanor's heart rate to slow down, too. "The class is put out to be voluntary."

"Oh." Eleanor sighed. "Um… I… I guess that could work. Fair exchange for the priest allowing us to use his building… until I can get something more suitable." She was warming up to the idea until Sam erupted into a laughing fit. "Did I say something funny, Sam?"

"No, just the idea of it!" He guffawed.

"What?" Eleanor pressed her lips.

"That ya sincerely believe such class would be voluntary!" he chortled. "I can assure ya, folks 'ere don't consider 'emselves free to choose *not* to sign up their kids for the padre's religion class. Only takes a public shamin' of 'em in his Sunday sermon to get any renegade parents back in line. That is, if a personal visit to the family fail to do the trick." Sam continued chortling.

Eleanor heaved a sigh. "What do you suggest, then?"

A sober expression took over Sam's countenance. "Eleanor, if there's one piece of advice I could give ya, it's this: Don't get on the wrong side of the padre. My second piece of advice? Don't mess with el presidente, either. An' if ya 'ave to choose 'tween 'em? Choose the priest! For I tell ya—he hold power over heaven an' earth 'ere."

Eleanor slumped in her seat.

Just as they were leaving the plaza, she spied a dark, ragamuffin figure emerging from one of the alleys. He was a cruddy old man with long, unkempt, graying hair and beard, dressed in filthy, tattered clothes, shambling shoeless, gesticulating, as if he were arguing with someone walking beside him. Yet, he was alone. He approached a garbage pile from which the same dog she'd spotted earlier was still scavenging for food scraps, and the mongrel growled at him. Eleanor blenched as he kicked the stray on the belly. The animal yelped and scuttled away.

Sam drove the carretela to a street behind the plaza and pulled up to a property enclosed by a bamboo fence. A pair of tall, ancient-looking trees with wide canopies stood diagonally across the yard, marking the front and back ends of the property. There were also a couple of coconut trees abundant with pea-green globes and some banana trees—one of which was heavy with clusters of fruit that looked like fat, brown fingers.

To her delightful surprise, there was also a frangipani tree that bore the fragrant flowers the Hawaiians strung into leis. Planted along the fence were hibiscus, bougainvillea, and other flowering plants. Providing contrast to the red, fuchsia, orange, and ivory colors of the blossoms were lush, green shrubs whose foliage ranged from ferns to fronds, lance-like to curvy, spotted to striped. Everything framed a fetching view of the house at the center of the yard.

Eleanor's heart pounded and quickened. The modest yet charming abode had a metal hip roof, wood-paneled walls, and, to Eleanor's delight, capiz shell windows and turned-wood balustered parapets. It was built on robust timber stilts about four feet from the ground, allowing for ample crouching space underneath, screened with a bamboo trellis skirt.

"Sam, is this where I'm staying?" she asked with wide-eyed anticipation. "I mean, at least until I find a place to lease?"

Sam grinned. "Act'ally, this is it, Eleanor! This be yer new home— that is, if ya like it."

"Like it? Love it already!" Eleanor exclaimed. "Thank you! I was told I'd be in some dormitory while I looked for long-term lodging. How'd you get me this pretty house?"

"We figured ya'd want to be close to town. An' this was the only house available. An' my Cristina—she got ya a great deal! Only twenty dollars a month, fully furnished. Ya'd easily pay twice for this in Manila."

At that moment, a door opened and a young, smiling, and very pregnant Filipina emerged and slowly stepped down the stairs, cheerfully calling, "O, Samuel! Yoo-hoo! Samuel!" She said his name like a Spanish-speaking person would. Following behind her was an even younger-looking, stick-thin native woman. Both of them were dressed in traditional, yet humble-looking camisas at sayas.

"Ah!" cried Sam happily. "Is ma' missus! Said she'd 'ave the house cleaned for ya. Didn't expect 'er to still be 'ere."

He climbed down from the driver's seat and limped over to Eleanor's side to help her step down from hers. "What ya doin' 'ere, darlin'?" he hollered as his wife approached. "Ye should be restin'!"

She smiled brightly and rapidly replied in a language Eleanor couldn't comprehend. It must be the mixed Spanish and Vicolano that Sam mentioned. Draping his arm around his wife's shoulders, he said, "Eleanor, I'd like ya to meet ma' wife, Cristina. Tina, honey, this is la maestra Americana."

She glanced up at her husband, who was about twice her height, and turned to Eleanor, smiling timorously. With her left hand caressing her huge belly, Cristina extended her right hand to Eleanor. "P-please… to m-meet… you, ma'am. W-welcome!" Her husband coached her through her little speech.

Eleanor shook her hand enthusiastically. "Why, thank you, Cristina! I'm very happy to meet you, too. Please—do call me Eleanor."

Cristina glanced alternately between Eleanor and her husband. "El…?"

Sam repeated Eleanor's name.

"El… leo… no…. Ah!" Cristina exclaimed, nodding vigorously, as though she'd just received an epiphany. "Iyó! ¡Sí! Leonor! You—Leonor!" Her sweet, round face bounced like a ball on her short neck to the cadence of her sing-song voice, and her eyes twinkled with child-like excitement.

Sam chuckled. "I think ya'd just been chris'ened with yer Spanish—or, I should say, Filipino name! Leonor."

"Leonor." Eleanor paused to consider it and smiled. "I like it! Thank you, Cristina."

Cristina beamed and pulled the other woman from behind her and said something to her husband.

"Cristina wants me to tell ya that this 'ere be Yolanda," Sam said. "Yer muchacha."

"My what?" Eleanor exclaimed with arched eyebrows.

"Muchacha," Sam repeated, smiling. "She's sort of a maid an' housekeeper all in one."

"A maid? Housekeeper?" Eleanor echoed, shooting perplexed glances at Cristina and Yolanda. "Please tell them I appreciate it, but I don't need one."

"Oh, trust me, ya'll need one, Leonor," Sam said.

"I'm pretty sure I can manage," Eleanor retorted. "I can't think why I'd need help running my own house."

"Well, then, let me explain," Sam replied. "First, it saves ye a lot of headache an' heartache figurin' out where to get stuff an' how to do things 'round 'ere. Yolanda will take care of all the marketin,' cookin,' cleanin,' washin,' an' all ya need so ye can focus on yer teachin.' Second, ye be givin' this poor, young, hard-workin' girl a badly needed job. Fin'lly, an' most important, 'avin' a servant or two is a necessary status symbol 'ere. It's expected, 'specially for someone in yer position, to 'ave at least one muchacha. Or…"

"Or, what Sam?" Eleanor interjected.

"Or folks 'ere will think yer strange! An' trust me, Leonor—ya don't want that!" Sam shook his head.

"I see," Eleanor said, sighing. It was the old issue of conformity challenging her again—this time, telling her it probably wasn't prudent to insist on presenting herself as too different. "Well, I want to fit in, of course. But how much would this… this fitting-in cost?"

Her salary was about a hundred dollars a month, yet she had no idea of the cost of living in the area. Although she had some cash left from the funds she withdrew at a bank in Manila, she suspected the superintendent was just relying on the Thomasites to shoulder the initial cost of establishing their schools because he hadn't mentioned advancing any monies for the purpose. It seemed a silly extravagance now to hire a maid she didn't need.

Sam turned to his wife and glanced back at Eleanor. "Don't ya worry, says Cristina. Not much. Only five dollars a month."

"What! Five dollars?" Eleanor exclaimed. "Why, that sounds ridiculously low, Sam! Are you sure?"

Yolanda frowned, looking anxious.

Cristina nodded vigorously again and said something to Sam, who said, "Cristina suggests to start with that, an' if ya like Yolanda's work enough, then it's up to ye if ya wanna give 'er a raise."

Cristina said a few more things to Sam, who glanced back at Eleanor. "To be clear, the five dollars is in addition to free room an' board."

"She lives with me, too?" Eleanor raised her eyebrows and glanced at Yolanda, who was now shifting her weight between her legs, rocking side to side, and pulling at her fingers.

"It's customary 'ere," Sam said. "Besides, we would'na want ya to be by yerself. It's safe enough in this town, but havin' a muchacha will give ye—an' me an' Cristina—extra peace of mind. That's if ya don't mind the extra expense?"

"No—I mean, it's not that," Eleanor replied. "I... I suppose I'm just not used to having a maid. Never had one. But I see what you mean. Appreciate you and Cristina thinking of my needs." Eleanor glanced at Cristina and smiled.

"De nada, Leonor!" Cristina surprisingly replied, beaming.

Eleanor realized she understood more English than she'd let on.

Cristina spoke to Yolanda, who glanced at Eleanor, smiling with seeming relief.

"Good, that's settled!" Sam exclaimed, clapping his hands. "Now, shall we show ya yer home?" His thick mustache rose with the arching of his bushy eyebrows.

"Please!" Eleanor exclaimed, smiling back at him.

Sam and his manservant took down Eleanor's crate and luggage from the carretela. "Where'd ya want these, Leonor?" Sam asked.

"Please bring my trunk and portmanteau to the bedroom. And the crate? Is there a storage area, perhaps?" Eleanor asked.

"Only under the house."

"That'll do. Thank you."

Yolanda grabbed the Gladstone bag, and Eleanor exclaimed, "Oh! I could carry that, Yolanda. Gracias." She tried to take her luggage from the muchacha, but Cristina said something to Yolanda that made the latter hang on to the bag.

Sam intervened. "Leonor, it's Yolanda's job now to be carryin' yer things. If ye insist on this yerself, ya'll make 'er feel useless."

Eleanor acceded, for she had no energy left to argue.

Cristina grabbed Eleanor's hand and pulled her up the bamboo stairs to the house, as if they were already the best of friends. From the solid wood front door, they entered a spacious *sala* or "living room." Cristina gave instructions to Yolanda, who opened the windows and sliding panels behind the parapets to let in the afternoon sunlight and breeze.

At the center of the dark, polished, wide wood-plank floor, a pair of plantation chairs and a rather ostentatious baronial sofa surrounded an oval, marble-topped center table. A crocheted doily covered the table, at the center of which sat a terracotta-potted fern. When Cristina wasn't looking, Eleanor subtly ran a finger across some of the surfaces. Sam's wife had certainly ensured the house was clean and ready for her.

She noticed the seats and backrests of the sofa and chairs weren't upholstered but rendered in woven cane, a style she supposed was more suitable for a warm climate. Opposite the windows that faced the front yard was a hallway into which Sam and Pedro disappeared, carrying her steamer trunk. An empty bookcase stood in front of one of two walls flanking the hallway entrance. Set against the second wall was a console, above which hung a huge, stunning painting of Mayon Volcano.

Cristina pulled Eleanor next to what she called a comedor, which appeared to be the dining room. It was accessible from the living room through a doorway. Four windows, a pair of which were on the long side of the rectangular room, allowed abundant natural light. Six elaborately-carved throne chairs surrounded a dark, oblong dining table under a painted, glass-shaded oil lamp hanging from the center of the ceiling. A sideboard, over which a Venetian-style mirror was hung horizontally, sat against the wall on the other long side of the room. The tables here were again covered with crocheted runners.

Eleanor noted that all the furniture she'd seen, so far, was ornately carved—a surprising luxury for a rented house.

A second doorway led from the dining room to the *cocina* or "kitchen"—a small, dark room in the middle of the backside of the house. Its sole source of ventilation and light came from a single window with a hinged, thatched shutter propped up by a rattan cane. Between the kitchen and a short hallway leading to the bathroom, there was a door that opened to the backyard, which was accessible by another set of bamboo stairs. Eleanor was glad to see an artesian well with a hand pump in the back garden.

Before the kitchen window, a pair of charcoal braziers sat on one side of the counter wrapped in tin. On the opposite end of the counter sat a glazed, bulb-shaped, terracotta pot. "Para agua," Cristina explained, pointing to it. Water. This told Eleanor there was no indoor plumbing and that water had to be pumped from the well outside and stored for kitchen use inside the pot. A faucet was fitted into the clay jar, which was placed over a sunken rectangular box with a bottom consisting of bamboo slats. Eleanor guessed this must be where the dish and hand washing were done, since there was nothing else in the tiny space that looked or functioned as a sink. She was aghast to realize the waste-water simply drained between the slats straight to the ground below.

Displayed on shelves opposite the cooking counter were cans of corned beef, sardines, and various bottles of what appeared to be condiments that emitted exotic and fishy smells. Cristina lifted the cover of a huge, squat, clay urn on the floor to reveal where they stored the rice grains.

A pair of baskets hung from the rafters. Yolanda stepped on a stool, unhooked one of them, and showed Eleanor what it contained: some green, leafy vegetables, a bunch of bananas, garlic, and onions. The other basket contained fresh eggs and, wrapped in newsprint, two kinds of fish: dried and smoked—which assaulted Eleanor's nose with such a rotten smell, it almost made her gag. She refrained from covering her nose with her handkerchief for fear of offending her guides, who appeared quite proud of what they had prepared for her arrival.

Eleanor smiled and nodded appreciatively at both women, and they beamed.

"Cristina, you thought of everything. ¡Muchas gracias!" Eleanor said. "Por favor—how much do I owe you? ¿Cuánto...?""

Cristina vigorously shook her head. "¡Nada, nada, Leonor!" She giggled and playfully slapped Eleanor's arm.

"What!" Eleanor exclaimed. "No—this is too much! Please, tell me. This all must have cost you something."

Cristina continued shaking her head and said something that included the word, *regalo*. Sam startled her from behind and said, "Cristina says it's a gift. To get ye started an' all." He grinned. "Besides, she didn't have to pay cash for any of it. Came from her family's farm."

"Oh, Cristina," Eleanor said, "thanks so much, again!"

Cristina startled her when she hugged her.

Sam looked upon his wife adoringly before he glanced back at Eleanor. "Would ya wanna see yer bedroom?"

Eleanor nodded eagerly and followed Sam through the hallway that would have led them back to the living room. But Sam opened a door along the way, which led to a big bedroom. Eleanor realized the space was equivalent to the size of the dining room on the opposite side of the house.

"Well, Leonor, what ya think?" asked Sam with an expectant smile.

"Oh, Sam, it's wonderful!" Eleanor replied.

The bedroom featured a four-poster wooden bed that had, Eleanor was glad to see, not only a caned platform, but also a feather mattress. The arched headboard was carved with a design of coconut palms, while the finials capping the barley-twist posts mimicked little coconuts. At the foot of the bed was where Sam and Pedro had set her steamer trunk. Perfect!

The bedroom also had a caned throne chair and writing desk in front of a window overlooking the side garden. Set against one of the walls was a dresser and an armoire. Cristina opened the armoire's mirrored door, showing a hanging rod for dresses and lower shelves for towels, blankets, bedsheets, pillows, and a mosquito net.

Sam's wife then said something that seemed to include Yolanda's name, which her husband translated. "Cristina says Yolanda will set up the 'skitter net when yer ready for bed."

"Thank you, but I know how to do that myself," Eleanor replied, briefly glancing at Yolanda who stood by the door, smiling timidly.

"I know ya do, Leonor," Sam retorted. "But make sure ya leave 'nough work for Yolanda to feel useful. They got lots of pride—these people. And 'spite of what the Spaniards say 'bout 'em, most are happy to work for their meal if ya let 'em. They're some of the best hard-workin' folk I know."

They returned to the sala where Eleanor examined the Mayon Volcano painting. Portrayed in the landscape's foreground was the ghostly ruins of a church. Only the bell tower and a portion of its façade wall remained—survivors, she assumed, of what must have been an especially devastating eruption of the volcano. The work appeared to have been painted long after the calamity, as could be deduced from the moss, vines, ferns, and other plants, including what appeared to be tree saplings, growing on the stone walls.

The tranquil scene evoked violence, latent yet powerfully present in the unsullied image of a turquoise volcano spearing a clear, blue sky. The stream of white smoke rising from the crater suggested its continuing capacity for destruction. *Behind every paradise lie hellish truths*. It was then that Eleanor noticed a signature on the lower right-hand corner of the canvas. *L. E. G.*

"That's by a local artist," Sam said.

"Is that so? Marvelous! It's gallery quality," Eleanor remarked. "I'm surprised the landlord left it in a rented house."

Sam grinned. "No surprise when ya consider yer landlord is the artist. Don Luis Gonzaga."

Eleanor raised her eyebrows and smiled. "What kind of landlord paints like this?"

Sam grinned again. "Ya tell me—after ye meet 'im this Sunday."

"Sunday?" Eleanor swung around to face Sam. "This Sunday?" She shook her head. "Sam, I don't know how many more surprises I could take."

"Don't look at me!" Sam chuckled. "Had nothin' to do with it! See that envelope on the table?"

Eleanor turned to where he was pointing. She didn't notice the envelope at the center table earlier perhaps because it was partially covered by the potted fern's leaves. She picked it up and saw her name handwritten in elegant cursive. In classic calligraphy and English, the card inside stated:

Don Luis Enríquez Gonzaga and Doña Ximena Gonzaga y Enríquez
request the honor of your presence
at a dinner at Villa Gonzaga
on Sunday, the 8th of September, 1901
at six o'clock in the evening
to welcome the honorable Maestra Americana,
Señorita Eleanor Karsten.

A handwritten note accompanied the invitation.

Dear Señorita Karsten,

We hope to have the pleasure of your company at the welcome dinner we are proud to give in your honor. We shall send a carruaje to fetch you at five thirty in the afternoon.

Sincerely yours,
Doña Ximena Gonzaga

Eleanor glanced up at Sam. "Please tell me all you know about my hosts."

Eleanor remained awake under the mosquito net tied to the four posts of her bed. The strangeness of sleeping in a strange house was testing her tolerance for novelty. In Manila, such newness was exhilarating. Now, with no friends to help absorb the shock of novelty, she felt restless.

She found herself bristling with delayed resentment for being forced to agree with things she normally wouldn't have agreed to. While motivated by good intentions, Cristina got her a maid without her consent. Eleanor went along with it because she felt sorry for Yolanda.

It all smacked of emotional blackmail. She liked Cristina, but disliked the Filipina's sly coercion.

Similarly, the reception her landlords were giving her upset her, for she was hoping, instead, to spend the weekend resting, unpacking, familiarizing herself with her new environment, and perhaps visiting the local U.S. infantry station to avail of commissary supplies. How strange for her hosts to have scheduled such an important event, supposedly in her honor—without consulting her! This suggested the affair wasn't really meant for her benefit, but theirs. They created an occasion to size her up—on their terms!

Yet, she knew this was one event she couldn't miss without offending what, possibly, could be the town's most prominent denizens. Still, this didn't prevent her from feeling dismayed at everyone's lack of etiquette. Elite or not, people here appeared accustomed to having their way or manipulating others to achieve it. She resolved to assert herself better next time.

Homesickness then hit her with renewed vigor. The little conveniences she took for granted in the states now appeared to be impossible luxuries. She didn't get the bath she wanted but what appeared to be the natives' version of a shower. Without indoor plumbing, the lone bathroom offered, instead, another huge clay urn that Yolanda had filled with water from several pail runs to the garden artesian well. To take a "shower," Yolanda explained through hand gestures that one scooped water from the urn with the bamboo ladle and poured the water over oneself. When Eleanor took such a shower earlier, she shrieked from the shock of cold water streaming down her naked body. To aggravate the situation, Yolanda barged into the bathroom to see what was the matter with her mistress and ran out screaming, "Que horror! Bruja! Que horror!"

Yet another superstitious native mistaking her for a witch! Eleanor surrendered to the only thing to do under such circumstances: laugh. She must have presented a frightful sight to the muchacha: a horrific vision of a nude Lady Godiva wrapped in wet, snake-like hair— laughing like a mad woman.

Eleanor should have foreseen it was unheated. If she wanted a warm shower next time, Yolanda would have to heat several pots' worth of water. But she didn't have the heart to burden the muchacha with such a tedious task. Hence, she resigned herself to cold showers.

The bathroom floor presented another issue she never anticipated until she felt a draft between her legs. Like the pretend sink in the kitchen, it was made of bamboo slats with gaps where water could drain through directly to the ground below. Eleanor grimaced thinking anyone could just sneak up from under the bathroom floor and see her naked as she showered. The only solution she could think of was to wear a slipdress next time, telling herself it wouldn't be different from wearing swimming attire at the lake or beach.

She was thankful the toilet, at least, was inside the bathroom, not at an outhouse. The wooden commode sat on terra-cotta tiles at ground level next to the elevated shower floor. It appeared to empty directly into a hole in the ground. She imagined the septic pit had to be regularly cleaned out to prevent an overflow. A malodorous smell from the pit made her wonder when the last maintenance service was done. Recalling the bathroom and toilet were next to the kitchen, she dared not even imagine the disgusting consequences of an overflow.

Earlier that evening, Yolanda prepared them a dinner of smoked fish stew with vegetables and what Eleanor now recognized as the staple of Filipino meals: boiled rice. The stew had a sour-salty flavor she didn't think she'd like, yet enjoyed—except for the tiny red-green peppers in the broth. Eleanor isolated the spicy culprits, showed them to Yolanda, and shook her head and forefinger to convey to the cook that she wanted such ingredient excluded from their food.

Yolanda first reacted with a defiant, gaping mouth—followed by crestfallen eyes, before finally nodding. The muchacha's slow, half-hearted acquiescence, however, warned Eleanor to remain alert against quite possibly continuing, covert, treacherous assaults by the potent spice.

The town and house were not yet electrified; only candles or oil and kerosene lamps provided illumination after dark. Eleanor thus ate her dinner by lamp and candlelight, which could have made for a romantic first meal at her new home, until moths attacked the lamp above the dining table, fell, and then perished by candle flame before her eyes.

The melancholic bugle that sounded the lowering of the US flag at the infantry station reverberated across town and added to the poignant ambiance. Frogs and crickets serenaded her from the garden, reminiscent of Iowa summer dinners with her parents on the porch of their farmhouse. Loneliness besieged her again. She tried to persuade Yolanda to join her at the table, but the muchacha repeatedly shook her head and kept to the kitchen, where the maid ate her dinner after Eleanor had finished hers.

At bedtime, another surprise struck Eleanor. She realized there was just one bedroom in the whole house. She asked Yolanda through clumsy hand gestures where the maid intended to sleep. The muchacha responded by showing her the *banig* or "woven mat" she planned to set down on the kitchen floor. Eleanor glanced up at the food baskets hanging from the rafters above the spot where Yolanda intended to sleep, reminded that such a food storage system was likely also a preemptive defense against critters. Imagining cockroaches and mice crawling all over the maid as she slept so repulsed Eleanor that she insisted on Yolanda sleeping in her bedroom. Yet, the maid demurred with equal persistence. Thus, Eleanor tried to persuade Yolanda to sleep on the caned sofa in the sala, instead. The muchacha then nodded with a smile.

Tired yet still unable to sleep, Eleanor got up, lit a candle, and went to the kitchen to get a cup of drinking water. She startled both herself and Yolanda when she accidentally stepped on the maid who'd apparently been sleeping on the kitchen floor despite Eleanor's objections. The muchacha, scared out of her slumber, launched into a shrieking fit and ran around the house, screaming, "Ay, multo! Multo!"

Unable to comprehend what Yolanda was shouting about, Eleanor chased after her and caught her just in time before the maid was about to step out of the house, which could have caused her to fall down the bamboo stairs. Eleanor grabbed and hugged the crying, screaming maid, who squirmed in her arms.

Finally, the young woman looked up at Eleanor and, perhaps realizing it was none other than her mistress holding her, calmed down. Through tearful, incorrigible speech aided by rather creative hand gestures and expressive facial expressions, Yolanda communicated that, upon being jolted out of her sleep and seeing Eleanor's pale, candlelit face; pale, long snake-like hair; and pale, long nightdress in the dark, she mistook her mistress for a *multo* or "ghost."

Eleanor chuckled and embraced the young woman. The muchacha couldn't be more than nineteen or twenty: a woman just past girlhood. She caressed the maid's back and sighed. "Oh, Yolanda, we have a long way to go before we could convince you there are no such things as witches and ghosts—don't we? Well, then, we'll just have to include you in our adult classes. Let's begin by teaching you English and you teaching me Vicolano. So we could understand each other better. All right? Meanwhile, I insist we share the bedroom."

Eleanor returned to the kitchen, picked up Yolanda's blanket and pillow, and gestured to the wide-eyed maid to roll up her mat and follow her to the bedroom. There, they set Yolanda's banig, blanket, and pillow on the floor beside Eleanor's bed. "There, Yolanda," Eleanor said, smiling, "I hope you sleep better for the rest of the night."

Yolanda gazed upon her mistress with thoughtful eyes. She took one of Eleanor's hands and kissed it.

Next morning, Yolanda prepared Eleanor a breakfast consisting of rice and fish—again, but different from last night's dinner. It looked like dried fish fried in lard, with the rice likewise fried but with garlic and seasoned with salt and pepper. Eleanor didn't want to disappoint Yolanda by criticizing the meal and planned on simply asking the cook to reduce the grease in their food next time.

She was surprised she enjoyed the garlic fried rice, yet hardly touched the fish, for where it still had some flesh, it was practically a petrified, salty fossil. Frying it had reduced it to crispy crumbs when she tried to slice it—additionally rendered almost impossible by the fact she had no table knife to begin with. It seemed Yolanda expected her to eat with a fork and spoon. When Eleanor asked for a table knife, the maid handed her the kitchen cleaver.

Yolanda must have noticed Eleanor's dissatisfaction, for she produced a pair of fried eggs in no time. Although they were also greasy, Eleanor ate with gusto, and the cook smiled. Instead of coffee, however, Yolanda served her a hot beverage brewed from toasted rice, which had a smooth and pleasing nutty flavor, yet was nothing like coffee. Thus, she planned on going to the infantry station in town to inquire about purchasing some of its commissary supplies for herself.

After breakfast, she wrote letters to Miss Covell, Maude, and Arabella, assuring them of her safe arrival in Magayon, and set herself on unpacking. She hung her dresses in the armoire and put away folded clothes into the dresser drawers. Yolanda appeared by the open bedroom door, and by way of fists rubbing against each other, asked her mistress for clothes that needed washing, and Eleanor handed her a few.

Wondering about what to wear to the Gonzaga dinner, Eleanor thought of the pale blue gown that Maude had lent her during the Waterhouse Honolulu reception, which the Radcliffe girl gifted to her as they were repacking to travel to their assigned school areas. "I brought too many dresses, anyway," Maude had said. "I hope this brings you luck where you're going." While the frock didn't bring up good memories for Eleanor, recalling how badly she felt at the Waterhouse mansion, Maude could be right. Maybe, she'd have better luck with it, this time.

Eleanor found it and hung it up in the armoire. But it was too feminine and whimsical. Perhaps a less severe version of one of her Victorian spinster outfits, as Arabella had called them in jest, was best. She decided in favor of the high-necked, lace-trimmed Victorian blouse and linen skirt she'd worn at Miss Clendenin's tea party on the *Thomas*. She'd put up her hair in the fashionable Gibson style that Arabella and Maude taught her to make. She would be the image of la maestra Americana who was voguish yet conservative. *Perfect.*

She was digging for the attire in the steamer trunk when she heard Yolanda's now familiar shriek. What, on earth, had frightened the muchacha now?

CHAPTER 8

The Serpent in the Garden

She ran to the backyard where the screaming came from. She'd earlier glimpsed the maid setting down a wide, scalloped-edged tin basin full of clothes for washing under the artesian well's spout. But Yolanda wasn't there. Instead, the muchacha was standing, seemingly frozen in place, under an ancient-looking tree. Eleanor slowly approached the maid, who was staring upward. She touched Yolanda's shoulder. "Yolanda? Why—what's the matter?"

The muchacha jumped behind Eleanor and pointed a trembling finger at something dangling from one of the tree branches.

It looked terrifying. At the same time, it was magnificent. A magnificent snake! It was huge and long—although, on account of Eleanor's almost zero knowledge about snakes, she wasn't sure if its size was normal for its kind. Its scalloped brown, black, and golden scales blended with the tree bark. No one would have noticed it if it didn't hang as it did. It seemed to be contemplating the two women, just as the women were contemplating their next move.

In all of her visions of a tropical paradise, Eleanor didn't count on encountering snakes as she probably should have. What was a Garden of Eden, after all, without the serpent? She thus resolved to learn about the local wildlife. For instance, was the snake venomous? In the meantime, it seemed a good idea to do as Yolanda did. Remain still. Any abrupt movement could provoke it to strike.

Both women jumped out of their skin when the snake suddenly spoke with a man's voice—in a language that sounded to Eleanor as a combination of Spanish and, possibly, Vicolano. It sent Yolanda shrieking anew and hopping in fright.

When the snake spoke again, Eleanor realized it wasn't the snake speaking but a native man standing outside the chest-high bamboo fence directly behind the tree where the snake had coiled itself around one of its branches. He appeared taller than the average Filipino but no taller than Eleanor by perhaps an inch or two. He wore a peasant's shirt with sleeves rolled up to his elbows and a straw hat that kept his face in shadow. All she could see was his round, brown nose with slightly flared nostrils, full, shapely russet lips, and square jaw.

A verbal exchange transpired between him and Yolanda, before the man climbed over the fence and jumped into the yard.

"W-wait, wait! What does he think he's doing?" cried Eleanor. "Yolanda, we don't know this man!"

But neither Yolanda nor the man bothered to address her concern. Instead, the stranger took off his hat and hung it on the fence, slipped off his leather sandals, folded the hem of his long pantaloons up to his big calves, and climbed the tree like a cat. He crawled on the branch on which the snake had coiled itself, pried it off the tree limb, and, to Eleanor's astonishment, draped the reptile around his neck and jumped off the tree, landing solidly on his feet.

When he glanced up at Eleanor, he twisted his lips into a smile and winked. She noted his dark, sparkling eyes, his black, wavy, jaw-length hair, and his sinewy forearms flexing as he pushed his hair from his face and tucked it behind his ears. He put on his hat and sandals and approached the women, holding out the snake to them as if it were an offering.

As he stepped forward, Eleanor stepped backward. "N-no, no! Please! We don't want it!" she exclaimed, shaking her head.

Yolanda screamed again and ran to the house.

The man replied with what, again, sounded like a mix of Spanish and the local language. When Eleanor failed to respond, he continued— to her great amazement—in English. "No poison. Good eat. Taste like chicken." He smiled and mimicked pushing food into his mouth with his fingers, chewing, and rubbing his belly.

Eleanor waved her hands in declination. "Oh, t-thank you, but no, señor. Could you just… please put it away somewhere? Like… like in those woods, perhaps? Yes, far away from here!" She gestured in sweeping, shooing motions.

The man tilted his head, as though trying to comprehend what she said, looking quite amused. Without saying more, he walked past her toward the street and left, whistling a happy tune, with the docile snake wrapped around his shoulders like a stole.

"Señor? Excuse me? Señor!" Eleanor hollered. But the man did not look back as he disappeared into the dusty haze of another warming day.

The carruaje sent by the Gonzagas to fetch Eleanor was a well-preserved vestige of a late eighteenth-century carriage, pulled by a pair of horses. It was fully enclosed with doors that had glass-paneled windows covered by curtains. The coachman sat perched up in front, while a footman stood on the rear platform that served as a place to stack luggage, steamer trunks, and other cargo. The carriage doors were painted with a family crest consisting of the letter *G* in calligraphy style, topped by a rather pretentious crown. A pair of coconut trees flanked and arched over the letter. Beneath the coconut trees was what appeared to represent an undergrowth of banana trees.

In the late afternoon, it was still warm and humid, especially inside the enclosed carriage. Eleanor opened her reticule and realized, to her lament, that she forgot to bring the fan that Arabella and Maude gave her. She was about to tap the carriage ceiling to ask the driver to return to her house so she could get it. Yet, she refrained from doing so as it occurred to her that she didn't know how long the ride to the hacienda would take. She didn't want to be late. To ventilate the carriage cabin, she drew the curtains open and slid down the glass panel.

She thought again of the native man who'd rid her garden of the snake. He demonstrated intelligence and initiative. His ability to speak some English was additionally surprising. His playful personality bordered on irreverence, however. It suggested an independent mind and lack of fear. Specifically, a lack of fear of her. This stunned her, for it meant she may have expected to be feared or revered by the natives.

She peered out the window, curious to see if she might spot him among the peasants walking home from the fields on the dirt road into town, carrying sacks and baskets or pulling ropes tied to their beast of burden, the carabao. Most of them glanced up at her with fierce, if not wary, expressions on their faces. Clearly, she had a lot of winning of hearts and minds to do. Yet, the Filipino yesterday didn't seem to care what she did or didn't do. He just went about his way as he pleased, and she found his indifference both annoying and beguiling.

The carruaje passed rice, corn, and sugarcane fields—a breathtaking view of the Mayon never failing. Sweeping swathes of fertile land mapped out paths of ancient lava flows, while more recent eruptions had scarred the landscape with charcoal bands of seeming barrenness. The shifting terrain was a centuries-old record of the Mayon's history and a reminder to the people that, before long, Daragang Magayon would prove yet again she was a living goddess—still smarting from love's loss.

A formidable fence of lava rocks topped by arrow-tipped iron bars told Eleanor she was near her destination. Yet, the banded route seemed to stretch on endlessly, until the carruaje slowed down and turned toward a pair of manorial wrought-iron gates. The metalwork words, "Hacienda" and "Gonzaga," marked the left and right side panels, respectively. Monumental volcanic stone columns capped by lighted metal oil lamps flanked the gates that screeched as a group of servants pulled the two gate panels open and separated "Hacienda" from "Gonzaga."

The approach to the villa was as impressive as one might imagine the entrance to a grand American Southern plantation, except that its carriage road was lined by bountiful coconut trees, instead of majestic old oaks. When the villa finally revealed itself, it struck Eleanor as something that belonged in Spain or France, perhaps, instead of the boondocks of Vicol. It was a two-story mansion with a terracotta-tiled roof, ivory stone walls, and European-style detailing in its pilasters, pediments, and balusters. Elegant wrought-iron scrollwork secured and accented its second-floor Juliet balconies. Its windows featured leaded glass panels instead of wooden grids of capiz shell. The carriageway turned around a three-tiered stone fountain that spouted and cascaded water in the center of an expansive circular pond. Eleanor stuck her neck out of the carriage window to see water lilies floating and golden koi darting in the pond's greenish waters. A low, trimmed hedge dotted with bright orange globes of star-like blossoms delineated the pond from the stone-flagged driveway.

Eleanor gathered from Sam that the Gonzagas had descended from pure-blooded Spanish insulares who could be traced to pioneering pen-insulares who arrived with the first galleons filled with adventurers from the Old World determined to make their fortunes in the New World. From what Eleanor could see of the mansion's exterior, the family had indeed made their fortune. The source of their wealth lay in the production of copra, from which oil was extracted, and of abaca fiber, which was essential to rope and marine cordage production.

When the driver stopped the carruaje in the arched *porte cochére,* the footman opened the door for Eleanor and helped her step down from the carriage. Almost immediately, at the top of the stone stairs that led up the villa, a pair of massive, elaborately-carved double wooden doors swung open, and a distinguished-looking Spanish mes-tizo couple emerged from them. The gentleman was tall, handsome, and bearded, and wore a Barong Tagalog. Holding onto the crook of his arm in a rather possessive way was an older lady dressed in an excellent example of an embroidered camisa at saya rendered in purple and gold. Behind the couple were other elegantly-dressed people who craned their necks or tip-toed to get a better look at Eleanor.

Eleanor focused her scattered breaths. She realized she was sorely underdressed in her cream, lace-trimmed, Victorian shirtwaist and blue linen skirt. She touched the golden locket resting on her breastbone under her blouse, reassuring herself as she climbed the few steps to meet her hosts.

When she reached the top, the gentleman smiled and declared in English laced with a Spaniard's accent, "Welcome to Hacienda Gonzaga, Señorita Karsten!"

"Thank you for having me," she replied, forcing a bright smile.

"Allow me to introduce ourselves," he said. "I am Luis Gonzaga, and this is my mother, Doña Ximena Gonzaga y Enríquez." He extended his hand to her, and she accepted it, but instead of shaking her hand, he performed a gesture of a kiss that a traditional Spanish gentleman might give.

Turning to his mother, she extended her hand and said, "I'm so pleased to meet you, Doña Ximena. Thank you so much for this kind reception."

The matronly lady briefly touched Eleanor's fingers and, with a semblance of a smile, said in a startlingly sharp voice, "De nada, Señorita Karsten. Bienvenida."

A corpulent, balding Spaniard in a brown friar's cassock stepped forward, prompting Don Luis to say, "And may I also present our reverend parish priest, Padre Damián Benitez?"

The friar extended a bulbous hand in front of Eleanor's face, as if he expected her to kiss it. She ignored the priest's look of dismay on his pockmarked face as she shook his hand, instead, and pulled away from his sweaty grasp—remembering, too late, Sam's warning not to antagonize the padre.

Next came a short, enthusiastically smiling man wearing, to her great surprise, a European gentleman's three-piece tweed suit. His eyes suggested he could be a Filipino Chinese mestizo. His richly pomaded hair was tautly brushed back from his small head. Sweat trailed down his brow and beaded upon his nose and upper lip.

Don Luis announced, "And this is our honorable el presidente, Don Basilio Dizon."

The mayor enclasped Eleanor's hand and declared with as much vigor as he shook it, "Encantada, señorita! Muy encantada! Bienvenida a Magayon!"

Eleanor gently yet firmly withdrew her hand from his painful grasp.

A petite, plump woman who'd been staring with seeming fascination at Eleanor's golden Gibson-styled hair stepped beside the mayor, who declared, "Tengo el honor de presentarles a mi esposa, Doña Hermosa Dizon y Henson." Eleanor caught enough of what he said to understand that he was introducing his wife.

The indigenous-looking woman was shorter than her short husband and, like the villa, looked like an anomaly of place and time. She wore an outdated European frock that was so frilly and bulky, it threatened to swallow her up at any moment. Her face powder was, in stark contrast with the dark brown skin on her neck, in a shade of ivory. Her red coiffure wig, though, matched the rouge circles on her cheeks and the crimson stain applied beyond the outline of her lips that, altogether, lent her a clownish appearance. What irony the woman's name was the Spanish word for beautiful!

Doña Hermosa likewise reeked of cheap French perfume as if she'd bathed in it. Overwhelmed by it, Eleanor involuntarily sneezed as she was offering to shake her hand. "Oh! Excuse me! Pardon me!" Eleanor exclaimed, quickly retracting her hand to pull out her handkerchief from her reticule and wipe her nose. The poor woman appeared suspended between confusion and embarrassment. Thus, Eleanor declared with more than usual geniality, "I am pleased, so very pleased to meet you, Doña Hermosa." She extended her hand again to the mayor's wife who simpered as she took Eleanor's hand by the fingertips and bent her knees in what seemed to be an attempt at a curtsey, such as one did for royalty. Eleanor pulled up the mayor's wife, exclaiming, "Oh no! Please, señora! That's not necessary."

The woman glanced quizzically between her husband and Eleanor. Don Luis translated what Eleanor said in what sounded like the hybrid Vicolano and Spanish. Doña Hermosa smiled again at Eleanor and, this time, only bowed her head.

"May I escort you inside?" Don Luis offered his arm to Eleanor with an expectant smile.

"Yes, thank you," Eleanor replied.

He folded her hand into the crook of his arm, while his mother continued holding onto the other. The rest of the guests followed after them. He led them past a broad, tiled hallway into a large drawing room, which he referred to as their "grand sala." A huge, circular, wrought-iron chandelier with lighted candles hung from the center of the high ceiling and, together with the light of several Victorian oil lamps spread around the room, shone upon the gilded details of Asian porcelain, European artifacts, and frames of landscape, religious, and portrait paintings.

A male servant wearing a white tunic shirt and dark trousers approached them, carrying a silver tray of frosty-looking champagne flutes. Don Luis picked one and offered it to Eleanor.

She welcomed it, for the warm, dusty ride to the hacienda had rendered her quite parched. As she sipped, the quality of the cold, effervescent drink impressed her. It could have only come from a dealer of fine French wines and must have been cooled in an ice box. She recalled the European food and wine merchants in Manila's Escolta district who'd advertised shipping to other islands and surmised that this was perhaps how Doña Ximena procured the champagne.

Don Luis introduced her to the rest of the guests and aided her by translating the exchange of pleasantries. Everyone sparkled in their finery. Here, again, were the usual displays of ample pearl and yellow-gold jewelry—now encrusted with diamonds and other precious gems, besting those worn by Manileña socialites at the Exposition. Even the female servants looked enchanting in their sheer, butterfly-sleeved camisas and fastidiously paired tapises and sayas. If she squinted her eyes, Eleanor could almost imagine she was in a fairy ball where ladies flitted about with iridescent, gossamer wings.

She felt less self-conscious now about her conservative choice for a garment, for although her simple Victorian outfit appeared understated for the occasion, it lent her a professional image that was just right for her introduction to what, undoubtedly, was elite Magayon society. In comparison, the décollette of the blue frock Maude had gifted her might have been seen as almost scandalous, for while the ladies appeared to revel in their femininity through their highly-ornamented camisas at sayas, they also seemed careful not to let their cleavages show.

Seeing the ladies incessantly fanning themselves with their Spanish fans, Eleanor longed for her abanico. The most she could do was to fan herself lamely with her dainty, lace-trimmed handkerchief and occasionally dab the sweat beads on her brow and nose. She glanced across the room at el presidente who, remarkably, was still smiling in his three-piece woolen suit. He constantly wiped his face with a handkerchief as his wife alternately fanned him and herself.

Soon, the heat from the oil lamps and chandelier combined with the heat of the crowded room to transform the social niceties into a sea of blurry faces incoherently chattering above a fuzzy array of dazzling attire. Exacerbating the suffocating atmosphere was the inclination of most guests to wear a profuse amount of perfume and cologne. This, together with the occasional whiff of malodorous body scent, nearly made Eleanor gag a few times.

Although the glass windows were open, the lace curtains covering them restricted airflow. Feeling choked, Eleanor strained to breathe.

She tugged at her high-necked collar, yearning to escape to the garden outside, visible from the glass French doors. She wondered why her hosts kept the doors to the courtyard shut until she spied a shadow or two of what could be bats flying into the eaves. From this, she realized the lace curtains were perhaps intended not for privacy as they were meant to inhibit the entry of the chiropterans, also moths and mosquitoes.

She was about to ask Don Luis if they could go outside when he exclaimed, "Ah, just the couple I wanted you to meet!"

A smiling, middle-aged, Caucasian gentleman in a European evening suit approached them, along with a smiling, matronly yet attractive Spanish mestiza at his arm. She was dressed in an exquisite camisa at saya dyed in pastel shades of rose and lavender. Unlike the other ladies, however, she didn't seem shy to show a little cleavage.

"Tío William! Tía Beatriz!" Don Luis exclaimed. "I was beginning to think you forgot."

"Wouldn't have missed it for the world, old boy!" the gentleman said with a British accent. "So sorry for our delay. Just returned from seeing a patient in Legazpi." Turning to Eleanor, who was smiling brightly, for she already liked the couple, he said, "Well, well! And who do we have here? Is this our lovely la maestra Americana?"

"Indeed," Don Luis replied. "Señorita Karsten, I have the honor to introduce..." He paused, glanced around, and, as if confirming it was safe to speak, continued under his breath, "The most important person in Magayon: our esteemed medico, Doctor William Langford!"

Doctor Langford interjected in an equally hushed tone, "What the good fellow meant to say, my dear, is that I'm the most important—next only to his mother, Padre Damián, el presidente, and him—in that order!" He chuckled, along with Don Luis and the lady.

Eleanor extended her hand to Doctor Langford, who responded with a gesture of a kiss, saying, "Charmed!"

"And this beauteous lady," Don Luis said, "is not only Doctor Langford's wife, but our chanteur d'opéra par excellence, Doña Beatriz Langford y Escudero."

"Opera singer?" Eleanor exclaimed, extending her hand to the lady. "How marvelous to meet you, ma'am!"

"Enchanté!" the elegant matron replied, beaming. She surprised Eleanor by kissing her on both cheeks, continental style.

Don Luis waved a servant over to serve the couple frosty champagne flutes. Doña Ximena joined them, declaring, "Ah, Beatriz, Doctor Langford. You are here, at last. ¡Muy bien! Now, we can have dinner." She clapped her hands twice and, on that cue, a group of servants simultaneously opened the four sets of French doors into the outdoor courtyard garden.

Eleanor breathed in the cooler, fresh air deeply.

Don Luis again led his mother and Eleanor by the arm, followed by everyone, toward the rectangular courtyard by passing through a loggia banded with alternating columns and pointed arches. The pattern of columns and pointed arches repeated in the wrap-around second-floor balcony overlooking the courtyard garden, which featured a bubbling fountain flanked by a pair of white-painted wrought-iron settees. Pots of ferns, palms, and other tropical plants clustered around the four main columns at the courtyard's corners, where jasmine and bougainvillea vines grew and climbed to the upper balcony. Colorful, geometric tiles paved the courtyard floor that, together with the tapered arches, lent the villa a distinctly Moorish feel.

The party crossed the courtyard to the opposite side of the villa and, by another set of French doors that mirrored those of the grand sala, entered a room of similar dimensions as the drawing room. Yet, instead of a chandelier, what hung at the center of the high ceiling was a tapestry punkah that served like a giant fan to circulate the air in the room. Wooden battens framed the tapestry's top and bottom, and the ends of the bottom frame were tied to ropes gently being pulled back and forth by servants crouched in a shallow mezzanine above them, careful not to blow out the flickering flames of the candelabras spread across the long dining table.

Eleanor doubted the benefit of merely recirculating warm air inside an enclosed space. She pitied the punkah pullers who surely had to bear up with the heat that had nowhere to go but rise to the crawl space where the attendants lay prostrate, surely soaked in sweat. The setting, however, was magnificent, as if attesting to the necessity of human sacrifice to achieve anything both grand and beautiful. Yet, such success was increasingly becoming clear to Eleanor as having been attained by her hosts through the labor of a dedicated servant class that catered to their needs in a manner uncomfortably reminiscent of Black slavery in America.

Sixteen baronial chairs surrounded the dining table laden with French porcelain, English silverware, and Venetian glassware. Name cards informed everyone where to sit, written in a familiar elegant hand that Eleanor recognized as Doña Ximena's. White caladiums, golden chrysanthemums, and cream orchids, interspersed with greenery, spilling out of a multi-armed crystal and silver epergne at the table's center and weaving like a flowering vine around silver candelabras distributed in regular intervals across the table, end to end. Adding illumination were candle-lit wall sconces and candelabras sitting on pedestals along the room's perimeter.

The food was laid on two sideboards at opposite ends of the room. From this, Eleanor knew their dinner was going to be served *ambigú* or "Russian" style, where the food was brought to the guests by waiters who served individual portions of the various viands to each guest. The etiquette and charm course that Eleanor's mother had forced her to attend that summer after high school graduation was finally paying off.

One of the serving tables displayed a culinary feast of land and sea offerings laid on various tiers of porcelain platters and tureens. The spread was a gourmand's collection of roast turkey, grilled fish, steamed crabs, vegetable dishes, and the familiar hair-thin, greasy noodles sautéed with pork cutlets and mixed vegetables. As Eleanor expected, there were also pots of what was now clearly the staple of every Filipino meal: boiled rice. What shocked her was the culinary centerpiece that appeared to be a braised boar's head.

On the other sideboard lay a selection of desserts that included meringues, cakes, egg custards with caramel, and various tropical fruits—some of them familiar to Eleanor, such as pineapples, papayas, and bananas.

One might have assumed, considering the lavish setting and bountiful feast, that no less than royalty was hosting the dinner somewhere in Europe, until one remembered the venue was nowhere in the European continent. Eleanor supposed this wasn't extraordinary at all, if one considered the Gonzagas were perhaps the closest to royalty in that corner of the world.

What she found intriguing was that whoever had built the villa didn't seem content to construct it in the colonial style that dominated the grand homes in the former Spanish colony. Instead, the builder appeared to ensure that the New World, represented by this strange mansion in the boondocks of Vicol, mirrored the Old World to the most minute detail.

A large portrait hung vertically on the long wall of the dining room, suggesting clues to who may have built the villa: a Spanish nobleman dressed in a hose and doublet, decorated with badges of military conquest and royal favor—medals, insignias, and other ribbons of distinction. He stood erect, chin up, next to a table that held a Bible on which he rested the long, tapering fingers of his right hand, while his left hand clutched the grip of a sword hanging from his hip. His affectation reminded Eleanor of Pastor John.

The way his eyes looked down on the viewer and eerily followed wherever one moved in the room instilled a sense that the Old World nobleman continued to lord over the present world. His features remained vividly sharp, despite the few hundred years that had darkened and dulled the painting. Eleanor saw his likeness in Don Luis's statuesque build, bearded oval face, slim nose, and deeply-set eyes. She also gleaned something else from the portrait—something about the man's jutting chin, firmly set jaw, and brutish stare suggested a cruel streak. Ruthlessness. She hoped that Don Luis did not likewise inherit such a trait.

Don Luis seated his mother at one end of the dining table. Padre Damián immediately sat to the hostess's right, while el presidente occupied the left. The mayor's wife sat next to her husband, ever more dwarfed as her short torso made her look like a child among adults. As Don Luis led Eleanor away to the opposite end of the table, she breathed a sigh of relief, glad to see that the triad composed of Doña Ximena, Padre Damián, and el presidente—whom she'd privately dubbed The Three Musketeers—were installed away from her. Their appraising eyes had been surreptitiously following her all evening, as did the haunting gaze of the man now in the portrait. Don Luis pulled out a chair for her to the right of where he sat, which had the tallest backrest that marked the cabeza de mesa or "head of the table." Eleanor smiled as Doctor Langford and Doña Beatriz sat directly across from her, and everybody else occupied their assigned chairs.

The table was abuzz with a babel of languages and watchful eyes. Eleanor noticed that the various personalities appeared to conform to a social hierarchy that recalled what she'd observed from the Manila socialites who visited the Exposition. From the almost sycophantic regard the guests displayed toward their hostess, it was clear that Magayon's queen, as Doctor Langford had earlier intimated, was Doña Ximena. Eleanor looked at the mayor, who seemed to be animatedly pontificating again. She remembered that Chinese mestizos like him were accepted in local society mainly because of the wealth they'd amassed from their business enterprises, by which they likewise gained political influence and power. Perhaps it was by the same token that his seemingly pedestrian wife was accorded the same courtesy by elite society.

The way the place settings and silverware were arranged also informed Eleanor that she was in the company of people accustomed to European etiquette. The salad fork was laid left of the dinner fork, recalling that continental-style dining served the salad after the entrée. Servants poured each guest a glass of *vino comun* or "house wine" meant to complement the first course that Eleanor expected would be some kind of soup, as suggested by the soup bowl on her charger plate and the soup spoon laid at the rightmost of the silverware to the right side of her plate.

The chatter faded as Don Luis tapped his spoon lightly on his crystal goblet and stood. "Amigos, damas y caballeros, my mother and I thank you for joining us tonight in honoring a young American lady who carries an immense and noble responsibility: teaching Magayon's children. Please join me in welcoming la maestra Americana, Señorita Eleanor Karsten. ¡Salud!" He raised his glass to her, as did everyone. Eleanor acknowledged the toast with a smile and joined everyone in sipping the dry white wine.

She was about to reach for her napkin when Doña Ximena declared, "Now, we ask Padre Damián to lead us in saying grace."

Eleanor glanced at the Franciscan friar who stood and put on a solemn expression as he drew his hands together and prayed—in Spanish. Eleanor bowed her head and clasped her hands upon her lap.

It certainly wasn't the time to betray herself as not religious. After the prayer, everyone reached for their napkins and the chatter returned.

Don Luis turned to Eleanor. "Are you finding the house to your satisfaction, Señorita Karsten?"

His tone and countenance assured her that his question was sincere. It briefly crossed her mind to mention her longing for a bathtub. She responded, instead, with a smile. "Yes, thank you. And thank you also for letting out the house to me. It's quite a charming abode."

"De nada. It is our honor and pleasure for you to reside at the former home of my late aunt, who left it to my mother, her sister. We were just wondering what to do with it when Sergeant Munro approached us about your need for lodgings. It is we who must thank you. You know what they say about an uninhabited house becoming the critters' den?" He laughed the refined laughter of one who'd learned to modulate even an expression of mirth. Eleanor wondered whether his art thus became his outlet for unbridled sentiment.

She grinned. "I know! Why, just yesterday, a snake scared the wits out of me and my maid." The words, my maid, sounded strange to her ears, even stranger that she uttered them.

"A snake!" he exclaimed. "And what did you do?"

"Someone kindly helped to take it away."

"Ah! That must have been Diego, my foreman. I asked him to keep an eye out for you and anything you may need. Funny—I saw him roasting a python yesterday with the other campesinos," he chuckled.

"Diego?" She smiled. "An interesting character, he was."

"You could say that again. Yet, without him, it would be like losing my right arm."

"Yes, he did seem very capable." Eleanor nodded, smiling, thinking of how the man called Diego had unsettled her precisely because he seemed so settled about himself. "Thank you for your concern. But, barring more pythons and other snakes, Yolanda and I are fine."

"Yolanda?"

"Yes. As I said, my… maid. But really, a sort of all-around house-keeper. Sergeant Munro and his wife insisted I needed one."

"I agree," he remarked. "I cannot imagine anyone in your position not having one. The muchacha would surely help make your transition easier. I am almost embarrassed we did not think of it first. If this girl does not serve you well, please let us know. Mamá can recommend a suitable replacement."

Eleanor smiled wryly. "Tell me, Don Luis, since it's customary to have live-in maids here, isn't it also customary to provide a separate bedroom for them? I mean, I feel bad for Yolanda. Didn't your aunt have live-in help, too?"

He smiled. "Your concern for… what is her name… Yolanda?… is understandable and commendable, Señorita Karsten. I mean, America— land of the free, democracy, and all that." He grinned. "You know, I spent some time there."

"Oh? Did you? Where?" she asked, while likewise noting he dodged her question.

"Nueva York. I was enamored with the romantic landscapes of the Hudson River School. So, I studied with some of the style's aficio- nados. After a few years, I went to Inglatera to study John Constable's paintings. And, finally, Madrid." His smile faded. "If Papá did not get sick and… well, I couldn't possibly leave Mamá to manage the plan- tation alone. Or, I would have stayed in Europe longer."

"I'm sorry about your father," Eleanor said.

"Gracias." He pressed his lips. "It has been many years ago now."

She smiled. "But did you really need all that schooling to be able to paint that excellent landscape in the sala?" On seeing his seeming perplexity over her question, she grinned and added, "You see, Don Luis, I find there's only so much a teacher could teach a student. The protégé must have something more—like natural talent and passion or, at least, a curiosity that propels him to pursue the answers. I found all that in your painting."

He smiled, flushed. "Oh, you are too kind, señorita—as was my dear late aunt in showing off my work. When she passed, I did not have the heart to remove the painting from her house because she was so attached to it. Now, I am happy it remains there because I like to believe it is through the painting that her good spirit watches over her previous home—and, now, you."

Eleanor chuckled. "Well, that's surely something not to share with Yolanda!" Noting his and Doctor and Mrs. Langford's puzzled expres- sions, she added, "Forgive me, Don Luis. I didn't mean to laugh at what you said about your aunt. I was just thinking of my maid. She's of the nervous and superstitious sort, I'm afraid. Why, just the other night, she scared herself thinking there was a ghost in the house! I assure you, it wasn't your dear aunt, but rather I whom she mistook as this phantom! I guess she's not used to pale-skinned women like myself."

He and the Langfords burst out laughing. As his laughter faded into a smile, he gazed into her eyes and said, "Nor to blue-eyed, golden-haired angels, I see." His velvet voice matched the admiration in his hazel eyes. The golden specks of his irises reflected the brass highlights of his burnished hair. He appeared to be younger than his beard earlier suggested. She estimated him to be only in his early thirties.

She looked away, smiling, and felt her face redden as she caught Doña Ximena observing her and her son, oblivious to el presidente's chatter. Padre Damián, Doctor Langford, Doña Beatriz, and a few other guests also appeared to be eyeing her and Don Luis with keen curiosity.

"¡Hijo!" Doña Ximena startlingly called out. "You remember Padre Damián's lovely niece, Maria Teresa, don't you?"

Don Luis appeared stunned. He craned his neck around the candelabras and floral centerpiece. "What's that, Mamá?"

"I said, Maria Teresa—remember her? Padre Damián's beautiful niece? She has been studying in a convento in España these recent years," his mother broadcast in a louder voice.

Don Luis replied, "¡Ah—si, Mamá!" He turned to the parish priest. "And how is your fair niece, Padre Damián?"

The padre answered rapidly in Spanish, which Eleanor failed to catch. Yet, as though to ensure Eleanor understood it, Doña Ximena volunteered in English, "He says she will be coming back soon! I was surprised to learn this only now from our good padre. Tell me, hijo, that you will be the usual gentleman and fetch Maria Teresa from the port when she arrives?"

A subtle unease seemed to wash over Don Luis, but he smiled at his mother when he replied, "¡Por supuesto, Mamá!"

Doña Ximena nodded and smiled with a satisfaction shared by Padre Damián.

Turning back to Eleanor, Don Luis cleared his throat and remarked in a hushed, clipped tone, "Maria Teresa is… er, like a sister to me."

"Well, then, I'm sure, it would be a happy reunion," Eleanor said, smiling.

He smiled back briefly and averted his gaze, finishing his wine.

Two servants took off the covers of a pair of soup tureens on the sideboard. They carried the serving bowls to opposite sides of the dining table and served a ladle of the soup to each guest. The milky broth appeared to have prawns and vegetables in it. Soon, another set of servants each took their positions beside some guests. They fished out the prawns from the guest's soup with perforated spoons and set both spoon and prawn on a small plate beside the plate charger. Eleanor had assumed the plates were for bread and then wondered why no bread was served. It shocked her to see the servants shelling the prawns with their fingers and returning them to the guest's soup bowl. She ignored the oddity and took her first sip of the soup.

"Mmm… what is this?" she exclaimed.

"You like?" Doña Beatriz asked, smiling expectantly.

"Indeed!" Eleanor replied. "What is it?"

"Guinataang langostino," Doña Beatriz said. "With coconut milk."

Eleanor picked up the Spanish for prawn. "It must be the coconut milk that makes it creamy?" Eleanor asked, eyebrows arched.

The woman nodded with a big smile.

"Oh! And there's a piquancy to it, too!" Eleanor grinned as she reached for her glass of water and sipped.

"Is it too spicy for you?" Don Luis asked with a tone of concern.

"Not too bad," Eleanor said, clearing her throat and drinking more water.

Some guests seated nearby grinned. Doña Beatriz said something to Don Luis in the hybrid Vicolano and Spanish, and the host turned back to Eleanor, saying, "Tía Beatriz apologizes that our cuisine is more spicy compared to the Tagal dishes you may have sampled in Manila. We have a fondness for sili pepper. The galleons had brought it from Mexico, and we came to like it so much we cultivated it right here."

"Believe me, there's nothing to apologize for," Eleanor demurred. "It's rather delicious. The spiciness will take some getting used to, but I'm more than fine with it, I assure you."

She worried about how to shell her prawns. She observed what Don Luis and Doctor Langford did, for they were among the few guests who didn't avail of a servant to shell their langostinos for them. Picking one prawn at a time, they set it on the small plate and, holding it down with a fork, used a knife to slice off its head and legs. This appeared to loosen the orange husk, which then allowed them to easily pry out the crescent peaches-and-cream flesh.

Doña Beatriz must have also been observing Eleanor, for after her servant had shelled a couple of langostinos for her, the mestiza gestured for the muchacha to go to Eleanor. The servant was about to fish out a prawn from Eleanor's soup, when Eleanor held back the servant's hand, saying, "No—please!" She glanced at Doña Beatriz, who looked mortified. Eleanor smiled at her reassuringly. "Doña Beatriz, thank you, but I would like to learn how to do this myself."

The mestiza sighed in seeming relief and smiled back.

Her husband said, "You must excuse my wife, Miss Karsten. She just can't help herself. I mean, she would lend you her chambermaid, if you asked! You can say it's a family malady. But, frankly, I'm not sure how long I can continue with a medical practice forced to accept payment in fruits, vegetables, and eggs! I feel quite the wealthy man if they offer me fish or chicken!" He laughed, as did his wife and Don Luis.

The doctor added, "Beatriz says it's customary practice for country folk. Therefore, being the obedient husband I am, I just smile and say to my patients and their families: ¡Muchas gracias! So, my dear, when you require fresh provisions, please look no further than our pantry!" He guffawed, and his wife affectionately slapped his arm, chuckling with him.

Eleanor grinned. "That's very kind of you, doctor! I'll remember to send Yolanda if we ever need anything we can't find elsewhere." She proceeded to mimic how Don Luis and Doctor Langford shelled their prawns.

Doña Beatriz smiled at Eleanor's attempts. "More easy—with fingers!" she said.

"Yes, thank you," Eleanor replied. "But I'm up for the challenge. If Don Luis and Doctor Langford could do it, why can't I?" She grinned as she continued her efforts to triumph over the crustacean.

Everybody looked on with amusement as a prawn jumped from Eleanor's plate to the floor and another to the napkin on her lap. It took a couple more messy attempts before she finally succeeded in getting a completely shelled prawn into her mouth. "See? I'm no shrimp!" Eleanor declared, inciting laughter from those around her.

Doña Beatriz and her husband and Don Luis applauded her success to the smiles and grins of the guests seated farther away.

After the guests finished their soups, the servants poured them their glasses of sherry.

"Doña Ximenez gets this shipped all the way from Jerez!" Doctor Langford volunteered.

Eleanor sipped. "Mmm… That explains why it's so good!" She glanced back at Doctor Langford. "Tell me, doctor, how did an Englishman like you find your way out here?"

The doctor and his wife exchanged tender glances, smiling. He turned back to Eleanor and replied, "I heard her sing in Madrid, and I was smitten for life! Right, mi amor?" His wife nodded, smiled, and glanced down, flushed as a bride. He added, "I asked her to marry me, and she agreed—on one condition!"

"What?" Eleanor arched her eyebrows, alternately glancing between the spouses with an expectant smile.

"That we come and live in her hometown," the doctor said. "And, being the devoted husband I am, I followed where my wife led. You can say I was led like lamb to slaughter!" He chuckled, and Doña Beatriz slapped him again on the arm, shaking her head and wagging her finger at him as she covered her mouth to modulate her laughter.

Don Luis remarked, "How fortunate of you—Tío William, Tía Beatriz—to have found each other. Across an ocean at that!" The couple nodded and smiled at him. Don Luis stunned Eleanor when he turned to her and said, "Would that some of us here could be as lucky!"

Eleanor was relieved when another gentleman chose that moment to grab her attention. "Señorita Karsten, por favor, díganos cómo piensa enseñar a nuestros hijos."

Eleanor turned her head toward the center of the table where the voice came from. When she found its source, a Spanish mestizo, she replied, "You want to know how I intend to teach your children, señor?"

"Sí, señorita." The mestizo smiled—a smile closer to a sneer. "Por favor."

Everyone, including The Three Musketeers, turned to la maestra Americana, as though this was the question everyone was itching to ask all evening.

CHAPTER 9

Pockets of Perilous Wilderness

*H*ow, *indeed, do I plan to teach their children? She recalled from the* superintendent's letter of instructions that, although the Spaniards had established some kind of public education system by mandate of a late nineteenth-century Spanish royal decree, the Office of Public Instruction wasn't sure of the actual attendance numbers and level of instruction. This was partly because the poor were known to pull out their children from school and put them to work in the fields or factories or as domestic helpers to supplement the family income. Thus, the superintendent advised the Thomasites to conduct a careful and comprehensive assessment of their students' individual abilities to determine their proper grade placements.

Eleanor clasped her hands and replied, "It would depend on the student's proficiency in the three R's: reading, writing, and arithmetic." Don Luis duly translated what she said, and she continued at a pace that allowed him to keep up with her. "I'm assuming they're all at beginner's level, although I'm sure Sergeant Munro has done an excellent job introducing them to the basics. Then, I'll test them to determine their individual level. If I see significant variances among them, I'll divide them into groups according to their abilities. Then, I'll develop teaching plans for each group."

"But they not beginners!" objected a woman seated across from the mestizo. "Students learn before the same things you teach."

Eleanor craned her neck to get a better view of her interrogator. "If that's so, then the test would show that. I would then create proper lessons for them."

"And this lesson—in English?" the same woman asked.

"Yes, I'm afraid so," Eleanor replied, smiling apologetically.

"But why English?" the woman demanded.

After a brief pause, Eleanor said, "That's a good question, ma'am. And the answer is, simply, because most American teachers only speak and write in English."

A gentleman, who appeared to be another Chinese mestizo, asked, "Why, then, you not just hire the old teachers again?"

What now struck Eleanor was that many of the guests now appeared to know more English than she assumed. She recalled that the ilustrado class, of which most of the guests probably belonged, was a well-educated group. Many of them may have also studied abroad like Don Luis. She wished she had Miss Covell by her side to help her address their seemingly civil yet pointed questions. After another tension-filled pause, she said, "Please correct me if I'm wrong. I understand there is no common language for the islands."

A Spanish mestiza scoffed. "¡O, pero tenemos Español!"

"True," Eleanor replied. "But I also understand it's only elites like yourselves who are literate in Spanish. While your children enjoy the same privilege, a greater number of other children don't. And for them, there are as many languages as there are islands, it seems. Educating the children in one language would thus allow everyone to communicate with, and understand each other. Yet, whose language, among those of your many tribes, should be that common tongue? Should it be Vicolano? Or Tagal? Or Spanish? For lack of a national language, English seems to be the practical choice. It's the bridge between the teachers who have come a long way to teach your children and the necessity for a common language."

A few murmurings followed the brief silence.

Eleanor added, "An educated population makes for a stronger nation. Having a national language can unite different tribes and people into one nation. If this isn't enough for you, consider this: English is the language of American bureaucracy. Don't you want your children to qualify for the new civil service positions that would soon open? Wouldn't you want them to be among the country's future leaders?"

A buzz erupted, spilling into various expressions of approbation: sí, por supuesto, or yes, of course, or that makes sense, accompanied by vigorous nodding. Eleanor smiled. She may have finally reached a breakthrough with her critical audience. Thus, she was taken aback when the same woman who raised the issue of English as the medium of instruction shrieked, "¡Ay, un momento! You mean—our children study with the *other* children? ¿Con hijos de campesinos y sirvientes? With… with children of… peasants? Servants?"

Eleanor's breath hung suspended between incredulity and dismay. "Why, of course, señora. That is, after all, the essence of an education system under a democracy. Each child, whether rich or poor, should be able to enjoy the same quality of education."

"¡Ay! ¡Que horror!" the woman cried, inciting similar objections from others.

Don Luis tapped his crystal goblet. "¡Por favor! ¡Por favor!" He addressed the table in the hybrid language, which he reiterated in English for Eleanor's benefit. "Please, why don't we all just give Señorita Karsten a chance to do her job? Let us be patient. Wait and see. And then, if any of us still have concerns, I am sure Señorita Karsten would be more than happy to address them. Am I not right, Señorita Karsten?" He sent Eleanor a knowing smile.

Eleanor smiled back at him. "Why, yes! Yes, of course!" Turning to her fellow guests, she said, "I welcome anyone with any question about their children's classes to see me anytime."

Doctor Langford and his wife nodded in approval, along with Don Luis.

Everyone appeared relieved when the servants returned to serve the next wine, a Bordeaux, and prepared to serve the entrees. "Jolly good and about time!" exclaimed Doctor Langford, grinning.

Eleanor thanked Don Luis for his assistance with the group, which was friendly one moment, contentious next. The new round of eating and drinking became a welcome distraction from an issue that had never occurred to her could be anyone's problem: equality. She wondered whether this indicated that democracy was incompatible with the culture, thus posing a challenge to establishing a democratic system of government among Filipinos. Most Americans simply assumed all people wanted democracy. For who wouldn't want the freedom and equality it promised? Everyone wanted to be free, but not everybody, it now appeared, wanted equality. Eleanor may have just identified the first seed that wasn't ready to be planted on the islands.

The wine flowed as the evening progressed. Eleanor couldn't remember a more bacchanalian feast. After her first glass of vino, she took care to sip only some of the later wines. Already, her face felt unduly warm, and she worried she looked red as a grape. A dull ache in her temples that she blamed on the wine began to bother her.

Servants picked up the various entree platters from the sideboard and approached each guest with an offering. Eleanor was mindful to accept a small portion of each dish, knowing it was customary in the culture to show one's hospitality through food, and that a host may consider it an insult if a guest didn't try at least a little of everything. She did so, and showed her appreciation for each dish—until the last. The braised boar's head!

It took two servants to carry the huge platter to her and another to offer a portion of the brain from the open skull. Eleanor held up her hands to decline, when the sharp, booming voice of a smiling Doña Ximena startled her. "It is our custom to give this special delicacy to our honored guest, Señorita Karsten! No one can have it until you first have some of it."

Eleanor must have worn an expression of disgust because Don Luis rose to her rescue. "Mamá, perhaps we could let Señorita Karsten become more accustomed to our customs first? She has, after all, been such a good sport in partaking of everything else." He smiled, as though charming his mother to relent, yet Doña Ximena appeared unmoved.

All eyes fixed themselves on Eleanor, who turned to the servant with a smile, saying, "Sólo… un poco, por favor." The servant smiled back at her, yet served her a big lump of the boar's brain.

Eleanor fed herself a slice of it. It landed on her tongue with a savory flavor that left a gamey aftertaste on her tongue. What impressed her first was its odd texture that combined that of ox tripe and bone marrow. Nonetheless, she chewed and swallowed it, smiled, and declared, "Mmm… remarkable, indeed! And certainly not for the faint of heart and palate!"

Much of the room burst into laughter and applause. By the end of the meal, Eleanor sensed she may have earned everybody's respect—except Doña Ximena and Padre Damián, who both remained aloof, yet civil toward her.

At the end of the meal, Doña Ximena invited everyone back to the grand sala where, she announced, a little show awaited them. There, the servants had re-arranged the settees and chairs into rows facing the pianoforte at one end of the room. As the guests settled into their chosen seats, the servants offered the ladies glasses of muscatel; the men, tumblers of rum. To those disinclined to drink more alcohol, like Eleanor, there were tazas of hot cocoa served. Passed around were small plates of coconut macaroons and candied nut sticks that Don Luis called, turron de pili. He sat beside Eleanor on one of the love seats and explained that the turron was made from honey and the nuts of the pili tree that grew mainly in the Vicol region. Eleanor found it much to her liking.

Doña Ximena stood before the audience and stated, "Damas y caballeros, el presidente will now honor us with a recitation of Doctor Jose Rizal's immortal poem, 'Mi Último Adiós.'"

Don Luis whispered in Eleanor's ear, "Doctor Rizal, if you don't know, is a Filipino hero and martyr in the revolution against Spain. He wrote the poem on the night before his execution."

Eleanor lit up. "Why, yes! I know something about him. Is this the poem where he calls the islands Perla del Mar de Oriente?"

"Indeed!" Don Luis exclaimed. "I'm delighted you're acquainted with his works."

"Not all, I'm afraid." Eleanor smiled ruefully. "I've only heard about this poem. And I have yet to read it."

"Then, this should be a treat, señorita!" He smiled, tapping her hand.

Everyone clapped as the short man took the stage. The mayor straightened his coat, adjusted his tie, and cleared his throat. In the characteristic bravado Eleanor had learned to expect from him, he raised his arms in oratory style and declaimed, "*Adiós, Patria adorada, región del sol querida...*"

Don Luis startled Eleanor when he placed his arm around the back-rest of the settee they shared and leaned close to her, whispering his translation. "Farewell, my adored land, region of the sun caressed..."

He was so close that his breath tickled the skin on her ear and cheek. His lavender cologne overpowered her and almost sent her into another sneezing fit. Eleanor straightened up and inched away from him, but he only moved closer.

Doña Ximena, who was seated in the front row, glanced back at them and frowned. Yet, her son ignored his mother's stare. Eleanor fidgeted in her seat. She couldn't wait for Mayor Dizon's performance to end. When it finally did, she stood to applaud, inciting everyone to do the same, hoping to restore the physical space between Don Luis and herself when she sat back down. Yet, Don Luis returned his arm to the backrest and continued leaning on her body.

She sensed him gazing at her profile, seemingly forcing her to meet his eyes. She briefly glanced at him and said, "Thank you for the translation, Don Luis. You didn't have to do that."

He replied in a throaty voice, "Oh, but it was my pleasure, señorita! Anytime you need me to be of service to you, just let me know—and I will soon be at your side." His eyes mapped her face as his words and smile dripped with honey.

Eleanor forced her attention to the next performance, determined to ignore Don Luis's continuing attempts to seduce her.

A concert of *zarzuela* pieces and native ballads followed—performed, as Eleanor had hoped, by Doña Beatriz. Accompanied by one of the gentlemen on the pianoforte, the erstwhile opera singer sang like the virtuoso she was reputed to be. Doctor Langford looked adoringly at his wife as though he were falling in love all over again with her.

Between songs, Eleanor asked Don Luis from which side of the family his Tía Beatriz belonged, knowing "tía" meant aunt. She hoped that by engaging him in quotidian conversation, he would stop flirting with her.

He grinned softly. "She is actually not a blood relation. In our culture, we refer to our parent's friends as aunts and uncles. If they are about the age of our grandparents, we address them ápo. And if they are our grandparents, we call them lolo and lola."

Eleanor smiled. How charming it was that a society called its members in terms of family relationships! She noticed that even the servants addressed their masters in the language of love—calling them *amo,* as though their employers were their family. Eleanor wondered, however, how much filial piety factored into what, essentially, was a transactional relationship.

Nonetheless, there was an undercurrent of romance in the culture she couldn't help admiring. She noted a prevalence of bittersweet love songs in Doña Beatriz's repertoire, composed of Spanish zarzuelas and Filipino ballads. Although she couldn't understand the lyrics, the melodies moved her.

Don Luis caught her dabbing the corners of her eyes, and she flustered, abashed. The dull ache in her temples worsened into a throbbing vexation. Just as the tall case clock in the entrance hall struck the midnight hour, the show ended. Secretly grateful, she stood, clapping and shouting, "Bravo!" The other guests followed suit.

Don Luis offered to accompany her home, citing the lateness of the hour. Doña Ximena glowered behind her son, and Eleanor declined. All she wanted was to be alone—free of Don Luis's pawing attention and his mother's disapproval—and go to sleep. She was relieved when Don Luis didn't insist and bid her goodnight. But when he took her hand for what she expected was the usual gesture of a kiss, what he did stunningly deviated from custom, shocking not only her but his mother and everyone else who witnessed it: He pressed his lips on her skin.

The carruaje rattled along the long, dark, dirt road toward Eleanor's house. From afar, the twin kerosene lamps on its upper anterior sides must have appeared like the glowing, red eyes of a large, nocturnal creature crawling to stalk its prey. No other lights shone amid the fields, not even in the farmers' huts where the residents had been asleep not long after dusk to recoup the energy needed for another workday that began at dawn. And neither did the moon and stars shine behind the clouds that foretold of rain.

Eleanor reflected on the various personalities she met tonight. She knew what the Three Musketeers wanted: to maintain their spheres of power in the community and influence on each other. And Don Luis— what did he want? Was it just cheap conquest he was after? Eleanor feared she may have unwittingly complicated her role in the community by appearing to have condoned his flirtation with her. She certainly did not score points with his mother. She'd have to tread on a tightrope that was braided from conflicting yet interwoven strands of individual and community interests, including those of her government. But how could one walk balanced on such a tightrope of interests without falling or stepping on someone's toes?

She massaged her temples. Such ponderings weren't helping with her pulsating headache.

She stuck her head out of the window to breathe in the cool night air—a refreshing relief from the choking atmosphere inside the gilded, cultured walls of Hacienda Gonzaga, which held treacherous pockets of perilous wilderness. She closed her eyes to listen to the symphony of crickets and frogs playing among the rows of rice, corn, and sugarcane. The occasional hooting of an owl and chirping of a night hawk provided a musical counterpoint. She imagined herself back in her family's Iowa farmstead, her parents tucked and snoring in their beds, and she, pausing from her bedside reading, relishing the evening concert.

Suddenly, the driver cried, "Whoa! Whoa!" He reined in the horses, and the carriage lurched to a stop, causing Eleanor to hit her head against the window frame.

"Por que?" she yelled out to him, caressing her bruised cheek. "What's happened?"

She glanced around and realized they were at a section of the road walled in by six-foot-high stalks of sugarcane on both sides. She craned her neck to peer at what lay ahead. There appeared to be a barricade of people holding torches. Soon, they surrounded the carruaje, and she realized they were all men in peasants' clothes. She couldn't see their faces that were half-covered by bandanas; neither their eyes that were shadowed by their straw hats. The flames, however, shone upon the sharp outlines and deadly arcs of the bolos that hung from their hips.

Eleanor was acquainted with the bolo as an instrument of terror due to mainland newspaper accounts of the battles between American soldiers and Filipino insurrectionists. The articles featured illustrations depicting the bolo's blade as half the length of a sword's, but wider and thicker. Yet, precisely because it was shorter, it was said to be a nimbler weapon to wield. Although primarily used as a tool for taming the wilderness, it had the notoriety of being efficacious in cutting down men as it was in felling down trees. Thus, the American soldier came to dread the Filipino's bolo more than the Spaniard's gun and bayonet. This inspired great dread among Americans, who imagined the barbarity it took to hack a man into pieces, and inflamed already impassioned calls to subdue the Philippine insurrection and civilize the savage Filipinos.

Eleanor trembled as she gripped the handle of the carriage door and grasped the seriousness of the situation. All her preconceived notions of a noble and exciting adventure flew in the face of the horror that was about to be unleashed by the bandits, insurgents, or whoever the masked men were. Being raped and chopped into pieces weren't part of what she'd envisioned when she volunteered to be a teacher to little girls and boys in faraway islands. The throbbing in her head felt as though it were cracking her skull.

One of the men yelled something that forced both the driver and footman to jump down from their perches and hold up their arms. The same man yanked the carriage door open and shouted similarly to Eleanor. She stepped down from the carruaje and raised her arms—her reticule hanging ridiculously from the crook of her left arm; her fear patent in her shaking hands.

The man approached her, and she saw in his eyes not only torch flames but lust as they roved her body. Her breath shuddered as he stepped closer and sniffed her like an animal about to eat its prey. He glanced back at his gang and casually said something, and they snickered. She cringed and turned away from him, but he grabbed her by the shoulders to face him again. As she squirmed and writhed in his hold, he sniggered and yelled something to his comrades that incited lurid laughter.

He grabbed her reticule and broke its handle in the process. He seized the cameo pinned to her collar with such force, it ripped her blouse, thus exposing her chest. Fortunately, her breasts remained half-covered by her chemise, secured by her corset. He slipped the cameo into his shirt pocket and his eyes darted to the milky mounds of her bosom, where they spied the locket gleaming golden on her cleavage. The man's eyes shone brighter with brazen greed and craven desire. He moved toward her in a manner that suggested he didn't only intend to rob her of the necklace but also molest her.

"No, don't! You bastard!" she cried, pushing him away with all the strength she could muster. He shuffled back, and Eleanor wasn't sure what possessed her to do what she did next. During the few seconds as the man tried to regain his balance, she lunged at him, shoved him to the ground, and pounced on him, crying, "That's my mother's cameo, brute! Give it back to me! Give it back!" The men gathered close around them, chortling and hooting in amusement.

She pounded on him with one fist as she felt around in his shirt pocket with the other hand. But before she could retrieve her cameo, he managed to swing both of them around and rolled on top of her. She blindly flailed her arms at him as he straddled her. While pushing his arm away from her chest, her fingernails caught on the rolled-up hem of one of his sleeves and tore off part of it, uncovering a tattoo on the underside of his upper right arm. It appeared to be a triangle with some kind of wavy script at its center.

The man looked stunned before anger flashed in his eyes. She heard the pounding on the ground of approaching horses' hooves as she braced against the pounding she expected to receive from the man. He was poised to hit her when another man's voice barked from behind the pack. The savage immediately jumped to his feet, while his comrades stepped back and parted to make way for the other man—whom Eleanor now suspected was the true ring leader. He stepped into the clearing and, in a grim, commanding voice that sounded vaguely familiar, said something to her attacker that compelled the latter to move away from her. The leader approached, and bent over Eleanor, scaring her into thinking he was about to claim her for himself and rape her before his men before he allowed them to take their turns with her.

How true that, at Death's door, one's life passed before one's eyes! She thought of her father and mother, and Miss Covell, Arabella, and Maude. She closed her eyes and prayed to Daragang Magayon to save her from a fate worse than death.

When she opened her eyes again, to her astonishment, the leader was holding out his hand to her, as though offering to help her stand. She hesitated to accept it, yet he kept offering his hand to her. She raised her hand to him, albeit with great trepidation, and he firmly grabbed it to pull her up to her feet. Yet, the strength with which he pulled on her was so disproportionate to her weight, it sent her body colliding with his—face to face. His eyes gazed into hers, shining not only with the light of the flames but also with a strangely familiar gleam.

She pushed away from him, and it seemed for a moment he was almost reluctant to release her. She became conscious again of her near nakedness and vainly tried to return the torn flap of her blouse over her chest. He frowned and glanced around, as if looking for something, until he glanced down and removed the scarf around his neck. He dusted it off and, holding up its ends with each of his hands, approached her. A vision of the python being offered to her flashed in her mind, and she stepped backward. But the man advanced toward her again, continuing to offer the scarf to her. She allowed him to come close enough to let him secure the scarf around her neck, thus covering her chest.

The leader turned to the tattooed man and stated something that forced the thug to surrender the reticule and cameo to him. The leader faced Eleanor again, holding out the objects to her. She grabbed them from his hands and dropped the cameo into her reticule. When she glanced up at him, she caught the familiar sparkle in his eyes again. But before her memory could process the perplexing recognition, he grabbed her and turned her around to face away from him. With a single arm wrapped around her arms and waist, he pinned her to his body. The more she struggled, the more tightly he held her—so tight, she could feel the muscles on his arms, torso, and thighs flexing and folding as he gave and gestured instructions to his men.

As his body moved against hers, she smelled him—the smoky musk of him, a mixed scent of salt, sap, and soil. Creature of the earth he was. Eleanor's father had taught her how to read the land and weather through her nose. Her olfactory sense rose to heights of great awareness, especially in times of great stress. Thus, she recalled the most distressing events by the scents she associated with them—like the sweet-sour pungency of newly-plowed earth that pervaded the land immediately before and after the tornado had hit their farm and killed her parents. This, too, was how she knew she would never forget the scent of this man.

Two of the men forced the driver and footman to their knees and tied their hands to their feet behind their backs. Another pair cut the horses loose. Some of the marauders then threw their torches into the carriage, setting it on fire. When the carruaje was fully ablaze, the men raised their fists and shouted, "Ibagsak ang imperialistang Cano!

Ibagsak ang piyudalistang Kastilya!" Some words sounded close enough to Spanish such that Eleanor picked up on "American imperialists" and "feudal Spaniards."

As the flames consumed the carriage, the men doused their torches and dispersed into the fields, where they disappeared from view. Their leader released her. She swung around planning to pull off the bandana from his face to confirm who she suspected him to be. Yet, he, too, disappeared into the shadows—leaving her alone, standing, and shaking, with the driver and footman groaning and wriggling helplessly at her feet.

The rain that had threatened to fall now poured. Without a tool to cut the driver and footman loose, Eleanor struggled to set them free, breaking some of her fingernails. The sharp, coarse ends of the thick rope pierced her skin, adding her blood to the slippery mess. When, at last, she succeeded, she instructed the footman through a combination of English, broken Spanish, and hand gestures to run back to the hacienda and get help. She also conveyed that she and the driver would proceed to her house on foot. She wasn't willing to risk the possibility that the thug who tried to rob and molest her would return to do them greater harm.

The previously dusty road turned muddy in the rain. She and the driver had traversed only a third of the distance when she heard galloping horses and the wind shouting her name. She turned around, relieved to see Don Luis at the head of a group of riders carrying torches that burned despite the downpour. She was stunned to likewise see, riding beside him, the man who'd helped her get rid of the snake in her garden. She recognized him by his jaw-length hair that now framed his square face in soaked, stringy strands. With help in sight, Eleanor's body surrendered its struggle, shaking uncontrollably until her knees buckled.

Don Luis and Diego leaped down from their steeds. A revolver bounced at Don Luis's hip as he ran toward her. "¡O, señorita!!" He must have seen the bruise on her cheek and the blood on her clothes. "¡Dios mío, Eleanor! What did they do? Where did they hurt you?"

She shook her head and showed him her bleeding fingers.

"Whoever did this will pay!" he cried as he took off his coat and wrapped it around her. He picked her up and carried her until he handed her to his foreman so he could mount his horse. Diego lifted her to his master, who seated her sidesaddle in front of him with an arm wrapped around her waist and rode toward her house.

Diego was already waiting with Yolanda outside the house when they arrived. The foreman must have gone ahead to prepare the maid, who was ready with an umbrella and blanket. Don Luis handed Eleanor to Diego, who carried her into the house, followed by Yolanda, who threw a blanket over her mistress and held the umbrella over her. The muchacha told Diego where the bedroom was, and he gently laid Eleanor on her bed.

His scent was unmistakable. His eyes no longer sparkled with amusement but burned with concern. "You... it's you, isn't it?" Eleanor mumbled.

He remained silent as Yolanda removed the wet coat wrapped around her mistress and the soaked scarf around her neck and chest. Diego stepped aside to make way for his amo.

Don Luis bent over Eleanor and placed his palm on her forehead. "¡Dios mío!" He exclaimed. "Eleanor, you are burning up!" He turned to Diego and said something about a doctor.

Eleanor wanted to say, no, please don't go—I have so much to ask you. But her parched throat refused to release her voice before Diego left.

Yolanda took over the care of her mistress, pushing Don Luis out of the room. She stripped Eleanor of all her clothes and dressed her in a nightgown.

Eleanor gladly surrendered to the fevered blackness that claimed her.

The scene played out in fragments, continued where it left off, each time—with Eleanor willing it to the next part, yet unable to direct it to where she wished. The story had a mind of its own. She saw herself dressed in a bridal frock, marching solo on the aisle that separated the girls and boys in her Iowa classroom, except that her American students now appeared to be the urchin mob at Legazpi Port—tugging at, and pulling on her hair as she walked by them.

A flower girl sauntered ahead and turned around to glance up and smile at her with a lit cigar dangling from her mouth. Instead of flower petals for Eleanor to walk on, she left a trail of ashes and smoke that induced a sneezing and coughing fit for Eleanor.

At the aisle's end was a make-shift altar set against a blackboard inscribed with a huge, chalk-drawn, upside-down cross and the statement, "Knowledge is danger." Standing there, smiling smugly, was Pastor John—holding his trusty, old Bible over his heart. Standing on his right, dressed as maids of honor, were Miss Covell, Maude, and Arabella, all wearing décolleté frocks, blissfully smiling with yellow-stained teeth and half-eaten mangoes in their yellow-stained hands.

On the pastor's left stood Don Luis, dressed in a hose and doublet, smiling with adoration at her; a man with sparkling eyes, wearing a python as a scarf around his neck, who Eleanor couldn't tell was smiling or not, for a bandana half-covered his face; and a faceless man who wore a tattoo of a triangle with an eye at its center—where his face should have been.

When Eleanor reached the altar, a shadow fell upon her. The bulky figure of a man blocked the sun's rays from streaming through the capiz shell windows. When she glanced up, it was Mr. Borg—wearing a bridegroom's coat-and-tails and a lecherous, toothless smile.

"Eleanor, we're so proud of you," her mother's voice said from behind her. Eleanor turned around and saw a pair of open coffins containing her parents' bodies.

The man wearing a bandana on his face and the man with a tattoo for a face then threw a torch into each coffin, setting them ablaze.

Eleanor's screams were what roused her from her burning slumber.

"There, there, Miss Karsten. There, there," a man's voice tenderly said—with a British accent.

"You have malaria, my dear," Doctor Langford informed her when she finally awoke and stayed awake long enough to comprehend what he stated. She'd been in and out of consciousness for a week, delirious with fever. But she wasn't out of the woods yet, he warned, for the fever appeared to return every forty-eight hours. Thus, he decided to give her something better than quinine.

The British Royal Army had known it for decades as a more effective malaria treatment: Warburg's Tincture. It wasn't widely known nor available to Americans because its inventor had sold it as a secret proprietary medicine for the exclusive use of British troops in India, Ceylon, and Africa. Doctor Langford, nonetheless, had procured a discreet supply for himself and his wife and patients during his last visit to London.

Eleanor suffered through fitful fevers interspersed with chills, vertigo, vomiting, and diarrhea. Yolanda proved devoted to her, seldom leaving her side unless it was to prepare her meals or clean out the chamber pot. She gave her mistress sponge baths, kept her hydrated with coconut juice, and nourished her with a chicken soup cooked with green papaya, ginger, and the piquant leaves of the sili plant.

Doctor Langford praised the muchacha's home remedies as complementing the medicine he administered to Eleanor in one-ounce bottle dosages, twice daily, for the past week, precipitating Eleanor's promising recovery after a fortnight. Yet, she remained very weak.

She had visitors, Yolanda informed her in the hybrid Vicolano and Spanish. Sergeant Munro and his wife supplied them with all cooking and household necessities, so that Yolanda needn't ever had to leave the house and her mistress alone. Don Luis dropped by almost every day with flowers to place in Eleanor's bedroom, such that Yolanda ran out of vases and had to throw out the old, yet still fresh flowers, almost as soon as Don Luis returned. Doña Beatriz came along with her husband when he administered Eleanor's medication, at which time, the former opera singer relieved Yolanda of nurse duty. Surprisingly, even Doña Ximena visited once with Padre Damián and el presidente.

Eleanor had a vague recollection of the priest praying and splashing holy water over her and The Three Musketeers chatting in low voices. They discussed Magayon's volatile situation regarding the soldados Americanos resulting from the attack on la maestra Americana—especially now that Presidente McKinley had been shot. The president—shot? Eleanor also remembered Doña Ximena saying that while she welcomed rooting out those who'd torched the Gonzaga carriage, she was concerned about how Señorita Karsten's ambush provided the

Americanos with the excuse to throw their weight around, proving who was really in charge in Magayon. Eleanor had pretended to be asleep.

During one of Doctor Langford's visits, she asked, "Doctor, was I just dreaming, or do I recall someone saying President McKinley was shot?"

Doctor Langford looked at her gravely as he prepared her dose of Warburg's Tincture. "I regret to say it's true, my dear."

"When?" Eleanor exclaimed.

"The sixth of this month," Doctor Langford said matter-of-factly.

"Why, that's when I arrived here!" Eleanor exclaimed. "How is he?"

"What we know, so far, is he's undergone surgery," the doctor replied. "He's said to have been shot at close range—twice. I understand one bullet hit one of his brass buttons and ricocheted to his sternum, which reportedly only caused a superficial wound. But there was a second bullet that entered his abdomen, which his doctors oddly said they never found. That McKinley does look like one hefty fellow!" He smiled yet soon turned serious. "But if I was there, I would have insisted on finding the second bullet's exit wound and, if there isn't any, then… Well, anyway, the doctors assumed it was a clean shot and now claim to have sutured his wounds and stopped the hemorrhage. Everyone hopes for his full recovery."

"May it be so!" Eleanor sighed. "But what about the shooter?"

"An anarchist! Caught and arrested on the spot and instantly confessed. Proud of his crime, too, he was!" Doctor Langford shook his head. "I heard the cretin's been sentenced to death by electric chair—set up with the assistance of Mr. Edison, no less!"

On the day Eleanor was strong enough to go to the bathroom by herself, Yolanda surprised her with warm water to shower with. The maid had boiled and collected several pots of it in the bathroom urn. By the time she filled the vessel, the water's temperature was just right.

Yolanda had become indispensable to her mistress, who now worried the muchacha had irrevocably spoiled her. *A servant was a seducer away from self-reliance.* As Eleanor poured water on her notably thinner body, she noticed her skin still exhibited the yellowish pallor that Doctor Langford told her was a symptom of the disease. Her recovery would be slow, he cautioned her. Thus, he advised her to likewise take it slow in resuming any activity.

But Eleanor was determined to get on with her mission.

She called Yolanda to help her dress, for she needed help with her corset. Her fingers still shook from the task. The blouse she intended to wear also had buttons on the backside, one of two that she still owned. The other was ruined during the ambush. It was incomprehensible to her how makers of ladies' outfits seemed determined to keep women dependent on others to accomplish the simplest personal tasks. It was as if they assumed all women had chambermaids, or that only those who could afford one had the right to beautiful things. This occurred to Eleanor even as she and her mother still had each other for assistance with the intimate aspects of their wardrobe. Hence, she'd long resolved to purchase only things that fostered her independence. Still, there was the corset and this one blouse.

Yolanda glanced blankly at the pre-strung corset around her mistress's midriff, seemingly clueless as to what Eleanor expected her to do. The girl appeared to have no notion of the undergarment's function, though she'd already laundered it twice before. Eleanor grinned and gesticulated her instructions. Yolanda gingerly pulled on the strings, constantly glancing at Eleanor to check if she was hurting her mistress when she pulled on the cords.

"See how fortunate you are—not to be tied to these strings?" Eleanor said, grinning. "You may pull tighter, Yolanda. You aren't hurting me. I've lost a few inches too many."

As Yolanda tugged at the strings, Eleanor noticed a strange, new reticule on her dressing table. She picked it up and examined it. The pouch was hand-sewn of beautiful python skin, accented with a crescent-shaped handle made of polished tortoiseshell. "Yolanda, what's this?"

The maid burst into a barrage of what Eleanor assumed was Vicolano language, prompting Eleanor to touch Yolanda's arm to ask her to speak slowly. "Dará ni Diego," Yolanda repeated. "Para sa imo."

"What?" Eleanor was surprised. "From Diego? For me?"

"Iyó!" Yolanda confirmed, as she secured the corset's strings into a bow knot.

"Why, it's… ¡Es hermoso! When did he… cuando?" Eleanor asked while she slipped on her blouse.

"Hmm…" Yolanda seemed to be struggling to slip the little fabric hooks around the tiny covered buttons on the backside of Eleanor's blouse. "Kuwatro aldaw."

"So, he visited… four days ago," Eleanor said—more to herself than to Yolanda. She grimaced upon seeing her sunken cheeks in the oval, brass-framed mirror on her writing desk, which now also served as her vanity table. Her skirt felt quite loose around the waist, so she searched for a pin in her jar of miscellany.

"Bakó!" Yolanda shook her head.

"No?" Eleanor glanced at the muchacha from the mirror. "What do you mean?" Finding a pin, at last, Eleanor stood, folded the excess fabric on the skirt's waistband, and pinned it to make the skirt fit better.

"No, señorita." Yolanda replied. "Diego dará este… kuwatro aldaw. Pero Diego… bisíta káda aldaw!"

"What?" Eleanor asked, grinning. "Repite, por favor."

It hadn't ceased to amaze and amuse her that while she communicated with the maid in a mix of English and Spanish, Yolanda replied in the hybrid Vicolano-Spanish; yet, in that mesh of languages, combined with hand gestures, both women managed to understand each other.

Yolanda restated everything slowly—from which Eleanor gathered that Diego left the reticule as a gift four days earlier, but also visited daily, dropping off freshly harvested coconuts, fruits, and vegetables from the hacienda.

Eleanor grinned. "Yolanda, sounds like you have a sweetheart! Hmm…?"

"¿Qué?" Yolanda frowned as she finished buttoning her mistress's blouse.

"¿Tienes novio? Is it Diego?" Eleanor smiled and winked at her.

The muchacha glanced quizzically at her mistress before soon snorting into chortling. She slapped Eleanor's arm in the same affectionate way Doña Beatriz did to her husband. Yolanda wagged her finger and pointed it at her mistress. "Bakó! Yo no. ¡Tú!"

"What do you mean… me?" Eleanor glanced sharply at the muchacha.

"¡Diego dába' tu!" Yolanda laughed. "Enamorado de ti."

"He—infatuated with me? No, that can't be!" *How dare he even think that...*

Yolanda left the bedroom, vigorously nodding her head, still chuckling.

Eleanor picked up the reticule again. Only a skilled and dedicated craftsman could have stitched the reptile's delicate hide, including its fine lining of piña cloth. It was likely made from the same python Diego had taken from their backyard—the same poor creature Don Luis said he saw the foreman grilling together with the other workers.

But a vision of the insurrecto leader, with his half-covered face and shadowed, yet sparkling, eyes reasserted itself. And his scent. She recognized them all in Diego as he carried her to her bed that night. Could he be the same person? If so, how and why did he gift her with so fine a piece? Was it an apology for the ambush? Or appeasement; a bribe? And why was he visiting her house daily, bringing gifts, if it weren't Yolanda he was after? What, then, was *he* after? Perhaps he was spying on her, making sure she hadn't connected him with the ambush—for fear she'd tell on him. Yes, that was it.

She continued mulling over the possibilities as she put up her hair in her usual chignon. The knocking on her door startled her out of her ruminations. "Yes, what is it?"

Yolanda peeked in, entered, and closed the door behind her, wearing a grim expression. "Es un soldado Americano," she whispered.

"Why are you whispering?" Eleanor asked, glancing at the maid from the mirror. "Is it Sam? Sergeant Munro?"

Yolanda shook her head.

"Then who?"

Yolanda shrugged her shoulders.

Eleanor tucked the last couple of pins into her hair. "Please tell whoever it is, un momento, por favor."

When she finally presented herself in the sala, a young soldier rose from the sofa into all six feet of him. He'd already removed his hat, as was a soldier's etiquette on entering indoors. He had short, middle-parted, platinum-blond hair and blue eyes. Despite his stunning features and almost perfect physique, he was rather plain-looking. "Miss Karsten?" he asked.

When Eleanor nodded in response, he added, "Ma'am, I'm Lieutenant James Waterstone. I hope you're feeling well enough for me to take your statement about the ambush?"

CHAPTER 10

Treading on a Tightrope

The lieutenant began by asking her how it all happened. She summarized what she remembered, leaving out details of which she wasn't certain. He wrote it all down with a short pencil in a little black pocket notebook. But he didn't seem content with what she shared. He asked her to repeat everything, walking her through it all with follow-up questions.

His general lack of an accent occasionally slipped into the compression of two vowel sounds in one, suggesting he was a Midwesterner like she was. Yet, she became wary of him and refrained from volunteering such kinship. Perhaps it was the aggressive manner by which he interrogated her, his unrelenting persistence, that bothered her about him.

"Are you sure this is all you remember, ma'am?" he asked for what seemed like the nth time. "Because with McKinley gone…."

"W-wait—what?" Eleanor interjected. "The president… d-died?"

Lieutenant Waterstone's brows arched. "Oh. I'm sorry, ma'am. Thought you knew."

"I only knew he was shot," Eleanor said. "Last I heard, he was expected to recover."

"That appeared to be so, at first," he said. "But he took a turn for the worse and died eight days later. From gangrene." Eleanor recalled what Doctor Langford said about the doctors not finding the second bullet's exit wound.

"So you see, Miss Karsten," he continued, "this attack on you has to be dealt with a strong hand, lest the insurrectos think the new Roosevelt administration is weak and could be played with." The way he said his r's made him sound like a pirate with a cold—further betraying his origins in the Northern Midwest. "Ma'am, is there anything else you remember about the men who attacked you that could give us clues on their identities?"

She remembered the scarf the leader had tied around her neck to cover her chest. "I'm afraid not, lieutenant," she replied. "It was too dark, and their faces were covered."

"Are you sure, Miss Karsten?" Lieutenant Waterstone insisted. "No identifying marks, odd features, anything out of the ordinary?"

She remembered the tattooed man. She shook her head.

"And you said there were about eight to ten of them but aren't sure, except they all appeared to be natives? You're positive you haven't left out anything?" The soldier persisted, his icy blue eyes probing her baby blues.

She averted her gaze from the glare of his scrutinizing stare. "Yes. I'm sure." She took care not to flinch when she met his gaze again. "You must understand, lieutenant, I was already suffering the onset of malarial fever when it all happened." She heaved a sigh and stood. "Now, if you'll excuse me, I must return to rest. I'm afraid I haven't fully recovered."

"Why, yes, of course." He likewise stood. "But if you remember anything, ma'am, anything at all—you *will* let me know, won't you? You'd be surprised how the smallest thing can be useful. We must catch and punish those damn n***ers!" His midwesterner's tongue brandished a steely edge.

Apart from hailing from the same region, Eleanor decided she shared nothing in common with this American. The Three Musketeers were, perhaps, right to be concerned. As she turned away from him to walk him to the door, he stunned her by grabbing her elbow.

"Miss Karsten, are you sure you didn't hear what those rebels shouted before they torched the carriage?" The driver or footman must have said something.

Eleanor glanced at the hand on her elbow and replied, "Lieutenant, it's one thing to hear; another to comprehend. Please remember I'm new here. I could hardly understand my maid."

"Right. Well, just the same, ma'am, I hope you come straight to me if you recall anything. Maybe when you're better?" He flashed his steely smile.

She pulled her elbow from his grasp and opened the door. "I really must rest, lieutenant. Goodbye."

"See you next time. Ma'am." He placed his cap back on his head, but before he stepped out, he glanced back at her, smiling a wry smile.

Eleanor closed the door firmly and returned to her bedroom. She sat on her bed and steadied her trembling breath, inhaling and exhaling—deeply, slowly. She refrained from sliding the windows open until she heard the lieutenant's horse trot away. Never had she lied to anyone before this. Why did she hold back on sharing her suspicions about Diego? Or the tattoo on the arm of the man who assaulted her? Or what the masked men shouted as they set the carriage on fire? *Because you're learning to walk balanced on this tightrope, Eleanor.*

Yolanda knocked again and peeked inside Eleanor's bedroom. "Señorita, you good?"

"Yes, thank you, Yolanda," she replied. The maid smiled, and Eleanor quickly added, "Yolanda, do you remember a scarf I was wearing that night I came home sick?" Yolanda looked puzzled, and Eleanor gestured what she meant by a scarf. Yolanda scratched and shook her head. "All right, but if you see it, could you please bring it to me?" Yolanda nodded.

Eleanor spent the next two days searching for the missing scarf in the house. She went to the garden, poking among the bushes. Perhaps it fell off there or on the road while Don Luis rode with her to her house. She proceeded to the backyard, where Yolanda had hung up clothes to dry on a rope tied from one tree to another. One of them was the tree where they found the snake hanging. It occurred to her that, maybe Yolanda just couldn't remember washing the scarf and hanging it up to dry. Now, she wondered if Diego may have secretly retrieved it—the one item that could be traced to him.

Sam came to fetch her to see her new classroom—a task delayed by her illness for a little more than a month. He had, in the meantime, filled in for her, continuing to teach basic arithmetic and English. She thanked him and he shrugged, stating that the more he helped the children know how to speak English, the easier her transition with them would be. She was tempted to tease him that she hoped the children didn't sound too Texan.

"Sam, I'm ready to work!" she announced, smiling. "But I don't want you to take me to the church school."

"What 'ya mean, Leonor?" His handlebar mustache rose with his arched eyebrows.

She smiled; she'd almost forgotten the name his wife gave her. "I have another idea."

The day after her interview with Lieutenant Waterstone, she asked Yolanda where she bought their canned goods, such as the corned beef they were then having for breakfast, which was especially good with garlic fried rice and eggs.

"Mr. Ang Kiok," Yolanda replied. "Instik man."

"What's that?" Eleanor asked.

"Chinaman. He give very good price."

"Could you bring me to him?"

If anyone possessed bold enterprise, Eleanor was sure it was the Chinese merchant. And many possibilities came with bold enterprise. If anything, the Chinese were a pragmatic people. Otherwise, they wouldn't have adapted and thrived, despite the prejudice against them, everywhere else she saw them—in Des Moines, Chicago, San Francisco, and the Hawaiian Islands. They had built the railroads that now connected the East and West coasts of the mainland, which, she believed, hastened the country's industrialization. Eleanor thus bet on Mr. Ang being agreeable, likewise, to work with the American presence in the Philippine Islands—or, at the very least, with the new American teacher in Magayon.

"Yes, amo," Yolanda said as she put away the breakfast dishes. "Take you Mr. Ang."

"Yolanda, please stop calling me that." Eleanor had decided she didn't like being called the natives' term for a master. "If you like, you may call me miss or señorita."

"Iyó, señorita."

Mr. Ang Kiok's establishment was not far from Eleanor's house. Located on the far side of the plaza, it occupied a two-story building with an iron-barred, double-window room on the ground floor. It sold a wide array of items ranging from fresh produce and canned goods to sundry household items. Eleanor was glad she didn't have to go to the army commissary to procure many of their necessities—not especially now with Waterstone there.

She peeked inside the store and spied a Chinese man and a mousy, little native woman busily catering to their customers' purchases. The man rushed out to meet Eleanor and Yolanda, while the woman craned her neck for a better view of the Americana and her muchacha. Their customers turned around with furrowed brows and curious eyes, checking on who was so important that the Chinaman abandoned them.

Mr. Ang was a short, slightly built man wearing a blue silk tunic over black cotton trousers and a round, black cap on the crown of his head, which was shaved, except for its backside. There, his hair was long and braided into a cue, secured with a bowed string at the end. *It looks like a kite's tail,* Eleanor thought with amusement.

She was acquainted with the iconic Chinese man's hairstyle from the Chinese on the mainland. She'd asked one of them, who spoke English, the reason for the uniform hairstyle. He said the Qing emperor had ordered all his male subjects to wear their hair that way. She found it curious that the Chinese who lived far beyond China's borders still considered themselves bound to the odd mandate.

Mr. Ang's flat, round face opened into a wide smile. His eyes crinkled and appeared to disappear into upside-down crescents flanking his delicately-sloped nose. Hands clasped in front, he bowed from his waist and surprised Eleanor by greeting them in English—with a British accent. "Madam, Señorita Yolanda—how kind of you both to come to my humble establishment. Thank you for your patronage. How may I be of service to you today?"

Eleanor surmised that Mr. Ang must have originated from British Hong Kong and, like many Chinese merchants who'd plied the junk trade between China and the islands, ended up staying in the archipelago.

Eleanor took her turn to surprise him when she said, "Mr. Ang, I'm here to request your assistance in procuring a suitable place for my school."

It took only two days after she'd met with Mr. Ang before she saw him again. He fetched her in his carabao-pulled carretela to go see a possible site for her school. He drove on her street to the end until they turned into another street behind the church, which led them to a dirt road.

As they passed what appeared to be a cemetery, Eleanor spied a familiar, dark figure climbing over the graveyard's wrought-iron gates. He seemed to be the same vagrant she saw upon her arrival in Magayon.

"Mr. Ang, who is that man?" she asked.

Mr. Ang glanced toward where she was pointing and grinned. "Ah. That is Toto. Or, at least that is what everyone calls him because he keeps mumbling, 'uto-uto,' which literally means, fool. But no one wants to be rude by calling him that. Thus, the name, Toto. No one knows who he is or where he is from. He appeared here a few months ago, out of the blue."

"But where does he live?" Eleanor's eyes followed the vagabond where he went: toward town, it seemed.

Mr. Ang chuckled. "Right now, it appears—the graveyard."

Eleanor glanced sideways at the Chinese man with arched eyebrows. "What? Is that allowed?"

The merchant continued grinning. "Señorita, in this country, people like Toto simply place their heads where they can lay them. I must say he is resourceful, though, for the cemetery is one of the best places where one could find shelter—rent-free! There are some mausoleums there bigger than many huts. As long as he does not behave violently, most people tolerate him. But, come to think of it, he tends to get agitated whenever he sees the padre. I cannot say I blame him, though." He chuckled.

Eleanor grinned. "But how does he feed himself? Just goes around begging?"

"Certainly!" Mr. Ang smiled.

"But isn't there some kind of philanthropic group here that could help him?"

Mr. Ang guffawed. "Señorita, this is not America where indulging in philanthropy is just one of the many pastimes of the rich. When people throw him food, they feel they have done their Christian duty. He often comes by our store. We do what we can for him, but other than that, we do not probe where he goes or what he does. He is no trouble to anyone, except to those who are troubled by his existence."

Eleanor shook her head, heaving a sigh of pity for the vagabond.

They crossed a quaint, little stone bridge built over a bubbling brook and emerged into a verdant rice field. Eleanor's heart leaped at the idyllic view. Her heart sank, though, when Mr. Ang stopped at what appeared to be a mere shed and announced, "Here we are!"

Long and low, the rectangular structure had bamboo-plaited walls and a thatched grass roof. He helped her get off the carretela and unlatched a door that was less a door than it was a stick-gate, which only prevented birds and free-roaming chickens, dogs, and pigs from entering.

Mr. Ang opened two pairs of windows facing each other on the long walls of the structure to let the sunlight in. They were similar to the window in Eleanor's kitchen. One "opened" them by raising their thatched flap shutters from their bottom frames by propping them up with a rattan or bamboo stick, and one "closed" them by simply removing the canes. It was a simple yet ingenious way of having windows, but it also meant the room could darken considerably when the windows couldn't be left open due to strong wind or rain.

Her heart further dipped on seeing the whole structure sitting on a mere dirt floor. The ceiling was no more than the underside of the thatched hip roof, supported by a bamboo frame layered with a sheet, again, of plaited bamboo. This suggested that the roof wasn't rainproof.

Stacked in a corner of the one-room space were a couple of poked-through caned chairs and a rickety old desk that prospective thieves had rightly adjudged as not worth stealing at all.

If she were to take this shed, she'd be back to a one-room school.

"This adjoins our modest rice field, over yonder," Mr. Ang explained. "We use this as a bagging station after we have sun-dried the unhusked grains roadside or to shelter them from the rain." He seemed watchful of her reaction that she took care to keep to herself. He continued, "I know it does not look much now, madam, but perhaps you can see its potential. It is ready for you to use, if you wish. You can perhaps put mats on the floor for the children to sit on and hang a blackboard up there." He pointed to the north wall.

Eleanor walked the dirt floor, which she estimated was about ten feet wide and fifteen feet long. It was, at least, a decent size. She could hold separate classes inside and outside for girls and boys, depending on the weather. *But could I really trade the church's stone school building—for this?*

A beautiful old tree stood outside one of the windows. It had a thick, gnarly trunk and wide-reaching branches that held up a cloud-like canopy of glossy, canoe-shaped leaves. "I have the same tree in my backyard," she said, thinking of the tree where they found the python.

"Then, you are fortunate, madam. For it is a mango tree, and it bears the sweetest, golden, heart-shaped fruits in May."

"Sweet?" Eleanor exclaimed, grinning. "That wasn't our experience of it in Honolulu."

He grinned. "That may be because they have a different kind of mango there. The Philippine mango is considered the fruit of the gods here, revered for its nectar-sweet, golden, velvet fruit. I have not tasted better, except perhaps the mangoes of India, which are, in my humble opinion, its closest rival."

"My, you've certainly traveled the world!" she exclaimed, smiling.

"Not the whole world, madam, but enough of it to know this land is as beautiful as the soil is rich, and equal to the best I have seen in my youth's adventures across three continents."

She looked out to the fields before turning back to him. "If I take this, what would you do when it's time to pack your grains?"

He smiled. "Thank you for your concern, madam, but it is no problem. We would simply haul the grains to the bodega beside my store and bag them there."

She walked around the structure again. "And... how much would you say you'll need to lease this place to me, Mr. Ang?" She turned around to face him.

He was looking down at the dirt floor, drawing circles on the bare earth with his feet clad in black canvas and leather-soled shoes. When he glanced up, he smiled. "None at all, madam."

"What?" She exclaimed. "But I can't possibly take advantage of your kindness like that, Mr. Ang! Surely, you require compensation?" She looked at him earnestly, and he met her gaze.

"Well, madam, if you insist," she said, smiling sheepishly. "Perhaps you can leave me whatever improvements you make to this place after you no longer need it? Or, start paying the usual rent for similar buildings at the end of five years—whichever comes first?"

Eleanor smiled. Just as she hoped, the merchant proved enterprising. Still, he did just offer a mere shack. She contemplated her options. *One could get an education under an oak tree,* her father had said the day she came home frustrated over being assigned the one-room schoolhouse at the edge of their county. Mr. Ang's, at least, stood beside a fruit-bearing tree! Moreover, it never snowed or got to freezing temperatures in the Philippine Islands as in Iowa.

"That sounds more than fair," Eleanor said, extending her hand to Mr. Ang, who firmly shook it.

Yet, Sam was not pleased. Not pleased at all.

"Ye must be jokin'!" he cried when he saw the dirt floor shed. "Leonor, 'tis insane! How can you exchange the church school for *this*? Come, let me show ya what yer givin' up!"

"No, Sam. I don't need to see it." Eleanor crossed her arms in front of her. "I've already made up my mind. I would rather have this shack and be free to teach my students as I see fit than have the priest monitoring us, teaching religion classes. It would confuse the children when we get to their civics lesson on what separation of church and state means in a democracy."

Sam looked her in the eye. "Ya 'member what I told ya 'bout not crossin' the padre, eh?"

She met his gaze. "Yes, Sam, and I'm prepared to face the consequences."

Sam rocked sideways, shifting his weight between his legs, hands on hips, head down.

"Look, Sam," she interjected, "who says change is easy? Isn't this what we're here for—to bring good change in these people's lives? Their children? If I simply conform, doesn't that make me complicit with the old order?"

Sam blenched. "Oh, and is that what ya thunk I done?"

"No, Sam!" Eleanor exclaimed. "That's not what I'm saying at all. You've done a great service. And, given the circumstances, it was the best anyone could have accomplished. I do appreciate it! But, now, we have an opportunity to bring this benevolent assimilation to the next level—*while* practicing our democratic principles! Isn't this what we're supposed to do? Practice what we teach?"

Sam shook his head, appearing unconvinced.

She approached him and gently laid a hand on his arm. "Look, Sam, can't you please just trust me on this? This is, after all, my call. I admit I'm going by my instincts here, but I also need all the help I can get. Do I have your support?"

He walked around in circles on the dirt floor, sighing and looking out of each window of Mr. Ang's shed. He went outside. She peered out to see what he was doing. He was circling the structure, appraising it up and down. When he returned inside, he shrugged his shoulders and heaved a sigh. He glanced at her and, with a seemingly reluctant smile, stated with a tone of resignation, "What the heck! All right, missy. You got what you want." He saluted, crying, "Aye, aye, captain!"

They both burst into laughter.

"Now, ma'am, what do you need?" Sam asked with a twinkle in his brown eyes.

As Eleanor had expected, Sam wasn't the last to challenge her decision.

She'd written to Padre Damián, thanking him for his offer of the church school building. She explained, however, why it would be contrary to her mission under now President Theodore Roosevelt's administration to establish a public school in Magayon on behalf of the United States government—for her to be seen as doing so under the shadow of the church.

"No less than one of the Founding Fathers of our democracy, Mr. Thomas Jefferson," she wrote, "had expounded on the Constitutional prohibition to 'make no law respecting an establishment of religion' as 'building a wall of separation between Church and State.'" Quoting Mark 12:17, she added, "'Give to Caesar what is Caesar's, and to God what is God's.' I acknowledge the community trusts you as the shepherd of its soul. Now, I request the same courtesy as the steward of its children's education."

On Sunday, after the priest would have long received her letter, Don Luis called on her. When she came out to the sala, he was standing in front of his painting of the Mayon, stroking his beard, seemingly judging his work. He wore a white linen poet shirt tucked into canvas breeches, with sleeves rolled to his elbows, and tan leather riding boots—the image of the ultimate plantation master. The sight, though, of his handsome, sun-kissed face rapt in contemplation, and his happy countenance on seeing her—cheered her.

"Don Luis, what a pleasant surprise!" she exclaimed. "Yet, why do you look so surprised at your talent?"

He grinned. "Señorita Karsten, I am happy to see that you are back to your usual lovely self. I, on the other hand, am but an artist who is a poor work in progress."

She extended her hand, and he performed a gesture of a kiss—without pressing his lips on her skin, like he did last time. She also noted he no longer called her by her first name as she seemed to recall on the night of her ambush and illness.

"You are too modest," she reprised. "This painting inspires me to go on a hike to the volcano someday."

"When that day comes, señorita, I hope you will honor me with the privilege of accompanying you. There are hot springs at the foot of the Mayon worth seeing. And I have just the right guide for us—my foreman, Diego!"

"Oh, thank you." She forced a smile. His mention of Diego stirred mixed feelings. "Yes, that would be something—wouldn't it?"

He continued to examine the painting—arms clasped behind his back, nose trained on the canvas, eyes fixed on some detail of the brushstrokes, as if he were a stranger to his handiwork. "Did you know that Magayon grew out of the town buried with the rest of this church?" he asked. "The survivors fled to these higher grounds, you see."

Eleanor shook her head. "What a tragic beginning for Magayon! And you've captured the sense of being haunted through that shell of a church and its bell tower."

"Perhaps," he said. "I am wondering, though, whether what I painted was what I saw in my mind's eye, or my heart's longing for what is, sadly, no longer there." He grinned. "Which is strange—because I did not yet exist when the town of Cagsawa was buried by the Mayon during the 1814 eruption." He looked into her eyes. "Is that not interesting, mi querida, for one to long for what one had never possessed?"

Eleanor picked up on the term of endearment. She turned away from his gaze, back to the painting. "It is normal to yearn for something we've never had, and yet wish for. But we're often confused because we don't know what that is. It inhabits us as a formless hope… a shapeless void." She glanced back at him. "That's why we need artists like you to help us see what that something is." She chuckled. "I'm sorry—I'm not making any sense, aren't I?"

"No—no! You are making perfect sense, señorita!" he exclaimed, nodding and smiling.

She smiled back. "When was the last time you painted?"

He sighed. "Alas, I lost that luxury when Papá died. Mamá expects me to fill his shoes. But I am afraid they may be too big for me."

"Oh, I doubt it!" Eleanor exclaimed. "But, surely, you find time to do what you love?"

"Making the time is not the problem," he said. "It is having the will and motivation. Unfortunately, this hacienda business is draining me of all energy and inspiration." He gazed into her eyes. "But now, perhaps, this could change. A little inspiration goes a long way."

She flushed, she was sure of it—and looked away in embarrassment.

He shook his head and grinned. "Basta, I did not come here to talk about me! It is you I came here to talk about, querida."

"Me? I hope not!" She spilled into a nervous chuckle. "For that would be a most boring subject!"

He smiled. "Not for me!"

"Now, please, won't we be seated?" She waved toward the sala.

He frowned and touched her arm. "Oh! Forgive me! Did I keep you standing too long, querida?"

"Not at all but, now, I do have to sit." She smiled as they occupied the opposite ends of the sofa. She still hadn't regained her full strength. She napped at odd hours of the day and, sometimes, the shivers started again and as soon stopped. Doctor Langford forewarned her about such recurring incidents, assuring her they were normal until she'd fully recovered.

Yolanda presented herself for instructions, glancing timidly at her mistress's guest.

Eleanor asked him, "May I offer you a limonada, perhaps, or some tea?"

"Might that be English tea?" His eyes widened with anticipation.

She grinned. "Yes, indeed! My stash of Yorkshire."

"Then, I am grateful to partake of the pleasure."

It only took a nod from her mistress now for Yolanda to know what to do. When Eleanor had dug up her tin of the loose-leaf black and her mother's porcelain tea set from her trunk, she set out to teach the maid how to make a proper cup of tea. At first, the muchacha put too much of the leaves in the kettle or too little; steeped them too long or too briefly; added sugar, or poured canned condensed milk into the pot, which made for an awful pot of tea. One day, having run out of the condensed milk, Yolanda used fresh carabao's milk, instead—and that, Eleanor found much to her liking. They'd since subscribed to a daily delivery of it from one of the farmers.

As Yolanda disappeared into the kitchen, Eleanor said, "Don Luis, thank you for all your help while I was indisposed. And the flowers were a welcome sight from my sickbed. I'm especially grateful for your visit today—for allowing me to thank you in person."

"I am the one who has to apologize for not having been able to visit you lately," he replied, smiling ruefully. "But I was assured of your progress by my foreman. Sent him here to check on you and anything you might need."

That explained Diego's visits. Or did it? Eleanor was reminded she hadn't seen him, although Yolanda had mentioned he still came by almost daily, asking about her as he dropped off vegetables and fruits from the hacienda. The fruits were now a regular feature in a

basket tray on their dining table. Among them, sometimes, were clusters of *lanzones* that looked like big grapes, except for their thick, blond
dermis that, when peeled, bled a white sap and revealed a translucent,
little egg of a silken fruit that tasted variably from tart to saccharine.

At other times, there was tamarind: laconic ropes of umber pods
encased in a smooth, bark-like shell that, when ripe, could easily be
cracked open with one's fingers to access their single-seeded, sweet,
brown meat. One day, Eleanor was pleasantly surprised to spot among
the fruits in the tray the red, spiky, anemone-looking fruit balls she
remembered from the Honolulu market. Yolanda called them, *ram-
butan*, and the large fleshy pearls they offered up, when peeled, tasted
almost like the scent of a rose—if the perfume of roses were edible.

First, a snake turned into a gift; now, exotic fruits that teased the
tongue. What was Diego up to?

Don Luis cut through Eleanor's reverie as he said, "Please forgive me. I have unfortunately been kept away by... matters beyond
my control."

Eleanor waved a hand in dismissal. "Oh, no need to apologize, Don
Luis! I understand you run an hacienda! By the way, please thank your
mother again for me. Yolanda said she likewise visited during my con-
finement. I wonder if she mentioned I sent you both a note of thanks?
I also appreciate all the delicious fruits you've been sending through
Diego. You and your mother have both been very kind."

His eyebrows arched and his eyes widened, as though something
she said surprised him. "Ah, sí—of course! Pero—de nada, señorita.
It is the least we can do. We are embarrassed and horrified that such
a shocking thing happened to you. You must think of us all as just a
bunch of bandidos! I promise you, we will make up for it. And we will
find the culprits and punish them!"

She heaved a sigh. "I believe the situation may be more complicated than you make it sound, Don Luis. I hope, in time, the people
could see me as their friend, not their enemy."

"Oh, but no one thinks ill of you, señorita! Some may just be...
worried about change. As for Mamá, she has been quite beside herself
about what happened. If it were not for some pleasant distraction to her
of late, she would be out of her mind. Completely loca!" He grinned.
"You remember Maria Teresa—the padre's niece?"

Eleanor noted his use of the lady's familiar name. "I seem to remember something about her visiting."

"¡Sí, sí! She is arriving soon. Mamá sends her regards and wishes you to join us at a welcome party for her."

"Oh, how nice!" Eleanor feigned delight. "When would this fantastic soirée be held?"

"During the harvest fiesta." He glanced at her expectantly. "Could you join us?"

She forced a smile. "Thank you, but I shall have to see. My illness has already much delayed the school opening. And, as you can understand, I have quite a bit of work to do before I could make that happen."

He glanced down. "Honestly, señorita, the school is another reason why I am here."

"What do you mean?" She willed him to meet her gaze.

He looked at her and heaved a sigh. "I am here to convince you to accept Padre Damián's offer."

"Oh, Don Luis, I'm sorry, but that is quite out of the question now." She shook her head and crossed her arms.

"¿Pero, por qué?" he exclaimed with a surprising tone of exasperation. He abruptly stood and walked to the window, massaging his neck. He appeared to contemplate the scenery before he turned around to face her again. "Señorita, let me be frank: You are in for a nasty war with Padre Damián if you do not accept. This morning, he devoted his entire sermon to bashing your school, calling it, La Escuela del Diablo."

Eleanor burst into laughter. "He said what?"

"The school of the devil! And that, mi querida, is no laughing matter!" He must have surprised himself by his outburst, for he softened his tone. "Need I explain, Señorita Karsten, that in this town—"

"Yes, yes, I know," she interjected, nodding. "Sergeant Munro explained as much."

"Then, why do you provoke the padre?" He raised his arms in a quandary.

Eleanor pressed her lips and heaved a sigh. "I'm sorry if that's what it appears. But I assure you that is not my intention. I can't help it if the good padre refuses to accept my perfectly good reasons for declining his offer."

"Sí, sí. I know." He smiled with a flash of amusement in his eyes. "He asked me to translate your letter."

His changed tone was reassuring, but it failed to predispose her to a tempered response. "Then, you should have understood!" Her chest heaved, rising and falling with her breathing.

Just then, Yolanda returned with a tea tray and a plate of *biscocho* biscuits that were among the snacks she liked to buy from Mr. Ang's store. To Eleanor, they were similar to, yet softer than the Italian biscotti she enjoyed during Christmas season. The maid set it all on the center table.

"Thank you, Yolanda," Eleanor said. Both she and Don Luis seemed grateful for the distraction. "I'll serve." She glanced at Don Luis. "Milk and sugar?"

"Sí, por favor." He returned to sit on the sofa. "And just a teaspoon, please."

Eleanor poured milk into his cup, then the brew, and a teaspoon of sugar, and prepared hers similarly.

"Aaah… delicious!" he exclaimed after his first sip. "I have missed English tea. Have not had this since my travels."

"And why should you do without it?" Eleanor asked, smiling. "Mr. Ang sells a good Ceylon. Even Doctor Langford loves it, I understand."

"Ah, mi querida," Don Luis interjected, chuckling, "although we have a patriarchal culture, it is the women who rule our homes. And Mamá very much prefers her tsokolate."

She chuckled and nodded. She took double sips of her tea, for she despised it getting lukewarm, even in that warm climate.

"Gracias." He smiled and likewise sipped. "Look, Eleanor…. ¡O, lo siento! May I call you that?"

She smiled. "Yes, you may, Don Luis. If you let me call you Luis?"

"¡Por supuesto! I would like that very much, Eleanor. It would proclaim our… friendship. After all, we have already experienced together what most old friends have not." He smiled with a mischievous glint in his eyes.

Eleanor felt flushed remembering the immodest state of her clothing when he found her after the ambush, and how he carried her in his arms and held her while riding to her house.

He seemed oblivious to her discomfiture. "Now, Eleanor… since you mentioned Mr. Ang… are you sure settling for that shed of his is wise? ¡Dios mío! It does not even have a proper door or floor! In the people's eyes, it would only confirm Padre Damián's claim it is the devil's school! No good parent could possibly see themselves sending their children to such a shabby place!" He shot her a pinched expression.

She chuckled. "Why, Luis—you sound like the devil's advocate! I see that news here travels fast."

"What did you expect, querida? Magayon and Legazpi, put together, would still a small town make! You must understand that here, even the coconuts have ears." He winked and smiled.

Which makes me wonder why you still don't know who attacked me that night. "I appreciate your concern, Luis. But it's *my* prerogative to decide what's best for my school and students. And, as my friend, I expect you to trust me on this. Leave the persuading of the parents to me. I have ideas on how to win them over."

"¡Dios mío, querida!" he exclaimed. "I can see you are bull-headed as you are lovely." He grinned and sighed. "I could offer you one of my bodegas, but I am afraid the hacienda is too far for most children."

She smiled. "I understand. And I appreciate the thought."

The superintendent certainly had to create more schools and send more teachers. Only children within a five to six-mile radius of her school could, realistically, attend her classes—and at great inconvenience, if not suffering. Most of them were poor. They couldn't afford the luxury of a personal carriage or public equipage for hire daily. Thus, those who lived at the outer rims of Magayon were practically denied an education.

"Bueno, mi querida, I am afraid I have to go," Luis said, standing. "In this war you have begun with the padre—may the best woman win!" He held out his hand to her, smiling.

Eleanor grinned and accepted his hand as she also stood.

He enveloped her hand with both of his and gazed into her eyes. "Whenever I can be of assistance, please, just send word." He brought her hand to his lips and kissed it—tenderly.

She returned his smile, wondering why now she didn't mind him kissing her hand that way. "I will, Luis. And, thank you—again."

As she accompanied him to the door, he paused and raised his index finger. "And one more thing, mi querida! Do not even think you can decline Mamá's invitation. Padre Damián may turn to the pulpit to battle with you, but with Mamá—well, *that* is a different war altogether you definitely want to avoid." He playfully wagged her finger at her, and she laughed.

CHAPTER 11

A Chiaroscuro of Like Images

S am fetched Eleanor in his carretela with Pedro. They stacked the bamboo carriage bed with carpentry tools, timber planks, bamboo canes, rolled bamboo-plaited sheets, and thatches of nipa grass roofing. They also loaded Eleanor's book crate and the now empty steamer trunk. Yolanda handed Pedro broomsticks, cleaning rags, and a picnic basket that contained pan de sal sardine sandwiches and bottles of filtered drinking water.

"We'll see you at noon," Eleanor said to the maid. Yolanda nodded and smiled. Her mistress had instructed her to cook lunch and deliver it to the school site.

When Eleanor, Sam, and Pedro arrived at Mr. Ang's shed, a young Filipino woman was standing there, as though waiting for them. Sam pulled up to the shed and said, "Leonor, meet Señorita Estrella Santiago. I understand she's to be yer assistant. She was the teacher here during the last couple 'a years of the Spanish."

Eleanor recalled the Superintendent's letter of instructions mentioning the possibility of sending her an assistant whom she also was tasked to train. She had expected another American and, therefore, was surprised by the presence of the Filipina. It appeared that the Office of Public Instruction had decided to employ the former teachers. The recent Taft Commission report suggested that the current 1,074 Thomasites were not enough to serve the more than 4,000 students enrolled in the twenty-nine schools of the archipelago. Given the mandate to put all school-age children in classrooms by year's end and establish more schools, Eleanor expected the number of enrollees to rise dramatically. Employing some of the former native teachers made sense. It eased the need to find enough recruits who already possessed some of the knowledge and training required for the job.

Eleanor hopped off the carretela. "I'm very pleased to meet you, Señorita Santiago!" She smiled and offered her hand to the attractive young lady, who shook it timidly.

"I am please meeting you, too, Señorita Karsten," she said with a quiet voice while bowing her head. "I come help." She smiled, and Eleanor noted a familiar sparkle in her eyes.

Señorita Santiago's long, thick eyelashes flaunted themselves whenever she lowered her gaze—which was often. She seemed to be about the age of Maude and Arabella. From afar, though, she appeared older because she'd put up her burnished hair into a pusod. She moved in the demure and dainty manner Eleanor had observed among upper-class Filipino ladies, but the young lady's modest and rudimentary camisa at saya belied her likely more humble social status.

The ladies set about cleaning the shed's interior. Meanwhile, Sam and Pedro verified its structural stability and repaired rotted woodwork. The men also patched gaps in the thatched roof and added hooks and latches to secure the windows. They removed the old stick door and built a new door made of solid wood planks and installed it with a padlock.

As the women teachers worked side by side, Eleanor learned more about her assistant. Señorita Santiago said she was an alumna of a convent school that prepared young women to be tutors and teachers. Convent-bred women and seminary-trained men had served as the main source of recruits for teachers in parochial schools ran by parish churches during the Spanish regime. Eleanor also gathered that, although college education was available under the Spaniards, such programs were offered mainly in Manila by *colegios* and *universidades* almost exclusively run by religious orders.

It seemed that everywhere Eleanor looked into the education of Filipinos, religion ruled. She began to doubt the feasibility of separating church and state in the Philippine Islands. She also wondered about how to teach science, particularly Darwin's theory of evolution, without confusing her students, who were likely taught to believe the Bible story of creation as literal truth. How to do this without further antagonizing Padre Damián would be a challenge.

Eleanor and Señorita Santiago cleared away cobwebs and abandoned birds' nests from the ceiling trusses. They swept the dirt floor, and Sam's muchacho compacted the ground with a building pestle until the floor almost looked like a polished slab of stone. Sam and Pedro also tightened the joints of the table and chairs and replaced the damaged cane backrests and seats. Now, all they needed was a blackboard.

Sam must have read Eleanor's mind. "I reckon the children could make do with mats to sit on," he said. "But what ya want to do for a blackboard?"

Eleanor had sent a letter to the superintendent requesting a blackboard and other school supplies, but had yet to receive a reply. She'd foreseen this problem as she packed for her journey and, thus, added some school supplies among the books in the crate. Packing a blackboard, however, was impossible because of its size.

"Maybe we improvise with what we have?" Eleanor asked more than answered Sam's question. "Perhaps we could create the panel using the crate boards. Then, cover it with the black oilcloth?"

Sam raised his bushy, silvery eyebrows and, with a glint in his eyes, replied, "Dunno how well that'll work, but ye never know till we try!"

They removed and set aside the crate's oilcloth wrapping. Eleanor and Señorita Santiago took out the books and school supplies from the crate and laid them on the table for sorting, after which they intended to store them in the trunk, which had a lock that Eleanor hoped would discourage theft. Among the volumes they pulled out were Baldwin's primers, Heath's *Primary Arithmetics,* and *Little Nature Studies.* There were also supplemental reader's series, such as *Grimm's Fairy Tales* and *Robinson Crusoe for Youngest Readers.*

In Iowa, just before Eleanor had resigned from her teaching position, the state superintendent was replacing the prescribed schoolbooks with new ones. He'd directed all teachers to send him the old textbooks for proper disposal. Eleanor examined the books and found most of them in useable condition. Some simply needed re-gluing at the spines, and most only required light cleaning with a damp cloth. In her resignation letter to the superintendent, citing her teaching appointment in the

Philippine Islands, she offered to buy the old books. The sale proceeds of her family's farm had allowed her a modest budget for the purchase. She told the superintendent that while the books showed some wear and tear and were outdated regarding minor aspects, they could still be of great service to her Filipino students.

To her surprise, the Superintendent replied, stating he was moved by her "mission of mercy" in the new U.S. territory. Thus, he'd negotiated and procured the consent of state officials to donate the old books to her, instead, "to benefit God's poor, little, brown children." He added, "Consider this our humble contribution to America's great evangelical mission in the Orient." Acquiring the books without cost allowed Eleanor to buy school supplies. She thanked her donors, unmindful of their motivation, for their religious fervor served her cause.

Now, as the books reemerged in the light of day from their months-long internment, it was as if they were greeting her like the old friends they were. The pencils, crayons, writing paper, notebooks, phonetic cards, multiplication tables, and boxes of chalk likewise presented a welcome sight. Especially dear to her was her father's Remington typewriter, which she planned to bring back to her house. Father had written his most important letters and other documents on the machine, which was among the few precious family heirlooms her parents had left her.

Señorita Santiago appeared to have paused from her chore and was leafing through a book with a wistful expression on her fair and pretty face. A shaft of sunlight shone upon her hair, revealing stunning golden highlights among the bronzed ebony strands, which suggested that Señorita Santiago was a mestiza likely of Spanish and Filipino ancestry. It also informed her that Sam still had some patching to do on the roof.

"Are you all right, Señorita Santiago?" Eleanor asked. "Would you like to take a break?"

"O, no, ma'am. I am fine, gracias." Her assistant smiled her timid smile. "I am just... surprise."

"Surprised?" Eleanor arched an eyebrow. "By what?"

The mestiza grinned timorously, as if embarrassed by her confession. "¡O, no, nada! I am just admire... I do... I mean, did... not know there be many book of American student."

"I see," Eleanor said. "May I ask what subjects you taught?"

"O, just simple… speak, read, write… en Español, por supuesto. Basic mathematic. The girls, we teach cooking and sewing—what important for to be good wife, good mother. Our book, just *Doctrina Cristiana*. Many girls reach only third, fourth grade."

"And how about the boys?" Eleanor asked.

"Boys, if parents can afford, they graduate primary school, then secondary. If they gente ilustrado, that even more good. Mean they can go to Manila, study at Dominican colegio o Jesuit universidad. And the dream… go study in España. En Madrid o Barcelona. Some boys choose seminary, become padre. Men… they has more… cómo se dice… opciones?"

"You mean, options?" Eleanor volunteered. "Choices?"

"¡Sí! More choice for boys." Señorita Santiago nodded, before glancing down again, smiling her timid smile.

Eleanor recalled that, even in the states, most universities and their libraries were still closed to women, although young, pedigreed ladies like Maude and Arabella had begun to access programs traditionally reserved for men through pioneering women's colleges like Radcliffe.

Señorita Santiago glanced up at Eleanor. "You know, Señorita Karsten, poor girls like me, if lucky like me—they can only study in convento o colegio if they have padron o padrona. Then, they can be maestra. I am bless. Don Luis, Sr. send me to study in convento. He, my ninong—godfather. He is so good to me. That is why I am sad when he die."

Eleanor smiled. "I'm so sorry. But I'm sure you made your god-father proud. I, for one, am grateful to him because by sending you to school, I have you now to help me teach the children, especially the girls."

The mestiza teacher beamed. "Sí. Me, also. Por favor, Señorita Karsten—please, just call me, Estrella." She reached out to touch Eleanor's hand.

Eleanor grasped her assistant's hand. "Then, you must also call me Eleanor."

"Sí. Gracias. That nice… Eleanor." Estrella smiled.

Sam barged into the room, startling both women. "Here ye are— yer new blackboard!" He and Pedro brought in the makeshift writing board. "Where ya want it?"

Eleanor asked them to hang it on the north wall. The board turned out to be a decent size—about four feet tall by five feet wide.

"Looks promising!" Sam remarked after fastening it to the wall with hooks. "Would ya care to give it a try?" he asked Eleanor.

"With pleasure!" Eleanor exclaimed, smiling.

Sam had thoughtfully pegged the boards together so that they formed straight, horizontal lines behind the snug fabric, thus providing guide lines for fledgling scribes. Eleanor took a piece of chalk and began writing the alphabet in capital and small letters on the black oilcloth. The chalk didn't glide as smoothly as it would have had on a regular chalkboard because the fabric had some give as one applied pressure on it. But the task proved manageable with some patience. If one made mistakes, one simply erased them with a damp cloth to avoid creating the messy patch that dry wiping created. After Eleanor finished writing the C's, she stepped back to inspect her work and turned to her assistant. "Well, Estrella, what do you think?"

The trainee inclined her head as she assessed the success of Eleanor's exercise. "I think… is good." She nodded slowly, then vigorously. "Muy bien! Brava!" she declared, giggling, clapping, and hopping in place. She reminded Eleanor of her Radcliffe friends, particularly, Arabella.

Estrella's head jerked toward the door where something or, rather, someone grabbed her attention. "Kuya!" she cried, before running to him.

When Eleanor turned around to see who it was, she felt the blood drain from her face. For there was the man she knew as Luis's foreman—who took away the python from her backyard and made a gift out of it for her; the man whom she also suspected to be the leader of the gang that ambushed her carriage and held her captive in his arms; and who carried her to her bed on the night she fell ill.

"Señorita Karsten—ay!" Estrella exclaimed and giggled, covering her mouth. "Sorry—I mean… Eleanor. This, my older brother, Diego. I think you know him?"

"Why, yes. Of course." Eleanor bit her lower lip. *But no, not really, Estrella. For who can truly say who this mysterious brother of yours is?*

Diego removed his straw hat, smoothed down his wavy, chin-length bob, and tucked the errant locks behind his ears. "Buenos dias, señorita.

I come help," he said, peering up at her from a slanted angle. His smile was measured, but the mirthful mischief in his eyes—he couldn't hide.

"Uh… g-gracias, Diego," Eleanor said.

Eleanor observed the siblings: One was fair, the other, dark. A chiaroscuro of like images. She saw similarities in the shape and sparkle of their eyes, the way they smiled, and their habit of inclining their heads—which could be contemplative and charming, like Estrella's, or coquettish and consternating, like Diego's.

"What you want… me do?" Diego asked, his eyes fixed on Eleanor's.

The intensity of his gaze returned the blood to her face, but also made her cheeks burn. "Uh… um… l-let's see. Sam, c-could you use Diego's help… somewhere?"

"Sure can!" Sam exclaimed. "Follow me, Diego."

When the men left, Diego's presence still filled the room.

As Eleanor and Estrella finished sorting and storing away the books and school supplies, the sounds of digging and shoveling called out to them.

"Sam! What on earth are you all doing?" Eleanor cried as she and Estrella went outside.

The men had dug a big hole on the backside of the shed facing the rice field.

Sam chuckled. "Well, ya don't wanna have to run to yer house to use the latrine, don't ya? An' ya don't want the proper gals to have an excuse to go home just for that. So we buildin' ya an outhouse!" he chuckled. "This hole 'ere is what ya call a pozo negro—where all the unmenshables go." He guffawed, inciting the two other men to chuckle.

"Oh," was all Eleanor could say as her eyes wandered toward Diego.

He looked up at her from the pit with that now familiar sparkle in his eyes and twisted smile. It was close to noon, the warmest part of the day, which explained why he'd taken off his shirt—baring his lean, brown, muscular frame. She was astonished by the almost absolute hairlessness of his body, except for the dark patches in his armpits. Sweat was streaming from his broad chest to his navel, down to the soaked waistband of his trousers that were folded to his knees, thus exposing the huge knots of his calves. She was seized with an urge to wipe it all off.

She turned her back on him and returned to the classroom.

Yolanda arrived in a calesin with their lunch. She suggested a picnic under the mango tree, and Eleanor agreed. A soft breeze made it especially nice and cool in the shade. The maid brought a few banigs so that everyone could sit on the mats. Eleanor and Estrella helped her gather sheets of banana leaves from nearby trees on which to lay out their mini fiesta.

The men went off to the brook under the stone bridge to wash up. When they returned, they all looked fresh and decent. Diego particularly appeared civilized now that he had his shirt back on. He glanced and smiled at Eleanor, but to Yolanda, he burst into a loud mouthful of their language, to which everyone else chuckled.

"What's so funny?" Eleanor asked, trying to look amused when, in truth, she was piqued at being left out of the conversation.

Sam replied, "Diego remarked on the quantity of food Yolanda brought. He said, by the looks of it, we may 'ave to spend the night 'ere to finish our work—coz we be all sleepin' a long siesta stuffed like pigs!" He chuckled again.

"Oh," was all Eleanor could say—again. She seemed to be at a loss for words when Diego was present, and she despised the way the hombre appeared to enjoy it.

Everybody gathered around the food. Eleanor and Estrella sat with their legs folded together on one side. Yolanda, as usual, perched upon her haunches. Eleanor was glad Sam chose to sit beside her, while Diego claimed a spot across from her, next to his sister. Sam's muchacho, however, appeared hesitant to eat with them. Yolanda said something to him which seemed to put him at ease and made him glance at Eleanor with an apologetic smile as he sat beside the maid. Whatever Yolanda told him must have assured him that sharing a meal with la maestra Americana was acceptable.

Yolanda lifted the covers of the still steaming clay pots of boiled rice, chicken stewed in coconut milk, grilled catfish, and a spicy yet savory vegetable dish called *pinangat* that consisted of layered leaves of the *gabi* plant, spiced with the tiny, hot sili peppers and likewise stewed in coconut milk. Spicy viands cooked in coconut milk seemed to be the signature of Vicolano cuisine, while adding sili to almost everything was Yolanda's mark.

Eleanor's palate had somewhat adjusted to Yolanda's culinary preference. But before this, it was a treacherous cat-and-mouse game with the cook. Whenever Eleanor had complained of too much sili in their food, Yolanda diminished the spice to near banishment, only to add a little of it at a time, until their meals reached hopping heat levels again. Through this tango, however, Eleanor's taste buds had adapted to Yolanda's palate until their meals settled into a comfortable compromise that only required the maid to simply add more sili to her portions.

Upon perusing the picnic spread, Eleanor asked, "Yolanda, where are the knives and forks?" Her trusty maid appeared to have only brought serving spoons.

"But is picnic, señorita!" Yolanda exclaimed. After a brief silence, she giggled, inciting the others to laugh, likewise.

"Well, Leonor," Sam said, "I guess ya'll 'ave yer first lesson eatin' with your 'ands!"

"Here, señorita. Wash," Yolanda said while suppressing her laughter by covering her mouth. She picked up one of the bottles of filtered and boiled drinking water she'd brought and handed it to their lunch companions.

It wasn't long ago when Eleanor discovered, to her shock, that her maid had simply been pumping water from the well and serving it straight to her. She thus taught Yolanda how to filter and sterilize their drinking water.

Eleanor presently held out her hands beyond the mat, and the maid poured some of the water over them. The others did likewise.

"Eleanor, please roll up sleeve," Estrella advised. "Can get dirty."

"Dirty?" Eleanor asked.

"I think she meant 'messy,'" Sam volunteered.

Eleanor smiled and did as her assistant suggested. She noted how everyone scooped rice from the clay pot with a flat wooden spoon and laid a mound of it on the banana leaf before them. They then served themselves portions of the various foods straight onto their respective mounds of rice, which absorbed the various sauces. No one seemed bothered that their meal hence became a hodgepodge of flavors. Eleanor, instead, laid the viands around her rice.

She next observed how her companions fed themselves with their fingers. It wasn't clear to her how they were eating the saucy foods along with the rice without everything crumbling or slipping off and dripping from their fingers.

To her surprise, Diego, who smiled at her without the usual mischievous glint in his eyes, said, "Señorita, like this." He showed her how to separate a small piece of the chicken with the fingers of one hand, placed it on his rice, pressed and molded both rice and chicken into a mouth-sized ball, and, with the same fingers, picked up and shoved it into his mouth.

Everyone turned to Eleanor to view her reaction. She smiled at them, inhaled and exhaled deeply—determined to prove herself equal to the task. On her first attempt, the rice fell in loose morsels between her fingers, and the chicken sauce trailed down her forearm. Estrella was right. If she hadn't rolled up her sleeves, she would have soiled her blouse. She tried, again, with some success. The group continued to grin and smile at her efforts, good-naturedly, cheering her on.

Deboning the grilled catfish proved trickier. She couldn't seem to achieve it single-handedly as everyone else did. She attacked her fish with all ten fingers and dipped the deboned pieces into the puréed tamarind sauce that Yolanda said complemented the fish. The muchacha was right. Eleanor's tongue bloomed with the savory fish flavor, balanced with the tamarind's tartness.

Though she kept failing, Eleanor kept trying until she was somewhat eating like everyone else, though messier than anyone. She soon achieved a harmonious rhythm of alternately eating portions of chicken, fish, and vegetables with her rice and taking swigs of her bottled water. Like at the Gonzaga dinner, she sensed she'd won her fellow diners' respect—just by trying. Diego especially beamed and nodded at her with enthusiastic approval. She supposed he was proud to have taught la maestra Americana something.

Throughout the meal, she noticed him snatching peeks of her, as she did with him. It occurred to her he was good-looking in his own way—a way she hadn't known would appeal to her. He was a wild, dark son of the earth, and she was everything he wasn't.

For dessert, Yolanda served miniature pineapples. They looked like baby versions of the ones in Honolulu, but their yellow-orange skins suggested they were mature and ripe. The maid sliced them into crescent pieces, skins intact. The idea seemed to be to bite into them as one bit a watermelon wedge. After Eleanor sank her teeth into the sunny, golden flesh, she exclaimed, "Oh, my goodness! These are even sweeter and juicier than the ones in Honolulu!" She learned to slurp the juice like the others did before it dripped from their mouths.

"You like, señorita?" Sam's muchacho asked with a timid smile.

"Yes, indeed, Pedro," Eleanor replied, smiling brightly at him.

She had no idea the fellow could speak some English, for he never said much, and when he did, he spoke almost exclusively in Vicolano. She surmised he learned some of it from Sam. Pedro appeared to be quite older than Yolanda, yet there seemed to be a quiet amity between the pair, who constantly chatted in their language with hushed tones.

"Yup!" Sam exclaimed as he bit into his pineapple again and wiped his lips on the back of his hand. "These pineapples are small but mighty sweet. They're another specialty 'round 'ere, ya know. By the way, Leonor, did ya see the padre's niece? She arrived 'ere some nights ago."

"Oh? No, not yet," Eleanor replied, trying to focus on eating her pineapple and wiping the juices from her forearm before they reached her elbows.

"Word come 'round she's some kinda beauty!" Sam smiled.

Yolanda chuckled. "¡Porque ella es la hija del Padre Damián!"

Eleanor's jaw hung open, while Sam snorted into laughter and exclaimed mockingly, "What? The padre's niece is really his daughter? You don't say, Yolanda! Why, you naughty little tsismosa!" He wagged his finger at the maid and laughed along with her.

"All right. Stop, you two!" Eleanor declared. "Yolanda, I would have you know I don't approve of gossip. Especially nonsense like this!"

"¡Pero es verdad!" Yolanda whined, pouting. She glanced at Estrella and turned back to Eleanor, pointing her pursed lips at the native teacher. "Ask her—she know!"

Estrella frowned at Yolanda and shook her head. Diego and Pedro looked away with faint smiles on their faces.

"Enough, Yolanda!" Eleanor exclaimed. "No more of this." But the unsolicited suggestion lingered in her head. Could Señorita Maria Teresa truly be the padre's daughter? How was that possible? Yolanda reminded Eleanor that Magayon was a small town, and small towns knew their people's secrets, although they pretended otherwise.

Eleanor was startled by a half moan, half groan she heard from behind her. Yolanda gasped, and Pedro shooed away whatever was behind the mango tree. Eleanor turned around and saw the ragamuffin, Toto, peeking from the tree and gesturing as if he were eating imaginary food. Pedro stood to drive him away, but Eleanor interjected, "No, Pedro, please. He only wants food. Here, give some to him."

She picked up one of the empty serving tin plates and filled it with the remaining viands and rice and handed it to Pedro. As soon as Pedro offered the plate to the beggar, the latter grabbed it and sat on the ground, shoveling the food into his mouth, unmindful of his long hair falling all over his face, dipping into the sauce-filled plate. A breeze that blew from his direction carried scents of foul body odor and urine toward the group. Yolanda grimaced and pinched her nose. Toto paused from eating to glance up and smile at Eleanor, unmindful of bits of food around his mouth and lodged between his stained, rotted teeth.

Eleanor told Yolanda to hand him a bottle of water. Pedro grabbed it from the maid and did it himself. The vagrant guzzled the water as though he hadn't drunk in days. When he finished drinking and eating, he burped loudly, stood, tapped his belly, and handed the empty plate and bottle to Pedro. After bowing several times to Eleanor, Toto mumbled something unintelligible and shuffled off toward the cemetery.

Everyone exchanged glances, smiling. Yolanda shook her head. When Eleanor turned to Diego, he was smiling at her with a seeming new light in his eyes.

After lunch, everyone retired to their siesta spots. Yolanda and Estrella gathered and packed up the picnic litter and brought some of the mats inside the classroom. Eleanor surmised that was where the women planned to nap. The men were already slumped against the mango tree, their faces covered with straw hats. Sam started snoring, and Eleanor grinned. He had certainly embraced the afternoon custom. She, however, found it difficult to adopt the practice, unable to shake off thinking of what else she could be doing to expedite the school opening. Yet, it was especially warm now, and with everyone satiated by their hearty lunch, it seemed a good time to take a break.

"Señorita?" Yolanda called from the new school door. "Gusto?" She puckered her lips and pointed them at the blankets in her arms.

Eleanor grinned. Pointing to something, someone, or somewhere with one's lips was a habit among the natives that always amused her. "It's okay, Yolanda. You and Estrella go take your siestas. I think I'll take a walk and wash at the brook."

"Bueno. Pero, no go far," Yolanda warned, wagging her finger.

Eleanor grinned. "I won't."

She traversed the dirt road toward a section of the brook located in a beautiful woodland. When she reached the pebbled banks, she bent down to wash her sticky arms and hands. The water brushed against rocks and washed over pebbles, producing a soothing sound. It occurred to her how refreshing it would be to dip her feet in the cool water. She took off her stockings and Balmoral ankle boots and laid them on one of the huge volcanic rocks scattered around. It was amazing to think such behemoths had been slung from as far as the mouth of the Mayon.

She lifted her skirt and waded into the shallow water. She recalled that the last time she did this was with Maude and Arabella at Waikiki Beach while Miss Covell watched and laughed at the younger ladies playing like children in the ocean. And how she missed them! She wondered what her friends were doing at that moment. She prayed to Daragang Magayon for Maude to be safe from the headhunters of the north, Arabella from the harems of the south, and for Miss Covell to continue holding her own against the men of the Office of Public Instruction.

She was swinging her feet, splashing water against the rocks, when she heard crystalline wheet-wips from the treetops. She turned around and sought the source of the bird call. Suddenly, blue patches on glossy black lifted from a branch and disappeared into the denser canopy. The Asian fairy bluebird! She remembered it from a visit to Chicago's Lincoln Park Zoo. One of its aviaries featured a few specimens of the bird—memorable due to its stunning chromatic combination and distinctive sound. A squawking from another tree turned her attention to vibrant plumes of orange and green. Parrots! Perhaps she should look for a book on native fauna and flora. That would make for an excellent series of science classes.

The cool water washing over her feet triggered a sensation that validated Sam's wisdom in building an outhouse near the schoolhouse. But where to go? She scanned her surroundings for any unwelcome presence and grinned at her silly anxiety about a lack of privacy in the woods. She went to the opposite bank and hid behind one of the big rocks to relieve herself.

When she emerged from her cover, she lifted her skirt again to wade back to the other side of the brook. It was time to go back to the group. But when she returned to the rock where she left her boots and stockings, her things weren't there. She looked for them at another rock—to no avail. Her heart raced as her eyes frantically searched her surroundings. What if that crazy Toto took them? And what if he was still around—hiding and stalking her?

She swung around as she heard the crunching of pebbles underfoot from behind her. Her heart pounded out of her chest and heat shot up from her gut to her head when she saw, to her utter astonishment and dismay—Diego, holding her boots with one hand and her stockings with the other, asking in an innocent tone, "This—your?"

How long had he been watching her? Did he see her naked legs? Might he have spied on her as she retreated to necessary privacy behind the rock? She grabbed her apparel from him. "How dare you!"

"Que?" he asked with a perplexed expression.

"Leave me alone!" she cried.

His eyebrows met. "Lo siento, señorita. Pero, not good for you solo here."

"That's none of your business, and I don't need your help!" She sat on a rock, lifted her skirt over her knees to wear her stockings, and remembered he was still there—smiling with seemingly increased amusement. "If you won't go, then at least look away!" she exclaimed, gesturing for him to turn around.

He grinned and did as she asked, and she hid behind a rock. As she began putting on her stockings and boots, she was further enraged when she heard him whistling a happy tune. She peered from behind the rock to see if he was cheating and peeking at her. Just then, he glanced back at her, still smiling his stupid twisted smile.

"You like?" he asked, when she emerged from behind the rock.

"Like what?" she snapped back.

"El bolso." His eyebrows arched with a twinkle in his eyes.

"¿El… b…bolso?" She frowned.

"Iyó—sí!" He mimicked how a lady might walk, carrying a reticule—swinging his hips in an exaggerated feminine manner.

She surprised herself by snorting into laughter. When she managed to suppress her laugh, she said, "You meant—the reticule? The one you gave me? Sí. Muchas gracias. It's hermoso." She smiled ruefully.

"Iyó—magayon, eh? Like you." He pointed at her.

Magayon… the Vicolano word for beautiful. She felt flushed, and he reached out to touch her forehead with his palm and said, "¿Tienes fiebre, señorita?"

"Don't touch me." Eleanor slapped his hand away from her face. She shook her head. "I don't have a fever." She glanced up at him again and noted his concern. "Um. Sorry. Just warm, I guess." She fanned her face with her hand.

"Ah, iyó! Here…" He went off to pluck a fan-shaped palm nearby and fanned her and himself with it, sending his distinctive scent toward her—that smoky, earthy musk of him, now sweetened with the perfume of pineapples.

Her mind returned to the night of the ambush. *Who are you really*, she wanted to ask. But she doubted they had ample vocabulary between them to conduct such a conversation. Uneasy at finding herself alone with him in an isolated place, she said, "We better return to the others."

She turned to walk back toward the school when he grabbed her arm and swung her around to face him. Gazing into her eyes, he asked, "¿Por qué?"

She tried to push his hand away, but he kept his hold on her. "Listen, mister," she said, "if you think I don't know what you're up to, then you're in for a surprise! And stop touching me!"

"¿Por qué?" he repeated, his searing gaze—unrelenting.

"Why?" She shrugged. "Well, because we have to! Siesta time is over, and we should return to work. Trabajo. ¿Entiende? Plus, our friends may be worried about us."

"Da'í—no!" He blenched and winced. "Not that! Why you say nothing la emboscada?" His fingers tightened around her arm.

"Em… boscada?" Eleanor considered what he may have meant. "The ambush? Why I didn't say… more about it?" He nodded and she took a deep breath. "I… I don't know! No sé." She shot him a defiant look. "What do you think?"

"What I think?" He pointed his forefinger to his temple, as though it were a revolver's muzzle. "I think I dead if you tell. Pero, me no dead. So, you no tell. ¿Por qué?"

Why, indeed? Eleanor grasped at the threads of her thoughts and emotions. *Because… because you're part of my tightrope act, Diego.* Yet, even this wasn't the whole truth. Knowing he was also Estrella's brother added complications. And, if she was completely honest with herself… "I'm not sure why, Diego." She shook her head, biting her lip.

He sighed and released her arm. "Bueno…. segúro, mañana… we see." He nodded slowly, his countenance brightened with a glint of levity in his eyes and a confident smile.

What was he so sure of? And who did he think he was? His confidence in his cleverness piqued her. She acknowledged he was no simple peasant. After all, Luis trusted him as his foreman. Yet, he was no simple foreman either! If he was indeed the secret leader of the local insurrectionists, then he'd also outsmarted everyone. Including Luis. And Lieutenant Waterstone. Except her. She'd show him!

On the other hand, discounting his complicity in the ambush, he'd also proven only helpful to her. Even thoughtful and kind. If he meant to harm her, he'd have done it already. He hadn't. Therefore, she was inclined not to do anything that would harm him, either. That is, until the situation required otherwise. But she resolved to be wary of him.

Together, they walked in circumspect silence. When they returned to the group, she sensed everyone appraising her and Diego. Yet, none asked about where they'd been or what they did together.

CHAPTER 12

The School of the Devil

Eleanor anticipated the first day of school with great excitement. The classroom wasn't perfect, but it wasn't bad either. An old American flag Sam had hung in his previous church-sponsored classroom was now hoisted on a bamboo pole he'd erected in front of the building. The red, white, and blue lent the school an official image—with a decent outhouse, to boot.

She recruited Sam to oversee the gardening and carpentry classes and appointed Estrella to teach cooking and sewing. She explained to the assistant native teacher that their training sessions were meant to sharpen her English skills, review the day's class, and go over the next day's lessons. She planned some of that time teaching Estrella some of the lessons themselves.

Eleanor created and tacked a typewritten class schedule on the school door so the townspeople could see the wonders of learning in store for them and their children.

Morning:

7:00 - 7:30: Calisthenics

7:30 - 8:45: Gardening

8:45 - 9:00: Recess

9:00 - 10:00: Reading & Writing

10:00 - 11:00: Arithmetic

11:00 - 12:00: Science & Hygiene

Lunch Break: 12:00 - 1:00

Afternoon:

1:00 - 2:00 History, Civics & Geography

2:00 - 3:00: Girls' Domestic Arts & Home Economics; Boys' Carpentry

3:00: Class Dismissal

3:30 - 4:30: Teacher Training

4:30 - 5:30: Adult classes

In the prior week, Eleanor had asked Sam to accompany her to the *ayuntamiento*. They delivered a courtesy copy of the class schedule to Mayor Dizon and requested his help in announcing the school launch. They also raised the issue of funding, informing him about the mandate to put all school-age children in classes by the end of the year. El presidente wasn't ecstatic about the need to fund the school, yet regarding their request to broadcast the school opening, he appeared to have acted no later than the next day.

After breakfast, drumbeats rolled and roused everyone out of their houses. Yolanda cried, "¡Es el bandillo! ¡Vamonos!" She pulled her mistress to the street.

The bandillo appeared to be the equivalent of a town crier. Three native policemen marched throughout Magayon, armed with terrifying revolvers that may have been confiscated from seventeenth-century corsairs. It wasn't a far-fetched idea, for Eleanor had learned that San

Miguel Bay, northeast of Legazpi Port, used to be a pirate's lair until the Spaniards reclaimed it as a galleon repair dock.

Heralding the bandillo was a scruffy-looking runt of a fellow. Shoeless and dressed in ragged clothes, he nonetheless held up his chin and puffed on a big cigar as he beat his drum robustly as though he was announcing his importance. When the troop reached the street corner, they paused their little parade, whereupon one of the policemen unrolled a paper and read it aloud—announcing the day and time of the opening of the new American school.

The people gathered there variously glanced at Eleanor—without smiling at, or greeting her. When it was all over, everyone somberly walked away as in the aftermath of a funeral. Eleanor smiled at them, but they seemed reluctant to even acknowledge her presence. She recognized some of them as her neighbors, who seemed content to pretend she didn't live among them. They hid their curiosity behind their capiz shell or nipa grass-shuttered windows as she walked by their houses daily.

Eleanor had thus warned Yolanda to be discreet. But she assumed they already knew much about her, for she often caught the muchacha cheerfully chatting with them at the corner *sari-sari* store. There, on a pair of bamboo benches facing each other, store patrons sat at morning and afternoon *merienda* time, merrily munching on snacks and gossiping.

When Eleanor passed them on her way home from school, she always greeted them with a bright, smiling, *hello, how are you today*, yet they always turned away or pretended they didn't hear her. She had attributed their seeming snobbery to shyness or to simply not understanding English. Yet, after the school opening announcement, she was sure something else was afoot, for she had never known a people to be ruder for no apparent reason.

A familiar voice cried out as she and Yolanda walked back home. "Oh, Miss Karsten!" It was Mr. Ang—carrying a roll of banigs under each of his arms. Eleanor had ordered a dozen of the woven mats for her classroom. She now recalled him saying he would deliver them that day. Yolanda grabbed a roll and went ahead to their house.

"Well, Mr. Ang, what did you think of that?" Eleanor asked, grinning. "I wish I knew what these people are thinking."

"They are not thinking, madam," he replied. "They are feeling—afraid, that is."

"But what are they afraid of?" Eleanor asked.

Mr. Ang smiled tentatively. "I don't know if I am at liberty to answer that, madam."

"Please, Mr. Ang," Eleanor said, "tell me. I feel I'm fighting an enemy I can't see."

He glanced at her sideways. "During your confinement, in the aftermath of your ambush, the soldiers were rather rough on the people. They searched their homes, interrogated them, and detained some of them in prison, where they were roughed up some more. Lieutenant Waterstone put the fear of the American eagle's claws in them. Now, they say that the Americano has two faces: the one that smiles, and the other that pecks your eyes out."

"Oh. I'm sorry to hear that," Eleanor said. "I'm aware the lieutenant may have conducted some searches and interrogations. Perhaps some of them got a little out of hand. But why would the people respond to my school opening as though I were Lieutenant Waterstone?"

Mr. Ang grinned. "Oh, but you see, madam—to them, there is no difference. You are both Americanos. You may be the American who smiles, but the lieutenant is the American who pecks at their eyes. The people cannot be in a more difficult position. The padre is another problem. If they allow their children to attend your school, they stand to be condemned by the priest. But if they refuse to let their children go to your school, they are worried the soldiers would punish them. It is the classic 'damned if you do, damned if you don't' situation."

Eleanor turned silent, and Mr. Ang continued, "Even el presidente knows he is risking the padre's goodwill just by announcing your school opening. He needs the church's blessing to maintain his political influence. Yet, he also needs to implement the new American government's policies to retain his post. That is why they also say el presidente rows his boat in two rivers."

The Instik man and la maestra Americana continued to walk to her house. When they arrived, Yolanda ran down the stairs and freed Mr. Ang of his remaining load of mats. And Eleanor continued to ponder upon what he said.

October 6, 1901

Dear Miss Covell,

I hope this finds you well. I, on the other hand, had a bit of an adventure with malaria. Thus, forgive my delay in responding to your last letter. Please don't worry. I'm fine now, I assure you, and, as they say here, fit as a carabao!

I'm also happy to share I'm about to launch our school. In this regard, I'm concerned, though, that the superintendent appears to be merely relying on our personal resources to shoulder the initial costs of establishing our schools. I hear this has inspired some innovative ideas on school funding.

A recent article in the Manila Sun (which we, unfortunately, receive almost a week late), for example, reported on the successful partnership between our Manila colleagues and their local officials to fund their schools. Municipalities that are already electrified passed resolutions requiring their residents to install lightbulbs in front of their houses to serve as street lighting. The regulations impose a fine on those who fail to obey the mandate, and it's the fines that then fund their schools.

I chuckled over this rather creative school funding measure. Unfortunately for us, Magayon is far from electrification. Although I've raised the issue of school funding with our mayor, he hasn't done anything about it. It may well rest on me to create my own innovative solution. However, since my illness has already much delayed our school opening, it seems more important for me now to launch the school and address its funding later.

My friend, please forgive me for asking about another delicate matter. Have you heard when the superintendent might be sending our paychecks? I inquire not for myself, as I still have some of the cash I'd withdrawn from the bank in Manila. It's rather for my assistants, Miss Estrella Santiago, and a former army sergeant, Samuel Munro, who have graciously been serving without pay and volunteering the services of their family and domestic help.

I'd written the superintendent requesting confirmation of Mr. Munro's appointment to teach carpentry and gardening classes. Unfortunately, I have not received a reply, nor an answer to my query about the status of our paychecks.

The superintendent's lack of response makes me feel especially guilty about declining the padre's offer of the parish school building, for it is my obstinacy on the matter that's now imposing the material burden on my assistants to support my decision. I know you, most of all, understand why I couldn't abide running my school under the church's auspices. But, I must confess, there are times I doubt the wisdom of my choice. Oh, my dear friend, how thorny is our path, we who try to live by our convictions.

At the risk of leaving you with the impression I only wrote to whine about my problems, I'm sorry to have to end my missive here. I have an early start tomorrow, our first day of school. Next time, I hope to share better news.

*Until then, please take care. If you hear from Maude
and Arabella, please give them my love, too. I miss you
all so very much.*

Love,
Eleanor

On the first day of classes, Eleanor and her assistant teachers arrived at the school at six thirty in the morning. It was now quarter past eight — and, still, no student had arrived. Eleanor pretended to be writing in the register, as if there was anything to record. Estrella, for the umpteenth time, it seemed, straightened the mats on the floor. Sam stationed himself outside, as if allowing the Thomasite the privacy she needed to lick her wounded pride. After fifteen more minutes without anyone coming, Eleanor knew they had to devise a new enrollment strategy.

She was about to call in Sam to discuss it, when he barged into the classroom declaring, "Miss Karsten, behold! Your first student!" She'd have to talk with him about his seeming habit of barging in and startling them out of their skins. She was glad, though, that Sam remembered to address her as "Miss" and not its Spanish equivalent, given the superintendent's order to establish English as the mandatory language of schools.

Their first student was a little girl dressed in a very adult camisa at saya. Her carefully combed, oiled hair fell in loose cascades to her waist, further dwarfing her. Nonetheless, she carried herself with the grace and dignity of a princess, which made her look almost tall. Yet, she moved with such fastidious, self-conscious pomposity as to render her comical. Eleanor and Estrella exchanged glances, suppressing their laughter while signaling silent agreement over the girl being simply adorable.

Following behind the girl, carrying a child's chair, was a woman who, judging from her humble clothes, appeared not to be the girl's mother but, likely, her nanny. The nanny set down the chair on the mat at the front and center of the classroom. The girl then sat on the chair while her nanny sat on the mat beside her. How progressive of the child's parents to have sent the nanny to school along with their daughter! Yet, the nanny was an adult and, therefore, in the wrong class. Eleanor thus asked Estrella to inform the servant accordingly, and to invite her to attend the afternoon adult classes, instead.

"But she not come to study, Miss Karsten," Estrella explained. "This yaya come to chaperone her alaga."

"All the more reason to exclude her from the classroom," Eleanor retorted. "We aim to foster confidence and self-sufficiency in our students."

Estrella explained to the nanny why she couldn't stay. The girl protested her yaya's departure, pulling on the servant's arm. Eleanor wondered whether she should intervene, but was curious to see what would happen if she didn't. After what sounded like multiple reassurances from the nanny, the girl finally let go of her. The servant exited the classroom and instantly reappeared outside the window closest to her charge, smiling encouragingly at the girl.

"Good morning, señorita," Eleanor said to the girl. "Please state your name and age."

The girl glanced at her with a puzzled look.

Estrella helped by saying, "¿Cómo te llamas, niña?"

The girl turned to her nanny and, after some coaxing and prompting from the yaya, replied timorously, "Mi nombre... es... Asunción Alarcon."

"Thank you, Miss Alarcon," Eleanor smiled, writing the student's name on the enrollment register. "And how old are you, please?"

Estrella translated the question to the girl, who answered, "Once años, po."

"Eleven years old?" Eleanor glanced at Estrella, who nodded.

A squat and stocky boy suddenly entered the classroom, dressed in short pantaloons and a *camiseta,* a simple white cotton shirt that Eleanor had observed was worn by native men usually as a mere undershirt to their Barong Tagalog. Yet, it was clean and presentable.

After surveying the room, the boy came forward and sat beside the girl, who reacted with surprising disdain for him. With a "hmph!" she stood, picked up her chair, and moved it away from him while keeping to the front of the classroom.

Eleanor asked Estrella to tell the girl she shouldn't put her chair in front because she would be blocking the view of her classmates. Estrella communicated the instruction to the girl, who, again, stood, picked up her chair, set it under the window where her nanny was watching, and sat. Thereupon, the boy also stood, surprisingly left the classroom, and, after about ten minutes, returned with a small wooden crate, set it down beside the girl, and sat on it—looking proud of himself. The girl harrumphed again, turned her back to him, and crossed her arms.

"Well, well," Eleanor said, grinning. "I say that's enough musical chairs for the day! What is your name and age, young man?"

The boy stood and replied confidently, if a bit too loudly, "My name is meester Bayani Burgos, ma'am! And I am twelve years old!"

Sam peeked from behind the door, grinning. "I guess ya met our little hero! That's what he done tell me his name means when he was ma' student."

"Yes, I can see that he is, indeed, quite the little hero." Eleanor chuckled and noticed that Bayani suddenly lost his smile. She went to him and placed her hand on his shoulder, saying, "Bayani, I wasn't laughing at you. In fact, I'm delighted you seem to speak English so well."

The boy recouped his beaming countenance and exclaimed, "Yes, ma'am!" He ribbed Miss Alarcon and raised his chin at her. The little princess harrumphed again.

Sam chuckled. "Well, if y'all are ready for more, there are other children out here lined up with their parents. Should I ask the adults to remain outside?"

"Yes, please, Mr. Munro," Eleanor replied. "And do explain to them that today's first lesson is about independence!"

Sam saluted. "Aye, aye, captain!" His chuckling continued to reverberate from the outside. He addressed his yet unseen audience. "¡Atención, por favor!" he said and relayed Eleanor's instructions in the hybrid language.

Two more girls and three more boys from the ages of about seven to thirteen entered the classroom. Together with little Miss Asunción Alarcon and Mr. Bayani Burgos, that made seven students in all. Seven! They must do better than this. Eleanor tried not to show her disappointment by focusing on registering each student with Estrella's help.

Some parents followed the example of Asunción's nanny and watched the class from outside the windows. They sporadically sent smiles of reassurance or scolded their children, who frequently turned their heads to the windows, checking to see if their guardians were still there, and, upon confirming the adults' continued presence among the spectators, sent them anxious and, sometimes, tearful glances.

When the registration process was complete, Eleanor stood from behind her desk and walked around it to stand close to where her students sat on the mat-covered floor. Except for Bayani, who appeared to be enjoying himself, they wore faces of stone or dread. She invited Estrella and Sam to join her in front of the classroom and requested the native teacher to translate her speech as she delivered it.

In a slow, enunciated manner, Eleanor stated, "Welcome to your new school, boys and girls! I am your principal teacher, Miss Eleanor Karsten. And these are your other teachers, Miss Estrella Santiago and Mr. Samuel Munro."

The assistant teachers smiled and nodded as their names were called, and the children glanced at them with wary countenances.

Eleanor continued, "Here, we shall learn to speak, read, and write English."

Bayani raised his hand. Eleanor was pleased to see that Sam had already taught him classroom etiquette. "Yes, Bayani?"

He stood, back straight, chest out, declaring, "But, ma'am, I already know English!" Putting his hands on his hips, he glanced around, smiling. Asunción grunted another harrumph, which didn't deter him from continuing to look pleased with himself.

Eleanor smiled. "Yes, and that's very good, Bayani. But you will know English even better. For example, you will learn how to read, write, and pronounce the alphabets that you see on the board behind me. Then, you will be able to read books like this." She picked up one of the Baldwin's primers and held it up to them, leafed through some of its pages, and showed them some of the illustrations inside.

The children let out a collective expression of awe.

"We will give each of you a book to study, if you promise to take good care of it."

After Estrella translated this, the children jumped into standing, clapping, and chattering.

"Children!" Eleanor interjected. "¡Silencio, por favor! Settle down, please, and sit." Her palms patted down the air, and the children immediately obeyed. "Thank you! Now, for the sake of peace and order, we have some rules to follow. And our first rule is this: Pay attention. Can you repeat that for me so I know you heard it?"

The students turned to Estrella, who coached them into declaring in timorous, near unison, "Pay attention!"

"Good!" Eleanor exclaimed. "In addition, we will be respectful and helpful to each other. We will be disciplined and devoted to our studies. And, if you dedicate yourselves to learning, you could become great men and women—leaders who, then, can be of great service to others."

Bayani raised his hand again. Eleanor gestured his permission to speak. "You mean, ma'am, I can be like Admiral Dewey?" He had the countenance of a child on Christmas morning.

Eleanor smiled at the boy. "Yes, of course, Bayani! You can be like Admiral Dewey or any other hero you want to be if you study and work hard enough for it."

The boy's face glowed with delight, as if his wish was already granted.

Turning to all her students, looking them each in the eye, Eleanor declared, "Remember: Each one of you, whoever you are, no matter what your or your family's circumstances are, can be whoever you want to be if you put your mind and heart into it. But, first, you must get a good education because a good education is your key to success. It will help you realize your dreams. It is also the one thing that no one can take away from you—whoever they are. And we, your teachers, can help you attain this in this school that, contrary to rumors, is not the School of the Devil, but *your* school: La Escuela del Buen Conocimiento—The School of Good Knowledge!"

October 11, 1901

Dear Eleanor,

> *I received your letter about you getting malaria
> with much concern. I pray you are fully on the mend,
> especially now that you're opening your school, at last.*

In my case, I'm happy to report my head remains safe and secure from the northern tribes.

In all seriousness, these people are far from their reputation as decapitators and cannibals. They're not cannibals at all, though they may have begun that way in their history. And their headhunting forays are limited to revenge killings between rival villages, which serve some kind of basic, ritualistic justice. An eye for an eye, you could say. Yet, I confess I secretly check for a certain bluish tattoo among them, the mark of a successful headhunter. Overall, they are the friendliest people with a great sense of humor and a good lot of common sense. We Americans could learn a thing or two from them.

They have here, for example, a festival of the maidens where girls old enough for marriage get to choose their husbands. The selection process would strike our puritan sensibilities as libertine or "uncivilized," but, on careful consideration, is simply pragmatic. All girls and boys eligible for marriage gather at a big party where the young stags present their best selves by way of dance skills and adornments of beads, feathers, and carved bone trinkets to impress a maiden to choose him for a trial marriage later that night.

Yes, dear, you read it right: trial marriage. The young women who've chosen a partner are assigned individual honeymoon huts to allow them to test the young men's "other skills" to ensure they're compatible in this most intimate of human encounters. To me, this bests the New York debutante season.

Among my greatest pleasures is being carried around here in a sedan by a pair of warriors wearing only gee strings. It's a comfortable way to travel to mountain village schools or go sightseeing at the stone-walled rice terraces that these people's ancestors had literally carved out of the mountainsides with their bare hands and primitive tools.

Supplies are conveniently carried on the backs of "polistas" who are capable of bearing loads of up to a hundred pounds in baskets called "chuggies," which have shoulder straps. They use a staff to balance themselves against their load and for climbing steep mountain trails. The polistas also carry bolos for clearing vegetation and defending us against robbers.

Overall, I'm content with my conditions here, except for the superintendent's failure to provide me with textbooks. I have had to write everything on the blackboard for reading and writing classes. I pick a short poem or paragraph from books or English newspapers and copy it on the board. It is a tedious, time-consuming process. I cannot wait to get the supplies we've been promised by month's end. I hope books are among them.

Though this has been an interesting and rewarding experience, I cannot wait to return to the mainland. With or without Father's blessing, I'm set on going to Cambridge for MIT's architecture program and fulfilling that dream, hatched in Honolulu, prompted by you.

I bid you farewell for now and wish you best of luck in your school launch! Tell me all about it next time.

Yours truly,
Maude

Every day since the school opened, Eleanor received a few more students. According to Estrella, this could be due to the rumor that la maestra Americana promised the children their own schoolbooks—a privilege which, the native teacher stressed, used to be enjoyed only by the *cacique* or ruling and wealthy classes. By the end of the first week, the school had gained ten more students. Yet, for Eleanor, this wasn't enough.

Through Yolanda, Eleanor utilized the grapevine at the corner store to spread the word that if parents wanted their children to qualify for the civil service monthly-salaried positions, graduating from The School of Good Knowledge was required. By the end of the second week, the school added ten students to its roll.

Still, Eleanor was dismayed. Estrella informed her that their problem was Padre Damián, who had been spreading his own rumors. He told his congregation, which was the whole town, that no book equaled the *Doctrina Cristiana*, except the Bible, which only priests had the authority to read and the wisdom to understand. He also claimed that La Escuela del Buen Conocimiento was a false name that the devil, through la maestra Americana, gave the school to confuse and deceive God's people into desiring forbidden knowledge and making them believe mankind originated from a mere monkey. "Tell me, any of you, whom God created greater than the angels: Can you really believe you only came from a matsin?" he'd reportedly roared from the pulpit, instigating the faithful to likewise roar into laughter. Eleanor could almost hear them from her house.

One afternoon, while Eleanor and Estrella were going over the next day's lessons in the schoolhouse, someone came by to see them.

"Why, Lieutenant Waterstone!" Eleanor exclaimed in surprise. "To what do we owe this... visit?"

"I understand you're having problems with school attendance." He removed his hat and pinned it under his left arm. "I've come to help."

Eleanor noticed him eyeing Estrella as he spoke. "Pardon my manners," Eleanor said. "May I introduce my assistant, Miss Estrella Santiago? Estrella, this is Lieutenant—"

"James," the soldier interjected, smiling at the assistant teacher in a way Eleanor hadn't seen him smile: the smile of a man who very much liked what he was looking at. "Lieutenant James Waterstone at your service, Miss Santiago." He reached for Estrella's hand and performed a gesture of a kiss.

With seeming trepidation, Estrella replied softly, "T-thank you, s-sir." She bowed her head and kept her gaze downward.

Eleanor broke the ensuing awkward silence. "Lieutenant, what do you mean by wanting to help?"

The officer's eyes reluctantly peeled themselves away from Estrella and turned to Eleanor. "Ah. Yes. Simple, Miss Karsten. I offer the persuasive force of my troop to herd the little ponies to your school." He glanced around the classroom and added, "I assure you, after we're done, you'll need a much bigger classroom. Heck, perhaps an entirely new school!" He laughed, while the two teachers stayed mum.

Eleanor recalled what Mr. Ang, including what Sam and Yolanda, later, had shared—about how, during her malarial confinement, the lieutenant and his men terrorized the natives with brusque searches and seizures, sweeping arrests and detentions, and torturous interrogations. She was convinced that this, more than Padre Damián's rhetoric, was why the people did not trust her. They blamed her for the actions of the soldados Americanos. She could not allow Waterstone to further damage her relationship with the community.

"I appreciate the offer, lieutenant," Eleanor replied. "But I'm sure the current situation just demonstrates the natural human tendency to be wary of newcomers. Like us. Their fear of change is also understandable. They just need time, like we do, to show them we're sincere."

The officer snickered. "Yeah, but it don't hurt to give them a little push!"

"I'd hardly call pointing your guns at them a little push, lieutenant!" Eleanor exclaimed, surprising herself. "How can they see us as different from the Spaniards, if we're using the same tactic of forcing them 'by the sword,' so to speak? If these people love their children as much as we Americans love ours, and I venture to say they do, then it's simply a matter of time before they realize it's for the good of their children to send them to school."

Lieutenant Waterstone scoffed. "I wish I could be as optimistic as you, Miss Karsten. Besides, I understand you're at war with the padre. And during a war, a show of force is necessary. Why don't you use all the resources you have at your disposal—namely, me and my men?

Shock them into following the rules, I say!" He grinned and turned to Estrella. "What do you think, Miss Santiago?"

Estrella glanced up, her face blanched. "W-who, sir… m-me?"

"Yes, you, miss!" Lieutenant Waterstone pointed at Estrella, smiling.

"But I not s-sure… I h-have… say in this," Estrella said.

"Well, I happen to be interested in what *you* say about this," Lieutenant Waterstone reprised. "So, señorita, do share with us your valued opinion."

Estrella clasped her hands. "I t-think… m-mees Karsten is r-right." She returned her gaze downward.

Lieutenant Waterstone chuckled. "Is that your opinion or your obedience speaking?"

Estrella glanced up at him—this time, with defiance. "L-lieutenant, I no s-slave to nobody! I just believe Miss Karsten correct!"

The soldier's laughter turned into a sarcastic smile. He shifted his gaze between the two ladies. "Oh, I see. I see what's going on here. It's women versus man, isn't it?"

"Lieutenant," Eleanor interjected, "a battle of the genders is *not* what this is. You asked us what we think, and we told you. If you insist on this show of force despite what we said, you will definitely set me up for failure in my mission. And if that happens, I would have to deliver a full report, including an account of your unnecessary use of force, to the superintendent, who would surely raise it with Commissioner Taft. Now, please, we have much work left to do!" She waved her hand to the door.

The soldier smirked. "Thought I'd give you ladies a helping hand. Seems you don't want it. But if you change your mind, just come and see me. I'll be waiting—just as I'm still waiting, by the way, for you, Miss Karsten, to tell me if your memory has improved enough to remember any more details about your ambush." He shot her that steely-edged smile of his. "Well, has it? Don't you remember anything that could be helpful to me in *my* mission?"

Eleanor was flustered. "I… I have said all I could say on the subject!"

"All right, then." He smiled as he returned his cap on his head. "You ladies know where to find me, as I sure do know where to find you—both of you!"

He sauntered to the door. When he closed it behind him, Estrella slumped in her chair, covered her face, and burst into crying. Eleanor sat beside her assistant and caressed her back, though she, too, felt shaken.

Eleanor decided to accept Doña Ximena's invitation to her welcome dinner for Señorita Maria Teresa. It was an opportunity to make up for her faux pas with Padre Damián. She realized that, instead of sending him a letter, she should have met with him in person and recruited Luis's help not only as a translator but advocate. She might have had a better chance of persuading the priest to respect her point of view or, perhaps, reach a compromise. Now, her punishment was proving steep, for it was the children who suffered by her imprudence.

She understood now what Sam and Luis meant by not making an enemy of the priest. Yet, she also couldn't believe anyone could be so gullible to the padre's outrageous claims. The damned priest truly held the people's souls in his grip! The sari-sari gossip vine informed her that most parents "would rather keep their children ignorant than have them go to hell," citing Padre Damián's sermon quoting the biblical passage, "For what doth it profit a man to gain the whole world, yet suffer the loss of his soul?"

Where is my precious independence now? How should I bend to the padre without betraying my principles? She was still clueless about what to say or do to convince Padre Damián to agree to a truce. Yet, she also needed to talk with him—now, in person, and, preferably, in a congenial setting. A festive celebration hosted by the Gonzagas in honor not only of Our Lady of the Harvest but also of the padre's niece was an auspicious occasion to induce the better angels of the padre's nature to prevail.

At class dismissal on Friday before the fiesta weekend, Bayani approached Eleanor. "Miss Karsten, for you," he said with a bright smile as he handed her a folded piece of paper. The black, shining orbs of his irises reflected Eleanor's delighted countenance.

"What's this?" She unfolded what appeared to be a page torn off a notebook she gave each student. In neat and careful cursive, heavily pressed on the paper as to seem almost etched, the note said:

Dear Miss Karsten,

Please come to my home for lunch on fiesta day. My mother cook best food! I hope you come. I want my family to meet my favorite teacher.

Sincerely yours,
Bayani Burgos

"Why, thank you, Bayani!" Eleanor exclaimed. "This is a well-written invitation! Did you write it yourself?"

The boy beamed and nodded enthusiastically.

"Congratulations on an excellent job!" she said, reaching out to ruffle his short, spiky mop of thick black hair. "I'll be happy to join you and your family."

The boy flashed an even brighter smile before skipping and hopping out of the classroom.

CHAPTER 13

Our Lady of the Harvest

The whole town dressed in grand and festive attire like a lady all decked out to go to a ball. Houses, great and small, decorated their windows and fences with coconut palms folded and woven into artistic designs of scallops, pinwheels, and scepters erupting into joyous sprays. Women and children created flowers from a dyed, woven material that Yolanda called *sinamay,* embellishing everything with the vibrant blooms. The men hung colorful paper buntings from house to house, which connected and seemed to unite everyone in the fiesta spirit.

Yolanda made a few coconut palm sprays and adorned them with red and yellow sinamay roses. Eleanor helped put them up on the front of their house and fence entrance. The Thomasite was pleasantly surprised when their neighbors began acknowledging her with nods and smiles.

The feast of Nuestra Señora de la Cosecha was launched on the eve of the saint's feast day with a religious procession around the town plaza. Eleanor and Yolanda went to watch the spectacle, along with what seemed to be hundreds of people, some of whom, the muchacha claimed, came all the way from surrounding hills and mountains and neighboring towns.

The religious faithful paraded around the quadrangle, holding candles and fingering rosaries—the intonations of their rote praying humming to the solemn beating of a drum by the bandillo drummer, who was now wearing shoes and clean clothes. The señoras and señoritas looked like queens and princesses veiled in Spanish lace and dressed in their Sunday frocks, while the men, rich and poor alike, seemed to be all caciques in their Barong Tagalogs.

A pair of shoeless acolytes in white tunics announced the arrival of the high priest of the august rites by sanctifying his path with clouds of incense. In his red silk vestments embroidered with gold and silver, Padre Damián appeared no less than a medieval king. Marching at a ceremonious pace, he sprinkled both sides of the crowd with holy water from an aspergillum. Those who got drizzled blessed themselves with the sign of the cross.

Eleanor ducked as the padre passed her—not so much to avoid the holy water as to prevent being seen by him and the Gonzagas, who followed close behind him.

Oddly, it wasn't Doña Ximena who held onto her son's arm, but a young Spanish mestiza whom Eleanor guessed was the padre's celebrated niece. Señorita Maria Teresa wore an ivory *peineta* comb under a pearl-white lace veil and a gown of emerald silk that shimmered in the light of a thousand candles and accentuated the red highlights in her hair. She was an image of Spanish royalty. She and Luis looked made for each other. To one who just chanced upon the scene, the parade might have seemed to be the couple's wedding march.

Eleanor was struck with a surprising shot of jealousy. How reassuring it must be to be certain of belonging to a place and people! While she valued her independence, she sometimes wondered if she was missing out on the consolations of social convention—particularly, a husband and children to call her own.

The parade culminated with the appearance of the elaborately decorated *carro* or "float" of the Nuestra Señora de la Cosecha, hoisted on the shoulders of men dressed in the ominous-looking black uniform of some religious fraternity. The people knelt and crossed themselves as the glorious statue of the Mother of God, akin to a harvest goddess, passed by them. The saint was bedazzling in her silvery blue tunic embroidered with lustrous seed pearls and brilliant rhinestones, cloaked with a mantle of gold brocade. The saint's carro was ablaze with countless candles and oil torchieres and skirted with garlands of fresh flowers and coconut fronds. Leafy sugarcanes and rice stalks heavy with grain wrapped around the four columns that held up a white silk canopy over the saint.

Eleanor's eyes widened with shock on seeing that the Lady of Good Harvest was clutching an exposed, bleeding heart—pierced by a dagger. Ropes of tiny yet fragrant miniature-like white roses that Yolanda called *sampaguitas* were arranged as if dripping from the goddess's wounded heart, radiating like crepuscular rays shining on baskets of fresh vegetables and fruits. The blossoms' achingly sweet perfume saturated the air around the carro and left a trail of olfactory blessing behind it.

Suddenly, a woman shrieked from the front end of the procession, shattering the solemnity of the religious cortège. A wave of troubled buzzing swept over the processionaries and spectators, and the parade abruptly stopped. A dark tatterdemalion pushed his way through the crowd, dragging a fair, young lady by the arm. Eleanor was stunned to realize they were none other than Toto the vagrant, pulling a screaming and disheveled Maria Teresa. Chasing after them was Luis who grabbed and punched Toto, knocking him to the stone-flagged floor. Bombinations of disbelief and concern reverberated across the plaza. Padre Damián soon appeared, yelling and cursing in Spanish. Maria Teresa ran to her uncle and tucked herself into his arms, sobbing. With her sleeve torn off, her veil gone, and her peineta comb hanging loosely on her tangled locks, she almost looked like a ragamuffin herself.

Lieutenant Waterstone arrived galloping on a princely white steed, accompanied by infantrymen. A couple of the soldiers pulled up the half-conscious tramp to his feet. Eleanor gasped as Toto's head briefly swung back on his limp neck, showing a bloody nose and mouth, before it hung back down again, curtained by long, stringy, and greasy graying hair strands. Eleanor spied a flash of recognition and terror in Padre Damián's eyes as he, too, saw Toto's face. He immediately blessed himself with the sign of the cross.

Toto suddenly cackled and screeched, shouting what sounded like invectives at Padre Damián, who ran away with his niece toward the rectory. Luis followed after them, along with Doña Ximena. Lieutenant Waterstone ordered his men to take the hellion away and announced to the crowd, "All right, folks! Show's over! Disperse peacefully and go home!"

Eleanor glanced at Yolanda. "What was that? Did you get what Toto yelled at the padre?"

Yolanda snickered. "Toto say Padre Damián es el diablo."

Eleanor grinned. "Well, we can't blame Toto." She added in a whisper to Yolanda, "That priest could very well be the devil himself!"

Yolanda chuckled. "Toto also say to padre: You steal my angel, now I steal yours."

"Hmm. I wonder what that means," Eleanor said.

Yolanda shrugged her shoulders, heaving from laughter. "¡Toto está loco!"

On fiesta morning, the shocking incident during the preceding evening appeared to have been forgotten in the jubilation of ringing church bells and rousing beats of a marching band that went around town announcing it was time to eat, drink, and celebrate the blessings of Our Lady of the Harvest. Eleanor braced herself for a full day's schedule that included lunch at Bayani's and dinner at the Gonzagas.' Yolanda sounded as if she was also totally engaged that day, on invitation from some of her fellow muchachas serving in other households.

Yolanda called for a calesin to take her mistress to Bayani's house. She informed Eleanor that she'd arranged for the same cochero to fetch and take her to the Gonzagas in the afternoon. The maid also handed Eleanor a food basket that contained various fruits and canned corned beef and sardines. "Is pasalubong, señorita," Yolanda explained. "Good to bring gift to Bayani family."

As the calesin drew near Bayani's house, Eleanor saw her favorite student sitting at the bottom of the bamboo stairs of a nipa hut. He was alternately cupping his chin and wringing his hands. Seated at the top of the stairs was a man holding and massaging a white rooster while puffing on a cigar. To one side of the hut, on the ground, a woman sat on her haunches stirring a clay pot balanced upon three rocks over a wood fire. A girl stood beside the woman, handing her condiments and other ingredients to add to whatever was cooking in the pot.

As soon as Eleanor's calesin pulled up to the hut, Bayani hopped to his feet and hollered to the house. A brood of children ran down the steps with the man holding a rooster. The woman and girl looked up and paused from their cooking. Everyone lined up in front of their hut, smiling in the direction of their approaching guest.

"Welcome! Welcome, Miss Karsten! Thank you for coming to our humble home!" Bayani cried, pulling Eleanor to his family, who stood like a welcoming committee. He waved his hand to them as he introduced each to Eleanor. "This, my ináy. This, my itáy. This, my brother and sisters. Lolo and Lola are upstairs." He smiled ruefully. "Is hard for them to go downstairs."

Eleanor's head swam in the swirl of faces before her. She counted seven girls younger than Bayani, in addition to an older sister holding a toddler boy saddled on her hip. The siblings looked like a ladder—each rung, a child shorter and younger than the one preceding her.

Bayani's father was a thin, toasted man, holding the rooster in one hand and his cigar in the other. He wore a big smile that displayed tar-stained, crooked teeth. A slim, short, and graying woman with sunken eyes and cheeks was Bayani's mother, who obscured her timorous smile with her fingers. Eleanor warmly shook each of their shy hands and handed the gift basket to Bayani's mother, who flushed and grinned nervously and bowed her head repeatedly to Eleanor.

Bayani pulled Eleanor up the steps that led to the hut. Seated on one of two rattan chairs was a shrunken, old woman with an extremely bent back, watery eyes, and ashen hair gathered into a pusod. Bayani gestured toward her and said, "This, my lola." The old woman grabbed her cane and attempted to rise from her seat with trembling knees.

Eleanor vehemently shook her head, exclaiming, "Oh, no, señora— please don't bother!"

Bayani rushed to his grandmother to help her sit back and translated what Eleanor had said into Vicolano. The old woman bowed her head at Eleanor and slumped back into her chair.

Bayani next pointed to an old man in a hammock that appeared to be simply a bedsheet gathered and tied at the ends and secured to the rafters with ropes. "And that, my lolo," said the boy. The old man raised his pigmented bald head to peek at Eleanor. He smiled and smacked his lips that soon receded into his toothless gums before he sank back into the hammock.

Apart from Bayani's grandfather, who was wearing a camiseta and pajama bottoms in his sling bed, the whole family appeared garbed in their best attire. Bayani's mother, grandmother, and older sisters wore humble camisas at sayas in cotton and linen, while Bayani and his father donned long-sleeved cotton tunics over canvas trousers. *All this just for la maestra Americana,* Eleanor thought. There didn't appear to be guests other than herself.

The hut was a tiny one-bedroom house, where all three generations of Bayani's family seemed to reside. The bedroom wasn't so much a room as it was merely a cubicle set apart from the rest of the space by a shell curtain. Eleanor couldn't see a bathroom, and the kitchen was obviously what she'd already seen outside. Pillows, folded sheets, and rolled banigs were stacked and piled against one of the bamboo-plaited walls. The hut probably turned into a communal bedroom at night, where most of the family slept on mats set on the bamboo-slatted floor, while Bayani's parents occupied the curtained niche and the grandfather resided in his hammock.

Bayani seated Eleanor on the unoccupied rattan chair beside his grandmother. There appeared to be no other pieces of furniture, apart from an open-shelf cupboard that held coconut shell tumblers and bowls, tin plates, and a kettle.

Eleanor glanced at Bayani's father, who was still massaging his rooster. She was reminded of a recent *Manila Sun* article about cockfighting being the most cherished sport in the islands and wondered whether Bayani's father entered his rooster in cockfights. The article deplored how most Filipino men were addicted to the gambling sport. This and liquor consumption, according to the journalist, were the worst vices among the poor that entrenched them deeper in poverty.

Bayani's mother soon joined them, offering Eleanor a tin cup filled with coconut juice. Eleanor thanked her, and the woman covered her mouth again with her hand as she smiled, as though ashamed to show her grossly incomplete teeth. *She must have lost a tooth for each new child,* Eleanor thought, glancing at the children of various ages sitting around her feet, staring at her like the urchin mob at Legazpi Port.

She smiled at them and turned to Bayani. "Bayani, how come I don't see your sisters in school?"

Bayani smiled sheepishly. "Oh, sorry ma'am. My mother and father need their help."

Eleanor glanced at Bayani's mother again. She certainly looked like she needed all the help she could get. This suggested to Eleanor another reason for low school attendance. Families like Bayani's, who appeared to live hand-to-mouth, required their children's help in both house and farm work to ensure they had something to eat daily.

She recalled what Luis had said about the culture being primarily patriarchal outside the home. From this and the way Bayani's family seemed to treat him as the source of their family pride, Eleanor surmised that Filipino sons likely enjoyed favored family status. This allowed sons to attend school if their parents could spare them from work—which seemed mainly possible if the family had daughters to sacrifice to the fields and factories. Bayani was fortunate because he had many sisters who provided the help his parents needed.

Eleanor looked upon the innocent faces of Bayani's sisters and turned to the boy again."Bayani, perhaps you could ask your parents to send your older sister, at least, to the after-school adult classes?" She glanced at the girl, who appeared to be about thirteen or fourteen years old, wiping her toddler brother's nose with her fingers, which she then brushed against her overskirt.

Bayani glanced at his parents with trepidation before conveying what Eleanor suggested. His mother shook her head and said something in Vicolano, glancing at Eleanor with an apologetic smile. Bayani turned back to Eleanor. "Sorry, Miss Karsten. Ináy say this is most busy time when she need Å'te Maria's help for cooking dinner and giving brother and sisters bath."

"I see," Eleanor said, smiling reassuringly at Bayani's mother. "If she can't send Maria, could she spare two or three of your younger sisters? I mean, to go to school with you? Girls need education, too." Eleanor looked at Bayani's mother, as though addressing her directly.

The woman avoided Eleanor's gaze and mumbled something to Bayani. Eleanor caught the Spanish word, seguro. Bayani dutifully translated his mother's reply. "She say maybe."

Eleanor nodded sadly, for she had come to understand that the natives' use of the word, which, in English, meant "sure," ironically meant "maybe." It was the natives' polite way of saying "no." She turned again to her student. "In case that, too, isn't possible, Bayani, perhaps you can help your siblings by teaching them how to read and write?"

"I will try, ma'am," the boy replied somberly, glancing downward.

It was the first time Eleanor saw him look almost despondent. That word *try* she also knew, meant that whatever was promised to be attempted was likely not going to happen. She realized she was imposing responsibilities on the boy in addition to the burden of his family's hefty expectations of him. "Hey, Bayani?" Eleanor said, smiling reassuringly. The boy glanced up at her with an anxious expression. "Just try your best—all right?" she said. "That's all you need to do in everything you do. I'm proud of you as I'm sure your family is. You are a great blessing to them!"

He beamed and grinned, seemingly back to his usual jovial self.

When the food was ready to be served, the girls spread out sheets of banana leaves on the floor, on which they laid a clay pot of boiled rice, a bowl of winged beans in coconut milk, and a platter with a whole roasted chicken. Eleanor bet the hen was a former pet—sacrificed to be the centerpiece of the family's fiesta meal.

The family gathered around the spread. Bayani's mother chopped the chicken into small individual portions on a cutting board, but set aside a thigh and drumstick. She placed the smaller pieces back on the platter and the thigh and drumstick on a tin plate. She added some rice and winged beans to the plate and had Bayani pass it to Eleanor. One of Bayani's sisters also handed Eleanor a fork and spoon.

"No, thank you, Maria. I know the drill!" Eleanor said, smiling.

The family's jaws dropped as la maestra Americana joined them on the floor. Eleanor asked Bayani's mother for her cutting board and cleaver. Although the woman appeared confused, she passed the items to her guest. Eleanor rolled her sleeves to her elbows and chopped the thigh and drumstick into two smaller pieces each. She retained one piece and added the rest to the platter that contained the rest of the chicken. The *O*'s of the family's mouths turned into crescent smiles.

With her fingers, Eleanor picked some of the rice and winged beans, which appeared to include pork cutlets and anchovies. She pinched the combined food into a bite-size ball and pushed it into her mouth. She nodded her approval to Bayani's mother, exclaiming, "¡Deliciosa!"

The whole family clapped and giggled. The grandfather sat up in his hammock, as if checking on what all the excitement was about. He smiled his toothless smile, and the children giggled again. Bayani's mother went to the old man with a small plate of rice soaked with the sauce of the winged beans and fed him with her fingers like a baby.

Not much happened by way of communication during the meal, except through seemingly endless smiles and gestures catering to Eleanor's every possible need and desire.

Come dessert time, one of Bayani's sisters briefly disappeared and returned with a bamboo steamer stacked with what Bayani called *suman*, which he described as steamed sweet, sticky rice rolls wrapped in coconut leaves. Bayani's mother passed a coconut shell bowl to Eleanor that her son said to his teacher was the topping for the rice rolls.

Eleanor noted how the family unwrapped their suman by unwinding only enough of the coconut leaf to expose a bite-sized portion of the six-inch long roll. They dipped the unwrapped part into their serving of the topping and bit into the roll. She followed their example and discovered that the suman rice was chewier and stickier than the staple boiled rice. Through the help of Bayani, his mother explained that the topping consisted of grated mature coconut meat toasted with brown sugar. The suman and its topping, together, made for a perfect, sweet finale to their fiesta lunch. Eleanor liked the suman so much, she planned on asking Yolanda to prepare it for them sometime.

When it was almost time to leave, Eleanor asked Bayani where the latrine was. The boy appeared to hesitate, yet accompanied her outside. The toilet turned out to be a mere hole in the ground, enclosed behind a bamboo screen. The school outhouse with its wooden seat was a luxury compared to it. The pit was topped with sand and lime to mask the sight and smell of old feces—done likely for Eleanor's benefit. She figured that she had to spread her legs to straddle the hole and sit on her haunches, careful to position her body over the pit, where she could then relieve herself. Instead of paper to wipe with, there was a bucket of water with a short-handled bamboo ladle probably meant to wash with. Eleanor was glad she only needed to urinate, for it was tricky squatting over the hole in her tailored, long skirt while avoiding either one of her feet slipping into the pit.

The family again gathered in front of their house and the grand-mother looked out the window to bid Eleanor farewell. "Gud by, Miss Karsten! Tenk yu! Come see us again!" they cried, smiling and waving at her as she rode away in the calesin that fetched her as Yolanda said it would.

She smiled and waved back at them. *Good job teaching them the words, Bayani.* Something tugged at her heart and stung her eyes as they disappeared from view.

Two men were roasting an entire pig skewered with a bamboo pole over a fire pit in the Gonzagas' yard. It was a scene Eleanor witnessed a few times as her calesin passed by other houses. It must be the fiesta specialty for any family who could afford it. What disconcerted her was realizing that one of the men was Diego. She pretended not to see him, but it was too late. He smiled at her with that usual twisted smile and impish glint in his eyes. She acknowledged him with a nod, and he beamed as his eyes wandered to the python reticule hanging from the crook of her arm.

She couldn't understand why his familiar attitude toward her made her feel less sure of herself. Not even her position as la maestra Americana seemed to shield her from him. Perhaps he saw her for who she was—just a small-town girl, no more special than him, although they were from two different worlds.

To her delight, the Munros also arrived, and she sought security in their company. Cristina's belly had noticeably dropped—a ripe fruit about to fall from the tree. She waddled while holding onto her limping husband's arm. Together, they managed to trudge on solidly.

"Hello, Cristina!" Eleanor exclaimed. "How are you?"

"Fine, tenk yu, Leonor." Sam's wife smiled and placed a hand on the small of her back while massaging her stomach with the other.

"She's ready to burst!" Sam chuckled. "We may 'ave to leave early. Frankly, she don't feel so good. But she says we can't refuse the 'onor of an invitation from a grand fam'ly."

Today, the Gonzaga feast was served in one of the villa's gardens. What appeared to be a mandolin band was playing lively Spanish melodies under a tree. Beneath the wide canopy of another tree were two long tables put together, covered with sheets of banana leaves laid out with what was once a sumptuous buffet. Now, the centerpiece was an almost-consumed roast pig. Only its head remained. Its mouth looked comical stuffed with a *pomelo*—one of the fruits that Diego sometimes dropped off at Eleanor's house. It was similar to a peach, except it was bigger and had thicker skin awash with vibrant ruby and coral hues. Most of the serving platters appeared almost empty of food. A pair of servants stood behind the buffet, languidly waving flies away with straw-woven, heart-shaped fans. One of them appeared to have recognized Eleanor and ran toward the villa.

Underneath crisscrossing strings of colorful paper buntings, rattan tables and chairs were spread across the lawn, where many of the guests were now just picking on the food remainders on their plates or from between their teeth and sipping from their tumblers of limonadas or bottles of *cerveza* or "beer." They glanced at Eleanor and her companions, following the newcomers with their eyes while chewing their food or drinking their beverages. Eleanor recognized some of them as having been present at her welcome dinner. She nodded and smiled at them. Only then did they acknowledge her with restrained smiles. Many more, still, were strangers to Eleanor. She was surprised that neither Luis nor Doña Ximena appeared to be around.

The sun was now at its descent, no longer searing, yet it remained warm under the shade. The ladies fanned themselves furiously with their abanicos, pausing only when they spotted Eleanor, whereupon they drew their fans over their mouths and leaned to the person next to them, as if whispering.

A familiar voice called out to them. "Miss Karsten! Sergeant Munro! Over here!" Doctor Langford cried, waving them over to the table he shared with his wife. Doña Beatriz sat smiling and likewise gestured with her Spanish fan for them to join them. The erstwhile opera singer stood to kiss both Eleanor and Cristina on the cheeks, while the doctor and Sam shook hands.

Eleanor noticed the empty, used plates in front of the couple. "Are we late?" she asked as she sat.

"God, no!" Doctor Langford exclaimed. "Fiesta is served all day long, that is, until all the food is gone—which, in the Gonzagas' case, never happens." He chuckled.

The servant who'd earlier left the buffet now re-appeared with other servants who took away the old roast pig and empty dishes and brought out fresh replacements.

"Why not go and get food?" Doña Beatriz urged.

"Shouldn't we greet our hosts first?" Eleanor asked, still scanning the crowd for Luis and Doña Ximena.

"Don't worry. They'll come around sooner or later," Doctor Langford said. "It's customary to just go ahead and eat. The hosts expect it. They're busy circulating among their other guests, anyway. Perhaps they're inside the villa now."

Diego and the other man, who wore a sleeveless shirt, carried in the new pig, now roasted to caramel perfection, and laid it at the center of the spread. An excited buzz arose from other guests, who stood and rushed toward the buffet.

"Dáli'-dáli'!" Cristina exclaimed under her breath, pulling Eleanor up from her chair. "Let's get lechon! Hurry—before they beat us!"

"Le… what?" Eleanor exclaimed as she tried to keep pace with the briskly-walking pregnant woman.

"Lechon. The roast pig!" Sam volunteered and chuckled as he, too, tried to catch up with his wife rushing toward the buffet with Eleanor in tow. The other guests looked their way with frowns and sneers.

Eleanor glanced at Sam, who laughed and shrugged. "What can I say, ma' dear? Gettin' to fiesta food is a racin' sport!"

Cristina shushed Sam and lightly slapped his arm, grinning.

The buffet table was now brimming with roasted chicken, boiled crab and shrimp, grilled fish, and pots of what Cristina said was goat stewed in coconut milk. Cristina grabbed plates for both Eleanor and herself and went straight to the lechon.

Diego stood next to the other man, who began chopping the roasted pig. Both of them wore scarves twisted into slim bands tied across their foreheads and knotted at the backside of their heads. The other man's hair was cropped close to his skull, which was glistening with sweat. Eleanor surmised the scarves were meant to prevent the men's sweat from dripping down their faces onto the food.

With a scarf around his head that pinned his chin-length hair at his temples, Diego appeared almost like a warrior from one of the American Indian tribes. She observed his scarf and wondered if it was the same one he'd tied around her neck to cover her chest on the night of her ambush. She forced herself to look away from it when she caught him stealing glances at her, which was how she also became aware of the other man surreptitiously peering at her. Whenever she caught the other man looking at her, he lowered his gaze, pretending to focus on his task.

The other man's right hand gripped a huge, heavy-looking cleaver that fell in rapid yet precise hacks upon the pig's roasted body. When he got to the breast bones, he wielded the blade with a savagery that sent bits and pieces of meat, skin, and bone flying in all directions and landing on some of the guests' hair and clothes, inciting cajoling protests or chuckling from them. Yet, the man appeared oblivious to them, except to Eleanor. He continued to watch her as she watched him, and Diego watched both of them.

As the man prepared to chop the pig's head off its body, he raised his right arm higher and paused mid-air, as if making sure the cleaver in his hand would land precisely upon a spot he'd targeted on the pig's neck. Yet, he blenched and his head jerked toward the direction of Eleanor, who gasped as her heart lurched when she spied something on the underside of the man's upper arm. In the light of day, the tattoo revealed itself as consisting of a wavy script that looked like a horizontal K in the center of a triangle. Eleanor's breath shuddered as the tattooed man glared menacingly at her. A vein that ran vertically in the middle of his forehead was pulsating in seeming sync with the expansion and contraction of his nostrils as he breathed. He was a snorting bull. He lowered his arm and gripped the cleaver as if he was about to hack her next.

Eleanor bit her lip and glanced at Diego, who looked at her with dismay. He whispered to the tattooed man, who left abruptly—disappearing into the woodland beyond the yard. Diego took over chopping the lechon and startled Eleanor out of her stupor when he addressed her brusquely, "What you want, señorita? Tell me! I give you!"

Eleanor turned to Sam. "S-sam, I… I'm sorry. Could I leave you with my plate? I have to go… and sit."

"What's the matter?" Sam asked. "Are ya all right?"

Cristina glanced at Eleanor with concern.

"Yes… I… I just need to sit," Eleanor replied.

"No worry, Leonor." Cristina nodded, smiling reassuringly. "I get you good food!"

Eleanor turned around and returned to Doctor Langford and Doña Beatriz. She felt Diego's eyes burning her back as she walked away.

"What happen?" Doña Beatriz asked as Eleanor returned without a plate in hand. "You look like you just see multo!"

Eleanor chose a chair that had its back facing the buffet to avoid Diego's glare. "Oh, nothing," she said. "I just suddenly felt… dizzy."

"What!" the doctor's wife exclaimed. "William—check her!"

Doctor Langford went to Eleanor to feel her forehead and press his thumb to her wrist.

"I'm all right," Eleanor said. "Please, no need to fuss."

"Well, you feel warmer than normal and your heartbeat is racing," said Doctor Langford.

"It must be just the heat." Eleanor forced herself to grin. "I suspect I've also eaten too much already—at another reception." She glanced up at the doctor and added, "Perhaps a cool drink might help."

"Allow me, my dear," Doctor Langford said and proceeded toward a table where servants were handing out beverages.

Doña Beatriz moved next to Eleanor to fan the teacher.

"Thank you, Doña Beatriz. I have mine." She fished out her abanico from her reticule and fanned herself.

"Oh! What a beautiful purse!" Doña Beatriz exclaimed. "May I?"

"Of course," Eleanor said and surrendered the reticule to the doctor's wife.

Doctor Langford returned with a tumbler of iced pineapple juice.

"Thank you, doctor!" Eleanor smiled and sipped the cool, tangy-sweet drink. "This is exactly what I needed."

Doña Beatriz interjected, "Is python skin. ¿Sí??" She wore a strange smile as she caressed the texture of the reticule.

"Uh… yes, I think," Eleanor replied, averting her gaze as she continued to sip her juice casually, pretending Doña Beatriz's appraisal of her reticule wasn't bothering her.

"Where you get this?" the doctor's wife probed.

Eleanor breathed deeply, willing herself to relax. It certainly wasn't wise to share that Luis's foreman gave it to her. Even thinking about it sounded ridiculous in her head. "Um… actually, it's a gift. From a friend. Don't know where it's from."

"Are you sure?" Doña Beatriz continued to dig. "Must be from here—because look: lining is made of piña cloth!"

Eleanor looked away and turned around, glancing in the direction of the buffet table. "What could be keeping Sam and Cristina?" she said. Her heart jumped again as Diego glanced up from his task and caught her looking his way. Eleanor swung back to the couple at her table.

"Do you not think so, William?" the doctor's wife asked her husband.

"What about, my dear?" he replied.

"That this reticule could be from here?" she said.

Doctor Langford scoffed, grinning. "What do I know of ladies' accoutrements?"

"But, see here, William," his wife pressed on. "Is this not fine piña cloth? And this handle—it's tortoiseshell! Look like something from here!"

Doña Beatriz turned back to Eleanor. "Your friend must like you very much. This—very special!" She nodded vigorously and smiled triumphantly, as if she'd just discovered Eleanor's secret. "Maybe your friend's name is… Don Luis?"

Eleanor burst into a coughing fit. Some of the juice slid down her windpipe and filled her nostrils. She grabbed her reticule from Doña Beatriz and took out her handkerchief to cover her mouth—and kept the reticule. Eleanor decided it was time to drop the subject by simply ignoring the doctor's comments. To her relief, Sam and Cristina returned, providing necessary distraction.

Cristina handed Eleanor a plate loaded with various viands jumbled over a large mound of rice. The individual dishes were almost indistinguishable from each other. The lechon, however, stood out. Eleanor remarked on its incredibly crispy skin, moist, tender meat, and the savory gravy that enhanced its flavor. Sam explained it was slow-roasting over an open fire that made the skin crispy. "An' brushing salted pork lard on the pig at every turn," he said. Cristina volunteered through Sam's translation that the gravy was made from mashed pork liver sautéed in the roast drippings. "Then add salt, crushed black pepper, bay leaf, and brown sugar," the pregnant woman said through her husband, seemingly proud to show off her culinary knowledge.

Eleanor glanced toward the buffet table. To her relief, Diego appeared to have left.

Eleanor had just spooned some strange dessert into her mouth, when a voice from behind her startled her into near choking on the gelatinous seeds of the nipa palm that Cristina described as having been boiled in sugary water.

"Ah! So, that is where you all have been hiding!" Luis cried. "¡Bienvenidos, amigos!"

Eleanor turned around and saw Maria Teresa holding onto Luis's arm, looking remarkably unscathed by the previous night's incident with Toto.

The young Spanish mestiza presented a vision of angelic pulchritude. She wore a Parisian-style frock in peach silk, accentuated with cream lace. A golden cross hung from a black silk ribbon tied around her long, slim, milky neck. The pendant stopped short of her modest, scooped neckline, which nonetheless hinted at the perky pomelos underneath. The pastel coral hues of her gown picked up the highlights of her hair that shone russet in the late afternoon sun. Sparkling upon the crown of her head was a bejeweled hair clip that pinned the upswept front and sides of her tresses into place but allowed the wavy cascades to fall loose on her backside, down to her waist. Framing her heart-shaped face were wispy locks that softly blew across her cheeks as she fanned herself with her Spanish lace and cream silk fan painted with orange roses.

"Eleanor, Sergeant Munro, Señora Munro," Luis said, "may I introduce our guest of honor, Señorita Maria Teresa Vasquez y Benitez!"

"Charmed, quite charmed, señorita!" Sam exclaimed, as he stood, bowed, held out his hand to the young lady, and performed a gesture of a kiss.

Eleanor was surprised. She'd not seen Sam do as much for any woman—not even for her. Cristina frowned, shifting her glance between her husband and the guest of honor, wearing a countenance of masked jealousy as she sucked her greasy fingers clean and forced a smile at Luis and his lady.

Eleanor held out her hand to Maria Teresa and said, "Pleased to meet you."

The padre's niece touched the tips of Eleanor's fingers in acknowledgment.

An awkward silence ensued, compelling Eleanor to add, "I hear you traveled all the way from Spain, señorita?"

Maria Teresa appeared confused and turned to Luis, who translated what Eleanor said. "¡Ah, sí! ¡De Sevilla!" the young lady declared, unsmiling.

Eleanor smiled. "Ah! Seville! From what I've read, that was where Magellan had sailed from to here, which he later named, Las Islas Filipinas. Right?"

The young lady now strangely looked agitated and glanced at Luis again.

"¡Lo siento, señorita!" Eleanor interjected, smiling apologetically. "¡Mi español… es malo! Not good."

Luis translated what Eleanor had earlier said about Magellan, prompting the padre's niece to reply, "Ah, sí. Magellan. ¡Pero, Magellan no era Español! ¡Él era Portugués!" She raised her chin and shot Eleanor a haughty stare, as if offended by the mere fact of being reminded that the first circumnavigating adventurer who'd claimed the Philippine Islands for the King of Spain was not Spanish—but Portuguese.

Luis chuckled. "Bueno. I think that is enough history for today. I hope you all have enjoyed the food?"

"¡Gustó mucho!" Sam exclaimed. "¡Siempre!" He smiled from ear to ear—at Maria Teresa. He hadn't seemed to have taken his eyes off the Gonzagas' guest of honor. Cristina tugged at his shirt and massaged her lower back and belly. "Oh! Yes, yes, ma' dear," Sam said to his wife. Turning back to Luis, he stated, "My regrets. Ma' wife tells me we may 'ave to be goin' soon. She's feelin' mighty poorly on account of 'er condition. Ya' know." He winked and smiled at Luis and the doctor.

"Is there anything I can do for her now?" offered Doctor Langford.

"Oh, no, but thank ye kindly, doctor," Sam replied. "Just the usual aches an' pains at this time, I s'pose."

Just then, Eleanor caught, out of the corner of her eye, another group approaching them. *Darn!* The Three Musketeers. It included the mayor's wife, Doña Hermosa, who was wearing a different yet still outmoded European frock.

Doña Ximena exclaimed, "Why, Señorita Karsten! I did not know you are here already!"

Eleanor stood and regretted not following her instinct to find and greet her hostess before she partook of the food. "Apologies, Doña Ximena. I was told you were busy with other guests." Eleanor smiled and nodded at the rest of the Musketeers and the mayor's wife. "I hope you've been well, Doña Hermosa? Mayor Dizon? And how about you, Padre Damián?"

Padre Damián chuckled and burst into a barrage of Spanish, laced with sarcasm. "¿Cómo se siente ahora, señorita?" he asked Eleanor, throwing her question back at her.

"Thank you for asking, padre," Eleanor replied. "I, too, am well." Eleanor smiled, ignoring the priest's suggestion that he was much better than she surely had been—which seemed to imply his success in keeping the children away from her school. She reminded herself to stay focused on the reason why she was there. She turned to Luis. "Luis, would you please help me communicate something to the good padre?"

"¡Cierto!" he exclaimed, smiling brightly at her.

Eleanor returned his smile. "Could you please tell Padre Damián I request to speak with him privately?"

"You mean, ahora?" Luis arched and knitted his eyebrows. "Now?"

"Yes, now. Please." Eleanor pressed her lips while maintaining a semblance of a smile.

Maria Teresa alternated between glancing at Eleanor and Luis. She tapped Luis's arm, demanding to be clued in on what was happening. Luis surprisingly ignored her and addressed Padre Damián in Spanish. The priest replied in the same language. Maria Teresa pouted, seemingly annoyed. And the priest looked at Eleanor with a self-assured smile.

Luis turned back to Eleanor. "The padre says that whatever you say to him can be said before all our friends here." He arched his eyebrows again and smiled ruefully. *The ball is now in your hands, Eleanor,* he seemed to say.

"No, no! Is not proper!" Doña Ximena interjected, wagging a finger at Eleanor. "Is not good talking business at party."

"No, no. ¡Esta bien!" Padre Damián demurred, waving his palms to calm down his hostess. "Adelante. ¡Habla, señorita!" He smiled and gestured for Eleanor to speak.

Everyone around them leaned in to listen, except Maria Teresa, who looked away, fanning herself. Even Sam and Cristina, who'd frequently been stating they had to leave—remained.

It's now or never, Eleanor told herself. She looked the priest in the eye as she declared, "Padre Damián, I realize I may have offended you by declining your kind offer of your school building. Please accept my sincere apologies. But please also try to understand my position. The U.S. government would never condone me running a school under the church's tutelage. Nor will it look kindly upon you teaching religion classes to my students. It's simply against our law."

"You can say," she continued, smiling, "that I was caught between the devil and the deep blue sea! And I was forced to turn to the devil—because, you know, I get seasick."

Except for Maria Teresa, who projected boredom, her audience variably smiled, grinned, or chuckled. They caught her reference to what the priest had been calling her school, School of the Devil. Even Padre Damián's lips twitched into a near smile.

Eleanor grinned before turning somber. "On an earnest note, Padre Damián, I am not, however, the one who's paying the price of my error. It's the children, you see. As you may be aware, their education is among the top priorities of the Taft Commission. Therefore, I, as their teacher, am authorized to call upon the resources of the government to help me fulfill my mission in Magayon. Specifically, I could ask for the local infantry's help to execute my mandate to bring all school-aged children to my classroom before the year is over. In fact, Lieutenant Waterstone has already offered his assistance—rather eagerly, I must say."

El presidente and Doña Ximena exchanged glances. "Yes, remember him?" Eleanor said, looking at each of the Three Musketeers. "Now, don't worry. I've declined the lieutenant's offer. I've also prevailed upon him to refrain from doing anything. I assured him I'm certain that you, Padre Damián, and I can arrive at a diplomatic resolution of our… little misunderstanding."

She added, "Please try to understand that I'm only after the children's welfare. I'm also here to support *our* community. Believe me, I do not want to give the soldiers any excuse to frighten the people again. But please note that Lieutenant Waterstone has the power to act on his own—with or without my request. Honestly, I don't know how long I could hold him off from what he's already keen on doing."

After a brief tension-filled silence, Padre Damián ranted rapidly in Spanish. Luis apologetically smiled at Eleanor. "Please excuse him, Eleanor. He is just frustrated. He says it is a problem for him to… countenance… an unholy school."

Eleanor lit up. "In that case, Luis, please tell him—I have an idea precisely on that." She flashed the sweetest smile to the priest she could manage.

"Bueno, entonces. ¡Habla, señorita!" Padre Damián cried.

Luis turned to her again with a rueful smile. "He said…"

"Thank you," Eleanor interjected with a palm raised to Luis. "I know." She turned to the priest. "Padre Damián, I understand and respect your concerns. Believe me—I do. Therefore, I invite you—no!—I humbly beg you to please come to our school and… bless it. Yes—that's it! Bless it! If you believe it is unholy, then I believe you have the power, as God's agent on earth, to make it holy. So—what do you say, padre? Could you, would you please—please!—save the children and me? From the devil?"

The listeners exchanged befuddled glances even before Luis finished translating Eleanor's statements.

Eleanor smiled at them. "Think about it! We could even make an event of it! A ceremony, perhaps? And, Mayor Dizon, you could announce it to the town so everyone can witness how our brave, good padre will surely cast out the devil from our school!" Turning back to the priest, she added, "Padre Damián, I have faith in you. I am sure no demon could overcome the power of your command!"

A slow clapping of hands followed—timid, at first; then, increasingly confident and robust. It started with Luis, Sam, and Doctor Langford; followed by Doña Beatriz and Cristina; and, finally, Doña

Ximena and el presidente. Doña Hermosa glanced at everyone with wide eyes and arched eyebrows, as though trying to comprehend what just happened. But she also applauded upon seeing her husband clapping. Maria Teresa, however, continued to pout while languidly fanning herself.

Padre Damián's expression was the best. His mouth gaped into a big *O* as his jaw dropped, and his eyes grew into a pair of plates on his plump, oily, pockmarked face, such that his almost hairless, shiny, globular head looked like a reflection of the harvest full moon rising behind it.

CHAPTER 14

A Grand Idea

The padre must have wished he'd kept his mouth shut. And his talk about the school with la maestra Americana private. Now, it had become a matter of public interest that he prove God's power over the devil—through him, no less. It was all anyone could talk about, according to Yolanda. Moreover, everybody was trying to outdo each other in pointing out how, contrary to everyone's mistaken assumptions, except theirs, Señorita Karsten was a good American, as demonstrated by her laudable Christian humility and repentance in begging for the priest's forgiveness in so public an arena as the Gonzagas' fiesta and allowing him to get rid of the devil in her school so that their children could study in peace—their souls safe from damnation.

In the week before the school's exorcism, all of Magayon anticipated the battle between good and evil as if it were a cosmic cockfight. Pious women said daily prayers to Archangel Michael asking God's champion to aid Padre Damián in his battle with the legions of satanas surely lurking in the nooks and crannies of La Escuela del Diablo. In honor of the occasion, the enterprising townsfolk held a special cockfight—with the church's blessing and a special permit from the ayuntamiento that granted a dispensation from municipal taxes.

Everyone placed their bet on St. Peter's white rooster defeating Satan's red rooster. San Pedro's rooster, Eleanor discovered, was none other than that owned by Bayani's father. She worried about what it would mean to Bayani's family if the white rooster lost. Yolanda assured her that God had ways of ensuring success. Apparently, God's plan was to rig the match in favor of St. Peter's rooster through an inconspicuous yet sharp little blade attached to the heel of the preordained victor.

The designated loser did meet with a gory end, but its owner was so richly compensated that he, too, felt like a winner. And because he displayed such convincing devastation over his bird's death, he was offered a coveted role in the nativity play next Christmas—as one of the Three Wise Men. Bayani's father was also paid for his part in the charade, though not as much as the red rooster's owner, for the privilege of being chosen winner by God Himself was deemed compensation enough.

During the night of the exorcism, Padre Damián wielded his aspergillum of holy water on the school walls as if he were dousing the very fires of hell, which turned the dirt floor into a multitude of muddy puddles. Fortunately, Eleanor and Estrella foresaw this cataclysm and hid the banigs safely away, thus saving the children's mats from drowning in the great deluge. The acolytes smoked the structure with a great fog of incense, so that mice, lizards, cockroaches, spiders, beetles, and ants came crawling out of the walls and ceiling. On witnessing the exodus of the pests, the faithful who had gathered in a prayer vigil outside, saw it as the devil's flight itself. It imbued them with a religious fervor that fired them up to throw the full weight of their faith into the supernatural battle as they stepped upon, and squished the demonic critters underfoot, triumphantly crying with each kill, "Hallelujah!"

When Padre Damián, at last, exited the shed, he proclaimed victory by pronouncing the school liberated from the devil—prompting everyone to rejoice into singing and dancing. There was so much celebration that the mayor was, in turn, inspired to invent his own event: a ribbon-cutting ceremony, wherein he cut the ribbon, declaring the Magayon Public School for Boys and Girls finally, truly, and officially open.

November 1, 1901

Dear Miss Covell,

Thank you for your kind letter last. I hope this, too, finds you well. I believe I've recovered from malaria, although Doctor Langford warns me that chills and dizzy spells could still attack me occasionally, especially if my health is compromised. Please don't worry. I've no intention of compromising anything.

I've regained most of the weight I lost during my illness. I'm not sure if this is a good thing, considering it's not likely the end of it. The weight gain, that is. How easy this happens here, where fresh vegetables and fruits are available all year, and there's always a good excuse for good eating! Like earlier today.

As with you, we had no classes, this being All Saints' Day. I was surprised to discover this is an especially-revered holiday among the countless holidays celebrated by the people based on the religious calendar. It seemed everybody went to the cemetery to clean and decorate the graves of their beloved departed with flowers and candles. Between you and me, I suspect it was just another ruse to have another fiesta, for there's no better way to describe it.

I went to the school to retrieve a book and inevitably passed the cemetery. There, I saw the most bizarre spectacle. The living appeared to be partying with the dead! Festive buntings hung across the whole cemetery, and the air was filled with the scents of flowers, candles, food, and liquor, as well as the sounds of praying, weeping, laughing, and singing. A band provided musical entertainment to which many literally danced on the graves of their departed loved ones!

In stark contrast with the persona non grata I used to be, it appears my initiative on the school exorcism has made me popular overnight. As I was walking by the cemetery, many of the people hailed me over to join them. I prepared to comport myself to be equally amiable with my 'hosts' by resigning myself to saying a few rosary and novena prayers with them in honor of the souls of their beloved dead. Yet, it soon became clear they intended me to join them not so much to pray but to feast with them.

Although communication was difficult due to my poor grasp of their hybrid Vicolano-Spanish, in the end, hardly any communication proved necessary beyond my acceptance of their offers of food and drink, by which they appeared immensely pleased. There seemed to be a silent understanding among my various hosts to share me equally among themselves, for after spending time with a family, a representative of another also invited me to partake of their fare.

In indulging everyone's hospitality, I became so engorged I felt I could burst. Yet, I worried about declining other people's invitations and hurting their feelings. Nonetheless, I discovered that when I shook my head, caressed my stomach, and projected a look of utter misery from being stuffed, they conveyed their understanding with laughter and granted me a reprieve.

It's admirable that this culture embraces the coexistence of life and death, not with the cynicism or apathy to which most Americans are inclined, but with a passion that, I believe, is at the heart of these people's celebrations. On the other hand, I also think they could do more with less superstition. Although I achieved a truce with the padre by orchestrating a school exorcism, the absurdity of it should behoove us to stress the critical importance of science to win the people over from beliefs that are ultimately harmful to their well-being.

Nonetheless, I'm happy to report that my tightrope balancing act with Padre Damián has paid off by tripling our enrollment. This, of course, has raised the new problem of inadequate school space that promises to worsen by year's end when we expect to receive an even larger number of students not only from Magayon but neighboring towns.

I, thus, intend to meet with the mayor again to pursue the matter of school funding. I shall keep you apprised of developments. In the meantime, we're off to what I now hope are routine operations.

Please stay well and take care, my friend.

Love,
Eleanor

Eleanor divided her students by placing the girls on the right side of the classroom and the boys on the left, closest to the door. She also assigned their seats according to their height, with the shortest in front. In the spirit of democracy that she wanted to instill in them, she disallowed Asunción from bringing her chair and Bayani, his stool. All had to sit on the floor mats, which didn't sit well with the parents, for when it rained, the banigs soaked up the moisture that seeped up from the dirt floor. Despite Sam's careful patching of the thatched roof, proof of the repair's adequacy was tested in the pudding of precipitation. And it failed to make the grade. Eleanor and Estrella kept clay jars on hand to catch the leaks, yet parents still blamed the school for the influenza that accompanied their children home and spread to the rest of their families.

This compelled Sam to plan on building school benches and desks for the boys' first carpentry project. Luis donated cartloads of timber and came by, one day, to deliver the boards, assisted by his foreman and other plantation workers. The tattooed man wasn't with them, to Eleanor's great relief.

However, she continued to experience a peculiar unease whenever Luis and Diego were both present. The native man continued to inexplicably make her feel keenly self-conscious, and his master seemed to instinctively pick up on this and treated his servant with irascibility. To appease Luis, Eleanor tried to pay more attention to him—which, in turn, seemed to earn Diego's ire. Exhausted by such mind games, she dismissed it all as the shameless contest of manhood, to which all men, whether master or servant, appeared ridiculously predisposed in the presence of an unattached young woman.

Mr. Ang generously allocated a portion of his rice field for the gardening class, which provided Eleanor with another opportunity to teach the democratic principle. On the day they were to build the vegetable plots, an unusual number of students arrived with their muchachas and muchachos. Eleanor soon learned why.

After Sam demonstrated how to dig the irrigation trenches and use the displaced soil to build the planting beds, the spade-wielding servants readily took their young masters' place in the dirt.

"Wait, wait!" Eleanor cried. "What do you all think you're doing?"

Estrella smiled a knowing smile, and Sam snorted into a chortle, exclaiming, "I could 'ardly wait to see yer face when this happened!" As his laughter subsided, he took Eleanor aside. "Leonor, people 'ere consider manual labor fit only fer servants. An' while some of these students are no more than peasant folks' kids, sendin' 'em to the American school raised their parents' expectations their children were now practic'ly ilustrados."

"But how could so many of them afford servants overnight?" Eleanor exclaimed, looking at the troop of helpers.

"Ma' dear," Sam said, "in this country, there's always somebody poorer than ye—no matter how poor ye are!"

Eleanor marched to where the muchachos and muchachas were poised to dig. She grabbed the shovel from Asunción's yaya and shoved it into the little señorita's hands. "Here, missy!" she said. "Time to learn self-reliance!" Turning to all the servants, she declared, "Now, away with all of you! From now on, you're going to just drop off the children at the school door and fetch them at dismissal time. Also, no one is allowed anymore to linger around the school premises and stand by the windows watching over your charges."

Estrella translated Eleanor's statement to the servants, who walked away tongue-tied and open-mouthed like many of their young amos.

Asunción burst into sobbing, and Bayani approached her, laying a gentle hand on her shoulder, murmuring sweet consolations. The girl pushed him away and wiped her tears. The boy, nonetheless, flashed her an adoring smile, which only seemed to incense the girl further. Asunción jutted out her chin and dismissed Bayani with an emphatic "Tsè!" The rest of the students giggled. Bayani, however, smiled proudly, as though the way Asunción responded to him was some badge of victory.

Estrella grinned, remarking, "Oh, first love!"

Eleanor raised her eyebrows. To her, it was the strangest demonstration of love and courtship. The children's canniness over matters appropriate only for adults alarmed her. She recalled the young ladies of Manila—really, only girls, as Maude had rightly observed—freely and openly entertaining suitors from their balconies with surprising sophistication. She blamed it on the culture that appeared to promote girls getting married as soon as they could have children of their own, which ran against her aim of inculcating among her female students an interest to figure out and forge their personhood before they lost themselves to marriage and children.

As Thanksgiving approached, a grand idea hatched and grew in Eleanor's mind. It occurred to her that the best way to impart the importance of the holiday to her students was for them to stage a play about the first meal shared by the Pilgrims and American Indians. It also presented the opportunity to educate the community about American history by sharing a turkey dinner with some Magayon denizens. She invited el presidente and Doña Hermosa, Doña Ximena and Luis, Padre Damián and his niece, Doctor Langford and Doña Beatriz, and Mr. Ang and his wife, whom Eleanor learned was the mousy, little Filipino woman she'd glimpsed at the store.

She also realized that, in connection with her education mission in Magayon, promoting peace and harmony in the community was essential to creating an environment conducive to learning. Thus, she was compelled, despite her personal feelings about Lieutenant Waterstone, to also invite him. A shared meal could be the perfect catalyst for fostering better community relations between the natives and American soldiers.

She wrote a short Thanksgiving play that doubly aimed at sharpening her students' English skills, which were already vastly improved due to an English-only speaking rule enforced by Asunción. Eleanor had appointed the girl as class sheriff, confident that the exacting señorita would serve as effective language police. Asunción did not disappoint her.

The girl had established both a retributive and rehabilitative system for dealing with any classmate she caught speaking a language other than English: after-school detention. Her cleverness demonstrated itself further by surprisingly, yet rightly recruiting Bayani to teach English lessons to the offenders during their detentions. The boy was ecstatic in obliging his lady love. In almost no time at all, the Vicolano-Spanish chatter among the students faded into fragmentary baby English-speak that soon spilled into schoolyard contests of who could churn out the greatest number of English words and sentences.

Nevertheless, the extraordinary number of children eager to participate in the play surprised Eleanor. She recalled how American parents had to cajole and coerce their children to join the annual school play. Estrella explained this wasn't surprising at all in Magayon because there was already a deeply-rooted love for storytelling through theater among the people. The assistant teacher cited the popularity of the annual Christmas play and Lenten pasión among the townsfolk who competed and campaigned for available roles as though they were running in an election for municipal council positions. Coveted roles, when won, then became family heirlooms where the actors who'd performed them for decades passed the part to their descendants when they died or became too old, sick, or weak to perform.

Despite the great number of students who wanted to act in the Thanksgiving play, a problem arose in the casting. It appeared the children only wanted to play Pilgrims and none wanted to be American Indians.

"But why?" Eleanor asked them during the auditions. "Both roles are equally important to the play!"

Only Bayani dared to answer. "Respectfully, ma'am, no one want to be loser."

"What loser? There are no losers in this story!" Eleanor exclaimed. "On the contrary, it's a beautiful story of how the American Indians saved the Pilgrims from starving to death during the Pilgrims' first winter in America. If anything, it's the American Indians who were the heroes. By helping each other, however, *both* American Indians and Pilgrims proved themselves winners."

"But ma'am..." Bayani reprised, "how about Captain Smith?"

"Captain Smith?" Eleanor asked, unclear about how the hero of New England pioneers figured into the casting impasse. "What about him?"

Bayan replied, "I saw picture of him holding Indian by the throat and pointing pistol to the head of Indian. Then, he say, 'Your money or your life!' Maybe Indians give their food to Pilgrims because they afraid Pilgrims kill them. That make Indians losers."

"And where did you see this... this questionable picture, Bayani?" Eleanor asked.

Estrella cleared her throat and said under her breath, "Um, here, Miss Karsten." The assistant teacher timorously handed Eleanor a copy of the book they'd been reading in history class, opened to the page showing an illustration of Captain Smith and an American Indian with a caption below it that validated what Bayani said.

Eleanor was struck with dismay at her lack of attention which resulted in a crucial and negative impression on her students regarding the Thanksgiving story. The material had never been a problem for her American students, who rather found the cartoon funny. Now, she realized the same picture conveyed a different message to her Filipino students.

She glanced up at her pupils, whose faces screamed for an explanation. "This… um… this here, class, is… is what's called… a… a satire. Yes—a satire!" Eleanor said. "This means it really doesn't mean what it says. It… it's like a joke, you see. An exaggeration—for comic effect. You understand?" She nodded her head vigorously, as though willing them to agree.

Bayani was tenacious. "Sorry, mees Karsten. I do not understand. I am confuse. Why joke about history? And why it not mean what it say? Why book show something not true?"

Eleanor sighed. "Well, um, good questions, Bayani. But I'm afraid they would have to wait for another lesson reserved for a higher grade level for the answer. This touches on the different forms of literary and artistic exposition. You understand? No? Precisely. As I said, it's meant for a higher grade level. Our focus now is on the play. We need to cast both the Pilgrim and American Indian roles. So, again—who wants to volunteer to be American Indians? No? None? All right, then. I guess we just have to have a lottery on who gets what role."

The children groaned, yet meekly surrendered to the new casting system. This was one of those times when the predisposition for obedience to authority by Eleanor's Filipino students worked to her convenience. Yet, she vowed to remain mindful of Bayani's eye-opening revelation. He did her a favor by alerting her that the native audience would likely identify with the American Indians. The victims. From there, no great imagination was required for the people to view the soldados Americanos as the conquering Pilgrims. And here she was— about to stage a potentially controversial play before the whole town that she had intended to help bridge the divide between the natives and Americans. *How can I minimize the negative message and accentuate the play's positive theme?*

Ironically, it was Padre Damián who offered her the solution when he dropped by during one of the rehearsals. Through Estrella's translation, he suggested, "Señorita Karsten, do you not think Pilgrims look more real if they carry big cross of Christ when they land on American shore?" *Perfect.*

Apparently, the padre bragged to el presidente about how he'd greatly improved the Thanksgiving play by providing la maestra Americana with crucial suggestions. It was, therefore, no mere happenstance to Eleanor when Mayor Dizon likewise visited the school. Through Estrella's help, he proposed that the best venue for what was surely going to be a *fantástica obra de teatro* for everyone to see was the concrete stage in the town plaza. "We use it for our Christmas and Lenten plays and the crowning of the Maytime queen during the Santacruzan festival. Why should the Thanksgiving play deserve any less?" he reasoned—a reason that Eleanor could not rebut.

She was also keenly aware this was the first time el presidente expressed a strong opinion about anything to her. Although she preferred her original idea of an intimate Thanksgiving celebration between her students and select members of the community, she'd learned her lesson from her battle with the padre. It would cost her nothing, yet potentially gain for both the school and town what her mission ultimately aimed for: peace and prosperity through education.

Mayor Dizon was finally revealing his secret talent to Eleanor. Although he projected a sheep's personality, he was now proving politically shrewd. Usually, he was content to simply go along with whatever Padre Damián or Doña Ximena wanted. Now, it seemed he was attempting a little political coup that could tip the balance of power in Magayon in his favor. Embracing the American holiday will not only put him on good terms with the local U.S. infantry but also placed him in the good graces of the new administration in Manila. As if to prove Eleanor's assessment right, the mayor lost no time in inviting the Superintendent of Public Instruction and the *Manila Sun* editor to Magayon for the event. Stunningly, both had accepted.

Hence, el presidente developed a swagger in his walk. As he reveled in his new political success, creative ideas also seemed to freely flow out of him. He called Eleanor to an urgent meeting at the ayuntamiento. Through the help of Estrella's translation, the mayor proudly pointed out to la maestra Americana that the Thanksgiving play presented them with another excellent opportunity.

"Why not have a Thanksgiving dinner and dance after the play?" he said. "We could hold it in the town hall and sell tickets to those who want to attend! And you can be sure, Señorita Karsten, that everyone would want to attend. But since we can't accommodate everyone inside the ayuntamiento, we can charge premium ticket prices. Then, the proceeds of the ticket sales would fund our school expansion project! No one wants to be left out of anything special, especially one endorsed by Magayon's elite. Why, this is a rare occasion for people to be able to brag they had dined with the Gonzagas while supporting a worthy cause!"

The next day, el presidente ordered the bandillo to go around town, announcing Magayon's First Thanksgiving Fiesta at the Plaza.

The mayor's exuberance seemed limitless, for he also volunteered to underwrite the cost of the stage set, costumes, food, and whatever Eleanor needed to make the event successful. He only asked her, in return, to ensure the play was spectacular and the menu faithful to an authentic American Thanksgiving dinner. Eleanor responded with her own request: that the student actors would have free tickets to the dinner.

"¡No problema, señorita!" he cheerfully replied.

Between daily play rehearsals and coordinating the Thanksgiving event preparations, Eleanor found herself with hardly any time for classes. The situation was compounded by Cristina giving birth, which compelled Sam's scarcity at school. Eleanor was forced to depend on Estrella for most of the teaching. And she was gratified to see the native teacher wonderfully competent, despite her partial training.

Sam was holding his baby as though she were a precious piece of china when Eleanor went to visit the happy new parents. "Cristina's named 'er Gracias, she bein' born near Thanksgivin,'" he said. "But I call 'er ma' li'l piglet. 'Av ya ever seen a plumper or pinker li'l darlin'?" He chuckled—clearly lost in adoration of his daughter.

Eleanor nodded, grinning, and asked to hold the baby. As she cradled the child in her arms, she was struck with acute maternal yearning. She caressed the chubby cheeks and imagined having a child of her own someday. It occurred to her that the name, Gracias, not only signified the baby's birth proximate to Thanksgiving, but also likely represented everything Sam was grateful for: a secure, happy new life with a new family, which the old soldier might not have realistically achieved if he'd returned to the mainland.

"Sam and me 'ave mestiza now!" Cristina said as she reclaimed her baby from Eleanor's arms. "Thank God she look like Sam, no?" Her relatives gathered around her, gushing over the baby's fair skin, light brown hair, and slim, high-bridged nose.

Eleanor smiled, although the child would have nonetheless been beautiful to her had the child possessed her mother's looks.

When she left the party, citing the thousand and one things she had to accomplish before the Thanksgiving event, Sam said, "Don't forget, Leonor—christenin's next Sunday! And you're one of the ninángs!"

"Oh, yes—of course!" Eleanor replied.

In the culture, she'd learned, it was a great honor to be invited to be a godparent. Sam said accepting was akin to agreeing to be the child's substitute parent should anything happen to prevent the parents from fulfilling their duties. It was a great responsibility that had to be taken seriously. Thus, she stressed over the many other requests she received to be a ninang to babies whose parents were practically strangers to her.

She also worried about juggling her now impossibly full social life with schoolwork. Being expected to attend someone's birthday, anniversary, christening, or wedding had become a regular feature of her Magayon life. *Who knew I would be so busy in the boondocks of Vicol?* She often wondered whether there wasn't some kind of game at play underneath the obsequious invitations and constant offers of favors to her. *Beware the tyranny of the benefactor.* This was the other reason she kept to herself when she declined Padre Damián's offer of his school building. She feared the unseen strings attached to a stranger's gift.

While seemingly eager to please or assist, the dispenser of gifts and favors obliged the recipient to a debt of gratitude, rendering the latter vulnerable to manipulation by a fear of offending the offeror through rejection. Eleanor saw it as an ingenious yet subtle method of acquiring and wielding influence over another person—one that the natives appeared to have mastered to a degree worthy of Machiavellian nod. What was this? A natural talent? Or learned behavior by the colonized? Whatever it was, it was certainly a way through which the powerless acquired power—no matter how middling.

She realized another benefit from el presidente's now widely-publicized Thanksgiving event: It lent her the perfect excuse to decline new invitations to serve as a nináng for christenings or *madrina* or "chief witness" for weddings. Otherwise, she'd have no rest at all. Being a Thomasite was proving to be a twenty-four-hour job, seven days a week. A god! And she imagined what God must feel from being called upon to be everything to everybody, according to everyone's needs. Exhausted. Was it any wonder, then, that God was often portrayed as an angry, vengeful deity?

Yet, this was Sam—asking her to be godmother to his child. How could she refuse?

In addition to worrying about ensuring the Thanksgiving event was successful, Eleanor now also worried that the affair was going to be such a great success that it would hence become an annual Magayon project she would be tasked to oversee. Thus, she regretted her grand idea of it altogether. Her regret was almost enough for her to wish it to fail, if she didn't care that critical social and political interests depended on the town's success in staging what el presidente now touted as Magayon's event of the year.

She realized she needed help. She turned to Doña Beatriz, who appeared so flattered by being asked to assist in such an important project that she immediately agreed. The opera singer turned society matron invited her fellow Magayon socialites to form themselves into a Thanksgiving Dinner and Dance Committee, which she volunteered to chair, to Eleanor's relief.

Doña Beatriz coaxed and cajoled the mistresses of the town's best-fed households, including the Gonzagas, into lending their cocineras to help prepare the dinner. Now, all Eleanor had to do was ensure the performance of an entertaining play and the menu was authentic to an American Thanksgiving meal. Eleanor interpreted the second mandate as being true to the traditional fare as local ingredients allowed.

Fortunately, roast turkey was no novelty to native cuisine as Eleanor recalled from the Gonzaga dinner in her honor. It was spit-roasted, just like lechon. Yet, she wanted the star of the culinary feast to possess a local flavor rather than simply being seasoned with salt and pepper. Yolanda offered to experiment with it. She soaked the bird in a brine solution mixed with pineapple juice. While it was roasting, she brushed it with a glaze made of spiced and sweetened pineapple juice and lard.

Yolanda accumulated a big supply of lard she'd collected in a glazed clay pot each time she fried pork fat and skin into a crispy snack she called *chicharrón*. The maid loved it especially dipped in spicy vinegar. Eleanor considered it unhealthy, but her cook justified it as a way to make tasty food out of scraps that would otherwise have been thrown out. Yolanda explained that one principle of native cooking was an aversion to food wastage. Thus, a good cook always found ways to recycle food. "Our mothers and grandmothers always say: Think of people who have nothing to eat!" the muchacha said, grinning.

The same principle, Yolanda said, likewise justified *chorizo*, which was a sausage that originated in Spain. It consisted of the otherwise distasteful and normally discarded parts of the pig, which were chopped, seasoned, and stuffed into the intestines of the same animal. Eleanor stopped Yolanda from naming the pig parts, simply happy to enjoy the final product at breakfast, when it was perfect with fried eggs and her now favorite garlic fried rice.

What appeared to be a novelty to the native cooks was the American idea of "stuffing." Yolanda offered to try making it out of native ingredients, based on how Eleanor described it. She suggested adding chorizo and local vegetables to the mix and using pan de sal, instead of American bread. She sliced and fried the Spanish sausage, rendering enough oil in which she sautéed garlic, onions, and pre-cooked rice. She added diced carrots and green beans, cauliflower, and raisins. Finally, Yolanda stirred in toasted cubes of old pan de sal.

To make the gravy, Eleanor's cook collected the turkey drippings in an iron pan set on a grill beneath the roasting bird. She used the savory oil as the base to which she added the mashed, boiled liver of the turkey and seasoned it with salt, pepper, bay leaves, oregano, and the sili pepper ever present in her cooking.

Doña Beatriz volunteered her cocinera, Tekla, to help make the side dishes and desserts. Tekla balked at merely reproducing the traditional side dishes. She said that, based on what Eleanor said about them, everything sounded too plain and simple, if not almost primitive, and, therefore, would not please the local palate. She kept suggesting completely different dishes that were tried and true among Magayon's elite, yet Eleanor stressed el presidente wanted an authentic American Thanksgiving dinner—or one that was, at least, faithful to the traditional fare as native cooking ingredients and methods allowed.

Since corn, green beans, and sweet potatoes were already cultivated as staples in Magayon gardens, it was easy to procure them. Tekla, however, had no mind to replicate American "creamed" corn and suggested, instead, simply grilling ears of unhusked corn over a wood fire or boiling them in their husks—served brushed with salted *mantequilla* or "butter" and sprinkled with pepper. That, she said, was the only way to be faithful to måís.

Tekla likewise nixed the idea of poached green beans. She claimed it would strike their discriminating patrons as boring visually and bland to their taste. Her solution was to jolt the "sleeping" vegetable into waking by tossing it in hot lard with garlic, onions, minced *jamon* or "Spanish ham," and sili peppers. The red of the peppers would add a festive look, she added through her mistress.

The sweet potatoes, on the other hand, merited gentler and sweeter treatment, opined Doña Beatriz's cook. She suggested they'd be exquisite—peeled and sliced into wedges; sweetened with vanilla beans, cinnamon, and sugar; seasoned with a little salt and pepper; sprinkled with star anise and cloves for enhanced fragrance and aesthetics; and then slow-simmered in coconut cream.

For pumpkin pie, she used the native squash called *calabasa* or "pumpkin" as a substitute and used *pili* nuts to reinterpret the pecan pie Eleanor specified among traditional Thanksgiving desserts.

Eleanor was impressed by all of Yolanda's and Tekla's reinterpretations of the traditional Thanksgiving dishes and desserts that turned out to be better versions of their American originals. *Or has my palate adapted to my current environment? My body and, thus, my mind transformed by my new world?*

To test the success of their culinary experiment among the natives, Eleanor invited her neighbors to dinner at her house. She also asked

Sam and Christina, who begged off because poor baby Gracias was suffering from colic, and they hadn't slept in days. When she invited Estrella, the native teacher asked if she could bring her brother. *How could I say no?*

Yolanda suggested also inviting the corner sari-sari store owner, a middle-aged woman named Tomasa who'd been widowed young and, yet, continued to wear her widow's garb as a badge of eternal fidelity to her deceased husband because of her obstinate belief that marriage bound two souls not only in this life but in the next. The maid then also urged her mistress to include Senyong, who was a fine, full-time guitarist and part-time drunk, who would surely come with his inseparable guitar and provide them with musical entertainment if he knew Tomasa would likewise be present. Yolanda was certain of this because everyone knew, except Tomasa, that Senyong was in love with her and that it was the widow's stubborn refusal to shed off her black attire and remarry that made the guitarist a drunk—which, to many, was a perfectly good reason to be drunk. *Again, how could I say no?*

Eleanor recognized the significance of the occasion. She was hosting her first dinner in her first home. Thus, she prepared for it like a young and giddy hostess excited to give her first party. She obsessed over what to wear, how to do her hair. She anticipated that, with a house full of guests, it could get warm inside the modest space, and she didn't relish the prospect of getting choked again by a high-necked blouse. She also wished to look more youthful and relaxed than her usual schoolmarm attire suggested.

Thus, she decided this was the time to wear the blue muslin frock again. While it didn't bring up pleasant memories of the last time she'd worn it at the Waterhouse Honolulu reception, she recalled what Maude wished—that it would bring her luck wherever she got sent to in the Philippine Islands. Eleanor hoped tonight was that night. She would put up her hair, not in the Gibson Girl style, but gather it to the crown of her head and allow it to fall in long, loose tresses on the backside in the manner associated with young, unmarried ladies, such as Señorita Maria Teresa.

With her hairstyle and wardrobe issues addressed, Eleanor next worried about the china, flatware, and glassware until Yolanda revealed a stash of old porcelain, pewter, and glass tumblers, including a brilliant cut-glass punch bowl and *taza* set, stored inside the previously locked cupboard of the dining room sideboard. The sneaky muchacha had picked the lock! After pretending to scold the maid, Eleanor wondered aloud whether they should ask the Gonzagas for permission to use the dinner service.

Yolanda scoffed. "Why make problem when there no problem, señorita?"

The punch bowl inspired Eleanor to create a cocktail using pineapple juice. It was easy to procure the pineapples and sugar, even the ice, as there was a *planta de hielo* or "ice plant" located at the Legazpi border—but not the white wine, which only came to Magayon by special order from Manila. Tomasa suggested her home-brewed *lambanog* or "coconut liquor" as a substitute. Despite Eleanor's initial skepticism, the cocktail mix turned out surprisingly good. She planned to share the recipe of what she now called her "Sunrise in Paradise" in her next letter to her Radcliffe friends. The lambanog proved to be stronger than white wine, though. Thus, she added only as much of the coconut liquor as she could stand.

She unpacked her mother's pair of silver candlesticks and embroidered linen tablecloth from the few possessions she'd saved from her family's lost Iowa home. She covered the dining table with the linen and placed the punch bowl at the center, flanked by the candlesticks. She replicated the memorable floral centerpiece at the Gonzaga dinner by surrounding the punch bowl with flowers and foliage she picked in the garden, arranging them like a flowering vine that spread and wove around the candlesticks toward the opposite ends of the table. She chose blooms of Birds of Paradise and their smooth, long, lanceolate leaves. To add texture and color, she inserted asparagus ferns, magenta bougainvillea, and what Yolanda called *santan*—the orange balls of tiny star-like blossoms that Eleanor saw on the hedge around the Gonzaga fountain. She scattered frangipani flowers, which the maid referred to as *kalachuchi*, across the arrangement and showered the spread with sampaguita blossoms that grew on the bushes along the inside fence perimeter. The sampaguitas looked like miniature white roses that diffused a scent similar to, yet more fragrant than jasmine. Eleanor noticed their perfume lingered long on her fingers and set aside a few of them to tuck later into her cleavage.

Yolanda said that the sampaguita was their most treasured flower. Eleanor had often seen them made into leis to honor birthday, anniversary, and other special occasion celebrants. She also remembered them as the flowers that were strung into garlands that radiated from the pierced heart of Our Lady of the Harvest during the fiesta procession.

Eleanor and Yolanda laid the food buffet-style on the sideboard in the dining room. They put the magnificent, pineapple-glazed, golden-brown roasted turkey in the middle, flanked by the boiled and buttered maís, sautéed green beans, creamy sweet potatoes, and calabasa and pili nut pies. They decided not to set down place settings on the dining table, for there weren't enough chairs for everyone to sit and eat in the comedor. Instead, they piled the plates and lined the cutlery on one side of the table to allow everyone to freely serve themselves from the buffet spread and choose to eat either in the comedor or the sala.

Their neighbors arrived in simple yet elegant traditional attire: the women in their camisas at sayas, the men in their Barong Tagalogs or long-sleeved linen tunics with standup collars and dark or striped pantaloons. They conveyed through the aid of Estrella's translation how much they admired the table spread and how pretty, younger, and more feminine Eleanor looked in her blue frock and long hair. They expressed how flattered they felt by la maestra Americana fêting them in a manner known only among Magayon elites. Eleanor acknowledged their appreciation with cheerful niceties, while checking the door every time it opened, to see if it was Diego who came in. She finally asked Estrella about her brother. Her assistant speculated he may have been delayed by hacienda work.

Eleanor wondered at her disappointment over this. She'd vacillated between anxiety and excitement in anticipating his attendance. Now that he may not even make it, her spirits sagged. At the plantation's mention, Eleanor was struck with guilt for not having invited Luis, or even Doña Beatriz and Doctor Langford. But she'd relied on her sense of her neighbors likely being most comfortable limiting the party to their company. The uninhibited chatter and lively guitar music that filled her home proved her instinct right.

Everybody declared the hearty feast a triumph. One of them, an old woman called Nanay Auring, who'd been long widowed like Tomasa and appeared to be revered as some kind of communal grandmother and healer, suggested just slight modifications: to add soy sauce to the turkey glaze for a more robust color and taste, and mix mashed *camotes* or "sweet potatoes" into the calabasa pie filling for creamier texture and additional sweetness.

The evening culminated in the sala with a group sing-along of native and Spanish ballads accompanied on the guitar by Senyong, whose playing skills appeared to improve with every refill of his Sunrise in Paradise. Senyong urged Eleanor to sing an American song, but she declined—until she could no longer resist the unanimous insistence of her guests. *Or, perhaps, I am less inhibited now that I've had more than my usual serving of the cocktail?*

She recalled an old love song that her father used to sing to her mother during those warm summer nights on their porch while they all enjoyed tall tumblers of iced tea. A music teacher from Illinois had composed "I'll Take You Back Home, Kathleen" for his wife, which became popular in the late 80s—right about the time her parents were courting. Her father said he liked it especially because it had her mother's name in the title and lyrics. It also had a sweet and simple melody on the quarter beat suitable for a sweethearts' waltz to which he'd often cajoled his wife into dancing with him on their lawn under the starry sky.

Witnessing that romantic living portrait of her parents through adolescent eyes had struck Eleanor with both awe and fear: awe at the depth and steadfastness of her parents' love for each other, fear for the possibility she may not become similarly blessed. That fear, she now realized, was what compelled her to bury such desire to save herself from bitter disappointment. Singing the same song now strangely stirred the same ambition for herself.

She stumbled on the first lines and, thus, imagined her father singing it along with her to boost her confidence. Senyong picked up on her scale and rhythm until, to Eleanor's amazement, he was masterfully accompanying her on the guitar—which, in turn, improved her singing. Though far from the only home she'd ever known, she now felt surprisingly at home with her neighbors who now seemed no longer strangers to her.

I'll take you home again, Kathleen

Across the ocean wild and wide

To where your heart has ever been….

To where your heart will feel no pain

And when the fields are fresh and green

I'll take you to your home again!

Eleanor's voice quivered as she sang the last few lines. *How poignantly relevant the lyrics are to my new life!* Silence greeted her when she finished. She worried she sang badly until she noticed most everyone's eyes glistening. The men blinked back their tears, while the women unashamedly wiped theirs and blew their noses on handkerchiefs fished out from their cleavages or the folds of their tapises. One by one, they applauded—ending in resounding shouts of "Bravo!"

Eleanor was amazed by how her audience, for whom English was a foreign language, may not have understood the lyrics, yet grasped their meaning. To them, perhaps, it was similar to her experience of the sentiments evoked by the songs of the native Hawaiians. She basked in the warmth of their joyous camaraderie, convinced of the power of a shared meal to seal new friendships. This proved true tonight among her neighbors, who belonged to a people for whom feeding each other and singing together were the way to foster fellowship. She was enthused all the more for the upcoming Thanksgiving event to achieve the same between Americans and the whole town.

A look of delight on Estrella's face directed toward the door compelled Eleanor to turn around. Her heart lurched on seeing Diego. He wasn't looking at his sister but at her—applauding her performance, smiling with that same old twisted smile and mischievous glint in his eyes. His jaw-length hair was slicked back wet, and he wore a loose, long-sleeved, ivory linen shirt with a standup collar and cream-and-navy striped trousers. He struck a distinguished yet casual presence among her neighbors who, regardless of age, appeared to acknowledge him not just with respect but some kind of reverence. The men lowered their eyes before him after mutual acknowledgment through a nod and smile, while the women extended their hands to him, which he enclasped with both of his. The exception was Nanay Auring, whose hand he sought, instead, and to which he pressed his forehead in the manner Eleanor saw children do for their parents. Yolanda had once explained this was their gesture of respect for elders. Eleanor had then realized this was what Padre Damián must have expected her to do when she first met him.

Diego presently approached her with a rueful smile. "Disculpe, señorita. I am late." He smelled deliciously of coconut and lime.

Eleanor stood and smiled back at him. "I'm glad you made it, Diego. Please follow me." She led him to the comedor, where she poured him a cup of the punch.

Without taking his eyes off her, he sipped and exclaimed, "Mmm… this good!"

She smiled. "Gracias. I made it myself."

His sister joined them, and Eleanor said, "Estrella, do you mind helping me serve your brother some dinner? I need to return to the other guests. You may ask Yolanda to warm up anything he likes."

"No need," Diego interjected. "This good."

Estrella happily pulled her brother to one of the chairs at the dining table. Eleanor returned to the women in the sala, choosing a spot from where she could see Diego in the comedor. She glimpsed Estrella serving him a plate of what remained of the dinner fare before she sat beside him, affectionately watching him eat. Many of the men also sat and chatted with Diego as he ate. When Eleanor glanced toward the comedor again, she caught Diego gazing and smiling at her. And her heart leaped again.

Within the hour, Eleanor's guests expressed their thank-yous and goodbyes, except Estrella and Diego. Estrella insisted, over Eleanor's objections, to stay and help Yolanda clear away and wash the dishes. Diego, Eleanor assumed, remained somewhere in the backyard where she'd last seen him with Senyong and some of the other men, smoking their *cigarillos* or "cigarettes." She went outside to find and urge him to prevail on his sister not to bother helping with the clean-up, for she knew it was a long ride back to Hacienda Gonzaga where they lived.

There was a new moon tonight, dark and mysterious. She might have missed him were it not for the smoldering tip of his cigarette that rose and dipped in slow arcs behind the mango tree. She followed the pinpoint of light and found him leaning against the massive tree trunk, his leg bent behind him like a stork.

"Are you sure there aren't any more snakes up there?" she asked him, smiling.

CHAPTER 15

I Lub de Flag, de Dear Old Flag!

Diego straightened up with a start, slow to smile, but smile he did—the twisted smile that now twisted Eleanor's heart into knots. He'd rolled his sleeves to his elbows and unfastened the few top buttons of his shirt. His hair had dried, falling into loose waves to his chin. He tucked a side of it behind his ear. She found this surprisingly attractive, not unlike, perhaps, the seductive appeal of a girl doing the same with her hair.

He offered her a puff of his cigarillo, and she shook her head. He arched his eyebrows. "No?" He dropped the cigarette and crushed it under his leather sandal. When he glanced up at her again, his eyebrows arched and his full lips twisted again into that smile she loved. He patted her shoulder. "Good song. Good sing."

She grinned. "You mean I didn't make a fool of myself?"

"Fool?" He shook his head. "You, no fool." He grinned and added, "Pero sí. ¡Un hermosa tonta!" A beautiful fool.

She grinned along with him.

He reached out to hold her hand, and she let him. *Did I add too much lambanog in the punch?* She closed her eyes as he pressed his warm, moist lips on her forehand—which, for some strange reason, she expected. What she didn't expect was when he turned her hand over and kissed it again. Her breath caught as she felt the wet tip of his tongue on the soft center of her palm, as if tasting her. A current surged through her spine, giving her goosebumps. He pulled her close to him—so close, they were breathing each other's warm breaths. A gradual poisoning it must be, for she began to feel light-headed.

She became aware of her speedy, shallow breathing—a force at work between them, pulling them to each other like the opposite ends of a pair of magnets. They stood, face to face, holding hands, pondering each other. Words became passé. Irrelevant. The mischievous glint in his eyes turned into something else, a burning flame.

This must be desire, she thought. *An erupting, earthshaking volcano in one's pit!* Heat radiated from her chest and spread throughout her body like carmine dye in water. She felt the urge to sink her face into the slope of his neck; slip her hand under his shirt to feel his firm, brown chest; and drink from his mouth until her thirst was quenched.

He caressed her hair, pausing to examine a golden ringlet against a renegade ray of light from the house. She quivered as his fingers traced the outline of her face, shape of her lips, and hollow of her throat, before they traveled down her necklace chain to the locket on the threshold of the valley between her breasts. She gasped as he briefly inserted his fingertip into the dip of her scooped neckline and brought it to his nose to sniff the scent of the sampaguitas tucked in her cleavage. Her nipples hardened against her dress, betraying themselves to him whose breaths now matched hers—deep and rapid.

She was about to meet his lips when an owl's hooting startled both of them. Reason resurfaced and took control.

"Diego," she said breathlessly, "I think it's time for you and your sister to go." She turned around to return to the house.

"Pero, Eleanor…" He tugged at her hand, pulling her back gently, but she tore herself away from him and ran indoors.

Later that night, in bed, she could still detect the lingering scent of coconuts, lime, and tobacco on her skin. His earthy effluence. She imbibed him. Unquenched, she succumbed to restless dreams of falling from a tightrope.

Luis had volunteered to help Eleanor design and build the stage set for her Thanksgiving play. His exuberant availability to her, while Maria Teresa was still in town, presented a curious twist to the highly anticipated pairing of the town's most desirable bachelor and the padre's beautiful niece. Rumors resurfaced about the Spanish mestiza being Padre Damián's daughter, according to Yolanda. Eleanor refused to concern herself with the gossip, but Yolanda swore she only mentioned it again because the rumors now also involved her mistress.

The gossipmongers were casting la maestra Americana as a person of interest in a love triangle with the dashing, eligible haciendero and the pretty, Spanish mestiza. Some were throwing bets on who, between the Americana and Española, would hook Don Luis's heart. She warned her maid not to raise the matter again and stoke up the overactive collective imagination by tendering her speculations to the gossip mill. Since the besotted new father, Sam, had become unavailable to assist Eleanor after classes, she was grateful to have Luis on hand. And she wanted nothing to upset the fragile balance of the status quo, especially not before the big Magayon affair.

On the day scheduled to build the stage set, Luis arrived with Diego and a few other workers who included, to her great alarm, the tattooed man. Eleanor bit her lip and willed her breath to slow down. Having both Luis and Diego on the set, including the man who'd threatened her with fear for her life and honor, was one tricky tightrope for her to tread all day.

Diego kept sending meaningful glances her way, trying to hold her eyes. She ignored him. After he attempted to seduce her under the mango tree, she decided no good could come from allowing herself further intimate encounters with the man she now indubitably believed was the leader of the local insurrection. *I must draw the line between balancing and playing with fire!*

There was also a good chance some or all of the campesinos who were now working with them on the stage set could be some of the men who'd ambushed her and torched the Gonzaga carriage. How could Luis not know? And if he did, why did he appear so unperturbed? The potentially explosive implications were too much for her to process while racing to get everything ready by Thanksgiving. Thus, she decided the best strategy was to do nothing and continue feigning ignorance about Diego and his men, to not poke the hornet's nest.

Despite the initial unease of working in the midst of those who may have participated in the ambush against her, the tension seemed to dissipate, contrary to Eleanor's expectation. The men often smiled at her, seemingly eager to be helpful to her—including, to her shock, the tattooed man whose name she finally learned: Juan. As she was about to step on a ladder to help paint the top of the canvas, Juan extended his hand to help her step up. Sensing an offer of a truce, she accepted it. But she was no fool, as Diego rightly said once. She worried that the workers' tempered conduct was only due to the constraining presence of their amo, Luis, and their leader, Diego. Without them, there was no knowing what the men were capable of.

Luis had sketched a backdrop of sea, mountain, and cornfields in the foreground of a setting sun on the canvas. It could have been a coastal view from anywhere in the islands, were it not for the absence of coconut and banana trees. His love for the Hudson River-style displayed itself through the idealized landscape he was painting. She smiled as she appraised the developing scene. She could almost step into the canvas and find herself transported to the world Luis was creating.

She was assisting him to paint a portion of the foreground when the artist-haciendero startled her by holding her by the waist and grasping her hand. "Mi querida, bold strokes here, a lighter touch there. See?" he said in a mellifluous tone as he guided her hand across the canvas. His breath warmed the skin on her cheek and neck, while his scent overwhelmed her with the combined aroma of lavender, cigars, and turpentine. She wasn't sure if it was accidental or not when his body occasionally pushed on her backside. She inched away from him until the wet canvas left her no space within which to retreat, unless she was willing to ruin her clothes. Her breath caught as she felt his stiff crotch press against her buttocks.

She was dismayed with herself for managing a mere nervous grin in response to his brazen advances. And she became more upset when she caught Diego frowning at both of them, as though accusing her of condoning his master taking liberties with her. As if she was being unfaithful to him!

The ruination of my clothes be damned! She squeezed from under Luis's arm, swung around, and quickly climbed the ladder again—safely installed away from all the grasping, needy, and deceitful men beneath her. Eleanor breathed a sigh of relief and proceeded to paint the sky portion of the canvas, pretending impercipience of male schemes.

Later, while stepping down the ladder, she lost her balance, slipped on a rung, and fell. She would have surely broken a limb, had not someone miraculously caught her. She found herself in Diego's arms again—just like that night when malaria overcame her and he'd carried her to her bed. Both heaving from breathlessness, they gazed into each other's eyes, and the primal chemistry between them reasserted itself with a vengeance. Having led, thus far, a rational and ordered life, Eleanor detested herself. For this—this was far from rational and orderly! There was no question about it, she had to totally distance herself from Diego if she wanted to be successful in her Magayon mission.

"¡O, Dios mío, mi querida!" Luis cried as he rushed to claim her from Diego's arms.

Yet, Diego's hands tightened around her, reluctant to let her go. Hence ensued a tense and ridiculous comical tug-of-war between master and servant.

"Anyone else needs a helping hand?" shot a familiar voice from the plaza ground below the stage. It was Mr. McCauley, looking quite amused. And standing beside him was a bespectacled, mustachioed mestizo holding a camera, taking photographs of her in the arms of the two men.

Eleanor wasn't sure what or whom she should worry about first.

November 11, 1901

Dear Eleanor,

I am sending this through the kindness of Mr. McCauley, hoping it finds you well.

I understand the superintendent couldn't make it to Magayon and is sending Mr. McCauley in his stead. Neither could the editor of the Manila Sun, but I do not expect you to suffer any loss of publicity as the paper is sending you its best reporter to write a special feature about your Thanksgiving event.

I commend you on your program to promote our uniquely American holiday. I must tell you it has caused quite a stir around here. It is even being discussed as a possible model to endorse to other schools.

Teaching your students and community about American history through a play while creating an opportunity for school funding, and, at the same time, ingratiating the mayor and other luminaries to your school's advantage by placing your town in the public eye is a stroke of genius, the ultimate balancing act! I am very proud of you, my dear!

Your innovation and creativity have earned you your just rewards. The superintendent has approved your request for Sergeant Munro's appointment as one of your assistant teachers. I expect Mr. McCauley will hand you a confirmation letter, including your and your assistants' paychecks. Considering no one else in the provinces has yet received his or her pay, the superintendent made an exception in your case.

School supplies are another matter, however. You may wish to discuss this with Mr. McCauley. Until the Philippine Commission passes a budget to fund the schools, I am afraid we are left to our own devices. Our situation is regrettably also subject to the whims of our nation's politics that continue to debate the arguments of the imperialists and anti-imperialists. While I favor the latter, I find myself ironically held back by them as I, too, struggle to find funding for the Normal School.

Nonetheless, we must persevere for the sake of our students.

I wish you a happy Thanksgiving and great success in your event.

> *Your affectionate friend,*
> *Ida*

Postscript: You really must stop addressing me as "Miss Covell." Further, might you consider spending Christmas in Manila with me? I have also invited Maude and Arabella, yet doubt they could make it since their travel time alone would eat up most of the holiday break.

Sam and Estrella stood like guards at the rear of the classroom as Eleanor declared, "Class, today is very special, for we have some very special visitors who came all the way from Manila just to see us. Let's give them a warm welcome, shall we?"

Her students clapped enthusiastically until Eleanor gestured for them to stop. She pointed to each guest as she introduced him. Mr. McCauley sat facing the students, while the journalist walked around the classroom, taking photographs. Eleanor continued, "This is Mr. Nigel McCauley, who's here on behalf of our superintendent to see how we're progressing with our lessons. What do we say to him, children?"

"Welcome to our school, Mr. McCauley!" the students cried in unison, repeating what they'd practiced with their teachers.

Eleanor pointed to the Manila Sun reporter. "And that gentleman there at the back, wandering about with a camera, taking photographs—well, he's not just doing that as a hobby." The students turned around to look at him as Eleanor continued, "He is Mr. Ramon de Alcalá, who will be writing about our Thanksgiving celebration in his newspaper, especially about our play! So, let's make sure we give a great performance, all right?"

"Yes, ma'am!" the students replied, vigorously nodding.

Eleanor smiled. She found her Filipino students easier to manage in the classroom compared with her American students, who had no qualms about taking mischievous risks in their deportment. On the other hand, American children were inclined to ask more questions, instead of simply parroting what they'd read or what their teachers taught—a talent in which her Filipino students excelled.

This was the product, she suspected, of a culture that discouraged its children from speaking their minds while allowing them to be seen, quite liberally so, wherever and whenever adults socialized. Filipino parties were presumed to be family gatherings where children were also welcome, unless the hosts stated otherwise. Eleanor had been encouraging her students to ask more questions in class. Their lives depended on it.

"Mr. McCauley," she said, " would you mind saying a few words to our students?"

The superintendent's representative smiled and stood. "Thank you, Miss Karsten! Don't mind if I do." He faced the class and hooked his thumbs into the pockets of his vest. "Girls and boys, you're fortunate to live in this exciting time, for we are on the brink of tremendous changes...."

"Excuse me, Mr. McCauley," Eleanor interjected. "May we allow Miss Santiago to translate your statements as you speak? The children are progressing in their English skills, but may not yet catch all the wonderful things you're saying."

"Yes, of course!" he replied.

Estrella, dressed in her usual simple but regal camisa at saya, walked to the front of the classroom and nodded and smiled at all the visitors.

Mr. McCauley continued at a slower pace, pausing between clauses to allow Estrella time to do her part. "As I was saying, children, you are all lucky to be living in an exciting time when great changes are underway. These changes could pave the path to your success—but only if you study well." He thrust his index finger upward to emphasize the last clause.

"And your success," he added, "means the success of this country. You are lucky to have such wonderful teachers here, such as Miss Karsten, Miss Santiago, and, over yonder, Mr. Munro." The students turned around as he pointed to the back of the classroom at Sam, who made a funny face at the children that made them giggle. He had quit wearing his sergeant's uniform and taken to donning the native gentleman's shirt, which seemed to endear him even more to the students.

Mr. McCauley continued, "Now, we have come here to join you in celebrating a very special holiday: Thanksgiving. It's special because it reminds us of the importance of cooperation. Students, do you know what this term, cooperation, means?" He glanced around the classroom with a smile.

The children timidly shook their heads, variably replying, "No, sir."

"Would you like to know what it means?" Mr. McCauley asked, raising his eyebrows.

"Yes, sir!" the students cried in unison, nodding.

"It means working together and helping each other succeed in a common goal," Mr. McCauley explained. "The best example of this were the American Indians and Pilgrims. They helped each other survive difficult conditions. And then other people learned from their good example. Because of this, we now have the United States of America! Therefore, let us all—Filipinos and Americans—learn from this and cooperate so we can succeed together!"

Eleanor led everyone in applauding. "Thank you, Mr. McCauley! And would you please remain with me here for a few more minutes?" Mr. McCauley obliged, and Eleanor continued, "Now, class, do any of you have any questions for Mr. McCauley? Remember what we learned about asking questions and how it is just as important as knowing the answers?"

As she expected, Bayani raised his hand.

"Yes, Bayani!" Eleanor eagerly said.

The boy stood from one of the classroom benches and desks that he and the other boys built under Sam's direction—finished just in time for the superintendent's visit. "Mr. McCauley, sir," Bayani began, "we learn in our book how American Indians give Pilgrims seeds to help them. But we also learn that American Indians not like the Pilgrims and not want them there. Why then did American Indians help Pilgrims? It make no sense."

Mr. McCauley glanced at Eleanor with amusement before he turned back to the boy. Eleanor gripped her hands, sensing where this was going and dreading it. Yet, she wasn't going to silence her student.

Mr. McCauley said, "Well, Bay… Bayani, is it?"

"Yes, sir," Bayani replied, his lips seemingly slightly quivering.

So uncharacteristic of the boy, Eleanor thought.

"Well, Bayani," Mr. McCauley continued, "perhaps the Pilgrims paid for the seeds. And the payment helped the American Indians."

"But, sir," Bayani interjected, "the American Indians need no money. They already have everything they need before Pilgrims come."

"Now, Bayani," Eleanor intervened, "remember: We aren't sure how the Pilgrims got the seeds. We only know they got them."

"Ma'am, sir, sorry to ask… again," Bayani said, wringing his hands.

"Go ahead, son. Ask away!" Mr. McCauley said, flashing a reassuring smile to the boy.

"Thank you, sir," Bayani replied, shifting his weight between his legs. "But, um, uh… maybe this not really a question. Is just something… Miss Karsten, sorry, ma'am. Well, it just… about Captain Smith, again. I know you say book not really mean what it say. That it just a joke. But when Captain Smith hold American Indian to the throat, pointing gun to his head, and say, 'Your money or your life!'… well, I… I just thinking… about my people. The Filipinos." Bayani dropped his gaze, bowed his head, and clasped his hands in front of himself.

Mr. McCauley and Eleanor exchanged knowing glances. A brief, awkward silence ensued before Eleanor asked, "Is there anything else you wish to add, Bayani?"

"No, ma'am," Bayani mumbled, slumping back in his seat.

"All right. Thank you, Bayani," Eleanor said.

Mr. de Alcalá, a mestizo of uncertain heritage—perhaps a Filipino mixed with Spanish and some Chinese—was beaming. The tip of his tongue stuck out from the corner of his mouth as he recorded the exchange in a notebook.

Mr. McCauley leaned toward Eleanor. "I should tell the superintendent that if he intends to teach these children the history of the United States, he ought to provide them expurgated editions of the books."

Eleanor pressed her lips and glanced sideways at him, and he grinned as he returned to his chair.

"Now, class," Eleanor continued, "in honor of Thanksgiving, why don't we show our guests how well we've learned our patriotic verses, shall we? Any volunteers?" She surveyed the room and, as usual, only Bayani raised his hand—waving more avidly than ever. Intent on giving someone else a chance, however, Eleanor waited. To her surprise, a student whom she never expected would debut her talent so conspicuously, timorously raised her hand. Eleanor beamed. "Yes, Asunción! Please come forward."

The girl looked as if she immediately regretted her decision. Bayani, on the other hand, appeared dismayed to discover that his competitor was none other than the object of his affection. Asunción stood, straightened her tapis and saya, and pulled down her camisa to ensure her midriff wasn't showing. All eyes were fixed on the little princess as she gingerly walked to the front of the class.

To bolster Asunción's confidence, Eleanor reached out to her as soon as she was within arm's reach. She laid her hands gently on the girl's shoulders and turned her around to face her classmates. Eleanor bent to her ear. "Thank you for volunteering, Asunción. What piece have you chosen to recite?"

The girl cupped her hand to Eleanor's ear and whispered her answer.

Eleanor smiled at her. "That's a very good choice. Remember to say it with feeling and conviction." The girl nodded, and Eleanor turned to their audience. "Ladies and gentlemen, let's give a hand to Miss Asunción Alarcon who will now recite a verse from Baldwin's Primer!"

The room applauded, and Asunción glanced up at Eleanor—trepidation patent on her face. La maestra Americana nodded at her with an encouraging smile. The girl moistened her trembling lips and pressed them together. She surveyed the classroom until her eyes landed on Bayani who, in an apparent bid to intimidate the new upstart, crossed his arms and taunted her with a frowning gaze. This, however, appeared to give Asunción exactly what she needed, propelling her into a performance of histrionic proportions. Her shrill voice reverberated throughout the classroom as she declaimed with emphatic, albeit rigid gestures that stressed the end of every line with an upward arc of her hands.

I lub de name ob Washington!

I lub my country, too!

I lub de flag, de dear old flag!

Ob red and white and blue!

The girl remained standing, waiting for her audience's verdict. It arrived soon enough and gave Eleanor no time to preempt nor soften it. One by one, her classmates tittered. A few tried to be polite by suppressing their laughter—evident, however, from their heaving shoulders and cupped hands covering their mouths. Asunción glanced up at Eleanor, eyes welling up with tears. The girl seemed ready to bolt out of the room—if she wasn't frozen in place.

Suddenly, a student stood and clapped, softly and slowly, and turned clockwise, looking each classmate in the eye. The speed and volume of his applause increased until he'd shamed his peers into silence. Turning to Asunción, he cried, "Bravo! Well done, Asunción! ¡Muy bien!"

The adults followed Bayani's lead—standing, clapping, and nodding enthusiastically—which soon elicited a unanimous standing ovation. When the applause faded and everyone returned to their seats, Asunción changed back into the regal and confident princess she'd always been. She beamed, raised her chin, and declared, "Tenk yu! Tenk yu, ebree wan!" She then turned to Bayani with a frown and pointed at him, stating, "But yu! Yes, yu, Bayani Burgos! I not forget yu talk nun-Engleesh! That mean detenshun por yu!"

The students broke into riotous laughter, including Bayani, who rolled his eyes and palmed his face in jest disbelief. For the first time, it seemed, Asunción smiled at him.

Mr. McCauley turned to Eleanor. "Well, Miss Karsten, I congratulate you on a job well done. It's clear to me you're going to need a much bigger classroom very soon."

"Thank you, Mr. McCauley," she replied, smiling.

The Gonzagas had invited Magayon's celebrated visitors, including Eleanor, to a lunch and tour of the hacienda after the class presentation. Eleanor entrusted the rest of the school day to Estrella and Sam.

Luis arrived in the schoolhouse to fetch them, smiling at Eleanor, boater straw hat in hand. He turned to Mr. McCauley and Mr. de Alcalá. "I trust you all had a good morning?"

"Indeed!" Mr. McCauley replied. "We're very impressed!"

Mr. de Alcalá acknowledged Luis with a nod and smile before he returned to writing in his notebook, as if the words he had in mind would disappear if he didn't set them on paper.

"Splendid!" Luis exclaimed. "I expected nothing less from our illustrious maestra Americana. Madam, gentlemen—your carriage awaits!" He offered the crook of his arm to Eleanor. "Shall we, querida?"

Eleanor smiled. This was when she most appreciated Luis's charms. Magayon needed to put on a good show, and he was a master at it. She put on her brimmed straw hat, hooked her hand onto his arm, and went outside with him. Mr. McCauley and Mr. de Alcalá reached for their boater hats and followed.

A footman opened the door of the six-passenger open carriage, which bore the distinctive Gonzaga crest. Eleanor wasn't surprised to see Maria Teresa seated in the quiles. Eleanor smiled at the padre's niece, but the Spanish mestiza's eyes darted to Eleanor's hand hooked onto Luis's arm and did not smile back. The haciendero introduced the gentlemen to the padre's niece, who nodded at them with a curt smile.

The rainy season had ended, giving way to sunny yet cooler days. But with the sun at its zenith, it was still warm. Maria Teresa furiously fanned herself while holding a parasol over her Edwardian-hatted head. Loose wisps of her auburn hair, now gathered into a French chignon, blew away from her face as her Spanish fan waved to and fro before herself.

Eleanor pulled out her abanico from her python reticule and likewise fanned herself. She glanced at the cheery sight of the gentlemen in their carriage all wearing boater hats. In the mainland at this time of year, the men had long switched to their woolen bowler hats. She smiled to herself, for she liked living in the land of endless summer.

Luis seated Eleanor on the same upholstered bench where Maria Teresa was sitting and sat between the ladies. Mr. McCauley and Mr.

de Alcalá took the bench across from them, facing where the quiles would be going.

A pair of mounted escorts guarded the front and rear of the quiles. Eleanor was disconcerted to see that Diego was among them. He glanced sullenly at her. This was the first time he'd failed to acknowledge her with a smile. The other escort was the tattooed man, Juan. Eleanor recognized the cochero and footman as the same servants who were with her on the night of her ambush. Was it possible the driver and footman were also complicit in the attack?

It occurred to Eleanor that the people who represented the natives' past and present rulers were all practically held captive in the carriage. If there was ever a perfect time for another ambush that made for a more powerful political statement than the attack on her, this was it. Perhaps she should share her suspicions with Luis about his men? It would be better to raise the matter with him than with ruthless Lieutenant Waterstone, who would only escalate the conflict. How would that leave her students and their families?

Luis caressed her python reticule as if to feel its texture. "Beautiful!" he exclaimed. "Is it American or from here?"

Eleanor glanced at where Diego was leading the quiles entourage and leaned toward Luis. "Not sure of the nationality of the python, señor, but it's fair to say its owner is American!"

Luis chuckled. "What delightful wit you have, querida!"

Maria Teresa glanced sideways at them and abruptly looked away, raising her chin.

Luis launched into a commentary on the geological history of the lay of the land as it pertained to the volcano's eruptions. Maria Teresa kept her gaze on her side of the road, seemingly indifferent to whatever was happening in the carriage. Eleanor retreated into mulling over the issue about the insurrectos.

Diego suddenly directed his horse to trot beside the carriage in such a way she couldn't miss his gaze. It was as if he'd intuited what she was thinking. How could she even think of betraying him? He seemed to be reminding her that he'd protected her from harm during the ambush and had since only been helpful, if not disconcertingly attentive, to her. She avoided his eyes.

Perhaps she should confront him, ascertain the truth about his role in the ambush and insurrection? Persuade him to abandon the armed cause to fight for peaceful reform, instead? This would not only save his life, but Estrella's and many of his people, as well. Yet, why even bother talking to him? What loyalty did she owe him, anyway, that transcended her fealty to her government?

How dare she betray him, he seemed to insist—this time, appearing to allude to a different kind of betrayal, reminding Eleanor of how she'd allowed his amo to practically make love to her on the plaza stage as they were working on it. He gazed at her with knitted brows and she shot him a defiant glance. Did holding hands and a near kiss under a mango tree during one lambanog-inebriated night commit her in any way to him?

He appeared to counter, *But it wasn't just simply holding hands and nearly kissing—was it, señorita?* Consecutive waves of shame and relief washed over Eleanor as she recalled her near lapse of judgment with the foreman. She looked away from him. Diego responded by grunting a command to his horse to return to the front of the entourage.

Villa Gonzaga's French doors and windows were left open, this time. Moths and mosquitoes weren't nuisances at noon as they were at night. But the heat persisted. With the aid of the punkah pullers, the warm air ventilated outside and the fresh, outdoor air circulated into the dining room. Yet, again, though, Eleanor sympathized with the punkah pullers who must be suffering the sweltering noonday heat in the shallow mezzanine above them.

Padre Damián and Mayor Dizon joined the group lunch. To Eleanor's great surprise, so did Lieutenant Waterstone. It was a consolation for her to see that Doctor Langford and Doña Beatriz were also present. The couple was always a cheerful and calming presence in potentially contentious situations. Doña Ximena seemed to be performing a balancing act of her own.

It was, as usual, an impressive meal. A viand that appeared to be beef braised in tomato sauce proved particularly good, and Mr. McCauley expressed his appreciation. "This is beyond what I've enjoyed in Manila!" He glanced at the ladies, asking no one in particular, "What's the secret to cooking this estofada that makes the beef so tender and savory?"

Doña Beatriz traded knowing smiles with their hostess. "Doña Ximena only serve best food for special guest," she said. "But it is not so much how to cook it but what it is."

"What is it, then?" Mr. McCauley asked, looking unsure about taking another bite.

The opera singer grinned. "Lengua."

"Leng… lengua…." Mr. McCauley's eyes widened. "You mean…?" A piece of meat on his fork hung suspended before his face.

"Yes, Mr. McCauley," Doctor Langford interjected. "You think correctly. To me, it's the best native delicacy — though, admittedly, it originated from the Spaniards."

Eleanor chuckled. "I beg to differ, Doctor Langford! This ox tongue is nothing compared to the boar's brain!" She deposited a piece of lengua in her mouth and ate it in a fulsome manner.

Everyone chuckled, except Maria Teresa, who, since the carriage ride, adopted a silent and stone-faced demeanor, and Lieutenant Waterstone, who seemed to have lost his appetite.

Lunch chatter revolved around the upcoming Thanksgiving celebration. With the help of Luis's translation, Mayor Dizon proudly announced that dinner tickets were already sold out, to which everyone applauded. El presidente added, "Miss Karsten, you will be happy to know it is more than possible now to expand our school."

"Here! Here!" cried Doctor Langford, raising his glass of vino comun, inviting everyone to toast the good news.

Eleanor clinked goblets with Mr. McCauley and Mr. de Alcalá, who were seated beside her. Luis gazed at her across the table, smiling with admiration in his eyes.

Through Luis's translation services likewise, Padre Damián announced he would be holding a special mass before the play's staging. "But explain this to me," the priest said, grinning and glancing at the Americans at the table. "I do not understand why you Americanos give only one day of thanksgiving to God when you should be thanking Him every day, especially in church!"

Mr. McCauley likewise grinned and replied, "You make a good point, reverend! I guess it's no different from celebrating Easter on just one Sunday of the year, when we should be celebrating the risen Lord every day we wake up and find ourselves raised from sin!"

Padre Damián clapped and nodded vigorously.

"Why, Mr. McCauley," Eleanor said, smiling with eyebrows raised, "you sound like a preacher!"

The superintendent's representative chuckled. "Can't help it! Born and bred by a Baptist preacher, who was sorry I wanted to be a civil servant, instead of becoming a servant of God like he was."

Eleanor smiled. "That's nothing to be sorry about."

"This reminds me," Mr. de Alcalá interjected, "is it part of the Americans' mission to convert Filipinos into Protestants?" He turned to Eleanor and said, "I understand, for example, Señorita Karsten, that you declined the church school. Could you please explain?"

Everyone's eyes turned to Eleanor. She cleared her throat and replied, "Well, Mr. de Alcalá, it's well known now why I did. I think even Padre Damián now understands my reasons, which are simply grounded in our democratic separation of church and state. And out of what you call in these islands as delicadeza, I didn't want to be seen promoting religion—any religion. Thus, to answer your first question: No, we aren't here to convert Catholics into Protestants. In my case, I cannot espouse or be seen as espousing any religious faith in my class-room. Aren't I right, Mr. McCauley?"

"Right, my dear!" Mr. McCauley replied as he continued to eat his lengua with gusto.

"Then, how do you explain the increased presence of Protestant missionaries in our islands?" Mr. de Alcalá pressed, as he pushed the bridge of his spectacles higher upon his nose.

Eleanor and Mr. McCauley exchanged inquiring glances.

Luis surprisingly answered. "I suppose for the same reason Hacienda Gonzaga is in business, Mr. de Alcalá."

"And what is that, sir?" the journalist asked.

"What other reason should a business have? To sell something!" Luis exclaimed, chuckling. "The Protestantes, you might say, are engaged in the same activity, though in a different industry."

Except for Maria Teresa, again, everyone laughed, including Padre Damián, who nodded gleefully and leaned to whisper something to el presidente. Lieutenant Waterstone seemed to have caught what the priest said and declared, "At least, Father Damián, American Protestants aren't trying to baptize Filipinos by the sword as the Spaniards did. Protestant pastors may be preaching their faith, yet no one is being forced to accept it."

An awkward silence ensued before Eleanor broke it by saying, "Forgive me for saying so, lieutenant, but aren't you rather being facetious?"

"Do enlighten, Miss Karsten!" the soldier challenged, sipping his wine leisurely—his pale blue eyes now shafts of steel.

Everyone's eyes swung between la maestra Americana and el soldado Americano as though they were spectators of the increasingly popular British sport called tennis.

Eleanor smiled back at him. "Please don't get me wrong, lieutenant. I agree with you that the religious wield their own means of persuasion that could border on coercion. And I say this of all the religious." She glanced at Padre Damián, who scoffed and shook his head. "Yet, as Don Luis intimated," she continued, "they're also in the business of selling something. They call it 'faith.' I call it 'belief'—a belief that only makes sense if everyone is scared enough to buy into it and believe it. Which is exactly what you're doing, lieutenant."

The officer smirked. "And what might that be? Pray, tell, Miss Karsten!" As he breathed in, his blue uniform tightened around his chest as though it might pop out a brass button or two.

"It's simple, really," Eleanor declared. "The religious are selling belief in God by scaring people with threats of hell, while you're selling belief in democracy by threatening them with your gun. In this sense, you're no different from either the religious or the Spaniards, who only happened to be limited to the sword by history."

Lieutenant Waterstone's face flushed, as though Eleanor had thrown boiling water at it. And he looked ready to lunge at her.

"I... I should like to say," Doctor Langford intervened, "being the neutral British here...." He paused to allow the laughter of relief from most of the group to rise and fall before he added, "By golly! Enough now, please, with talk of swords, guns, and religion! I'm ready for dessert! Anyone else?"

Everyone chuckled and buzzed into merry agreement, except Lieutenant Waterstone. Doña Ximena smiled and clapped her hands twice, and servants appeared to serve each guest a blooming chrysanthemum on a dessert plate. On closer examination, the chrysanthemums revealed themselves to be whole miniature pineapples cut into wedges and arranged like the petals of the golden flower.

Eleanor gasped. "Oh, Mr. McCauley! This is that amazingly sweet, miniature pineapple that comes from this region!"

"We wanted to give you a taste of what Hacienda Gonzaga's produces, Mr. McCauley," Luis said, smiling.

"Why, thank you!" Mr. McCauley exclaimed, as he sliced a piece and placed it in his mouth. "This is almost like candy! I very much would like to see it in the field."

"It would be my pleasure," Luis replied. His eyes darted to Eleanor's with a velvet sheen.

After lunch, Mr. de Alcalá asked everyone to pose for a group photograph in front of the Gonzaga ancestor's portrait in the dining room. Padre Damián, el presidente, and Doctor and Mrs. Langford departed soon thereafter. Maria Teresa went upstairs, perhaps for a siesta, while Luis dispensed with the afternoon custom to give the visitors a tour of the plantation.

Before they left the villa, Eleanor excused herself to escape to the lavatory that, in a mansion such as the Gonzagas,' was thankfully indoors. It was furnished with a polished wooden commode set upon a marble base. There was also a tray of folded tissue paper, a glazed clay urn filled with water with a faucet set over a porcelain sink, a dish of French milled soap, and a hand towel monogrammed with the letter *G*.

Eleanor checked on her reflection in the small oval gilt mirror above the sink. She winced upon seeing her shiny nose, forehead, and chin. She pulled out her handkerchief and a miniature flask from her reticule. After wiping her face with the handkerchief, she picked up the flask and tapped out some of the rice flour it contained onto her palm and dabbed and blended the powder evenly on her face. She dipped her ring finger into a miniature dish of lightly-tinted beeswax and applied the stain on her lips to protect them from drying and chapping while it lent them some color and sheen. When she was done refreshing her appearance, she swung the door open and was startled by Luis's mother standing just outside the lavatory.

"Oh! Doña Ximena, sorry!" Eleanor exclaimed, smiling apologetically. "Were you waiting long? It's all yours." She stepped aside to allow the matron to pass.

But the Gonzaga matriarch stayed where she was and didn't return her smile. "Señorita Karsten," she began, "do you not think it is important for people to know their place? You can do this, you know, by keeping to your own kind." Without waiting for Eleanor's reply, she turned around and headed toward the staircase, where she disappeared from Eleanor's view.

The seemingly silent Maria Teresa must not have been tight-lipped, after all. Eleanor realized she was perceived as a threat to the anticipated betrothal of the padre's niece with the most eligible cacique bachelor in town. She thus resolved to conduct herself to allay such fears. She did not relish locking horns with Padre Damián again or being seen as the American bully who deprived the innocent, convent-raised girl of her divine destiny with the haciendero.

CHAPTER 16

Upon the Dark Earth, Still

When Eleanor went out to the porte cochére to join the men going on the plantation tour, she was surprised to find both Diego and Lieutenant Waterstone mounted on side-by-side horses beside the carriage. They both wore such grave countenances that struck her as so comical, it incited her to burst into laughter. Both men glanced at her with disdain.

Luis smiled at her with arched eyebrows. "What is funny, mi querida?" He stood by the open carriage door and helped her climb to her seat. He sat beside her, while Mr. McCauley and Mr. de Alcalá took the bench opposite theirs. The men, including Lieutenant Waterstone and Diego, appeared to be waiting for her reply.

"Oh, nothing!" she said, still grinning. "But if you must know, it was just a silly thought about whether I'm the only rose among the thorns here or the only thorn among the roses!"

Everyone chuckled, except the horsemen, who either did not comprehend her attempt at levity or ignored it altogether, resolute on remaining grim.

"Well, you, mi querida, are certainly the rose!" Luis exclaimed and held her hand and squeezed it.

Remembering her resolution, Eleanor gently pulled her hand from his grasp.

Diego led the quiles, while Lieutenant Waterstone followed alongside the carriage, as if ensuring he didn't miss out on any conversation.

The soldier also appeared to be especially vigilant of the path they were taking as they passed verdant rice fields and coconut tree-covered hills, with a stunning view of the blue Mayon grabbing the eye at every turn.

Mr. McCauley exclaimed, "This looks impressive, Don Luis! How big is the hacienda?"

The haciendero chuckled. "I must confess I do not even know that exactly. Maybe around 10,000 hectares? To be sure, I will have to consult the royal grant. But from here, it is safe to say the hacienda goes as far as the eyes can see."

An awed silence followed. Eleanor turned toward her seatmate. "And where do the workers and their families live, Luis?"

"It depends on the work they do," he replied. "For example, my foreman, there, lives with his sister in a small house near the villa. Makes it convenient for us to meet every morning on hacienda business. The housekeeper has a room in the villa, while the rest of the house servants reside in a bungalow adjacent to the main house. The campesinos live with their families in huts next to the fields they tend. There! You see?" He pointed to a few tiny nipa huts visible between the coconut trees.

Eleanor spotted a young mother sitting at the top of the bamboo stairs of one hut, nursing her infant on her bare breast. A few young children were playing what appeared to be a version of hopscotch on the bare ground below. The sight of the mother and child reminded Eleanor of another young, nursing mother inside a casco on the Pasig River. She visualized such young mothers' lives—filled with the tedium of housework, childbearing, childrearing, and the constant food, health, and resource insecurities, with no education or books to cultivate and entertain their minds, nor any notion of a bigger world beyond their tiny homes and villages. And Eleanor was seized with the angst of growing old before one's time.

Worse to her was the thought of girls having babies when they'd barely emerged from childhood themselves, and then becoming trapped in lives of poverty, along with their children, in a vicious cycle that carried onto succeeding generations. It may take just one person to break such a vicious cycle, she mused—the child who dared rise above his or her station through education. *And this is why I am a teacher*, she told herself.

"So, you see, my workers have a good life," Luis continued. "We not only provide them with good jobs but also good homes."

Lieutenant Waterstone, who'd been riding alongside the carriage ended his silence. "And where, sir, could your men be found?"

Luis glanced up at him. "As I said, teniente, they and their families live in huts nearest the fields they take care of."

"Don't you have some kind of barracks where the unmarried men live?" the soldier asked.

"No," Luis replied. "We are not an army, teniente. We consider ourselves a family with our workers. And, whether hacienderos or campesinos, it does not matter. Children live with their parents until they marry and, often, even after they have children of their own. That is why you will find several generations of the same family living under one roof."

Mr. McCauley said, "I'm curious, Don Luis, how do the hacienda children get to Miss Karsten's school?"

Luis smiled a rueful smile. "I regret they do not."

"But why?" Mr. McCauley exclaimed.

"It is a simple yet not so simple matter of distance," Luis replied. "The school is just too far for the hacienda children to walk to. Their parents start work at dawn and cannot take them."

Mr. McCauley grinned. "Oh, but American children walk to school for miles, even in the snow and, we like to add — uphill, downhill, with or without shoes!" He chuckled.

"Oh, Mr. McCauley!" Eleanor interjected, shaking her head yet smiling. She turned again to Luis. "May I suggest something, Luis?"

"¡Claro que si cariño! What have you in mind?" Luis asked as he likewise turned to her, draping an arm across the top back frame of the bench behind her.

She smiled timorously. "Would you be willing to provide transportation to the hacienda children? I mean, perhaps you have a carretela or two to spare?"

He burst into laughter. "Always the agent provocateur!" he exclaimed, shaking his head. "Mi querida, I cannot promise you anything now, but I can promise to think about it."

She smiled brightly. "Thank you!"

Mr. McCauley expressed similar delight, while Mr. de Alcalá remained focused on taking notes, as if he were tasked with recording a transcript of all that was said and done. Lieutenant Waterstone continued to survey the lay of the land, as if committing it to memory, constructing a map in his head.

"¡Disculpe, Don Luis!" Mr. de Alcalá interjected. "I'd like to return to how you run your hacienda, sir—if you don't mind." Mr. de Alcalá pushed the bridge of his spectacles higher on his nose.

Luis arched an eyebrow. "Well, that depends on what you want to know!" he retorted, sounding miffed.

The journalist continued, seemingly oblivious to his host's pique. "You said, sir, that you provide a good life to your workers by giving them good homes and jobs. Questions aside on what a good life means to peasants—what do you get in return for the work they do for you?" Mr. de Alcalá's eyes appeared to have disappeared behind his eyeglasses as they reflected the sun's glare.

Luis glanced at him and, with a dismissive flip of his hand, said, "Oh, the usual."

"You mean, the usual ratio? Meaning, ninety-five percent share of the yield in your favor?" the reporter asked. "Five percent to the workers, minus payments on loans and interest, I assume?"

Luis scoffed. "Bah! We give them better than that!"

"How much better?" Mr. de Alcalá persisted. "Six, seven percent? Maybe ten?"

Luis chuckled. "Now, that, Señor de Alcalá, I am afraid, is a business secret."

Mr. de Alcalá smiled a knowing smile as he recorded Luis's answer.

Eleanor didn't understand all that Mr. de Alcalá implied when he mentioned loans and interest, but was shocked at how little the peasants seemed to earn from their labor. She asked, "Luis, what happens in case of a drought, flood, or, God forbid, another destructive eruption of the Mayon? Does that ratio still hold?"

"Mi querida, we landlords are humans still capable of compassion—no?" Luis replied in a mellifluous tone, as though chiding a child. "A haciendero is respected as much as a good papá who cares for his children. I value my workers' love and loyalty, as I am sure they value mine."

You mean, like torching your carriage, Eleanor was tempted to say. "But what if the other landlords aren't as compassionate as you?"

Mr. de Alcalá was writing more frantically now in his notebook.

"That, fortunately," Luis replied, "is something my workers never have to worry about as long as they are in my poder."

Eleanor pressed her lips and looked away. Up ahead, Diego's horse nickered as the mounter directed the mountee roadside and waited for the carriage to pass until the rider gained a convenient view of Eleanor. This time, she couldn't resist being drawn into locking eyes with him, yet he looked at her only as if to inform her he was still very much displeased with her. He faced forward again and trotted ahead.

A sense of deflation filled her. Her eyes followed Diego, noting how straight was his back, how elegantly proportioned his torso, how she could almost see his back muscles flexing under his shirt while he rode his brown steed as though they were one and the same beast.

When they came upon a familiar sight, Eleanor cried, "Oh, look!" In her excitement, she unwittingly placed a hand on Luis's thigh as she pointed with another toward the three-foot-high plants growing in the fields on both sides of the first road. Green leafy blades with russet stripes that extended toward the tips radiated from the roseate-green pearls nestled at their centers. Pineapples!

Luis stayed her hand and squeezed it, stating with a bright smile, "You like to see the piñas up close?"

She nodded and smiled and tried to withdraw her hand, but Luis retained it in his hand and ordered the cochero to stop. The driver grunted his instruction to the horses and pulled in the reins. Diego turned his horse around. His eyes darted straight to where his amo held Eleanor's hand firmly—on his thigh. Diego shot Eleanor an accusing look, pressing his full lips into a slim, straight line, setting his square jaw squarely.

Luis got off the carruaje first and extended his hand to assist Eleanor to step down from it. Mr. McCauley and Mr. de Alcalá followed. It hadn't rained in days. Every step Eleanor took powdered her Balmorals with dust. The reporter was soon busy taking photographs of the fields, while Mr. McCauley and Lieutenant Waterstone huddled into a low-voiced chat, occasionally grinning and chuckling. Meanwhile, it appeared the soldier had entrusted his horse's reins to Diego, who looked all the more displeased. The foreman remained on his horse, which continued to nicker, as if it was restless from sensing its master's restlessness.

"Come, querida," Luis said, pulling Eleanor's hand.

The haciendero wandered farther along the carriage road and gazed at the horizon. He only released Eleanor's hand when he unbuttoned his vest and took off his linen jacket, casually folding it over his left forearm. His right hand shaded his eyes from the blinding afternoon sun. Eleanor lowered the brim of her hat over her brow as she, too, peered out to where the fields faded into a dusty white haze.

Luis squatted, pointing to the spiky gem of a fruit surrounded by spears of leaves. Eleanor bent to examine the plant, surprised by the tiny, razor-like teeth along the edges of its leaves. It seemed to be a plant determined not to give up its treasure. How impossible it must be for the campesinos to harvest such a crop without getting themselves cut and scraped!

"You see, querida, how the land is good to those who care for it?" Luis stated.

"I'm well aware, as my parents themselves were farmers," she replied.

"Were they?" He glanced up at her as he sat on his haunches and narrowed his eyes against the sun. "¡Ay, caramba! How come I only learn this now?" He stood and grinned.

She smiled. "You never asked."

He placed both of his hands on her shoulders. "I knew we could work well together, mi querida! But not how perfectly compatible we are!"

"Oh!" she said, grinning. "I wouldn't go that far, Luis!" She turned around to walk back to the group.

He chuckled and followed after her. When he caught up with her, he drew her close to him with an arm hooked around her waist. Eleanor instinctively glanced at Diego, who now looked livid. Unable to bear his searing gaze, she lowered hers.

Mr. de Alcalá asked everyone to pose for another group photograph. He placed Eleanor between Luis and Mr. McCauley, and Lieutenant Waterstone next to the latter. The journalist asked Diego to likewise pose with the group. The foreman pretended incomprehension, until Luis said something to him in Vicolano, which appeared to compel Diego to comply.

The photographer composed a vignette of them facing the sun, with the foreman seated on his horse at the center, directly behind Eleanor. She glanced up at Diego, who faced away from the camera, his nostrils flaring and contracting like a bull ready to gore somebody.

"Mr. de Alcalá," Eleanor hollered. "Can we not have… um… the native posing with us?"

"Why?" the journalist retorted. "He's a perfect backdrop. Our readers will love it."

"Oh, querida, do not worry about my man here!" Luis interjected. "On the contrary, I am sure he is proud to be seen lording over these fields, which he knows like the back of his hand! More than I do—right, Diego?" The haciendero glanced up at his foreman, smiling.

Yet, the servant ignored his master, keeping his fiery eyes fixed on some point in the northern horizon.

"Oh, Señorita Karsten!" Mr. de Alcalá hollered. "Look here, por favor! All right, now, everybody—hold steady. ¡Uno, dos, tres!"

The group returned to their carruaje and the lieutenant mounted his horse again. Diego rode ahead and disappeared from view. Eleanor wondered where he went. She wanted to give him a kind word to assuage his surely wounded pride. The carriage soon passed what Luis called *abaca* fields. The trees had sheaths of olive-green leaves that grew to about ten feet high.

"Luis, I don't understand," Eleanor said. "I thought these were banana trees! But you call them what?"

Luis grinned. "Abaca. Yes, it is easy to be confused because they appear very similar. But look, there, near that hut. Now, that is a banana tree."

Eleanor glanced at it and said, grinning, "I still don't get it."

"You see that?" He pointed to a maroon-brown, prolate spheroid on the tree.

"But that doesn't look like a banana!" Eleanor grinned.

Luis guffawed. "Because it is not yet the fruit! That is the heart of the banana tree that eventually becomes fruits that look like fingers. Like there, see?" He pointed to another tree that was already heavy with cascading bunches of bananas. "The abaca, on the other hand, does not produce edible fruit."

"Oh, I see!" exclaimed Eleanor, smiling, glad to learn something new.

"And did you know that the banana heart is also edible?" Eleanor shook her head, and Luis continued, "We eat it as a vegetable. Very good cooked guinataan style, with coconut milk."

"It's amazing to me how much the native cuisine makes use of most parts of an edible," Eleanor remarked. "I saw my maid cooking the other day with what seemed like calabasa flowers."

Luis chuckled. "As our elders always say, 'Waste not, want not!'"

"I know," Eleanor replied, grinning. "Yolanda says the same."

The carruaje pulled up to a group of buildings that Luis referred to as the copra and abaca bodegas. The structures were constructed of volcanic rock walls and nipa grass-thatched roofs. They sheltered the campesinos working on the bare earth floor inside them. The workers appeared to be all men. Eleanor wondered where the women were. In their huts, tending to housework and children?

Despite the cooler and drier November weather, it felt warm and humid inside the bodega. Most of the men had taken off their shirts. On sighting their amo and his guests, they skittered to the walls to retrieve camisas hanging on rods or nails. They glanced up from their tasks with ambivalent smiles, as though trying to decide whether the visitors were friends or foes. When they spotted Lieutenant Waterstone, they kept their eyes downward.

"Hello!" Eleanor greeted them. "¡Buen día!"

"Buen día, señorita," some replied, their apprehension assuaged by her cordiality.

The copra appeared to be processed from mature coconuts, distinguished by their golden husks. The men masterfully dehusked them on upright blades, revealing the brown, stringy-veined spherical shells at their core. The workers then poked the three penny-sized natural depressions on the pointy end of the shells, from which they poured out the juice into glazed clay urns. Flies and bees competed for landing spots on the wet rims and sides of the urns.

Luis explained they collected the juice to create other products, such as coconut jelly and lambanog. Eleanor smiled remembering her experience with the coconut liquor. There was no other explanation for her lapse of judgment regarding Diego.

The men used their bolos to split the shells, exposing the white meat inside. Luis explained that the halved shells then underwent a drying process. He brought them outside again to show them the split shells placed face down on a slatted bamboo platform above a smoldering fire. Elsewhere in the yard, some men were scooping out the meat from the half shells. Others were spreading the shucked meats on mats under the sun, where they were left out to dry some more, according to Luis. This was what turned the coconut meat into copra. "The copra kernels are then packed into jute sacks and shipped to Manila," Luis said, "bound for refineries that extract the oil for a variety of uses that include industrial, commercial, and residential purposes."

He led them a short walk away outside near another bodega, where men were tearing abaca trunks apart—the trunks, not so much trunks as they appeared to be thick stems consisting of multiple, tightly overlapping, fleshy leaf sheaths. The campesinos stripped off the first layer of dark, coarse fibers from the outer petioles, which they then hung up to dry.

"This is what you Americanos call Manila hemp—the raw material for making ropes," Luis commented. "Now, observe the finer fibers extracted as they strip off the layers near the center."

The group watched as the stripping of the petiole layers closer to the trunk core yielded fibers of a lighter hue and finer texture. These were washed and hung up to dry elsewhere.

"What do you do with the finer batch after it's dried?" Eleanor asked.

"I will show you." Luis grasped Eleanor's hand and led her and the rest of the group inside the bodega where, finally, they saw the women, many of whom looked like mere teenagers.

The women glanced up and acknowledged their visitors, bowing with demure smiles, briefly breaking away from their standard expression that seemed to vacillate between stoicism and suffering. They knotted the ends of the refined fibers and connected them into seamless threads reeled into spools. Some other women fed the spools into the looms that stood at the other end of the building. There, through a masterful dance of arms, legs, and wooden rods, another set of women wove the previously aimless strands into purposeful pattern.

"We call this woven abaca, sinamay. It can be dyed in many colors," Luis said to the group. "Eleanor, I am sure you are asking this in your mind, so I will just answer it now." Eleanor chuckled, and he grinned, as did the rest of the men, except Lieutenant Waterstone, who appeared focused on watching the workers, who, in turn, seemed focused on avoiding his eye.

Luis continued, "Sinamay can be used to make hats, bags, purses or pouches, sandal straps, including household items like table mats, runners, and decorations like flowers."

"It's what Yolanda used to make those flowers for the harvest fiesta," Eleanor remarked.

"Yes, that is correct," Luis replied.

Eleanor smiled as she ran her fingers against the bristly yet beneficial fabric, marveling at how human imagination and labor could transform what was once a seemingly useless, fruitless tree into a product of beauty and many uses. She glanced up at the haciendero and said, "Luis, someone told me in Manila that the material for some of your traditional attire comes from pineapple leaves?"

"Ah, sí—yes," Luis replied, smiling.

"I imagine the pineapple leaves undergo a process similar to what we've seen here?"

"¡Sí, exactamente!" Luis exclaimed. "The piña cloth is woven from the refined fibers of the pineapple leaf. And it may interest you to note that the best, most refined abaca fibers we produce here could also be woven into the piña fibers to create a premium fabric called, piña jusi. That is the preferred material for camisas at sayas and Barong Tagalogs worn for the most special occasions."

"Oh! Are you in the piña cloth business, too?" Eleanor asked.

"Sorry, no." Luis grinned, stroking his beard. "We sell the refined abaca to piña jusi weavers, but do not grow the kind of pineapple needed for the fibers from which the piña cloth is made. This pineapple is the red variety, valued not for its fruit, but for the strength, beauty, and length of its leaf fibers. I decided to stick to what could be eaten."

The group chuckled along with him.

"By the way, are you all thirsty?" he asked. "Would any of you like some coconut juice? I could have some boys pick some young coconuts for refreshment."

"I would love some!" cried Mr. McCauley, raising his hand as if he were a student in a classroom. "I mean, this heat does get to one, doesn't it?" he added with a rueful smile, fanning himself with his boater hat.

The group smiled and nodded their agreement.

Luis led them back outside where he asked a pair of young campesinos to fetch some coconuts from nearby trees. One of them, a boy who could not have been more than thirteen, wore the bright-eyed look of youthful verve and enthusiasm. Everyone watched, fascinated, as the boys climbed up the slim, fifteen to twenty-foot-high trees with the nimbleness of simians.

Many of the workers paused from their tasks and joined the visitors to enjoy the spectacle. They hooted, hollered, and taunted the climbers to prove who was faster and more skillful than the other. When both boys reached the palm canopies that were full of coconut clusters, another competition appeared to get underway: who could drop the most coconuts. Everyone applauded as each coconut dropped to the ground, accompanied by cheers and shouts that tallied the boys' respective scores.

Suddenly, an unearthly shriek shot from the fronded tops, followed by a dark shadow falling before Eleanor's eyes. A loud thud announced that something other than a coconut had landed. Eleanor's brain was struggling to process what her eyes were seeing: two astonished pools of light, dimming into clouds. The younger boy's eyes! She fell to her knees beside the boy's body. His skinny, brown limbs lay twisted in aberrant angles and arcs upon the dark earth, still, as if his body had pleached and merged with the exposed tree roots on which it fell.

It was one of those sleepless nights again. Eleanor lay in bed, lamenting that if only the boy was in school, he would not have been at the hacienda to climb the damned tree to pick stupid coconuts for them. The boy's eyes haunted her: shimmering pools of great expectation, ably contained by the dauntless body and spirit of his youth, until the life drained out of them before her eyes. He'd heeded his amo's call to serve without delay, trusting in his master to reward him for giving las bisítas Americanos a good show. It sickened Eleanor's heart. Learning that Luis would be paying for the boy's funeral and burial lent her little comfort.

She decided that the hacienda system was not much different than slavery. Not even the patriarchal kindness of a haciendero like Luis could dispel the cruelty inherent in a system that kept people impoverished and beholden—either by material debt or debts of honor—to a master. Now, she understood what Mr. de Alcalá meant when he asked about payments on loans and interests as he questioned Luis on the terms of his workers' employment. What debts people couldn't afford to pay off in money, they were expected to pay through labor.

Now, she also grasped the full sense of the term, padrino. When she'd first heard it from Estrella, little did she understand the extent to which native society was built on a web of tit-for-tat, where those who owned the majority of the resources possessed the power to force people to literally bow and bend to their will. How could democracy survive in such a society that not only depended, but seemed to thrive on inequality? The economics of a place had to change before its politics could. Yet how could change be attained when those in power refused to reform it precisely because the prevailing system was already advantageous to them? It was a vicious cycle that required something— or someone—to break it. Something had got to give.

When the first light of dawn filtered through her bedroom capiz windows, Eleanor forced herself from bed. Today was the last day of rehearsal for her young actors. Luis had had his men erect a screen around the stage set that allowed her students to practice their performance but disallowed the town from prematurely watching them. There was no time for grief. She folded her feelings and tucked them away. She couldn't afford to falter now.

On Thanksgiving Day, Eleanor decided to attend Padre Damián's special mass in furtherance of the goodwill that now reigned between herself and the priest. She dressed in the resplendent camisa at saya that Doña Beatriz had her seamstress make for la maestra Americana in anticipation of the event. It was sewn of the finest piña jusi embroidered with seed pearls. The camisa with its rigid bell sleeves was in cream, the panuelo across the shoulders was in royal blue, the tapis over the skirt was in navy, and the saya featured alternating vertical bands of cobalt and magnolia that flared toward the skirt's hem.

Doña Beatriz had insisted there was no better display of American support for the community than la maestra Americana proudly wearing the traditional native lady's attire during the uniquely American fiesta. The stylish matron likewise ordered a matching cream Spanish lace *velo* or "veil" and an ivory peineta comb from her favorite shop in Manila. When the veil arrived a few days ago, Doña Beatriz had her *costurera* likewise sew a few seed pearls on it.

Yolanda helped to complete the look by assisting her mistress in gathering her long, curly, golden locks and coiling them into an artful pusod. The maid-turned-lady's-dresser then crowned the bun with the peineta, which served to pitch and elevate the shimmering lace veil on Eleanor's head. As Yolanda appraised her creation, she jumped up and down, clapping, like a little girl. "¡O, señorita!" she cried. "Bee-yu-tee-pul!"

The maid ordered a calesin for her mistress to bring her to the church. Eleanor ascended the grand stone steps and entered the Iglesia de Nuestra Señora de la Cosecha through a pair of gigantic wooden castle doors, each paneled by eight equilateral crosses. Mayon Volcano loomed large, northeast of the structure—a giant witnessing something gigantic, for Eleanor hadn't been inside a church since her parents' funeral. The sun shone at an angle on the volcano, accentuating the pleats sculpted by centuries of lava flows on Daragang Magayon's turquoise skirt.

When Eleanor entered the church, a low buzz erupted among the people who spotted her and grew louder as it spread among the congregation. Eleanor lowered her gaze against the fawning admiration in the eyes and smiles that greeted her. What pride and joy they expressed from merely seeing her wearing their native attire!

There didn't appear to be any pews, for everyone simply stood where they found space in the crowded church. A legion of lace-veiled women appeared to be holding flapping doves captive at their chests as they beat their abanicos furiously upon their bosoms. Contrary to Eleanor's assumption it would be cooler inside the stone church, the heat from outside radiated through the porous rock walls and turned the church into an oven. She followed the women's example, unfurling the cream lace and ivory Spanish fan that Doña Beatriz had lent her. The erstwhile opera singer realized she'd forgotten to order a matching fan for Eleanor's camisa at saya. "A woman's abanico is a crucial part of what she is wearing," Doña Beatriz had said. And so necessary in this heat, aggravated by these snug and stiff clothes! At least, the camisa at saya didn't require Eleanor to wear a corset.

A stern-looking matrona dressed in a severe, drab, brown camisa at saya and a long, black lace veil, adorned only with a large silver cross pendant hanging from a leather string necklace, approached Eleanor and motioned to follow her. She led her toward the apse where two rows of benches were reserved for important people. Eleanor shook her head and remained standing with the crowd, until Doña Beatriz spotted her and adamantly gestured that she join her in the second row where Doctor Langford, Sam, Cristina, Estrella, Mr. McCauley, and Mr. de Alcalá were likewise seated.

Everyone whom Eleanor passed murmured praise for her appearance and attire. Doña Beatriz beamed proudly when her husband said, "Well done, my dear Bea!" Eleanor glanced at Estrella, who nodded at her, smiling with approval. Her brother didn't seem to be anywhere near. Eleanor was struck with both relief and disappointment at Diego's absence.

At the front row sat the town's most eminent denizens, among them—el presidente and his wife and Maria Teresa, who sat between Doña Ximena and Luis. They turned all their heads toward Eleanor, who wasn't surprised when the Spanish mestiza and the latter's future mother-in-law glanced at her with indifference, while Luis flashed her an especially radiant smile, unable to hide his admiration. Doña Ximena leaned to her son and nudged him to face the altar.

The altar echoed the Solomonic columns and niches on the church's façade. Each of the niches was dedicated to a different saint, and the topmost niche featured the image of its patron saint, Our Lady of the Harvest. From the gloriously glittering altar, one would have thought Magayon's Catholics were polytheistic and worshipped a goddess as their main deity, instead of the male god of the Judeo-Christian religion.

Soon, bells rang and the choir in the loft above the church entrance erupted into joyous song. Ushered in by his sacristans, Padre Damián appeared and approached the altar, dressed in dazzling raiment. He acknowledged Eleanor's presence with a subtle nod.

During the sermon, which Doctor Langford whispered to Eleanor, the padre declared, "We thank the good Lord for sending teachers to Magayon's children, like la maestra Americana, Señorita Eleanor Karsten, who has caused great things to happen in our humble town. I urge everyone to watch the play her students will perform later—to which, yours truly, gave a helping hand. It shows America was born in the light of Christ's cross, which can make the Estados Unidos a great nation if only it could rise from under the shadow of the heretical Protestants!"

Immediately after Mass, Eleanor went with Estrella and Sam to check on their students at the church school building, where the padre had offered a room in which the young actors could change into their costumes. A frenzied mess greeted them. Anxious parents crowded their excited children, fussing over their outfits and makeup. Bayani looked splendid as an American Indian chief. The feathers of the turkeys being roasted for dinner had supplied the material for his headdress, which Sam had helped to create. Eleanor had listened in while the former soldier regaled Bayani with tales of the Indian-American battles as they worked on the boy's costume. Although Bayani initially resisted playing an American Indian, Eleanor was finally able to persuade him to accept after promising him the role of the tribal chief.

Asunción assumed the perfect persona of a demure and devout Pilgrim woman, although Eleanor couldn't understand why the girl's mother thought the role meant dressing up her daughter as a Catholic nun. Overall, the children were a convincing lot of American Indians and Pilgrims, all thrilled to be playing a part in the town's pioneering play about the American pioneers.

As she and her fellow teachers descended the church steps to go to the audience section in the plaza grounds, Eleanor noticed how soldiers were installed at various spots along the plaza's perimeter. She hoped for no untoward incident tonight with the insurrectos, yet feared the soldiers' presence only increased such risk.

While the audience waited for the play to begin, the same mandolin band that played at the Gonzaga fiesta reception provided musical entertainment. Eleanor had since learned it wasn't a mandolin but a *rondalla* band because it didn't play mandolins. Instead, they played a similar-looking instrument called a *bandurria*. It teamed up with a brass band playing what the native musicians must have fancied as American patriotic music. Eleanor and Sam exchanged glances and grinned as the band played "There'll Be a Hot Time in the Old Town Tonight."

The reserved seating in front of the stage duplicated the hierarchy inside the church. Chairs were marked with the names of Magayon's luminaries, including Lieutenant Waterstone and the mayors of neighboring towns like Legazpi. The rest of the audience had to stand.

The people watched the parade of elites toward their designated chairs as if this was the highlight of the evening. It reminded Eleanor of a similar scene at the Luneta a few months ago. *How long ago and distant that now seemed!* She imagined what Miss Covell, Maude, and Arabella would say if they could only see her play performed by her students.

She removed her velo and draped it over her arms like a wrap. The large, gossamer butterfly sleeves of her camisa made her feel like a fairy queen approaching her throne. The people she passed greeted her enthusiastically. Those in the distance hollered, "¡Buenas tardes, señorita!" or "¡Gracias, Señorita Karsten!" or "¡Felicitaciones, señorita!" Those within reach touched her arm in the manner by which they caressed their saints' feet in the church. Then, there were her neighbors: Nanay Viring, Tomasa, and Senyong—the drunkard guitarist who, commendably, did not yet appear to be drunk.

From behind Nanay Auring suddenly appeared the face that somehow had the power to make Eleanor's heart jump. The sparkling dark eyes burned with a bitter flame tonight, the angular jaw set squarely, and the full lips pressed into a stern line, twitching ever so slightly. A scorned lover.

The stage set was just as marvelous, if not more so than any opera house backdrop. Luis had framed his colorful canvas of mountain, sea, and sky with real corn stalks, which appeared to be a continuation of the corn fields painted in the foreground.

Eleanor and Estrella went on stage to introduce the show. With the help of Estrella's Vicolano-Spanish translation, Eleanor explained what the play was about and concluded by thanking the students' parents and all who'd supported the school in the endeavor, naming Mayor Dizon, Padre Damián, and Don Luis Gonzaga. The three men acknowledged her recognition by standing and bowing to the audience as if they, too, were performing.

As Padre Damián had correctly predicted, the entry of a huge cross conveying the Pilgrims' arrival on American shores resonated greatly with the native audience. Some of them crossed themselves, bowed their heads, and even genuflected. What Eleanor did not expect was the startling revision of her script, which she neither authored nor authorized.

Someone—Bayani, she suspected—had added a segment wherein the Pilgrim girl, Asunción, pointed a wooden toy pistol to the head of the Indian chief, Bayani, and screamed in her signature shrill voice, "Your moanee or your life, meester!" Bayani, acting scared, handed the Pilgrim girl a bushel of corn. The audience roared into histrionic laughter and applause. Bayani turned to them and smiled before returning to his character.

Eleanor gripped the edge of her chair. Her bosom rose and fell with her quickened, shallow breaths, grappling with the shocking implications of what her students had just done. Bayani must have persuaded them to play along with his prank, taking la maestra Americana at her word that the cartoon that had inspired the rogue scene was meant as a joke—a joke that now proved quite appealing to the native audience's sense of humor. Yet, Eleanor wasn't sure if the spectators appreciated the scene as simple comedy or picked up on its covert, dissident message—and agreed with it. As the audience laughed, it was as if they and her students were laughing *at* the Thomasite and all other Americans—screaming, *ha-ha, the joke's on you!*

Bayani's surprise played well, too well—a stunning display of the boy's precociousness, including, clearly, his political canniness. Through this maverick act, he'd ensured Eleanor knew that he knew the cartoon wasn't simply an innocent jest, but one that, like all jokes, contained truth. A frowning glance from Lieutenant Waterstone told Eleanor he knew this, too.

At the end of the play, the young actors called upon Eleanor to join them on stage and share in the glory of their standing ovation. Eleanor looked upon her students with bewilderment. She vacillated between obliging and scolding them. She remained upset over Bayani's mutiny and his classmates' complicity.

Yet, the boy was talented and still so young. Her father's tolerance of her own youthful rebellions reminded her this was an age when a child was most vulnerable to criticism. Therefore, a wise mentor was careful not to crush the child's independent mind and creative spirit through harsh rebuke or discipline.

Thus, the Thomasite went on stage and held the hands of her students, Bayani and Asunción, who, in turn, enclasped their classmates' hands. Together, they bowed before their highly appreciative audience.

CHAPTER 17

The Turning

All who had bought tickets to the Thanksgiving dinner and dance eagerly lined up in front of the ayuntamiento and presented their proofs of purchase to the *damas* of the Thanksgiving Committee. A balustered, mahogany staircase led the excited patrons to the grand hall on the second floor. There, a stately reception awaited them, where Mayor Dizon and his wife greeted everyone as though they were royalty.

Doña Beatriz and her volunteer army of society matrons had transformed the space into an elegant dining hall and ballroom. They procured every table they could borrow from the great households of Magayon and arranged them around a space reserved as a dance floor. The damas covered the tables with heirloom embroidered linens and laid centerpieces consisting of brass candelabras—that were, again, loaned by elite families—surrounded by red, white, and blue sinamay flowers.

The combined bands played the American hits, "Just One Girl" and "After the Ball," followed by other lively and romantic Spanish and native ballads.

Seated at the presidential table were the town's top elite and special guests, including the mayors of neighboring towns and their wives. Eleanor was glad to find herself seated at another table with Sam, Cristina, Estrella, and the student performers, who'd changed out of their costumes into their Sunday best. Eleanor smiled at seeing Bayani seated next to Asunción.

Eleanor caught Doña Hermosa frequently glancing at her, pushing up her coiffure that appeared to be an imitation of the Gibson hairstyle Eleanor wore on other occasions. The mayor's wife also had to pull up the constantly dipping neckline of her gown. Since it was in red, white, and blue, Eleanor assumed the frock was specially made for the occasion. Yet, its voluminous bustled skirt betrayed the outmoded European style to which the mayor's wife seemed hopelessly stuck.

El presidente delivered a long-winded speech welcoming each of the special guests and thanking all who had supported *his* Thanksgiving event, continuing with the story of how he got the idea for it. His oratory threatened to turn the food cold, prompting Padre Damián to intervene with the prayer for grace. At the prayer's conclusion, a group of servants on loan likewise from Magayon's prominent households served the dinner.

Eleanor wasn't sure if the food was a success with tonight's elite crowd as it was with her neighbors. She feared, based on the lack of verbal praise, that the menu may have been unremarkable to the discriminating patrons. Some guests were pushing around the stuffing on their plates, as if they didn't know what to do with it. Mr. McCauley, nonetheless, said he liked everything—although he, like she, when she'd first arrived in Magayon, had to wash down the spicy foods with copious glasses of iced limonada. When the calabasa and pili nut pie desserts were served along with cafe and cocoa, however, some diners surprisingly clapped their approval, which caused a chain reaction into unanimous applause.

El presidente proudly stood to accept the praise and, in a rare sharing of the spotlight, requested Eleanor, Doña Beatriz, and the damas of the Thanksgiving Dinner and Dance Committee to stand with him.

Doña Beatriz then announced the commencement of the dance with an exhibition of a *rigodon de honor*. For the Americans' benefit, she explained it was a type of quadrille that the ilustrados among them who'd traveled and studied abroad adopted from the court dances of Europe. She introduced a long list of dance couples, who rose from their chairs and lined up on one end of the dance floor. The ladies—backs straight, chins high—looked regal in their glimmery camisas at sayas. Their gentlemen escorts, however, appeared strangely mismatched with them, for the men were curiously not dressed in their traditional Barong

Tagalogs, but in some peculiar variation of the European black tailcoat: They wore their pleated white shirts like tunics—oddly untucked from their trousers and sticking out from under their dinner jackets.

The rondalla played a festive tune to the rhythm of a quadrille reminiscent of American square dance music—performed to a slower beat. The couples held hands raised high and paraded around the dance floor in a light, march-like tempo. They congregated at the center where they formed a rectangle, facing each other. Their movements entailed much bowing by the gentlemen and curtsying by the ladies and alternated such dainty, genteel moves with a dizzying sequence of promenades, turns, crisscrossings, and exchanges of partners and positions. It struck Eleanor as less of a dance than it seemed to be a mimicry of how the native elite amused themselves with afternoon plaza promenades, parading in their finery while engaging in social niceties with people of their class.

When the rigodon ended, Doña Beatriz joined the band and announced she was going to sing a *kundiman* or "love song" called "Sarung Banggi," which meant, "One Night." She proudly said that a young Vicolano composer named Potenciano Gregorio composed the kundiman, which, she declared, was perfect for a waltz. She invited everyone to dance as she sang, eliciting shouts of delight and applause from couples who hurried to claim spots on the dance floor. An unexpected yet familiar voice startled Eleanor when it said, "Shall we, mi querida?" When she glanced up, she was surprised to see Luis holding out his hand to her, smiling expectantly. He had shockingly abandoned Maria Teresa to dance the first dance with her! If she didn't wish to humiliate him publicly, she had to accept.

He led her to the center of the dance floor and planted his right hand on the middle of her back. Eleanor lamented how a lady's position during a waltz allowed her little control over the way a man held her, for her left hand was meant to hold and lift the left side of her skirt, while the man's left hand grasped her right. Luis held her so close to him that she felt smothered by his overwhelming lavender and tobacco scent. All she could do was turn her face away from him.

She likewise felt helpless against the assault of his eyes. During her fitting for her camisa at saya, Doña Beatriz had declared how she despised false modesty that hid a woman's natural assets. She thus suggested that her seamstress lower the neckline of Eleanor's camisa just enough to show some cleavage, and Eleanor agreed because it wasn't any lower than the décolletage of her blue frock. Now, she cringed, for this allowed Luis to gallingly leer at the swell of her breasts. She glanced at Doña Ximena and Maria Teresa, who were both frowning at her. Fortunately, Padre Damián had left the ball immediately after the rigodon, or she'd surely find herself in another feud with him tonight.

"Is this not perfection?" Luis said, smiling at her with mischief in his eyes.

Eleanor continued to avert her gaze. "What do you mean?"

His voice softened. "You—in my arms."

She tried to loosen herself from his hold, but he only pressed her body tighter to his. "Luis—what are you doing?" She glared at him.

"What am I doing? I suppose I am trying to see if there is hope, mi querida." His tone sounded earnest.

Eleanor's eyes narrowed. "Hope for what?"

"What else—but for me?" He smiled coquettishly.

"For you?" Her brows arched as her eyes widened. "Oh, but Luis—how about Maria Teresa?" she exclaimed under her breath, remembering Doña Ximena's warning to stick to her kind.

He scoffed. "¡Basta! Maria Teresa is just a girl!"

"Shhh!" Eleanor interjected. "People might hear you!"

"I do not care," Luis said. "She is not a woman like you—whom I could talk to, be true partners with. Can you imagine, querida, what the two of us, together, could achieve—not only for ourselves, but for this town, these people? We would be unstoppable! And did I mention how much I desire you?"

"Oh, my goodness, Luis! I had no idea! I'm sorry if I misled you in any way, but I assure you—my only interest here is my teaching mission." Her eyes anxiously scanned the room, worried someone had already overheard their conversation. She glimpsed a couple tottering on the other side of the dance floor. It was Lieutenant Waterstone, dancing with Estrella, who looked mortified. The soldier appeared flushed, swaying and swirling the native teacher in a manner that could topple them both at any moment.

"I find that hard to believe!" Luis exclaimed, grabbing Eleanor's attention back to him. "Did you really have no idea of my feelings for you? ¡Mírame, querida, por favor! Look at me and tell me you felt nothing at all for me all these months!" His voice was thick and low, and he pressed her against him even more. She felt the familiar, yet nonetheless startling hardness in his groin she'd encountered on that day she helped him paint the stage backdrop.

"Oh, Luis, I wish you would stop. Or…"

"Or what?" he interjected.

"Or… I'll shame you by leaving you on this dance floor!" She tried to wriggle out of his hold, but he only held her more tightly — again.

A battle of wills between them ensued as they continued to dance. Eleanor kept her face turned away from him, refusing to meet his gaze, until he groaned and relaxed his embrace. "¡Perdóname, Eleanor! Please. Forgive my conduct to… to madness! I did not know how to ascertain your feelings for me, apart from… from being direct." He bowed his head.

Eleanor heaved a sigh. "Luis, I think we've had some serious miscommunication here. I, too, apologize for my part in the misunderstanding. Please understand — while I appreciate our friendship, I'm determined to remain focused on my job." *And becoming your mother's and Padre Damián's sworn enemy isn't my idea of doing a good job!*

"What? What is it?" He searched her eyes. "Is it because of Mamá? Or Padre Damián? Eleanor, know this: While I am a good son, I am also the master of my own desires."

"Luis, can you please take me back to my seat now?" She steeled herself against his gaze.

He grimaced. "Do I have to?"

"Yes." She pressed her lips in a firm line. "We shouldn't be having this conversation — especially not before all these people!"

A scream emanated from the other side of the dance floor. "¡Salvaje! Let me go!" cried Estrella, struggling to free herself from Lieutenant Waterstone's embrace. The soldier appeared to be trying to kiss her. From the corner of her eye, Eleanor saw Sam leap from his chair and, though limping, rushed toward the officer, whom he punched and sent crashing to the floor.

As if this wasn't enough ruckus, what sounded like gunshots reverberated from the plaza outside. Luis pulled Eleanor down to the floor. Together, they crept toward the window to peer out, as many did. What appeared to be a straw effigy of an American soldier, wrapped in the American flag, was burning on stage.

"Halt, you damn n***ers!" yelled one of the soldiers before firing another shot at the dissident shadows.

A sickening feeling filled Eleanor. Could those be Diego and his men the soldiers were after? It occurred to her that another attack by the insurrectionists while the town was distracted by the Thanksgiving fiesta couldn't be more perfectly timed.

Everybody crouched down as more gunshots and screams shattered the vitreous shell of the crystalline evening.

Back in school, Eleanor, Sam, and Estrella discovered their flag missing. Many students were also absent for the first few days after the Thanksgiving weekend. Estrella attributed it to fear—fear of the soldados Americanos who were again raiding homes, seizing fathers and brothers, and manhandling women who objected to their husbands and sons being taken away.

Lieutenant Waterstone practically declared martial law in Magayon, imposing search and seizure orders and a curfew that prohibited anyone from loitering or otherwise being outside their homes after the church bells rang the six o'clock evening prayers. The proscription lasted till the church bells rang again next morning, reminding everyone to attend six o'clock mass.

This suited Padre Damián well, Eleanor imagined, for it ensured everyone turned to God, forsaking sinful nocturnal activities—but not the farmers, who already had to be at the fields before sunrise; nor the merchants, who needed to be on their way to or from Legazpi Port; nor el presidente, who wasn't happy reigning over a tense town, with himself looking completely *inutil* or "useless" to his people.

Mayor Dizon was likewise reportedly livid over Mr. de Alcalá's article in the *Manila Sun* that wrote more about the effigy and flag burning than the virtues of Magayon's first Thanksgiving Fiesta at the

Plaza—particularly, el presidente's historic achievement in organizing the first municipal-sponsored American fiesta in the islands that also funded an American school.

Something had to be done. Eleanor asked Sam to accompany her to the ayuntamiento to talk with el presidente and, together, request a conference with Lieutenant Waterstone to de-escalate the situation. She would assure Lieutenant Waterstone the school wasn't pressing charges on anyone for the stolen flag and, therefore, there was no need to continue terrorizing the community over it.

"Are ya kiddin,' Leonor?" Sam exclaimed. "Me, go with ya and talk to Waterstone? After givin' that bastard a shiner, ya think he'd listen to me? An' remember—am retired an' all. 'Ave as much influence on those buggers as a monkey on a tree." He scoffed. "An' the mayor? I tell ya—as far as the United States Army is concerned, he's their puppet."

Eleanor sighed. "But, Sam, we can't go on like this—not with Christmas coming! It's a depressing state for the children, who are also missing much of their lessons." She noted that Bayani and Asunción hadn't returned to class. "I believe many of them are scared to even make the trip to school. Or their parents won't let them."

Sam scoffed. "Stop pretendin' the flag thievery is the only problem. Ya know as well as I do that the army can't take what happened lightly. Why, that whole effigy and flag burnin' was practically a declaration of war! Only way to appease Waterstone is to give 'im an offerin.'"

"Like what?"

"Hate to say this, but... a sacrificial lamb. Someone Waterstone could blame the whole thing on an' help 'im with Manila. Make 'em think he's doin' his job proper."

"Are you serious?" Eleanor exclaimed. "Just point him to someone—anyone? Where's our sense of justice? That can't be the answer!"

Sam reprised, "The feller doesn't 'ave to be innocent, ya know. The insurrectos would 'ave to offer one of their own. That's the only way to get back the peace. After all, like ya said, how bad could his punishment be? No one got killed or hurt. Someone has got to pay, somehow!"

Eleanor thought of the tattooed man. *Should I? Could I... give him up?* After all, Juan was someone with proven violent tendencies. Diego may have been able to restrain him, but it was only a matter of time before the man caused trouble again. She wouldn't be surprised if he was behind the Thanksgiving incident. But, if he was, wouldn't Diego be also complicit—if he was indeed Juan's leader? Perhaps it was time to have a talk with Diego. Meanwhile, she had something to say to Lieutenant Waterstone, with or without Sam. She needed to tell him to leave Estrella alone.

Next day, Eleanor entrusted her morning classes to her assistant teachers. There was a light rain. She held an umbrella over herself as she walked from her house to the infantry station. On her way there, a carretela came up from behind her. She paused roadside to let it pass. It carried soldiers and their captives, who may be campesinos from Hacienda Gonzaga.

As the flatbed bamboo carriage passed her, many of the prisoners glanced at her with mixed expressions of dread and defiance. Some of them were merely boys—almost as young, if not younger than the boy who'd fallen to his death. Their hands were bound behind their backs with rope. Eleanor recalled how Luis said that the abaca fibers his men produced were used to make rope—the same rope that now held the same men captive. Most of them were shirtless above their pajama bottoms or were wearing torn and bloodied camisa de chinos, suggesting they'd been dragged out of their beds and beaten up by the soldiers. The rain dripped from their stringy hair and swollen faces, but didn't wash off the blood from their cuts, nor the stain of their bruises.

She hurried after them toward the infantry station, along with a couple of yapping stray dogs that chased the carriage, likely provoked by the scent of blood. She passed several houses that appeared to be locked up and lifeless, whose inhabitants were surely watching the morbid parade from gaps in their shut windows. When she reached the station, the carretela was already empty of its cargo. She asked the guard at the door if she could see Lieutenant Waterstone.

"Pardon me, ma'am. But you can't be here right now." Sweat beads rimmed the young soldier's upper lip, and his blue flannel shirt was soaked around the collar and armpits. Eleanor couldn't believe the army hadn't yet supplied its soldiers with uniforms appropriate for a tropical climate. He looked like a mere teenager, which wasn't surprising to her.

She knew that many soldiers were boys barely out of high school, who often came from destitute backgrounds because some of them were her former students. They'd likely signed up with the army as a meal ticket and passage into exotic adventure more than as a patriotic act. The older soldiers were usually veterans of the Civil and Spanish-American Wars who'd turned their unsated blood lust on a new common enemy: the Filipino insurrecto.

Eleanor's head jerked toward where cries, yelling, and other violent noises came from inside the infantry station. She turned to the soldier and asked, "What's your name, young man?"

Looking straight ahead, as though he was avoiding her gaze, he replied, "Patton, ma'am."

"Please, Private Patton," she begged with urgency laced with honey. "It's of utmost importance that you inform Lieutenant Waterstone I need to speak with him. It's about the school, you see, and I am the principal."

The young soldier finally looked at her. "Oh. Well… I… I'll see what I can do, ma'am. But please—remain here."

"Oh, but it's raining! Might I not sit inside while I wait?" Eleanor smiled with eyebrows arched. "Please?"

Private Patton looked flushed and overwhelmed. "B-but there's nowhere for you inside, ma'am. It's not allowed."

Eleanor tilted her head and pointed to the space behind the soldier. "Then, may I just please stand in the hallway? You wouldn't want me to get drenched, would you?"

The soldier sighed. "I… I guess that w-would be all right," he said with a begrudging tone. "But please, ma'am, you have to wait here till I return."

Eleanor smiled and nodded, stepped inside, and closed her parapluie. Private Patton entered the room nearest the entrance to the building and surprisingly came back with a stool he set on the floor. "Here, ma'am."

"Why, thank you, young man! 'Tis kind of you." She smiled and sat.

He turned around and headed toward a staircase midway down the hall.

Eleanor rested her hands on the grip of her umbrella. Shouts and screams continued from the hallway's end. Unable to bear them, she stood and followed where they led. The hallway turned into another hallway, and then another. The aisle turned into a corridor banded on one side by what appeared to be prison cells. The opposite wall had an iron-barred transom window close to the ceiling. The noises appeared not only to be coming from the groaning and moaning men inside the cells but also from what sounded like women and children crying and wailing outside the wall. The place reeked of unwashed human bodies and their liquids and feces.

She ventured past cell blocks filled with the listless bodies of native men flopped down on the broken, grimy terracotta floors. Many of the prisoners glanced up at her with mouths agape. She recognized Bayani's father among them. His eyes lit up when he saw her, but she pressed her forefinger to her lips to signal him to stay quiet.

Farther, she was aghast to discover, alone in a tiny cell, none other than Toto, the vagabond. *Oh, my God! Has he been here, all along?* She scuttled toward him, exclaiming under her breath, "Toto! Toto! Are you all right?" The man looked at her with blank eyes. He appeared acutely malnourished. "I… I'll get back to you, Toto. I'll try to get you out of here, too!"

She continued toward the last cell from where the yelling, groaning, and chortling were coming. When she got there, two soldiers were standing by an open cell door—hooting and howling as they watched something on the floor. Eleanor peeked between them. A soldier with sergeant's stripes was hunched over a native man whose shoulders and arms were held down by another pair of soldiers squatting on opposite sides of him.

They had pried the prisoner's mouth with a conch shell, into which the sergeant was pouring water from a bucket. The officer yelled, "Well, n***er, are ya gonna talk now? Have ya had enough?" The prisoner's body jerked as if he was drowning. The pouring paused, and the prisoner coughed and raised his head, gasping for air. But the sergeant continued to bear down on the prisoner's chest with his knee.

Eleanor shrieked and slipped from behind the two soldiers. "Stop! Stop it, you savages! Can't you see he's drowning? Get off him, fiend! You're killing him!" She lunged at the sergeant with her umbrella, striking at the soldiers who tried to block her path.

One of them managed to grab the parapluie, while another pulled her away from the sergeant, who yelled, "What the hell! What's this b**ch doing here?" He touched his face and his eyes widened when he saw blood on his fingers. She'd grazed his cheek with the metal tip of her umbrella. The sergeant stood and approached her menacingly. He was about to hit her when recognition registered in his eyes. He retracted his hand and spit on the floor. "Ma'am, what do you think you're doing? You're not allowed here!"

She was panting from breathlessness and glared at him.

The sergeant glanced at the soldier who held her. "Corporal, take her away! And make sure you get that muttonhead who'd let her slip by him!"

"Sir, yes, sir!" The corporal grinned and dragged her out of the cell into the hallway.

Many prisoners stood, shouting invectives at the soldier pulling Eleanor past their cells.

"Get your hands off me!" Eleanor cried as she struggled to free herself. When they turned the corner toward the entrance hallway, Private Patton was at the other end, scratching his head, until he turned around and saw her with the corporal. When Eleanor saw the bottom step of the stairs, she bolted from the corporal's hold and ran upstairs. "Lieutenant! Lieutenant Waterstone! It's Miss Karsten! I need to speak with you this instant!"

"Ma'am! You can't go there!" yelled the corporal, who chased after her, caught her midway up the staircase, and held her in a bear hug.

"Take your hands off of me! Lieutenant Waterstone! We need to talk!"

The officer's head popped over from the stair balusters above them. "What's going on?"

"Sir! I'm sorry, sir!" The corporal glanced up at his superior while trying to detain the writhing Eleanor. "We… we caught this lady in the cells. She says she needs to speak with you."

Lieutenant Waterstone sniggered. "Why, Miss Karsten! Ready to talk now, are you? Let her come up, corporal."

The soldier freed Eleanor, who straightened her hat, pulled down her waist jacket, and tucked the loose tendrils of her hair behind her ears. Lieutenant Waterstone met her at the landing and waved toward the room behind him.

"Sit." The officer pointed to one of two armless rattan chairs facing an imposing desk that had a typewriter and stacks of papers on it. Maps of the Philippine Islands and the Vicol region were tacked on a wall. On a map of Albay province, a large area was encircled and marked, Hacienda Gonzaga.

"You said you wanted to talk. Now, talk!" Lieutenant Waterstone said as he sat behind the desk and raised his feet on it. His blue eyes shone with wicked amusement, one of which was still ringed with the bruise caused by Sam's punch. He looked like a raccoon missing an eye. Eleanor wanted to lunge at him and fix the anomaly.

She sat up. "Lieutenant Waterstone, I demand you tell your soldiers to stop what they're doing to that poor man downstairs and release all the prisoners—including that unfortunate vagrant you've been holding here since the fiesta!"

He sneered. "Demand, Miss Karsten? And what gives you that right?"

"Because… if you don't… I won't tell you what else I remembered about that ambush!"

He guffawed. "Finally jogged your memory, eh?" He stood and walked around the desk to where she sat. Resting his bottom on the table's edge, he set his hands on his thighs and bent from the waist to place his face in front of hers. "Tell me, Miss Karsten, what do you see in these monkeys that makes you so enamored with them?"

Eleanor neither flinched nor blinked, and declared with a steady voice, "Lieutenant, I'd appreciate it if you stopped using such language with me. I'm a civilian agent of the United States federal government with authority over the education, safety, and welfare of my students. Anything that threatens that, like this witch trial and torture prison of yours, is *my* concern."

"Ha! You really believe that?" He sniggered. "Even if that were true, then you're a civilian who now happens to be interfering with military justice—which is under *my* control. You must remember, Miss Karsten, that in this town, *I am* the law." A nervous tick under his left eye twitched as he spoke. He clipped her scrutiny of him by walking to the window and gazing outside. When he turned to her again, he crossed his arms and said, "Don't you realize I have the power to force this information out of you—without having to accede to any of your demands?"

She glared at him. "And how, exactly, would you do that, lieutenant? By subjecting me to the water torture you're doing to that helpless man downstairs?"

He chortled. "Boy, you're a spitfire aren't you? I'd hate to be one of your students and find myself at the end of your stick."

One of the soldiers entered the room carrying Eleanor's umbrella. "The lady's weapon, sir," he said, smiling. He glanced at Eleanor. "Did a number on Sergeant Pearson's face."

"Ha!" Lieutenant Waterstone guffawed. "You really did have my man at the end of your stick, didn't you?" His chortling grated in her ears. He nodded at his subordinate, who left Eleanor's parapluie by the door. The lieutenant sat behind his desk again. "Now, Miss Karsten, where were we?"

Eleanor grimly stated, "I'm serious, lieutenant. I won't tell you a thing until you release all the prisoners!" She leaned forward. "Think about it. What, after all, did happen? You're holding all these men and torturing them and destroying our relationship with the community! And for what? For an annoying, yet harmless prank?"

He scoffed. "You call what happened harmless?"

"No one stood to be hurt by it, except by your soldiers shooting indiscriminately! Why, you all could have killed innocent people! Thank goodness, no one was hurt! Except perhaps your egos."

She softened her tone, hoping to reach his better angel, in case he had one. "Lieutenant, we have to prove ourselves bigger and better than the pranksters if we're to show we're a civilized nation with the moral authority to govern and educate these people! It's your choice: Go after the real threat, or insist on this machismo contest with the natives over some tomfoolery?"

The officer regarded her intently. Eleanor breathed deeply, hopeful he was listening now and that she may be succeeding in persuading him with reason—until he howled in laughter again. "Oh, Miss Karsten, you are one funny lady! You really think you could negotiate and argue your way through this, don't you?" He was still grinning when he glanced at the hallway and yelled, "Corporal!"

The subordinate entered the office and saluted the officer, who declared, "Detain this woman in the store room! And keep her there till she's ready to talk!"

The soldier saluted. "Sir, yes, sir!" He glanced at Eleanor with apprehension, seemingly unsure of how to hold her.

"No, no!" Eleanor jumped to her feet, escaping the corporal's grasp and knocking down her chair. "Don't you, or you, dare touch me!" She pointed her finger at him and the lieutenant.

What looked like a game of tag ensued between her and the corporal, and the lieutenant laughed as he watched them.

"The superintendent will hear of this!" she screamed, zigzagging and outstepping the corporal before she rushed toward the door and grabbed her umbrella. Pointing the tip of the parapluie at the soldier, she cried, "Stop! Or I'm not responsible for what happens to your face!"

The lieutenant blindsided her and snatched her umbrella away, allowing his subordinate to seize Eleanor and turn her around to hold her in a bear hug. The corporal was about to drag her out of the room when Private Patton barged in and blocked their exit, pulling somebody from behind him.

The private cried, "Sir! Sir! This one claims to be responsible for the Thanksgiving racket!" The young soldier turned around and grabbed whoever was behind him and shoved him before Lieutenant Waterstone.

Eleanor gasped on seeing who it was—even before Private Patton announced, "He says his name is Bayani, sir!"

Most people probably couldn't say when their childhood ended. But not Bayani. He knew this the moment he confessed. Or, perhaps, even earlier—when he decided to steal the U.S. flag from the school, wrapped it around a straw effigy of an American soldier he'd created, and burned both items on the plaza stage during that Thanksgiving night for everyone to witness. In other words—when the boy, now a man, chose to make a stand against something he believed was wrong. This was what Eleanor had gathered from Bayani's statements.

She had insisted on being present while Lieutenant Waterstone interrogated her student. The officer refused to believe the boy, convinced he simply took the blame to free his father—which was the logical consequence of Bayani's confession.

El presidente, Padre Damián, and Luis, after learning of Bayani's surrender—which spread around town like its ubiquitous dust—arrived at the infantry station together and offered their counsel and assistance to the American officer. They all agreed Lieutenant Waterstone had no reason to keep holding the other prisoners. Eleanor earlier suggested the same to the lieutenant, but he, as most men were wont to do, was more willing to listen to his fellow men, especially those who represented the most powerful interests, than to a woman like her, no matter how educated or wise she was.

Bayani swore he acted alone and walked them through the steps he took to create the effigy, steal the flag, and burn them on the plaza stage. Eleanor remembered searching for her students during the dance and discovered the children had already been sent home. There would have been enough time for Bayani—while the Thanksgiving revelry was at its peak in the ayuntamiento, and the soldiers were getting drunk and glutted by the wine and food sent them by the damas of the Thanksgiving Committee—to have set up and executed the theatrical blaze.

Bayani admitted to getting angry at seeing the soldiers treating Filipinos as losers and calling them "bad names." "Just like what happen to American Indians; just like how Kastilyas treat us!" he declared, standing before his judges and jury. He shot Padre Damián a defiant glance.

The Spanish friar scoffed.

Lieutenant Waterstone ordered Bayani placed inside a holding cell, while the ad hoc court deliberated his fate.

To Eleanor, the boy proved himself a man among men, although she wasn't sure where her student's budding political philosophy put her were it pursued to its logical end. She attested to the credibility of Bayani's statements. Every school day, they held flag-raising and lowering ceremonies with the help of students who, in pairs, took turns at the popular task. She recalled how Bayani and Asunción had often volunteered together for the morning and afternoon rituals. Sam taught them how to never allow any part of the flag to touch the ground and how to fold it in neat rectangles and triangles until it became a compact red, white, and blue *empanada*—as Sam jokingly called it, referring to the students' favorite recess snack: a flakey pastry that looked like a triangular sandwich stuffed with a meat filling. While this made the students laugh, Sam helped the youngsters appreciate the taboo against the flag touching the soil—just as they never wanted their food to be soiled.

"Bayani knew where the flag was kept," Eleanor said. She further explained that he only needed to slide a knife into the bottom window frame to maneuver a hook latch and gain entry into the classroom. "It was simple, really, for such a smart and resourceful boy," she declared.

She paused to gaze at Luis in hopes of recruiting his support before she continued, "Gentlemen, please remember that the accused is only twelve years old—a boy in puberty who's likely undergoing a challenging time. I also confess I may have been remiss by not helping him sooner regarding his questions about the Pilgrim-Indian story. I believe this was what triggered him into acting on his resentments. If there's anyone you should punish, it's me."

She volunteered to take him under her wing and place him in her care and supervision. "That way," she reasoned, "I could better monitor his education. Before you know it, believe me, this boy will prove to be a valuable asset to this community."

"No!" Lieutenant Waterstone cried. "That's letting him off the hook easy! The punishment should fit the crime. This was nothing less than an act of rebellion! An example should be made of him. So others won't try this stupidity again."

"Goodness, gracious!" Eleanor exclaimed. "What do you suggest, lieutenant? Lock him up for the rest of his life? Execute him by hanging or firing squad?" She heaved a sigh of frustration. "His actions may seem rebellious, but he was merely acting out! Remember—he is still just a boy. Can you imagine the uproar when the world learns you executed a child?"

"¡Disculpe, sargento!" Padre Damián interjected. "May I suggest compromiso?"

Eleanor mentally smirked at the idea of the church compromising on anything.

"Please!" Lieutenant Waterstone cried.

Padre Damián replied through Luis's translation, "Perhaps some corporal punishment would do him good."

Eleanor scoffed and rolled her eyes.

Padre Damián glanced at her with annoyance. "It will set a good example for the people. And it would be instructive but merciful!" He thrust his forefinger upward, as though he was delivering a sermon in church.

Eleanor challenged, "And what, pray, tell, padre, do you mean by 'merciful' corporal punishment? I consider any bodily harm inflicted on a child as cruel and unusual punishment!"

Luis gently touched her arm, as if trying to calm her as he translated her statements.

Padre Damián ignored her, keeping his eyes on Lieutenant Waterstone as he added, "I say, forty whips on his bottom! It would be symbolic of Christ's forty days in the wilderness. Add another day for him to kneel in church before the altar to beg for divine forgiveness and pray for wisdom. That should make for a good penance that will surely teach the boy an unforgettable lesson and warn others against similar offenses."

"What!" Eleanor cried. She glanced at Luis and el presidente. "You gentlemen cannot possibly agree to such… such medieval punishment! What do you think, el presidente? Would punishing a child that way sit well with the people—especially parents?"

Luis translated her question to the mayor, who likewise replied with the haciendero's help. "I agree some punishment severe enough to discourage unruliness among the youth is necessary. But it also cannot be so severe that all the mothers would jump on me!"

Eleanor jeered. "Well! That's surely an answer that failed to answer the question!"

Luis smiled with amusement and abstained from translating her response.

"How about you, Don Luis?" she persisted. "What do you say?" After his brazenly intimate advances, she decided that resuming the formal manner of addressing him was best.

Luis sighed. "There is no easy answer, indeed. But, perhaps… detaining the boy for a few hours at the scene of the crime—on stage— where the town could witness his repentance?"

"I like it!" Lieutenant Waterstone exclaimed. "Combined with the padre's suggestion! He being your student, Miss Karsten—how about applying the schoolmaster's touch, eh?" He grinned. "Forty whacks on the palms and twenty-four hours' detention on the plaza stage!"

"You cannot be serious, lieutenant!" Eleanor screamed. "That's utterly barbaric!"

"Would you prefer I keep him in jail and try him as an insurrecto?" countered the officer, his eyes—gleaming shanks of steel again.

"No! I cannot abide it!" Eleanor cried. "Let's see what the superintendent has to say about that!" She stood to prepare to leave his office.

"Now, you just wait there, missy!" Lieutenant Waterstone yelled, blocking the door. "You got what you wanted. The other prisoners will be released. Now, I want your detailed statement about your ambush. You owe me!"

"No, I don't!" Eleanor retorted. "You have to release the prisoners because they are innocent. I don't owe you anything for doing only what the law requires. Plus, I have news for you, lieutenant: I lied! I don't remember anything more than what I've already told you about the ambush. What I really came here to tell you was: Leave Miss Estrella Santiago alone! Your conduct as an officer is appalling. I'm sure somewhere in army regulations, there is a basis for a court martial against you. So, you just watch yourself, Waterstone, because I'm going to come after you if you ever lay a hand on any of my assistant teachers or students again!"

The officer laughed.

"Oh! And, by the way," Eleanor added, "when you release the prisoners, make sure you also release that poor, homeless man, Toto!"

"No, not he!" Padre Damián suddenly cried in English.

"And why not?" she challenged.

Lieutenant Waterstone replied, "Because that hobo is being held on separate charges unrelated to the other prisoners."

"Which are?" she demanded.

"Attempted kidnapping of Miss Maria Teresa, among other offenses," the officer retorted.

"You only mentioned charges," Eleanor reprised. "Are you telling me you've been holding that man without a trial all this time? Why, that sounds positively unlawful! Can't you see that man isn't in control of his faculties? What he really needs is care, not prison!"

Lieutenant Waterstone glanced at Padre Damián, who interjected, "No! No release that man! ¡Es un peligro!"

"Dangerous, you say, padre? Or dangerous only to you?" Eleanor challenged. "Tell me, Padre Damián, who is that man to you, exactly? Because you do know him, don't you? Why are you so intent on keeping him imprisoned? Tell us, what has he got against you? What injustice did you do him that made him hate you so much? Specifically, who was that angel he'd accused you of stealing from him?"

Padre Damián's eyes widened in horror. He pointed his finger at her. "¡Esta mujer es imposible! ¡Está loca! ¡Ella es histérica!"

Eleanor grinned. "No, no padre—not crazy. Just angry—angry at all the evil, injustice, and hypocrisy I see here from men whose job is to be good, just, and honest!"

"Eleanor," Luis intervened in a soft, pleading tone. "Should not the matter about the beggar be discussed at another time, so we can resolve the issue about Bayani?"

"Resolve, Don Luis?" she countered. "What do you mean, resolve? Haven't you men already decided this? Look at you—the three of you presuming to act as judge, jury, and executioner all in one neat, little old boys' club!" Luis lowered his gaze.

She turned to Lieutenant Waterstone. "What fine specimen of American justice you run here, lieutenant! Perhaps it's time Manila learned of this!" With that, she left the room and flung the door shut behind her.

Luis ran out after her. "Eleanor—por favor!" He caught her arm just before she stepped down the stairs and gently pulled her back. "Mira, I understand how this must be difficult for you. But please understand, querida, it is the same for us, too. Why don't we address the issue about the vagabundo later, so we do not complicate the issues? ¿Bien? Entonces, as for Bayani, lo siento, pero a penalty cannot be avoided for him. We can only do our best to persuade the teniente to impose the most humane punishment."

"You call that humane, Don Luis?" she countered. "Beating up a kid in front of the whole town? And then leaving him under the sun for his wounds to fester?"

"Ahora, what… what is this thing you are doing—calling me Don Luis again? Are we not friends anymore?" His eyes, though tender, reflected the pain in his voice.

Eleanor looked away from him, her chest rising and falling in concert with the tumult of her emotions.

"Escúchame, querida." He grasped both her arms and turned her to face him. "I promise you, I will do my best to reduce Bayani's penalty as much as I can. Meanwhile, por favor, trust that things will become better. It is a good thing we were able to convince Waterstone to free the prisoners, no?"

She sighed, nodded, met his gaze, and let the tears that had been welling in her eyes fall.

He dabbed her tears with a handkerchief he produced from his trouser pocket. It smelled of lavender cologne. He hugged her, and she let him. He raised her chin to look into her eyes and smiled affectionately. "Let me go back in there and see what else I could do. ¿Está bien?"

She looked down and slowly nodded. "Thank you, Luis."

CHAPTER 18

Yesterday, Today, and Tomorrow

Bayani's designated day of atonement was set on a Monday to accommodate Padre Damián's desire not to hold a public execution of punishment on God's day of rest. The bandillo had gone around town at six in the morning, announcing Lieutenant Waterstone's mandate for everyone to gather at the plaza at eight o'clock.

Eleanor would have preferred not to witness any of it, were it not for her promise to Bayani she would be there for him and his parents. She stood by his mother and father as they awaited the horrid spectacle to start. Bayani's ináy was whimpering, while his itáy, absent his beloved rooster, looked like he had no idea what to do with his hands, such that he was rubbing his knuckles raw.

Eleanor rejected Lieutenant Waterstone's demand that she declare a school holiday and bring her students to the plaza to witness their classmate's punishment. She told him that subjecting Bayani to further humiliation before his peers and coercing the children to see such a barbaric display of military justice made him a candidate for the insane asylum. "And the children are under *my* jurisdiction, not yours!" she reminded him.

Lieutenant Waterstone reprised, "As long as they don't commit acts under my purview! For, then, they become mine." He laughed an evil laugh before adding, "Wouldn't you rather have them experience a cautionary reminder?"

Eleanor instructed Sam and Estrella to keep the students busy in school and not allow anyone to skip class.

At the plaza, she was appalled to see that Luis's painted backdrop for the Thanksgiving play had not yet been taken down. The idyllic scene presented a scandalous counterpoint to the scenario that was about to play out. Many people had already gathered before the stage. Standing in the front row was el presidente, Doctor Langford, Padre Damián, and Luis. Their women apparently didn't consider themselves obliged to witness the ugly exhibition, although there were those from among their rank who, like their social inferiors, simply couldn't resist a spectacle.

The well-dressed stood with their parasols hoisted above their heads. Some were stone-faced, others wore subtle smiles of amusement, and quite a few appeared excited to see the boy, who ruined their Thanksgiving event and caused Magayon to lose face before the whole country, punished—because to them, losing face was a fate worse than death.

It was for the same reason el presidente didn't object to the public demonstration of disciplinary action, Eleanor surmised. He was vested in discouraging anyone from contemplating ruining his next Thanksgiving Fiesta at the Plaza, despite the grapevine's assessment that many now believed such event was cursed and, therefore, would be impossible to repeat.

Many campesinos walked all the way from the hacienda. The women covered their heads with their bandanas and prayed their rosaries—their countenances conveying both hope and despair. The men with their upward-brimmed straw hats remained silent—their faces inscrutable. Only one wore his feelings for everyone to see.

Diego stood at a fringe end of the crowd—his chest rising and falling, nostrils flaring and contracting, teeth grinding. He didn't glance in Eleanor's direction, but she knew exactly how he felt. Above them, Mayon Volcano towered like some ancient citadel sending white smoke out of its chimney—signaling that the goddess was still in residence, likewise watching.

Luis scoured the crowd as if searching for somebody. When he glimpsed Eleanor, he nodded at her with a grave face, and she acknowledged him similarly. Notably absent was Lieutenant Waterstone. When

Eleanor glanced at the infantry station, she saw him watching from his window with a pair of binoculars. The beastly coward!

Soldiers marched out from the station to the solemn beat of a drum. They surrounded the base of the stage, standing alert with their rifles as though ready to fire at anyone who might dare disrupt the proceedings. A pair of guards stationed themselves before each set of stairs located at opposite sides of the stage.

A pair of soldiers, one of whom appeared to be Private Patton, escorted Bayani out of the station. The boy's hands were tied with rope in front of him. His usual bright-eyed, innocent, boyish countenance was gone, replaced with a stoic stare. The procession culminated with the arrival of the executioner, the sergeant called Pearson, whom Eleanor had struck with her umbrella while he was inflicting water torture on a prisoner. The gash on his cheek that marked where she had hit him was now a reddish-brown scab.

Eleanor was stunned to see Padre Damián and an acolyte stepping up the stage in religious vestments. The sacristan handed an aspergillum to the priest who sprinkled Bayani with holy water and mouthed Latin prayers. Eleanor's eyes pricked. She wanted to scream, to denounce such a crude show of religiosity as blasphemy. Yet, she sucked in her rage and pressed her trembling lips shut. She couldn't afford to show herself less civilized than the natives around her who, at that moment, were the paragons of quiet dignity and courage in the face of atrocity.

Sergeant Pearson read a statement listing and describing Bayani's offenses, including a confirmation of the boy's confession and sentence. Luis had apparently succeeded in persuading Lieutenant Waterstone to reduce Bayani's penalty from the forty smacks on the palms suggested by Padre Damián to twenty-five, followed by detention on the stage until sundown. The judgment statement concluded:

> *Be it known to all subjects of the United States of America in the municipality of Magayon, province of Albay, Luzon Island, in these herein Philippine Islands, that any acts of insurrection or incitement to insurrection, such as those to which the aforementioned Bayani Burgos had pled guilty, shall henceforth be punished with the maximum penalty allowed by law, including,*

but not limited to imprisonment and/or death by execution through hanging or firing squad, regardless of infirmity, age, or any other condition. Signed, this 9th day of December 1901 by Lieutenant James Ebenezer Waterstone, Commanding Officer, Magayon Infantry.

"Stretch out your hands, boy!" barked Pearson. "Palms up!"

Bayani extended his shaking arms, his palms facing the clear, blue sky. Even the exceptionally fine weather struck Eleanor as offensive, an insult.

Private Patton handed Sergeant Pearson a flayed bamboo reed, upon which the officer ordered, "Mind the count, private!"

"Sir, yes, sir!" cried the young soldier.

The drum rolled. In the split second before the first blow, Bayani appeared to search for someone among the crowd. His face crumpled upon seeing Eleanor. She sent him a look of encouragement, though her eyes were clouded by tears. She nodded at him, lip-speaking, "Courage, my boy! Courage!"

Sergeant Pearson delivered the first blow. "One!" counted Private Patton, his voice hardly audible above the collective gasp and groan that followed the crisp thwack of the reed as it struck the boy's flesh.

Bayani's mother wailed, reaching out to her son, "O, aki' ko! Diyós ko, po! Hírak man!" She begged for pity for her son and clemency from God, but it all fell on deaf ears as the beatings continued.

Eleanor held back and hugged Bayani's mother, and turned themselves around to face the opposite direction—away from the stage, away from the church that sat on the quaint hill above it, away from beautiful Daragang Magayon who proved herself no more than a capricious goddess who, like all other gods, was solely interested in her own desires, her own lost love—ruthlessly indifferent to the sufferings of her mortal subjects. In an attempt to protect Bayani's mother from hearing the sounds of her son's torture, Eleanor pressed her hands over the ears of the woman, who buried her cries in Eleanor's chest.

"Five!"

One by one, many in the audience—elites and peasants alike—did as Eleanor did. They, too, turned their backs on the barbaric display of power. Eleanor knew then, without a doubt, that the insurrection became stronger than ever. Big mistake, Waterstone! She glanced back at where she'd last seen Diego, but he was no longer there.

"Thirteen!"

Private Patton's voice started to give out, cracking with each new blow, as if he was suppressing his own weeping. When the young soldier's voice finally failed, Sergeant Pearson ordered him to leave and appointed another soldier to replace him. During all that time, Eleanor heard not one squeak from Bayani. She glanced back at him, worried he might have fainted. But he was still up there, eyes closed, standing yet swaying in place. His hands no longer appeared to be hands. They were cups broken, dripping with a thick, dark brew.

As soon as the twenty-fifth blow was called, Eleanor turned around in time to see Doctor Langford hurrying toward the stage, his black physician's bag in hand. A soldier blocked his entry to the stairs until the soldier glanced in the infantry station's direction and appeared to receive permission to let the doctor pass.

Eleanor handed Bayani's mother to her husband before she, too, rushed toward the stage, where the soldier refused her entry.

"Let me go!" she cried. "That boy is my responsibility, too!" She pointed to Bayani, who was now lying on his back, arms eagle-spread on the concrete floor, while the doctor was cleaning his lacerated hands and forearms in preparation for bandaging.

"Sorry, ma'am. Can't do it," the soldier said. "Sentence has not been completed."

Eleanor tried to push her way up the stairs, to no avail. Luis joined her, saying, "Come now, Eleanor. Trust that Doctor Langford is giving the boy what he needs." He pulled her away gently.

The people silently left in groups. The campesinos walked back to their farms, the rich to their stone villas, and the mayor and priest to their hallowed offices. Bayani's parents remained on their haunches on the plaza floor with some praying women.

Luis and Eleanor watched as Doctor Langford finished dressing Bayani's wounds. When the doctor was finished, he joined Luis and Eleanor. "Well, that's all I could bloody do for the boy, for now. I'll check on him later. He'll need more morphine."

On the stage, Sergeant Pearson tried to force Bayani to his feet, but the boy's legs couldn't hold up. The corporal had another soldier help him set the boy into a sitting position, legs crossed. Bayani's head was hanging forward; his bandaged hands resting limp, palms up upon his thighs. A Buddha.

Eleanor whimpered and covered her mouth.

"Don't worry, dear—he'll be fine," Doctor Langford assured her.

Eleanor nodded. "Thank you, doctor," she said with a voice barely above a whisper.

Luis squeezed Eleanor's shoulder. "Shall we go, then, mia cara? We can return with Doctor Langford later."

Eleanor shot him a piqued glance. "Luis, please—let me be!"

The haciendero gestured to one of his men, who was standing nearby. The servant left and soon returned with a chair for her to sit on. Luis said, "If you want to stay here, mi querida, allow me, at least, to make you comfortable."

She had no will left to argue and accepted the chair.

Sergeant Pearson and the other soldiers marched back to their barracks, leaving a pair of their comrades guarding each of the stairs that led to the stage. Shadows were disappearing as the sun climbed to its zenith.

Suddenly, Eleanor spied a dark, little figure approaching one of the guards, carrying something in her hands. It was Asunción, holding what looked like a water jug. The guard refused to budge from her path.

Eleanor rushed toward them. "Private, please, there's nothing in the sentence that forbids anyone from giving the boy a drink! He could be dehydrated by now!"

The soldier remained unmoved until Asunción pleaded with her little girl's voice, "Plis, o good en kine sir, plis let me gib my fren just a little water."

The soldier glanced down at the girl and looked warily in the infantry station's direction before he begrudgingly said, "Fine. But be quick!"

"O, tenk yu, good en kine sir!" Asunción lifted the hem of her saya with one hand while clutching the jug with the other, and climbed the stairs one foot, one rung at a time.

Eleanor attempted to follow her, but the soldier blocked her with his rifle. "Sorry, ma'am. Not you."

She harrumphed at him and ran around toward the base of the center of the stage from where she could see Asunción and Bayani. The girl knelt and whispered to the boy. Bayani's head juddered as he raised his face to the jug that Asunción lifted to his lips.

"Hurry up!" the soldier hissed, his eyes darting between the station and the children. "Or we'll all be in trouble!"

Eleanor likewise glanced anxiously at the station and turned back to her students. "That's it, Asunción. That's good for now, sweetheart. Bayani, is that all right? Are you…?"

The boy nodded and hung his head down again.

Eleanor waved Asunción toward the stairs where she met her at the bottom step. She hugged the girl, who broke into soft sobbing. Asunción's yaya approached to collect her ward.

Eleanor told the nanny, "Please return her home safely."

The servant nodded, but before she took the girl away, Asunción paused and handed the jug to Eleanor. "Plis, ma'am, when he need it…"

Eleanor held back from breaking down by embracing and holding onto Asunción. "I am so proud of you, darling girl!"

At sundown, Doctor Langford gave Bayani another morphine shot before his parents took him home on the flatbed carretela that Mr. Ang had lent them. The doctor said he'd come by Bayani's house the next day to check on him again and change his dressings.

Eleanor stood and watched, dazed, as the family rode away. An arm hooked itself around hers—Yolanda's. "Come, señorita," the maid said tenderly. "Time go home now."

December 5, 1901

Dearest Eleanor,

How are you? I haven't heard from you in a while and wondered how your Thanksgiving affair went. I heard from Miss Covell you've become quite the celebrity in the superintendent's office. Well done, chum!

From my end, rest assured, I'm safe from any sultan, rajah, or datu. I think I'm too old and ugly to the local taste for a wife or concubine. What I'll be good for here, if I wasn't the teacher, is governess for the chieftains' child wives.

You will not believe the pomp and revelry that attend such weddings! The girl brides are dressed up like some combination of a China doll and Mughal princess, crowned with a Chinese headdress, while wearing a sari and patent leather shoes! The girls here put me to shame with their prowess in the art of facial painting, a skill that rises to mastery on a child bride's face. You no longer see the child behind the white face and red lips, making it easy to forget that behind such face and finery sits a frightened little girl who's about to get ravaged by an ape of a geezer.

I honestly can't understand how anyone could justify this barbaric practice. It makes me think there's indeed something to our "civilizing" mission here. While I try to be respectful of the culture, I can hardly stomach another child wedding. Yet, as you know, we "las maestras Americanas" are pressed to show up as part of our diplomatic role in the community.

Now, on to cheerful news! I'm happy to tell you that Bud and I (remember my Harvard beau?) have continued our correspondence. Dare I say we might make go of it when we return to the states? I'm keeping my fingers crossed and ask you to do the same for me.

I wish you a happy Christmas ahead! I'm sorry I can't join you and Miss Covell for the holiday. As you can understand, the trip is too long and difficult for me. When I leave this place, it will be the last. I look forward to the day I see all of you again!

Goodbye for now, dear chum. More power to every-thing you do!

Hugs and kisses,
Arabella

Eleanor accepted Miss Covell's invitation to spend Christmas and New Year in Manila. The morose atmosphere in Magayon after Bayani's public lashing was debilitating to her. She needed the solace of an old friend.

She noted how Bayani had not returned to school. She visited him at his home before Christmas break, but his parents claimed he wasn't ready to see visitors. He was sleeping all the time, silent when awake. She handed them a box of *yema* candies, among a few that Yolanda had made for the holidays, including a book that was her Christmas present for the boy, accompanied with a note tucked inside.

December 15, 1901

Dear Bayani,

I hope you are resting well. I am going to Manila to spend Christmas with a friend who is also a teacher, though no ordinary one, for she is a teacher of teachers. I am going to see her because I miss her very much, as I'm sure you miss your friends, like Asunción, who I know also misses you a lot, as we all do. I hope we will see you back in school after New Year.

Meanwhile, I hope this book, The Adventures of Huckleberry Finn, will keep you good company during the Christmas break. I enjoyed it very much as a young girl. It's the story of a boy who goes on an adventure journey with his friend. I'm sure you, too, will enjoy it. I would love to know what you think of it when I see you again in school.

Please note, however, that the English in which the book was written is not what we teach in school. The author, Mr. Mark Twain, who is among our best writers, was simply making his book's characters speak in a manner true to how people in the southern part of the United States speak. Please do not be confused. Keep up with correct English grammar.

I wish you and your family a Buenas Pascuas!

Your devoted teacher,
Eleanor Karsten

She went to plead again with Lieutenant Waterstone to release Toto, to no avail. "Have you no mercy, no compassion, sir? Why, it's the yuletide season! If this man isn't being held for trial, then he should be freed!" she insisted.

Lieutenant Waterstone appeared unmoved. "I owe it to the complainant, who, as you know, is the padre, to hold him here till the prosecutor from Legazpi comes."

"What!" Eleanor exclaimed. "The wheels of justice may turn slowly, lieutenant, but this is downright ridiculous! You owe nothing to the priest over what the law requires! And I believe the law requires Toto's release because you've long held him here without proper procedure!"

The officer chuckled. "Oh, lighten up, Miss Karsten! As you said, it's Christmas! Besides, I rather think the hobo likes it here. After all, he gets free room and board, and a roof over his head. What more could he ask for? He lives better here than out there."

Eleanor left the lieutenant's office without another word. The name Waterstone was only half appropriate to him, for speaking with him was like bargaining with stone. No ounce of softness! She tried to see Toto in his cell but, as usual, the guard blocked her access.

When she arrived home, she instructed Yolanda to bring Toto a food basket for Christmas, including a blanket, because the nights were getting chilly. She handed Yolanda a red envelope, which she learned was the polite way to give gift money in the culture. "¡Feliz navidad, Yolanda! Thank you for all your help this year. You're truly my life-saver. I'm going to raise your salary to ten dollars a month starting in January, if that's okay."

"¿Diez dólares?" exclaimed Yolanda. "¿Cada mes?"

"Sí," Eleanor replied, smiling. "Every month."

Yolanda hopped in joy and kissed Eleanor's hand. She said she'd miss her favorite amo but was glad her mistress's trip would also allow her to visit her own family during the holiday. She promised not to be away too long, keep the house well-tended, and not forget about Toto.

Luis declared his displeasure over Eleanor leaving, complaining she'd be missing many fantastic feasts and pageants that made Christmas the most festive and happiest time of the year in Magayon. Eleanor bit her bitter tongue to avoid spreading her gloom. Thanksgiving had robbed her of all Christmas joy.

She stayed with Ida, who took over Miss Thompson's old quarters at the Escuela Municipal. The dormitory, converted from a girls' school, was part of a larger complex that included a normal school for male teachers during the Spanish regime. It all now comprised the new Manila Normal School where Ida conducted classes for both male and female teachers-in-training. The set-up gave Ida a perfect work and living arrangement.

Eleanor was surprised to see that her friend now needed a cane for ambulatory assistance. Ida's hair had also grayed considerably since the five months they'd last seen each other. Returning to the Walled City felt strangely like returning to an innocent, unsullied time. Walking the same cobbled streets they'd explored with Maude and Arabella made them keenly aware of their Radcliffe friends' absence. Their companionable presence to each other, however, was still a great consolation to Eleanor. Ida was her sanctuary from her Magayon troubles.

"Don't you just love those parols?" Ida exclaimed as she pointed to the festive star lanterns that decorated windows everywhere. She said they were symbolic of the Star of Bethlehem. Bright tissue paper, usually red and yellow, sometimes green, covered a bamboo frame shaped into an upright, five-pointed star that culminated in a pair of long strips of paper that represented the comet's twin dust and gas tails. Colorful buntings connected homes on opposite sides of the streets, making the whole world appear as if it were one big fiesta.

"Yes, I like them a lot," Eleanor said, managing a smile. "Ida, thank you. Your invitation to spend Christmas with you couldn't have come at a better time."

"I'm glad you came, my dear. But do I sense restlessness?" Ida glanced sideways at her.

Eleanor heaved a sigh. "I don't know if I'm doing right by my students and the town. I'm afraid I may have made a mess of things. The situation is complicated in Magayon right now. And I worry I'd be returning to more trouble than I could handle."

She told Ida about what had happened at Thanksgiving and about Bayani. "I may have been an unwitting accomplice to the boy's radicalization. And I seem to always find myself locking horns with the town's most powerful personalities!"

She left out sharing her uneasy, shadowy tether to the local insurrectos, especially her near indiscretion with their probable leader, over which she, herself, remained incredulous. How could she have even felt what she felt for Luis's foreman during that night under the mango tree? She thought she could just dismiss it all to too much lambanog, but that didn't explain what she felt for the man as he held her in his arms again since her illness—when she slipped off the ladder on the plaza stage. During the voyage back to Manila which, thankfully, took two days shorter in better weather than her experience on the opposite route, she found herself thinking of Diego even more.

The older teacher held onto Eleanor's arm and smiled one of those knowing smiles that Eleanor found simultaneously disquieting and quieting. "I confess I cannot help you with all the answers, my dear. All you can do is your best. The issue with the boy is tough, indeed. But you cannot blame yourself for everything. To be responsible for another's well-being, let alone a child's, is not for the faint-hearted. But you certainly did not arrive here by being one. I believe the circumstances in which you find yourself are such because you possess what it takes to face them. Life is both a riddle and an answer. Time is what differentiates one from the other."

Mr. McCauley invited them to dinner at the posh army and navy club which was located in a regal Spanish-style *palacio* on Manila Bay, affording its members one of the best water and sunset views in the city. Not since being on the *Thomas* had Eleanor found herself in what appeared to be exclusive American company, apart from the waiters. The Filipino servers were elegantly dressed in white jackets, black trousers, and white gloves, recalling the uniforms of Black butlers and valets on the mainland. Eleanor also noted another source of curiosity. "Mr. McCauley, don't Filipinos get to dine here?" There weren't even any mestizos or mestizas among the patrons.

"God, no!" Mr. McCauley exclaimed, grinning. "Isn't it nice to feel somewhat back at home, eh? It isn't exactly Washington, D.C., but it's not shabby either, don't you think? A happy Christmas to you both, ladies!" He raised his champagne glass to Eleanor and Ida, who did the same. Eleanor was grateful for his tactfulness in not mentioning the Thanksgiving incident.

A band played "Jolly Old St. Nicholas" on a platform stage in the dining hall. At a corner, there stood a spindly pine tree decorated with Victorian Christmas cards and trinkets. She wondered how Diego and Estrella were celebrating Pasko in Magayon.

On Christmas Eve, Ida suggested they attend one of the Christmas midnight masses celebrated in one of the many beautiful churches inside the Walled City. Ida chose the San Ignacio Church on Calle Arzobispo. "It is, believe it or not, the youngest church here," she remarked as they walked to the church. "It was finished just two years ago, rebuilt after three other churches built on the same site by the Jesuits were destroyed by earthquakes. I suppose earthquakes are the reason why, this time, the Jesuits decided to do things differently."

"Oh? How so?" Eleanor asked.

"They built it with a metal frame designed and built by no less than Gustave Eiffel!" Ida exclaimed.

"Eiffel?" Eleanor said. "You mean... Eiffel of the Paris Tower World Fair fame?"

Ida chuckled. "Or, infamy, you could say! His tower was very controversial at the time. Many Parisians, bound to tradition, considered it ugly. And the surrounding residents were scared the tower would collapse on them!" Ida shook her head, smiling. "It is truly never easy building something new, something that is both beautiful and meant to last. You know Eiffel also designed and built the metal structure for our Lady Liberty?"

"Yes, I remember something about that from the papers," Eleanor replied.

The crisp evening air of late December was as refreshing as a beautiful spring day in Iowa. People put little votive candles inside their star lanterns. Seeing every house and building flickering with the colorful stars could make one almost believe the heavenly hosts had indeed come to earth on this special night.

"The Church of St. Ignatius is also famous here for many other reasons apart from Eiffel," Ida volunteered. "It's also the first church in the islands to be lit by electrica luz!"

"I can't wait to see it!" Eleanor exclaimed. "It must be marvelous all lit up for Christmas!"

"Yes, and that is why tonight would be an excellent time to see it," Ida said. "But, you know, the church's Neoclassical exterior is rather restrained compared to its interior. An atelier of all-Filipino artisans carved its interiors and statuaries from native hardwoods and, in my opinion, their work rivals the best examples of Baroque and Renaissance style I have seen in Europe."

"You don't say!" Eleanor remarked, smiling—enjoying her friend's passionate interest in all things.

"I do declare it!" Ida replied, grinning. "But, to me, the best thing about the Iglesia de San Ignacio is that it is the first church entirely designed by a Filipino architect. For the Spanish Jesuits to entrust such a responsibility to a Filipino and commission an all-Filipino atelier to craft the church's interiors was nothing less than revolutionary!"

Eleanor smiled as Ida pointed to their destination now just ahead, feeling almost as excited as her friend was about seeing the church. White stone posts interspersed with black wrought iron fence panels enclosed the church's perimeter and delineated it from the street. Black metal electric lamps sat on the posts and shone their yellow light upon the church's simple yet elegant façade. Inside, lighted candles and candelabras combined with the electric bulbs of the chandeliers to make the ornately-carved wooden altars, pulpit, ceilings, and doors glow with an almost immanent light.

Arriving early secured Eleanor and Ida choice spots on the pews close to the main altar before the church soon filled to overflowing. The faithful, adults and children alike, came dressed in their most festive, shimmering attire. At the precise hour of midnight, the bells of the Iglesia de San Ignacio joined with the hundreds of other church bells ringing in the Savior's birth all over the capital. A choir belted out "Adeste Fidelis" to the accompaniment of a pipe organ in the choir loft, while a cherub in a white silk robe and feathered wings, played by a chubby, curly-haired mestiza girl, strode to the creche scene before the altar, cradling a statue of the baby Jesus, which she laid gently in the manger.

After the Mass, the air outside the church was saturated with the sweet, smoky scent of rice cakes being cooked by street vendors. The enterprising merchants installed themselves in front of the church, fanning their charcoal braziers, where the banana leaf-wrapped Yuletide treats called *bibingka* were broiling and tempting the faithful to buy some to bring home for their *noche buena* feasts with their families. According to Ida, the rice cakes were best enjoyed with cups of, hot, thick Spanish cocoa.

They, too, bought a few to share with Ida's dormitory mates whom they agreed to meet at the cantina across the Escuela Municipal that was serving a splendid noche buena feast of Peking roast duck, glazed Spanish jamon, and a sharp-tasing, spherical cheese from Holland so rightly called, queso de bola.

"I've never experienced such an extraordinary international meal!" Eleanor exclaimed as they feasted with Ida's new friends. That evening, Eleanor managed to temporarily forget her Magayon woes.

On New Year's Day, Ida took Eleanor to watch a new play being staged at the Teatro Nacional called, *Kahapon, Ngayon, at Bukas.* Ida translated it as, "Yesterday, Today, and Tomorrow."

"Aside from the play being written and directed by a Filipino playwright, the theater itself is unique because it is round, like Shakespeare's theater!" Ida raved.

Eleanor smiled at her friend's usual exuberance about art and culture.

"Not that I had seen Shakespeare's theater beyond illustrations of it, of course," Ida remarked. "That structure burned down in the seventeenth century, then rebuilt, until it was closed by an ordinance pursued by the Puritans." Ida grinned. "One could say in that sense that religion is the great killer of great civilizations. Let's see how this playwright, Tolentino, portrays the Spanish friar—shall we?"

Ida occupied the time it took them to ride to the *teatro* to brief Eleanor about the play. "Now, fair warning, my dear, it is written entirely in the Tagal language, although the playwright is a Kapampangan. You know—from Pampanga, the Central Plains?"

"Ah, yes," Eleanor replied. "Isn't that the province where the two other Radcliffe girls, Eliza and Mabel, were sent?"

"That is correct, my dear."

"But how come the playwright wrote the play in Tagal if he's Kapampangan?"

Ida smiled. "That is one of the reasons why I'm interested in it. Tolentino seems to be promoting Tagal as a national language. Important for national identity and unity, he says. I agree, since the different regions and provinces are often fractious, contentious tribes madly possessive of their cultural identities, always arguing about who is superior to whom, and all such nonsense."

"About the play," Eleanor interjected, "won't it be difficult for me to follow it, since it's in Tagal?"

"Ah, do not worry, my dear!" Ida grinned. "The characters, I understand, are all metaphorical. From this, you could follow the plot, more or less. If not, I will help you along. I imagine it is not every day you get to see a Filipino play in the ambiance of a premier theater."

"You're right." Eleanor smiled. "Thank you, Ida. Perhaps this would also lend me some insight into Filipino drama. I'm thinking of expanding our literature class to cover plays. The natives seem to especially love this art medium."

Ida nodded. "No doubt! Although this play, I suspect, would likely lean on melodrama, of which, if you haven't noticed, the culture is fond, equaled only by its penchant for slapstick humor!" She chuckled. "Filipino theater, to me, is the Sock and Buskin of classical comedy and tragedy."

When they arrived at the Teatro Nacional, Eleanor was impressed by its unique circular design and nipa thatch roof. It was a splendid example of the culture's capacity to adopt extrinsic influences and integrate them into its heritage.

According to the program, the play consisted of three acts—symbolic of the Filipinos' past, present, and future. "Oh, look!" Ida cried as she read it. "It seems the playwright himself may perform the role of the hero, Taga-ilog."

"Taga-ilog?" Eleanor wondered aloud. "How is that related to the Tagalogs?"

"The same! The character's name means 'people of the river'—essentially, the Tagalogs' origin."

Eleanor smiled. "Oh, Ida, I'm simply amazed at your knowledge of these people!"

"Thank you, my dear." Ida turned wistful. "It all goes back, I suppose, to my fondness for that first Filipino I met in Michigan. A fine fellow he was! I often wonder whatever happened to that young man. Would I recognize him, perhaps, if I met him again in the streets of Manila?"

The play began with the dramatic employment of a classic Greek chorus. Although Eleanor couldn't understand the language of the play, she was able to follow its plot, as Ida said, through the various characters who appeared to represent the major actors in the islands' history: the indigenous people of the islands, the Chinese, the Spanish and their Catholic friars, and the Americans and their government.

The audience hissed and booed characters they hated and rambunctiously cheered those whom they loved. There was a particularly gruesome scene in the second act where the hero, Taga-ilog, appeared to bury the characters representing the Spaniards—alive! The band in the orchestra pit played what was called the "Aguinaldo March," a reference to the last general of the Philippine revolution. Many in the audience stood and applauded.

A commotion started when some of the audience left or tried to leave in apparent disgust over the burying-alive scene, while fistfights erupted between those who tried to force others to stand and clap to show respect for the hero and those who refused to do so. Eleanor and Ida stood to recoup their view of the stage. However, the skirmishes among the audience soon spread to the performers on stage. This happened after a climactic scene where the hero, Taga-ilog, breaking free of his shackles, shouted, "Long live Freedom! Long live the Motherland!"

A mechanical device raised the Filipino flag which, like the American flag, was rendered in red, white, and blue colors. In addition, the Filipino flag had a golden-yellow sun with a human-like face at the center of a white triangle, surrounded by three golden stars. The triangle reminded Eleanor of Juan's tattoo and wondered whether there was a connection.

Pandemonium erupted when the device not only raised the Filipino flag but also floated it to obscure the American flag. The hero then pulled down the U.S. flag and trampled it. Some Americans from the audience rushed to the stage, attacked the actors, and smashed the stage set.

Eleanor recalled Asunción's oration of the Baldwin verse about a red, white, and blue flag. It now assumed a different and poignant meaning. Bayani's flag burning also came to her mind. Seeing adult Filipinos demonstrating equally passionate subversions of the symbols of American occupation hit her with the sense of being choked. It was as if Mayon Volcano had erupted, spewing sulphuric fury that reached her in Manila. Seized with a coughing fit, Eleanor tugged on Ida's sleeve, urging her friend for them to leave the turmoil of the theater.

CHAPTER 19

Camps, Construction, and Conciliation

When Eleanor disembarked at Legazpi Port after the new year, Sam was already waiting there with Pedro to fetch her. They rode along in relative quiet, which was strange, for Sam was usually cheerful and chatty. She asked him if everything was all right with baby Gracias and Cristina. "Oh, they be fine." For the first time since she saw him at the dock, he smiled his usual bright smile. "They be ma' bright shinin' stars." She chose not to probe further into the seeming sadness to which he soon returned.

At the approach to Magayon, what used to be small farms and planted fields were now occupied by nipa huts. Eleanor was amazed to see a great number of native men moving an entire hut on top of huge bamboo poles borne upon their shoulders. In another section of the field, soldiers and natives were building a new hut.

She turned to Sam. "What's going on?"

"Those be Waterstone's new project. Reconcentrados!" Sam snickered.

"Recon... what?"

"Reconcentrados. Or, hamlets, as the lieutenant likes to call 'em. To protect law abidin' citizens from insurrectos, he says. But really, internment camps. 'Cept the natives don't know it yet." Sam smiled wryly.

"What?" Eleanor said. "I don't understand..."

"Ha!" Sam interjected. "The genius thinks the best way to root out rebels is to put everyone in one place so he could watch 'em. He don't know how much watchin' he'd 'ave to do!" He guffawed into chortling.

"Why, that's terrible!" Eleanor cried. "And the mayor agreed to this?"

Sam sneered. "He don't 'ave any choice! Besides, I think he kinda like it. Peace an' order, he call it. The folks who need an improvement on their homes think they're gettin' a good deal. Some of them are getting a free, new house, an' security, along with it."

"But how about Luis?" Eleanor pressed. "He could not have agreed to have his men relocated so far from the hacienda."

"Right ye are! Them peasants an' their families were too many to be moved, anyway. So Don Luis agreed with Waterstone to put soldiers at his hacienda. It was the only way the lieutenant would back down on his order that everyone come an' live here in town. Fortunately for me an' Cristina, our house falls just outside the border, in Legazpi. An' lucky for us, General Kobbé hasn't yet seen the need to corral us into reconcentrados."

"But those farms, those fields!" Eleanor exclaimed. "Somebody must have owned them. Did Waterstone buy them?"

"Guess again!" Sam grinned. "Expropriation, he call it—for the greater good. Mr. Ang lost more than 'alf his field 'round where the school is."

"Oh, my goodness! Poor Mr. Ang! And he's been so good to us. Can't believe this is happening." Eleanor moaned.

"Ya preachin' to the choir, Leonor!"

Yolanda said she heard Lieutenant Waterstone had released Toto just before Christmas, but no one had seen the mendicant around, not even begging for food. This troubled Eleanor, but she was soon distracted by more pressing school issues to inquire further about Toto.

Classes resumed, yet Bayani hadn't returned. No one seemed to know what happened to the boy. And anyone who might know seemed strangely mum about it, according to Estrella, who said she'd already inquired about Bayani before Eleanor's return, certain her supervising teacher would ask about her favorite student.

Moreover, Asunción seemed to struggle to keep up with their lessons and kept mostly to herself. Eleanor often caught her in a daze, disinterested in whatever was happening during class or recess. She also observed how the girl's old entourage of fans, who used to fawn over Asunción's pretty dresses, idolized her pluck and confidence, and toadied to her wealthy family, now distanced themselves from their former idol, disenchanted by her dysphoria. Eleanor planned on having a private chat with her.

Sam was right about Mr. Ang's land. The area around the school had changed radically. The field was cleared to make way for new huts or old ones to be relocated there. Eleanor gazed upon the once refreshing sight of greenery, now a desolate swathe of dark trampled land. Even the mango tree beside the school seemed to be struggling. It hadn't rained in weeks. The earth looked like an old native's skin: toasted, cracked, and crinkled. When the wind blew, it brought dust into the classroom, irritating everyone's eyes and throats. Eleanor had to have the windows closed or opened, depending on the wind's direction.

What remained planted and thriving around the school were the students' vegetable gardens, except for a patch that may have been plundered by a wild boar, rabbits, or field mice. The sili plants needed more time to grow before their first little spears of glossy, green peppers matured. But the tripods of tomato vines and green beans and the arbors of bitter melons and string beans were already heavy with produce. If one lifted the plate-sized, jade green, scalloped leaves of the calabasa squash creepers, many ridged, orange spheres of delight revealed themselves sitting squat and fat on the soft, tilled soil. At another set of garden beds, one only needed to dig lightly to excavate their buried treasures of *patatas* or "potatoes," camotes, *gabi* or "taro," and a violet yam called *ube*. Sam organized a community harvest, whereby students and their families picked their share of the crops. The activity served to briefly clear away the fog of anxiety that hung heavily around the school.

Eleanor collected two baskets' worth of vegetables—one for Mr. Ang, another for Bayani. She asked Yolanda to bring Mr. Ang's share to his store with a message she would see him soon. She chose to deliver Bayani's portion herself. It seemed the only sure way to learn what had become of her favorite, albeit disgraced student. Fortunately, the boy's hut was close enough to town, so that his family didn't have to move to Waterstone's hamlets. When she arrived there, his parents said they had sent him to live with an uncle on Masbate Island to keep him out of trouble—Eleanor bet, away from the lieutenant's grasp. Though they appeared grateful for the vegetables, with Bayani gone—gone, too, it seemed, was their sparkle. He clearly was their golden boy around which their hopes and dreams had revolved. It was a brief and awkward visit, complicated by lack of communication, both parties being bereft of their translator.

Luis came by her house the next evening. Eleanor was uneasy about his visit. She'd learned from Yolanda that Señorita Maria Teresa had returned to Spain after Don Luis failed to propose to the Spanish mestiza on New Year's Eve. It appeared the haciendero failed to meet the young lady's deadline, and now, here he was—at Eleanor's door. What would Doña Ximena and Padre Damián think? Eleanor had too much on her mind and hands to add discord with the Gonzaga matriarch and the priest among her worries.

"I come bearing gifts!" Luis declared jovially. "Christmas presents, belated though they are."

"Oh, but you didn't have to," Eleanor protested, yet he proceeded straight to the comedor and laid a large package on the dining table. "Now I feel bad," she added. "I'm sorry, but I don't have anything for you."

"This is not about what you Americanos call tit-for-tat!" Luis retorted. "Frankly, this is my excuse to get to see you, mi querida." He grinned before turning somber. "I have missed you, you know?" He held both her arms, trying to hold her eyes, but she averted her gaze. He changed back to his cheerful tone. "And guess what? Yolanda gets to have something, too! Where is the muchacha? ¡Yolanda, ven aquí!" He hollered as he pulled out a red envelope from his pocket.

Yolanda appeared and approached him tentatively. Luis gestured for her to come closer and handed her the gift.

"Muchas gracias, po, Don Luis!" Yolanda smiled timidly and scurried back to the kitchen.

Eleanor shook her head and sighed. "Luis, are you trying to bribe my maid?"

"Bribe?" Luis chuckled. "Now, that is the difference between Americans and Filipinos. You see it as a bribe, while we simply view it as *pakikisama*. Paving the path to smoother relationships."

Eleanor grinned. "As long as you're aware, Luis, that you're paving nothing but a road to nowhere here."

"Ay-ay-ay, querida!" he exclaimed, chuckling. "As the Three Wise Men say, it does not hurt to give gifts to God himself! Sometimes, one has to tempt a goddess with an offering to lure her down from her pedestal to give this mortal man, who adores her, a chance to be noticed."

"Oh, Luis—you're at it again." Eleanor shook her head, smiling. "I have not changed my mind about... well, whatever we talked about during the Thanksgiving dance." She crossed her arms, but couldn't resist smiling at him.

"Ah, but I am not here to change minds, mi querida. I am hoping, instead, for your change of heart." He pouted like a sulking child, yet his tone was cheery. "Now, do you want to open your gift?" He slipped on a countenance of great expectation.

Eleanor grinned. "Oh, if I must!"

She untied the string bound around the brown paper-wrapped package. It was a curiously thick, heavy, and huge rectangular board that occupied almost a fourth of the dining table's surface. When the folds of paper fell away, what appeared was a framed portrait. A portrait of her! He'd painted her likeness dressed in the camisa at saya she wore during Thanksgiving, her face half-turned toward the viewer, poised at the start of a smile. The image clutched a book with one hand and a pen in the other, set against a capiz window slid open to show the majestic Mayon in the background, peering over her shoulder. Eleanor glanced up at Luis, whose eyes anticipated his reward. "Oh, Luis! I... I don't know what to say... except... I can't possibly accept it! I don't deserve it."

"Ay, ay, ay, mi querida! You truly have much to learn about love! It is freely given, deserved or not. As you can see, I have found my inspiration to paint again." He took her hand and kissed it—slowly and fervently.

Despite el presidente's misgivings about what happened on Thanksgiving, he proved true to his word. He surrendered the funds raised by the event for the school to Eleanor—minus costs, he said. She wasn't sure what costs he meant, since almost everything was donated. Still, she was grateful to receive what appeared to be enough money to build another classroom and purchase some badly needed school supplies.

It was time to see Mr. Ang again. She wasn't surprised to learn he'd converted the bodega next to his grocery store into a hardware shop.

"I thought perhaps I should take advantage of this building boom," the Chinese merchant said, smiling. He was admirably being diplomatic, for he was surely still suffering a loss of income from the loss of his land to the U.S. Army.

"Mr. Ang, I'm so sorry to hear about your rice field," Eleanor said. "I hope you're making Lieutenant Waterstone pay for what he took from you through your pricing on the materials he needs to build his hamlets." She smiled, and he grinned.

"Thank you," he said. "And thank you also for the vegetables. My wife made us a delicious stir-fry with them."

Eleanor beamed. "I'm happy you both enjoyed them. Now, I'm happier to offer you additional business. We're expanding the school, you see. Hence, your expansion into the hardware business is timely. I hope you can still accommodate us with preferential pricing? That is, if you also don't mind us occupying more space in the plot you've been generous to lend us?"

He sighed. "At this point, madam, all that land is practically under the control of the soldiers. Whether I agree or not is irrelevant. But I would appreciate you building under the same conditions we agreed upon. And, perhaps, this time, we could draw a document?"

"Certainly! Please prepare the papers, and I'll sign them." She understood that both the new and old structures would belong to Mr. Ang when the school no longer needed them, or the school would start paying rent after five years, whichever came first.

Mr. Ang added, "Do not worry, madam, I am most happy to supply whatever building materials you need—practically at cost. But promise not to compare notes with the lieutenant?" He glanced sideways at her and smiled mischievously.

"That, you can be sure!" Eleanor exclaimed, grinning.

Sam drew a plan for the new school building, with separate toilets for girls and boys. He integrated the projects into his carpentry class, but they needed adult men to help them. Eleanor was outside with Estrella and their students, conducting their morning calisthenics when Luis and some of his campesinos arrived at the building site. She breathed deeply upon seeing that the group included Diego and Juan. The men immediately began unloading the timber and other building materials and tools from two flat-bed bamboo carretelas.

Eleanor noted that Diego appeared intent on ignoring her, although he waved hello to his sister. *Who is he, and why should I care, anyway?* she thought. This, however, didn't lessen the sting of his snobbery.

Eleanor broke away from the calisthenics lesson to join Luis and Sam, who appeared to be discussing the building plans.

"Reporting for duty, ma'am!" Luis said, saluting her upon her approach.

She grinned. "Thank you for all your help, Luis. How long can you make yourselves available?"

"Unfortunately, I have to return to the hacienda. I just wanted to review the plans with the sargento before I go. But you have Diego and the rest of the men at your disposal for the duration of this project. I will drop by to lend a hand, now and then, and check on the progress—if you both don't mind."

"Not at all!" Sam eagerly shook the haciendero's hand. "We're grateful for yer 'elp, sir."

"De nada," Luis replied. "I am happy to be of service to the school and children."

"That's so kind of you, Luis," Eleanor said.

Luis looked into her eyes and smiled. "My pleasure, Eleanor." He turned back to Sam. "So, as I understand, we're raising the new building on foundation posts?"

"Yes!" Eleanor interjected. "I'm looking forward to not having to worry when the rains come. It's a good thing we've been enjoying dry weather lately for the construction."

"Don't ya worry!" Sam said. "We'll get ya in the new building long before the next rain. Then, we move onto elevatin' the old building an' makin' a proper floor for it."

"How wonderful for you to have not just one but two buildings!" Luis remarked.

"Indeed," Eleanor said. "My idea is for the new structure to serve as the girls' classroom, the old one, for the boys. We need to make room for more students who have been enrolling daily now. You know, with the new migrant families?"

Luis and Sam exchanged knowing glances.

"Ah, but do I note some gender discrimination here?" Luis said chuckling. "The girls get to have the new building, while the boys must be content with the old? Surely, you did not agree to this, Sargento Munro!"

Sam chuckled. "Please, sir, it's Sam to you. And yer certainly right 'bout this dang favoritism!" Both men laughed.

"Oh, please!" Eleanor cried, chuckling. "You men enjoy many more privileges than we women in society. Let my girls get theirs in my school!" Glancing in the working men's direction, she caught Diego looking at her. Both quickly averted their gaze from each other.

Work progressed on the new structure, as did classes in the old building—like two worlds existing side by side, yet hardly touching. The weather continued to cooperate. This allowed Eleanor to divide her enlarged class of ninety-two students into two sections—assigning the girls to the school building; the boys outside, under the mango tree. The funds raised by the Thanksgiving event allowed Eleanor to purchase a pair of blackboards, among other school necessities. She also bought a large easel on which to put one of the blackboards for the outdoor class. When it was her turn to teach the boys outside, Eleanor avoided Diego or pretended he wasn't around.

Eleanor noticed that Estrella seemed happier lately. Initially, Eleanor assumed this was due to the proximity of her brother, with whom the younger teacher shared a daily lunch at the work site. One day, however, she spied Estrella chatting animatedly with the tattooed man. The mestiza also began riding home with Juan, who drove the carretela in which the campesinos arrived every morning from the hacienda. Eleanor wasn't sure how to think or feel about this. *Should I tell Estrella what I know about Juan, what he did and tried to do to me during the ambush, what he may still be capable of?* She failed to see what the mestiza teacher saw in him. They couldn't be more different! A little voice reminded her, *so are you and Diego.*

It was one of those days when everyone had left school, except Eleanor. Estrella had gone home with her suitor, along with her brother and the rest of the workers. The adult class just ended, and Yolanda, who attended them, went home ahead to make dinner while her mistress caught up with class preparations that Eleanor had neglected due to the distractions that came with the school construction.

She was reviewing the next day's lessons when she heard a timid knock on the classroom door. "Who is it?" she called out. There was no answer, so she returned to her task. Then came another set of rattling—this time, louder. Annoyed, Eleanor stomped off to the door. "Whoever it is, I'm too busy for this!" she cried while unlatching the door. When she flung it open, the blood drained from her face.

"Uh…" She cleared her throat. "Diego. What… what is it?"

"Can we talk?" His English sounded quite improved. Estrella must still be teaching him.

"Please." She waved toward a student's bench and sat opposite him. She folded her hands on her lap and asked, "What can I do for you?"

"Not easy… to ask," he said. He clasped his hands, rested his sculpted forearms on his ample thighs, and leaned toward her. He bowed his head, as though embarrassed to say whatever he came to say.

"Please. Tell me." She fidgeted in her seat. She couldn't seem to find a comfortable way to settle her derrière. And her corset chafed against her backside, forcing her to sit upright.

He glanced up at her with grave eyes. "I ask… for my sister… to stay with you. Just for now."

"What?" Eleanor said. "I'm sorry. I don't understand."

"Estrella… she not safe in hacienda," Diego said. "I think she more safe with you."

Eleanor instantly thought of the tattooed thug. Diego was probably worried about Juan's courtship with his sister. "I understand, Diego. But this is… a most unusual request. I don't know. I have to think about it." She liked Estrella, but she also liked her privacy.

"Not think. Say yes!" he insisted. "Or big trouble come. To her. To us."

"What are you worried about, exactly?" she asked. "Why don't you just tell your friend to back off? After all, don't you control him?" He raised his eyebrows, and his forehead scrunched up. She added, "I mean—Juan."

Diego groaned and shook his head vigorously. "Ay, no! Juan not problem! Is Waterstone!"

"What!" Eleanor exclaimed. "I'm aware the lieutenant was bothering your sister before. Are you telling me he's still doing it?"

"¡Sí! He make trouble for her on road home. Always waiting for her. He also go to our house in hacienda. Visit her. I no like, she no like. Juan mad. If we not stop this, big problema para todos!"

Eleanor sighed. "I see." She stood, paced about, and turned back to him. "I guess she could stay with me…until things settle down. I suppose… I could share my bedroom with her. But I only have one bed."

"¡No hay problema! I bring her bed to your house." A semblance of a smile finally appeared on his face. "¡Gracias! ¡Muchas gracias, señorita!" He extended his hand to her.

She accepted it with trepidation, recalling the last time she allowed him to hold her hand. "De nada… Diego."

As he was about to leave, she grabbed his arm. He looked stunned as he turned around. "Diego… can't we be… friends again?" she asked.

"Friends?" He appeared puzzled, almost disappointed.

"Yes. Amígos—you and me." She pointed to him and herself.

He sighed and met her gaze. "Por supuesto, señorita. Yes."

"No. Not señorita, Diego. If we're friends again, then you must call me like before: Eleanor."

"Sí… Eleanor." He smiled. "You like I walk you home? More safe for you."

She smiled back at him. "I'd like that very much."

Eleanor gathered her things and padlocked the classroom door. Diego offered to carry her book strap, and she let him.

As they walked in companionable silence, it struck her how, in that plane of quiet amity, she felt no division or difference between them. His innate dignity and self-possession radiated from him like an energy that surmounted the ascendancy which, she now acknowledged, may have shamefully colored her attitude to him from the start, a mindset perhaps rooted in her elevated concept of herself in relation not only with him but all the natives—as a teacher, or American, or both. Yet, divested of race, language, and culture, they were, simply, a man and a woman—no more, no less than the other; yet, somehow, less than whole without the other. It was a puzzle that bemused her whenever Diego was near. Now, Eleanor bid herself to settle into the peaceable state of accepting his presence with her without solving the paradox that came with him.

They reached and crossed the plaza, and the early evening promenaders, natives and soldiers alike, turned their watchful eyes to them: a couple, walking with each other.

Next Saturday morning, Diego brought his sister and her things to Eleanor's house with the help of Juan. Eleanor would have felt uneasy with the tattooed man's presence in her home were it not for Estrella and Diego. He also seemed even friendlier now toward her. For Estrella's and Diego's sake, she responded in like manner to him. She supposed Juan and she were learning to accept they were inextricably part of the world they inhabited with people they cared about.

Estrella's bed, meant for a single occupant, was, fortunately, narrower than Eleanor's, and fit nicely in the bedroom, along with a diminutive night table set between the beds. Since the additional school funds enabled Eleanor to order lockable bookcases for the school in which to store the books that used to be kept in her steamer trunk, she was able to bring the box back home. It now sat at the foot of her bed and served as additional storage for her clothes and other things, which thus made room for Estrella's dresses to hang in the armoire.

It was strange having Diego back in her bedroom. The last time he was there, he'd laid her to bed as she succumbed to malaria after the ambush. She still felt flushed whenever she recalled how he'd covered her half-exposed breasts with his scarf, which she never saw again. Sometimes, she wondered if she'd just imagined it in her delirium.

Yet, catching Diego stealing glances at her again told her she wasn't just imagining such moments of intimacy with him. Her body remembered well enough. He occasionally glanced at her portrait, which hung on the wall to one side of the bedroom window that overlooked the side garden. She'd felt embarrassed to hang it anywhere else in the house. There was something akin to an invasion of privacy in someone painting one's image without one's knowledge. Thus, the bedroom, with the privacy it offered, seemed the only place for it. Now that other people saw it, too, Eleanor felt exposed again.

Yolanda served them lunch. It struck Eleanor as strange, after everything that had happened, to now find herself dining casually with Diego, his sister, and the tattooed man at her table. Their conversation, though conducted in broken Spanish, English, and Vicolano, was convivial, revolving around the natives' shared experiences growing up in Magayon. They asked about her childhood, and she told them she, too, grew up on a farm, to which they expressed surprise and delight. She also told them about her parents.

"O, lo siento," Diego said tenderly, reaching out to tap her hand.

After lunch, Juan and Estrella went to the garden, while Yolanda cleaned up in the kitchen. Diego and Eleanor sat on opposite ends of the sofa in the sala. She'd never known a more disconcerting moment during an otherwise normal human activity. They gazed down at their clasped hands upon their laps, as though grappling to come up with words to mask the loaded silence between them. Almost simultaneously, they glanced up at each other to say something, and they both grinned.

"You first, Diego," Eleanor said, still grinning. "What were you going to say?"

"O, nada," he replied, smiling. He tucked one side of his hair behind a perfectly-shaped ear and looked into her eyes. "Gracias. For help to Estrella."

She hadn't known him like this—almost meek. Yet, she sensed he was also struggling against some kind of inner demon. "I'm happy to help," she said. "What are friends for?"

"You happy… we friends?" he surprisingly asked, holding her gaze.

"Why, of course, I am!" she exclaimed. Meeting his gaze, she added, "Are you?"

He blinked and turned away. He stood and walked to the window, as though checking the garden for his sister and Juan. When he turned around to face her again, he replied by asking another surprising question. "Don Luis give you painting?"

"Yes," she said, and wondered at her sense of shame by her admission. "It was a Christmas gift." *And why do I even feel a need to explain?*

"Is nice," he said, "pero… no capturó todo sobre ti."

Eleanor frowned in puzzlement, and he added, "It not… cómo se dice… catch you." The fire in his eyes seemed to spark again. He approached the vase of sampaguita flowers on the center table and buried his nose in the blossoms. He glanced up at her from under his dark brows and lashes. "I see you, Eleanor," he said with an inscrutable smile. "All of you."

This time, it was she who couldn't hold her gaze.

Estrella likewise brought her own trunk, which she called a *bá'ol*. Her brother and Juan had set it down, following Eleanor's example, at the foot of her bed. It was carved out of *tanguile*, one of Vicol region's prized hardwood trees, Estrella said.

Eleanor ran her hands on the intricate carvings of flowers, butterflies, and birds, and her new roommate said, "Mi mamá said mi papá had it made for me when I was born. I never met him. He died when I was a baby. Mamá also passed away when I was only seven. That was when my *ninong*, Don Luis, Sr., adopted me. Paid for my education. He also hire Diego as his errand boy. Trained him to be *katiwála'*. When ninong died, Diego was ready to serve as foreman for his son, Don Luis."

Estrella's eyes wandered toward the portrait Luis had painted of Eleanor, smiling. "Don Luis must like you very much. He paint you… beautiful."

Eleanor smiled with unease, remembering what her brother had said about it. "Thank you. But I was surprised when he gave that to me because I never posed for him." She was determined to change the subject. "You never mentioned your mother before, Estrella. I'm sorry to hear you lost both of your parents so young. How good of Don Luis Senior to do what he did for you and your brother."

"Sí. It was his way to help mamá. She used to be the villa housekeeper, you know. Maybe, he pitied my mother—widowed so young, with two young children." Estrella sighed. "Now, I am sorry to be a burden to you, too. Diego and I quarreled about me coming here. Please do not think I do not like to stay with you. It is just that I do not want to trouble anybody."

Eleanor sat beside Estrella on the latter's bed and put an arm around her shoulder. "But you're not trouble, and you're not just anybody, Estrella. I'm happy to have you here. Truly. I'm just sorry I didn't realize earlier about Lieutenant Waterstone. I'd assumed he'd already stopped pestering you. I've been so absorbed with the school. I agree with your brother—this is a good arrangement. You and I can benefit from each other's company."

Estrella glanced up at Eleanor with misty eyes. "Muchas gracias, Eleanor. I hope I can repay your kindness. Please—let me share in the rent and other house expenses."

"Don't mention it!" Eleanor retorted. "As I said, this works for both of us. Now, you don't have to rise so early to get to school on time. And we could walk there together. You know, I sometimes wondered how it would be to have a sister. Now, I have you, and you have me."

Estrella burst into tears, and the pair of maestras hugged.

Later that night, as both women lay in their beds, what sounded like guitar playing came from outside their bedroom window. At first, Eleanor assumed it was Senyong, the neighborhood guitarist, who was perhaps now so drunk he might have wandered into her yard without realizing it—until a man, who didn't sound drunk, began singing with the guitar playing. He had the voice of an exemplary tenor. Soon, there was a frantic knocking on the bedroom door.

"What? What is it?" Eleanor replied.

Yolanda peeked in, eyes wide and bright. The maid had offered to sleep in the sala, now that Estrella shared Eleanor's bedroom. "Señorita—look outside!" Yolanda said. "Is harana!"

"What's that?" Eleanor asked.

"A serenade!" Estrella exclaimed as she jumped out of bed and slid the windows open. She giggled as he leaned on the window ledge, smiling at whoever was out there.

Eleanor and Yolanda followed her to the window, and what they saw, to Eleanor's astonishment, was Juan singing to Estrella. He was accompanied on the guitar by Senyong and a choral group of a few other men. Eleanor smiled at the sight of bright-eyed Estrella giggling with Yolanda. Their child-like excitement was reminiscent of Arabella and Maude.

She gazed at the luminous night sky. Translucent, billowy clouds sailed across the face of a waxing half-moon, creating a play of light and shadow on the landscape. A spell of enchantment seemed to have been cast upon everything and everyone. Eleanor followed the dappled shapes across the garden until she detected the smoldering tip of a cigarette. It hinted at the shape of a man standing in the shadows behind the serenaders.

Her breath caught. He was, without a doubt to Eleanor's trained sense of him—none other than Diego. Although she couldn't see his eyes, she could feel the heat of his gaze searing through the thin, cotton fabric of her nightdress, as though he'd stripped her naked. Unable to stand the sensation, she returned to bed, pretending to go to sleep. Yet, she remained awake—shivering and sweating under the sheets, long after the harana was over.

Each day, the new school building rose higher from its foundations, which consisted of two hefty pairs of bamboo pilings buried deep in the ground. Mortar had set them in place, which the men produced from an amalgam of crushed volcanic rock, sand, ash, lime, and, to Eleanor's amazement, egg whites. To keep the egg yolks from being wasted, Yolanda made them into *leche* flans and yema candies that she sold through Tomasa's corner store. Eleanor told the maid she could keep a third of the proceeds and apply the rest toward funding the lunch they now served daily to the campesinos who'd volunteered to help build the school.

Yolanda delivered their freshly-cooked lunch at noon, driven by Pedro in Sam's carretela. The men greeted Yolanda's arrival with cheers and applause, as though it were a hero's welcome. They placed long boards upon their sawhorses to make a table and gathered stools and wooden boxes around it. Cristina dropped by—presumably to see her husband and show off baby Gracias, who was now three months old, fat and pink as a prize suckling. Eleanor thus invited Sam's wife to partake in their picnic lunch. This happened often enough, such that Yolanda and Cristina agreed to divide the cooking between themselves.

In addition to the Munros, couples seemed to form spontaneously during the lunch seating. Juan sat beside Estrella, Pedro with Yolanda, and Diego claimed a seat next to Eleanor. In that space of a shared meal, there was no master or servant, no teacher or peasant, no American or Filipino. A sense of hierarchy only returned whenever Luis came by.

The haciendero visited the school site occasionally to check on the construction's progress. One day, he dropped by when the teachers and workers were just about to have lunch. Eleanor thus invited him to join them. He readily accepted and, on seeing Diego seated beside Eleanor, tapped his foreman's shoulder in the way a gentleman asked another man dancing with a lady to cede his time with her, thus compelling Diego to give up his spot.

Now, the foreman appeared agitated whenever his master came around, which also occurred more frequently, thus making Eleanor keenly aware of the heightened tension between amo and katiwála'. It was as if Luis had noticed and disapproved of his servant's familiar conduct toward the American teacher. Moreover, he seemed to be marking his territory, as though he was staking a precedent claim on Eleanor. The Thomasite resented being reduced to an object of competition between the two men. Thus, she took to taking her lunch later than everybody or having none at all, feigning class work as an excuse.

News of the fantastic meals being served by la maestra Americana to anyone lending a hand at the school construction site spread quickly among farmers now bereft of farms due to Lieutenant Waterstone's reconcentrado program. Sam and Diego had to turn away many volunteers who, hence, loitered around town, aimless and jobless. This, in turn, seemed to cause an increase in petty thievery and piles of garbage in Magayon.

The town denizens were furious and complained to el presidente, who issued a stricter edict against vagrancy. The new municipal regulation, however, was practically useless because there was no means of enforcing it without the help of Lieutenant Waterstone, who was the source of the problem in the first place.

On the bright side, the increased number of helpers in the school's construction advanced the project's completion. Within a month, Eleanor was conducting classes in the new building, which boasted of timber plank flooring, capiz shell windows, and a metal roof, in addition to the bamboo-plaited walls that were similar to what the old one had. Mr. Ang extended the school credit on all materials, thus allowing Diego and his men to immediately begin renovations on the old building and bring it up to the standards of the new structure.

Estrella started receiving flowers at the school from an anonymous sender. They were waiting in front of the classroom door by the time the teachers arrived each morning. An envelope with Estrella's name handwritten on it accompanied each bouquet. The first time it happened, Estrella threw out the flowers, tore up the envelope, and tossed the pieces to the wind.

"Why trash the flowers?" Eleanor exclaimed. "They're beautiful! They could, at least, decorate our desk. I think I may have a vase somewhere here we can use." She bent over, scrounging inside a storage box for one.

"No!" Estrella cried, startling Eleanor. "It is not proper," she added in a sober tone.

Eleanor straightened up and grinned. "Don't tell me you're still too shy to acknowledge Juan's courtship? I've seen you with him. You seem to enjoy his company."

"It is not him," Estrella replied. "These are not from Juan."

Eleanor raised an eyebrow. "How do you know? You didn't even read the note."

"No need. Because… Juan cannot read or write," Estrella said somberly.

"Oh." Eleanor looked away, pretending not to see how embarrassed her assistant teacher appeared about entertaining the courtship of an illiterate man.

Eleanor continued to wonder who was sending Estrella the flowers until one afternoon when an unexpected visitor came to the school and confirmed her suspicions. She knew Estrella suspected the same person, too, when the native teacher blanched and hyperventilated as she and Eleanor spied him riding his horse, heading toward the school's direction.

The workers, particularly Diego and Juan, stopped their hammering and sawing. They looked like deer in suspended animation—heads raised, necks stretched, ears pricked—as they listened for, and watched the predator approach.

Sam, who was outside teaching carpentry class, saw him, too. He limped toward the soldier who dismounted and hitched his horse to a bamboo post. The former sergeant appeared to confront the higher-ranking officer. To Eleanor's great surprise, Lieutenant Waterstone seemed to respond to Sam—who had punched him in the face, not too long ago—in a civil manner.

Eleanor wished she could listen to what both men were saying, but all she could hear were their deep, low voices. She and Estrella exchanged astonished glances as they witnessed the lieutenant offering a handshake to Sam, who appeared to hesitate before finally nodding and accepting it. Together, the two American men walked toward the new school building where Eleanor and Estrella were conducting a sewing class.

Sam entered the classroom and reacted to the female teachers' look of puzzlement with an enigmatic smile. "Guess who's come to see us, ladies."

Lieutenant Waterstone followed behind him, smiling and carrying a package. He removed his cap and pinned it under his left arm. "Good afternoon, Miss Karsten, Miss Santiago," he said.

"Lieutenant, what's the meaning of this?" exclaimed Eleanor. "I would have you know we still have class and can't have any disturbance."

Estrella turned her back to Lieutenant Waterstone and instructed the girls to pay attention to their needlework. The students' eyes flitted anxiously between their head teacher and the officer. A whimper escaped one of the girls. Asunción. Estrella went to comfort her.

Lieutenant Waterstone held up his palm to the ladies. "I'm sorry. I don't mean to bother you. But I only need a few minutes. I come with a peace offering." He glanced at Estrella before he approached Eleanor, holding out the package.

"What's this?" Eleanor asked.

"Please. Open and see," he replied in a conciliatory tone.

CHAPTER 20

Love and War in the Time of Cholera

Eleanor accepted the triangular package from Lieutenant Waterstone with trepidation. It was soft under its brown paper wrapping. She set it on her desk and took a pair of scissors to snip off the twine that secured the wrapping around the object. When she peeled away the paper, what appeared was a folded fabric of bright red, white, and blue. A brand-new American flag!

She glanced up at the lieutenant in disbelief.

"I thought your new school deserved a new flag." He smiled. "Please accept it with my sincere compliments and… apologies for any… misunderstanding." He smiled ruefully and glanced at Estrella, who looked away from him.

Eleanor glanced at Sam, who stood behind the officer, shrugging his shoulders and smiling in bewilderment. She cleared her throat. "Thank you, lieutenant. This is… a pleasant surprise."

He approached and extended his hand to Eleanor, who shook it. He smiled and turned to Estrella. "Miss Santiago, I hope… you liked the flowers? Please forgive me for upsetting you. I want you and everyone to know I only have the best intentions. Honorable intentions. I admit I have been boorishly clumsy showing it. But I hope, now, we could be… friends?"

He offered his hand to Estrella, who appeared dumbfounded. She glanced up at him and at Eleanor and Sam and turned again to the hand he continued to hold out to her. She moistened her lips and, in a slow, tentative move, accepted it.

Lieutenant Waterstone sighed and smiled as he grasped her hand and, instead of shaking it, surprised everyone again by bowing and performing a gesture of a kiss.

The officer turned to the other teachers. "Well, then, Miss Karsten, Sergeant Munro, I hope you all have a good evening. Please let me know if I can be of any assistance. Anything at all!" He turned again to Estrella with a tender glance and put on his hat. He tapped it on the right side as though saluting to her. "And you, as well, Miss Santiago."

Eleanor scuttled to the window to observe the officer's departure. Just as she feared, Diego and his men had gathered around Lieutenant Waterstone's horse and pressed in as the officer approached his steed. The lieutenant, looking quite unperturbed, met their fierce gaze with a suave smile.

Juan wore a murderous expression on his face, his shoulders heaving. Estrella joined Eleanor at the window and gasped, for Juan appeared about to lunge at the soldier. Diego grabbed Juan just in time to hold him back. Lieutenant Waterstone maintained his unsullied posture while both men struggled with each other. He unhitched his horse and mounted the animal with a single swing of his leg. He pulled on the reins and steered the steed around the men, tipped his cap to them, and cried, "¡Adiós, muchachos!"

Estrella ran outside to her brother and Juan. Diego caressed his sister's back and pointed to the classroom. As the assistant teacher headed back inside the classroom, Diego slapped the backside of Juan's head and shoved him toward the direction of where they were working.

Sam grinned as he peered out of another window. "I dare say, that Waterstone sure showed some cajones bigger than Mexican jumpin' beans! Makes ya wonder what he's up to."

"Why, Sam, don't you see?" Eleanor said. "Lieutenant Waterstone just officially declared his courtship of Miss Santiago." The students burst into giggling, reminding Eleanor they weren't alone. "Now, girls, I forbid you to say anything about this to anyone, you hear?"

"Yes, Miss Karsten!" the girls cried in unison, and continued tittering, whispering bright-eyed speculations to each other. Only Asunción appeared indifferent.

By the third week of March, the Magayon Public School for Boys and Girls began holding separate classes in two buildings. Diego and his men had raised the old structure from the dirt floor, placed it on bamboo pilings, and refitted it with new capiz windows, a timber plank floor, and a metal roof. The new and old buildings now looked almost like twins, except for the dark patina of the wood that marked the older structure.

Luis indulged Eleanor's request to provide the hacienda children with school transportation by having two horse-drawn wagonettes made for the purpose and assigning drivers from among the older campesinos no longer capable of heavy manual labor.

The various hamlets that had sprouted around town contributed to the increase in student enrollment, which now reached a record of 167 students. While Eleanor was ecstatic about this, she also worried she'd soon need additional teachers and to start planning for another school expansion to include a high school. This meant building new structures that required more resources—when her current resources hardly sustained their present operations.

Still, Eleanor was determined not to let their achievement pass without celebrating it. She dreamed of a launch ceremony to which she would invite Ida as the ribbon cutter. She envisioned the event as another community affair that could help people forget the ugly Thanksgiving incidents. She had just written to Ida about it when news arrived that rendered such a dream impossible for the foreseeable future.

Doctor Langford dropped by Eleanor's house and somberly said, "There's a cholera outbreak in Manila. I expect it'll be here soon. I immediately thought of you and your students. The school is vulnerable as a spreader."

Eleanor's hand went over her chest as her breath turned fast and shallow. Estrella's jaw dropped, and her hand flew to her gaping mouth.

The doctor said he had just come from Legazpi where quarantine measures had already taken effect at the port. No one was allowed to disembark from any boat or ship before passing the requisite five-day isolation. He said he was at the Regan Barracks when the soldiers received a dispatch from Manila about the grave news. He read a copy of it to the teachers.

> *The Board of Health was alerted earlier this month about a strain of Asiatic cholera first recorded in Guangzhou. The same was reported a week later in Hong Kong. By mid-March, it was confirmed in Manila. The surgeon general has ordered the capital's lockdown. No one is allowed to leave Manila without passing quarantine. Importation of vegetables is forbidden. Strict hygiene measures must be observed and enforced. Every case of cholera must be recorded and reported by the chief health officer of each town to the Board of Health.*

"In Magayon, that means me." Doctor Langford sighed.

"¡Sus, Maria Santissima!" Estrella cried, crossing herself. "What are we going to do?"

"First, understand and educate everybody about how the disease is spread," Doctor Langford replied. "It's passed by ingesting contaminated food or water caused by poor sanitation. Second, recognize its symptoms. Earlier hospital deaths were recorded as merely flu-related or caused by some other illness like dysentery. Yet, the rate at which the deaths happened within the same area in Manila provoked testing for the bacillus. If people only knew what signs to watch out for, it could have been identified earlier."

"And what should we look for, doctor?" Eleanor asked.

"First sign is watery diarrhea, which looks like rice water with a fishy odor. Then, vomiting of clear fluid. The sick person eventually turns bluish-gray due to dehydration. That's why cholera is sometimes called the Blue Death."

"Do we watch out for fever, doctor?" Eleanor added.

"It isn't a symptom of cholera if that's what you're asking," he replied. "On the contrary, cold clammy skin is an indication of the disease. Fever, though, is still relevant as a sign of secondary infection. So, we note all the symptoms of the person—lack of energy or weakness, deep and labored breathing, rapid pulse, sunken eyes, dry mouth, muscle cramping, wrinkled hands and feet. All signs of dehydration. Later on, there could be seizures, hallucinations, even coma, especially in children."

Estrella covered her mouth and closed her eyes.

"But, beware," Doctor Langford continued, "not everyone exhibits symptoms, though the person may already be infected. That's the hard part about controlling transmission. The asymptomatic could spread it unknowingly. And those who are symptomatic? Well, let's just say better call for the padre, because a majority of the infected do not survive. We still don't know why some recover and others don't. I'd venture to say it depends on the person's constitution. Thus, children are most vulnerable, and so are unhealthy adults and the elderly."

"And if we see the signs, doctor, what do we do?" Estrella asked with a panicked tone.

"Isolate that person immediately and call me at once! No one should touch him or her except someone who could be trusted to be disciplined about washing and sanitizing everything."

"But, doctor, that's almost impossible here," Eleanor interjected. "I mean—what with entire families living and sleeping in one-room huts!"

"I understand the problem, Miss Karsten—believe me. And these new hamlets, with their improper sewage and congestion, are no help at all. That's why I intend to talk with the mayor and lieutenant about them first thing tomorrow. By Jove, we don't even have a hospital here! We'd have to bring the sick all the way to Legazpi!"

"Doctor, what is cure for this?" Estrella pleaded with a pinched voice, hands clasped in prayer pose.

"I'm afraid there isn't any, Señorita Santiago. There's a Spaniard named Ferran who claimed to have developed a vaccine, but there's no consensus on its effectiveness. All we can do is try to lessen dehydration by continuously feeding the sick, especially with nourishing beverages, like coconut juice. Thank goodness, we have much of that here!"

"¡Sí, gracias a Dios!" exclaimed Estrella, crossing herself again.

"Doctor, how should we talk to our students about this?" Eleanor asked grimly. "And should I suspend classes?"

Doctor Langford heaved a sigh and bowed his head, caressing his forehead. When he glanced up at her again, the lines between his brows deepened as he shook his head. "I don't think that's necessary at this time. Last thing we want is for people to panic, which would only make the situation worse. But preemptive measures are critical. So, I would tell your students to be extra mindful of observing good sanitation and hygiene practices and to watch out for the signs I described. If they see them, they must immediately separate the sick and send for me."

Both teachers nodded listlessly. The doctor left them with the latest copy of the *Manila Sun*, which published an article by Mr. de Alcalá, who lamented the lack of national discipline that favored superstition and sentimentality over science. He blamed the epidemic on people skirting quarantine measures to return to their families outside the capital. People escaped confinement by traveling on bancas or trekking across fields to avoid the road routes monitored by the Philippine Constabulary enforcing the lockdown.

The next morning, Eleanor and Estrella conferred with Sam on how to prepare their students for an epidemic scenario. They explained to the children what cholera was and what they could do to help prevent it, such as educating their families about it. They reminded them what they'd already taught them in science and hygiene class: to frequently wash their hands with soap, especially after going to the latrine, and filter and boil their drinking water. They also warned them against eating unwashed and uncooked vegetables and fruits.

No one appeared more aggrieved than Senyong when the disease chose Tomasa as its first victim in Magayon. Yolanda said their neighborhood sari-sari merchant had gone to Manila to shop for supplies and returned before the quarantine measures took effect at Legazpi Port. Doctor Langford attended to Tomasa with the help of the childless widow's niece. He admitted the woman's condition was serious. Senyong lingered day and night on the benches in front of the closed store. According to Yolanda, he had also been seen lighting candles in church, praying on his knees, and wiping his eyes with a handkerchief so soaked with snot and tears, it left a big, wet blot where he kept it in his trouser pocket.

On Good Friday, the townsfolk reenacted the crucifixion and death of Christ in a passion play on the plaza stage as an offering and reminder to God, who had already sacrificed his son for them, that there was no longer any need to kill anyone else through cholera.

The next day, Doctor Langford called for Padre Damián to administer extreme unction to Tomasa and, on Easter Sunday, the poor woman succumbed to the disease. In his sermon, the priest declared the widow blessed for dying on the Lord's day of resurrection. "For she would surely rise again on Judgement Day!" he exclaimed. He also proclaimed Tomasa happily reunited with her husband after praising the woman's faithfulness to her spouse by wearing her widow's garb till the end. A howling cry was heard from the back end of the church. Senyong's.

The tragic speed by which the illness took Tomasa was outdone only by the speed in which she was buried: on the day after she died. No wake was held, and her body was placed inside a plain coffin, hurriedly made, and generously coated with lime. Only a few attended the burial: the padre, assisted by an acolyte, including Tomasa's niece, Nanay Auring, Eleanor, Estrella, Yolanda, and Senyong, who cried like a baby and had to be put to bed like one because he was too drunk to find his way home.

In school, more and more students were absent each day. News spread that Legazpi Port authorities found a *paraw* or "canoe" brought in by the tide with a corpse inside it. Everyone scared themselves to death speculating who might be next on Death's list. When Magayon's death rate exceeded ten a day, Eleanor closed the school per Board of Health guidelines.

She and Yolanda went to Mr. Ang's store and returned home with a quart of crude carbolic acid, a bushel of chloride of lime, a box of camphor, three dozen tea towels, and a huge pot for boiling water. Eleanor instructed the maid to spread a layer of lime on the front and back stairs that led up to the house. They placed a sign instructing everyone to refrain from visiting or, else, take off their shoes at the bottom of the stairs before stepping up to the house.

With Estrella's help, they wiped down all the furniture, floors, and other surfaces with *agua finecada* solution made from diluted carbolic acid. They filled a bowl with the same for everyone to wash their hands with on entering the house. They set the bowl on a small table by the door, along with tea towels meant for single use. Yolanda sanitized the towels in the big pot of boiling water she kept simmering over a wood fire near the well in the backyard.

Doctor Langford invited Eleanor to a meeting with him, Mayor Dizon, Padre Damián, and Lieutenant Waterstone at the ayuntamiento. She assumed it had something to do with her students or the school closing. When she arrived, she was surprised to see Doña Beatriz likewise present.

"Señorita Karsten," el presidente said, with the help of Doctor Langford's translation, "we invited you here as a courtesy to let you know we have decided to use the school buildings as a hospital during this epidemic."

"What!" Eleanor cried, recoiling from visualizing her precious new buildings subjected to the filth of the disease. "And you decided this without consulting me—which would have been the least courtesy you owed me? No, I cannot accept this! The school is too important!"

She glanced at the priest and added, "Why not use the church, instead? Isn't that the place to practice love, mercy, and compassion, Padre Damián?" She turned to el presidente. "And how about the town hall, Mayor Dizon? If it's big enough for public balls and feasts, it's surely big enough for the town's sick!" Turning toward the infantry officer, she said, "Or how about your barracks and prison, Lieutenant Waterstone? Use them for something good, for a change!"

The men shook their heads, smiling wryly, and Doctor Langford replied, "The reality, my dear, is that it's only the school buildings that offer the space and logistics for this undertaking. I confess I was the one who asked for them. If I'm to be in charge of all the patients in this town, I need ample facilities in one place. We need an integrated system of providing patient care. As you know already, isolating the sick from the healthy is a serious problem if people were left on their own."

Eleanor heaved a sigh. "I understand the challenges, doctor. But I plead with you to consider the possibility that you all are being shortsighted in so readily targeting my school to address these otherwise valid concerns. Think of the children! We were doing so well before this. We quadrupled enrollment and just began to give them a proper space for learning. I can't imagine opening the school again this year if you take over my buildings. Put yourself in a parent's shoes! How could you think of sending your child back to a place that was soaked in the miasma of a contagious disease?"

The men exchanged glances again, but it was Doña Beatriz who replied, this time. "My dear, we are very sorry. We understand. Pero, por favor, also try to understand us. The community help you build your school, yes? Now, do you not think it has right to use it to help save people's lives?"

Eleanor slumped back in her chair. Of course—the lady was right!

Doña Beatriz added, "I am here because I want to help my husband. Plus, the ayuntamiento appointed me to organize volunteer nurses to care for the sick. You and Señorita Santiago are welcome to join if you like."

Eleanor's head hung down. She felt terrible. Perhaps it was she who was being shallow, selfish, and shortsighted? She glanced up and looked everyone in the eye. "I understand you all don't consider yourselves subject to my wishes, but if I raise this matter with the superintendent, there's a chance I could prevail. I refuse to accept the school as your only option, and he may decide similarly. You might note that under military governorship, the Superintendent of Public Schools outranks the army when it concerns the schools. If you're not aware of this, just ask Lieutenant Waterstone." She glanced at the soldier, who curled his lips into a half-smile and whose eyes twinkled with amusement. "That said," Eleanor continued, "I'm willing to withdraw my objection—on one condition!"

"And what is that, dear?" Doctor Langford asked.

"That you return the buildings to me in the same condition you found them—as soon as the Board of Health declares it's safe to open the school. And if you fail to do this, then the town will promptly provide me with the same, if not better, facilities and resources as replacements," Eleanor declared. "Do we have a deal?"

"Deal!" Lieutenant Waterstone shockingly replied. "All will be arranged as you wish, Miss Karsten." This time, he wore a full smile.

April 13, 1902

Dearest Ida,

Thank you for your letter assuring me you're safe and well. I've been anxious to hear from you since news of the epidemic in Manila reached us.

Thank you, also, for asking about me. Although I've had to adjust to some radical changes, I, too, am well. My assistant, Estrella, now lives with me. She and I have joined a group of volunteer nurses formed by Doña Beatriz to help her husband, Doctor Langford, to care for the increasing number of cholera patients. Between fifty to a hundred now succumb daily to the disease. Doctor Langford could hardly cope with the demand on his time and energy. We've requested another doctor from Manila, but it appears none could be spared, as I understand the epidemic is at its peak there.

Because our town doesn't have a hospital, my two new beautiful school buildings have been expropriated as such. I'm grateful this happened after I'd already closed the school, per BOH guidelines. I worry, however, I may never recover the buildings. The possibility of reopening the school this year is doubtful. I am, frankly, despondent because we worked so hard to get those buildings erected and, now, they may be as good as lost to us.

Sadly, I've lost some of my students to the Blue Death. I grieve most for little Asunción, the lovely girl who so wonderfully recited a patriotic verse during our Thanksgiving class presentation to Mr. McCauley. I was given both the blessing and curse of caring for the child in her last days. It was heartbreaking, to say the least, to see such a beautiful, vibrant girl snatched from life, even before she'd begun to live.

My regret is not having had the talk I meant to have with her after Christmas break, when I saw her descend into melancholia, partly due, I'm sure, to what happened to her friend, Bayani, who never returned to school. I witnessed how their friendship developed from rivalry and antipathy (more on Asunción's side) into the friendship they shared in the end. For Bayani, though, I'm afraid, Asunción's death means more than a friend's demise. It's a tragically curtate first love.

This perhaps explains why I got to see him again after all these months. His parents told me he'd gone to live with an uncle on another island. But I doubted this after I spotted him at Asunción's burial on the day after her death. It wouldn't have been possible for him to have learned of her death and reached Magayon in time for her funeral if he had to travel from another island. I was devastated upon seeing how he, who once was my favorite and most outstanding student, did not care to even say hello to me before he disappeared again like the ghost he has become.

Oh, Ida, I can't shake off the guilt I may be to blame for the boy's alienation. If only I had not opened that Thanksgiving can of worms! I've underestimated the power of history to be a catalyst for change, which, in this case, has resulted in calamitous change for a boy who was so promising! Such, perhaps, is the wage of waking the sleeping before they're ready?

I take comfort in thinking that, although the story of Bayani and Asunción is tragic, it nevertheless shines a light on the road to building democracy in this country. It suggests that democratization of schools is indeed the path to equality in this society because it allows children from different social classes to interact with and learn from each other. Asunción and Bayani would probably not have met, were it not for our school. And even if they did, someone like Bayani, who belongs to the campesino class, would not have been able to freely mingle with Asunción, whose family, though not quite cacique class, hails from ilustrado lineage.

I agree with Doctor Rizal when he wrote, "The youth are the hope of the land." I wonder, however, if we adults aren't making such hope harder to realize.

I'm afraid I have to pause my pen here, my friend. There's still much to do in the land of the living. Please continue to be safe and well. And please do keep me posted about your situation in Manila.

Love,
Eleanor

April 20, 1902

Dear Maude,

Thank you for your note of concern. I'm fine, but as you can imagine, this epidemic has tested everyone. I'm glad to know you haven't seen signs of it yet in Benguet province. I hope this scourge never reaches you.

My assistant teacher, Miss Estrella Santiago, has roomed in with me, but instead of teaching, we now work with a group of volunteer nurses in the same buildings that used to be our school, now a hospital. I'm afraid the structures are lost to us now because—oh, the filth, Maude! The ruthlessness of this disease and the raw suffering it brings!

The living and the dying enter and exit our doors, riding a macabre carousel of death that won't stop turning. Within a matter of a mere two to three days, a new patient becomes a mere shadow of his or her old self: bluish-gray, puckered, sagging skin hung on a skeletal frame! One could hardly recognize the patients in the end, and, thus, the name tags on their toes. Yes, toes, my dear, because we don't even have proper beds to which we could hang our patients' names. What we have, instead, are native woven floor mats called banig.

In this connection, and in a rare act of selflessness, the local padre offered us church space to store all our school furniture. As for the books, I had them crated and stored under my house. This freed up space for us to lay down mats on the floors of our school-turned-hospital, lined up in multiple rows. When a patient dies, we simply burn the mat, pillow, and sheets used by the deceased.

Much of the patient care we provide involves the simple yet tedious regimen of constantly rehydrating and feeding the infected despite their resistance to food and beverage due to vomiting and diarrhea. We also sterilize and wash all materials that have been in contact with the patients and their caregivers. I lament these are the most we could do until an effective vaccine could be developed. I understand from Doctor Langford that a Spaniard by the name of Ferran may have developed a cholera vaccine, but he appears to be so vilified and steeped in controversy in Spain that even if the antipathy among Spain, the U.S., and Filipinos could be overcome, it's doubtful we could procure it.

All the kneeling and back-breaking work exact a toll on the body by end of day or night, depending on one's shift. We arrive home bone tired, with hardly any appetite to eat, yet we know we need to keep up our strength so we could be of use next day. My house-keeper thankfully keeps us well fed, and our house, clothes, and things properly sanitized and washed.

The hems of our skirts have become bleached edges eaten by lime-coated floors. We've mended them as best we could, cutting off the frayed edges and folding and sewing them into neat hems again. This has naturally shortened our skirts, which have raised quite a few eyebrows. Yet, this may very well point to where women's fashion might go, simply because shorter skirts are easier to keep clean and more convenient to move around in—an idea I imagine our dear Arabella would approve of.

I haven't heard from Arabella, and hope that she, like you, remains untouched by this epidemic. Your distance from Manila may be working in your favor in this regard. When this epidemic is over, we should all celebrate through a reunion. Perhaps on the anniversary of our arrival in Manila?

Meanwhile, my friend, I wish you continued good health and safety. When you hear from, and send word to Arabella, please give her my love, as well.

Love,
Eleanor

First came the cholera; next, the burnings; then, the outrage that invigorated the insurrection. Officially, Americans were still at war with Filipinos. Yet, Sam explained that, to the Filipinos, the war was a continuation of their revolution for independence against Spain, which they believed they could have won if their former colonial ruler had not sold the archipelago to the U.S. under the Treaty of Paris. "The natives feel we've cheated them of their victory," Sam said.

To Eleanor, however, it was all a shameful waste of human life regardless of what it was called. She glanced dolefully out of her former classroom window from which, only a few months ago, she'd enjoyed the beauty and tranquility of a pastoral field. It was now a wretched patchwork of burned and burning huts, amid a paroxysm of weeping and wailing. The mango tree beside the old school building had died, as if it, too, had lost its will to live. Bereft of leaves, with only its scraggly dark branches and gnarly trunk remaining, it was a ghost tree. A cross for Magayon.

To thwart many families' attempts to hide away their sick, Lieutenant Waterstone ordered house-to-house inspections and the burning of huts where the ill had been kept without proper isolation. The rest of the family was detained in a quarantine tent camp that soon also became a cesspool of contagion. Eleanor understood that the lieutenant's actions were harsh, but she also recognized them as a response to the naïve, undisciplined, or superstitious reactions of the community to the epidemic that further endangered public health. What no one, including Eleanor, anticipated were the unintended consequences of the take-and-burn campaign.

She couldn't stop thinking of Bayani since she saw him at Asunción's burial. She searched for one of her books, *Tom Sawyer*, which would make for a good companion to *The Adventures of Huckleberry Finn* she'd given him at Christmas. It also provided her with an excuse to see his family again. Perhaps, they would be more willing, this time, to tell her where she could find him. When she reached their hut, however, she was horrified to see it burning. She hopped off the calesin and ran to the soldiers holding the flaming torches.

"What happened?" she cried.

"Stay back!" one of the soldiers yelled, holding out his palm to block her approach.

She continued rushing toward the hut, screaming, "What have you done?"

The soldier grabbed her by the upper arms to hold her back. "Halt! You can't go there!"

She pointed at the burning hut. "But that's my student's home! Where's his family?"

The soldier's stern expression turned sympathetic. "Sorry, ma'am. Had to burn it all."

Eleanor paused to process what he said. Failing, she asked, "What do you mean—burn it all?"

The soldier averted his gaze. "They were all dead, anyway. From the cholera."

Eleanor's hands flew to her chest to still her pounding heart and catch her breath. She glanced up at the soldier, tears in her eyes. "But where are the bodies?"

The soldier's Adam's apple rose and fell. He glanced downward. "Um… sorry, ma'am. They… they were too far gone. Practically meltin' in their own rot. No one wanted to touch them. So… so we… they're all still in there… together."

Eleanor's knees shook. She felt as if her heart was wrenched from her chest. "God, no, oh no! How could you do this? All those children! How could you be sure they were all dead? And how did no one know? Or even tried to help them?" *Why did you, Eleanor, of all people, not have known and failed to help them?*

The soldier shrugged. "Poor families clam up an' just lock 'emselves in, ma'am. Everybody's just strugglin' to save 'emselves."

The fire crackled and the roof timbers crashed, surrendering to the ravenous flames. Wood smoke laced with the sweet scent of burning flesh filled the air. Eleanor choked and her legs buckled, prompting the soldier to catch and hold her up. Her tears fell like the ashes that rained upon them. She held up her palms like the scales of Lady Justice, weighing the incinerated particles in her hands, rubbing the gray ephemera between her fingers, amazed by how such lightness could feel so leaden; how the dancing ash petals could evanesce into the air; and how everything, even an entire family, could turn into nothingness as if they never existed.

Eleanor despaired over how the disparities among the living simulated themselves among the dead. Since it was the poor who lived in one-room huts where the infected couldn't be separated from the rest of the family, it was likewise the poor who bore the brunt of the burnings. In contrast, the villas of the rich, which had multiple rooms in which the sick could be sequestered, were spared. Sheer ignorance and lack of resources aggravated the plight of the destitute, rendering them helpless to ensure the safety of their food and water. Hence, the indigents suffered a vastly disproportionate number of deaths in the community.

So one-sided was this holocaust, and so great was the outrage from the injustice, that no amount of medical, scientific, or rational explanation could persuade the aggrieved who'd somehow dodged the disease, that they weren't intentionally targeted by the containment and conflagrations. Many of the survivors sought refuge in the forests and mountains, taking what remaining family and possessions they had. It came as no surprise to Eleanor that such people ended up joining the insurrectos who mounted new guerrilla attacks against the soldiers. They ambushed, looted, and torched army supply wagons—sometimes, with the soldiers still inside the vehicles. Thus began a new cycle of violence and hatred in Magayon.

Eleanor was also not surprised that Diego and Juan had seemingly disappeared. She assumed they'd both gone underground to pursue the insurrection. Estrella, however, said she was sure the men were just keeping to the hacienda. Luis confirmed this when he checked on Eleanor and her housemates and brought them fruits, vegetables, and other increasingly scarce supplies. He said he'd ordered his men confined to the hacienda—not only to protect them from the contagion but also to guard hacienda property against the rampant looting.

Nanay Auring came over and said that a local *babaylan* or "shaman," had called for a revival of an ancient custom called, *atang*, and asked Eleanor, Yolanda, and Estrella to join her. The native healer explained that the ritual was meant to petition the god, Gugurang, for help against the tragedies that were surely brought upon them by his evil brother, Aswáng. Eleanor agreed to go, if only to take her mind off all that was happening—by witnessing a subversion of another kind. It appeared that at a time of great tribulation and suffering, when not even the colonial Christ god could seem to help and, rather, may have even fomented the actions of the soldados Americanos, the Vicolanos remembered their pre-Hispanic gods—despite four centuries of Christianity.

On the appointed evening, Senyong, though hardly seen lately, fetched the women in the carretela lent by Mr. Ang. Nanay Auring advised that, if they were stopped along the way by anyone, they were to say they were going to assist her, a healer, who also happened to be a *partéra* or "midwife," to help a woman in labor deliver her child. They had to keep the atang a secret, she stressed, because Padre Damián was sure to come after them if he ever learned of it, and there was none crazier than the padre in confronting pagan practice.

The excuse that Nanay Auring suggested came in handy when a pair of patrolling soldiers halted them. They let the group go upon Eleanor's claim they were enroute to assist in a birth. After they'd long passed the soldiers, Eleanor wondered aloud what they might have said if the soldiers had asked for the pregnant woman's name. Nanay Auring chuckled. "No worry, señorita. I know many. This cholera keep people home—making babies all the time!"

Everyone burst into laughter, even Senyong. The old woman provided them with much-needed comic relief.

"Nanay Auring," Eleanor said, "please tell me more about this atang. I want to know about these ancient gods."

Nanay Auring answered through Estrella's translation.

> *The babaylan blames all the bad things happening now on Gugurang's brother, Aswáng. He is the evil and lesser god who makes people sin and suffer. He lives on Mount Malinao, an ugly volcano compared to Mayon where Gugurang lives, and an inferior one because it has no fire inside. Aswáng has always been envious of Gugurang's sacred fire. So, he probably created all these troubles to force Gugurang to give up his fire to him. This is why we are having the atang: to ask Gugurang to put an end to all the destruction that Aswáng is causing.*

"That's fascinating," Eleanor remarked. "Reminds me of the myths and gods of the ancient Greeks and Romans. I'm curious, Nanay Auring, do your people also have a creation story? I mean, like how the world began? How man was made?"

After Estrella translated Eleanor's statements, Nanay Auring chuckled.

The story is not about how man was made, but how both man and woman were created! Before the time of the Kastilyas, our people believed that man, whom they called, Malakas, because he was strong, and woman, called Maganda, because she was beautiful, were born from equal halves of a giant bamboo pecked open by the mystical bird, Tigmamanukan. Man and woman were born at the same time—not one ahead of the other, nor one lording over the other. In other words, man and woman were considered different, yet equal.

Eleanor smiled as one rejoiced over great insight. Different, yet equal. She loved it. No other religion she knew preached the principle of equality between men and women. She couldn't wait to get to the atang, wondering what other wonders awaited her.

CHAPTER 21

Darkest Before Light

Past the outskirts of town, they rattled along a dirt road that led to rougher terrain, in a field strewn with large volcanic rocks. The clouds obscured the moon and stars, making it difficult to find one's orientation. Were it not for the glimmer of a fire burning behind some rambling structure, it was difficult to determine where they were.

As Eleanor's eyes adjusted to the flickering light and shadows, she discovered they were at the Cagsawa Church ruins portrayed by Luis's painting. By day, there would have been a breathtaking view of the Mayon, yet tonight, she could only make out the dark, conical outlines of the volcano against the dim glow on the horizon. She marveled at the seeming poetic justice at play—where an animistic ritual was about to be performed in the shadows of the remains of a Christian church buried by the wrath of a pagan god.

They joined a motley band of other participants gathered around a bonfire. The sound of a small drum tapping a mantraic beat announced the entrance of someone whom Eleanor assumed was the shaman. She looked younger than Nanay Auring and unlike anything Eleanor expected. On closer scrutiny, she was, shockingly, not a she but a he. He wore an Indian woman's sari and a woman's necklaces, bracelets, and anklets. He had an androgynous face and frame, a high-pitched, feminized voice, and effeminate gestures. Eleanor glanced with puzzlement at Nanay Auring. The old woman nodded, saying, "Sí. He…

asóg." Eleanor turned to Estrella, who smiled and remarked, "He is one of those born a man with the spirit of a woman."

Eleanor turned her attention back to the babaylan, who stood in front of a low bamboo table. The ritual participants approached him, offering tributes of rice cakes and fruits that he put on the table. Nanay Auring requested Eleanor help her carry the rice cakes in coconut shells she brought as offerings. Yolanda and Estrella followed, bearing baskets of bananas and ube yam, which the natives considered special because it was the color of royalty—purple. When Eleanor reached the shaman, his eyes widened with fretful surprise. Perhaps he never expected to see an American at an unauthorized indigenous ritual and feared reprisal from the authorities. Nonetheless, he accepted her offering.

Eleanor returned to her spot in the circle. When she glanced up again, her heart lurched and her breath quickened at the sight of Diego, who was standing across the bonfire, looking at her. She was relieved to see he was alive and seemingly well. With reports of skirmishes between the insurrectos and soldiers, she'd been bracing herself for news of either his arrest or demise. His hair, which used to be chin-length, had grown to his shoulders. The fire cast dancing shadows upon his face, and the flames reflected in his eyes, so that he almost looked like some kind of demon. Standing beside him was Juan, whose eyes were focused on Estrella.

After the babaylan had received all the offerings, he knelt before the altar table, and everyone followed, kneeling in place. The babaylan chanted a series of prayers and stood. Holding a coconut shell in his hands, he danced around the bonfire in jerky motions and contortions to the drummer's primeval beat. As he danced, he picked up handfuls of what appeared to be crushed, dried leaves from the coconut shell and threw the potpourri to the fire, until he'd completed the circle. Whatever he tossed in the fire suffused the air with a fragrance akin to incense. He returned to the table, picked up the food offerings, and, one by one, gave them up to the fire.

The sweet-sour scents of burning fruits and cakes combined with the potpourri's perfume snaked themselves into the participants' nostrils and seemingly induced a trance-like state in some of them, who were now smiling at the fire while swaying their bodies. Eleanor felt scared, yet chose to trust her friends, who wouldn't have invited her to a ritual dangerous to any of them.

The shaman and his drummer picked up the offering table and also hurled it to the pyre. Soon, the multiple tongues of fire united into one, big, dancing flame. It stayed that way for a few minutes before it diminished and separated back into smaller flames.

Four pairs of men carried huge clay jars to the babaylan, who laid his hands on each vessel. The men then spread into four equidistant spots around the fire and began dousing it with what appeared to be water in the containers. When the fire turned to embers, the shaman and drummer solemnly marched away, cutting through the circle of devotees, melding with the shadows behind the ruins.

Everyone began to leave. Diego and Juan approached the women and Senyong. Estrella smiled at the sight of Juan, with whom she walked away. Diego took Nanay Auring's hand and pressed it to his forehead. The old woman smiled and blessed him with the sign of the cross, which struck Eleanor as a jarringly Christian act, considering the pagan rite they'd just attended. Diego smiled and nodded at Senyong, who escorted the old woman back to the carretela. Yolanda scuttered to catch up with Senyong and Nanay Auring, leaving Eleanor and Diego alone.

"Hello, Diego," Eleanor said. "How are you?"

"Estoy bien, gracias." He smiled his old, disarming smile, eyes twinkling. "You—komusta?"

"I'm fine," she said. "Thank you. I'm also glad to see that you seem all right, despite everything."

He nodded.

Finding herself alone in his company again, she felt at a loss for what else to say. How to tame her pounding heart? "Well, I think we need to get going," she said. She turned to where Estrella was chatting with Juan and hollered, "Estrella, time to leave!"

Diego detained her with a gentle pull on her hand. She stood frozen as he caressed, sniffed, and kissed it like some doting animal, awakening the same stirrings she'd felt under the mango tree. He gazed up at her with embers for eyes but said nothing as he walked her to the carretela, the silence between them was a cauldron brimming with unspoken things too dangerous to explore, lest they boiled over.

With the school now a hospital, Estrella's bouquet arrived at Eleanor's house, delivered every day by Private Patton. Eleanor spied him in the early mornings from a crack in her bedroom window facing the front yard. Yolanda arranged the flowers in a vase on the dining table so that Estrella could enjoy them while they ate breakfast. The bouquets consisted of whatever blooms were in season—lilies, gardenias, dahlias, daisies, and, on occasion, even roses. An envelope, as usual, accompanied each delivery, which Yolanda slipped under the vase facing where Estrella usually sat.

Eleanor observed Estrella's seemingly changing attitude toward Lieutenant Waterstone's attentions. The young lady initially ignored the envelopes, but no longer tore them up nor tossed the flowers away. She progressed into opening the envelopes and reading the notes during breakfast—blushing without comment before returning to the bedroom where, Eleanor was sure, her roommate stored the letters inside her bá'ol. Now, Estrella smiled while reading the messages, sometimes suppressing a giggle. On some nights, when Estrella must have assumed Eleanor was asleep, the young lady fetched the notes from her trunk and reread them by candlelight.

"Lieutenant Waterstone's courtship is gaining your favor, I see, " Eleanor commented one morning, eyeing her roommate.

Without confirming or denying it, Estrella smiled—before anxiety took over her countenance. "Please, Eleanor, do not tell my brother. Especially not Juan!"

"Why would I ever speak to others about your business, dear?" Eleanor retorted, adding in a somber tone, "As your friend, however, I have to say this: A tiger does not change its stripes."

Estrella crinkled her brow. "What does that mean?"

"It means most people can't change their nature," Eleanor replied. "They're ruled by emotion, not reason. Therefore, be mindful of their character, especially those whom you're letting into your heart. Unless, of course, you're prepared to have your heart broken."

Estrella looked away.

One late afternoon, while Eleanor and Estrella were walking home from the hospital, they noticed a crimson glow in the darkening sky above the town plaza. They also detected the acrid scent of smoke particular to buildings burning. This struck them as unusual, since the plaza had typically been exempt from torchings. Alarmed, they hurried toward the plaza's direction.

Fearsome shouts, shrieks, and small explosions assaulted their ears when they arrived in town. People were running from and to the source of the conflagration. They learned that what was burning were Mr. Ang's stores. Adding to the fear and confusion were soldiers who were shooting at, and chasing a group of men scurrying away from the scene. Mrs. Ang was sitting on the bare ground, wailing and sobbing, while her husband was frantically trying to put out the fire with the help of some neighbors equipped with puny pails filled from an artesian well nearby.

Eleanor and Estrella rushed to Mrs. Ang's side. "Mrs. Ang!" Eleanor cried. "Are you hurt?" She helped the woman to her feet and hugged her. After the merchant's wife had a good cry on her chest, Eleanor asked, "What happened?"

Mrs. Ang replied in Vicolano, which Estrella translated. "Men came and broke the windows, threw torches into the stores."

"Insurrectos?" Eleanor asked.

Mrs. Ang shook her head and continued with another barrage of Vicolano.

Eleanor glanced at Estrella, who said, "She said they were just people. But angry people. Some of whom she recognized as old customers."

"What?" Eleanor exclaimed. "But why target Mr. Ang?"

Estrella translated the question to Mrs. Ang, who replied again through the native teacher. "The men shouted something about the cholera coming from China. They are blaming the Chinese for the epidemic."

"That's ridiculous!" Eleanor cried. She wished she had a pail to help the people still laboring to douse the fire. Tongues of flames fanned out of the windows of what used to be the grocery and hardware stores. Bottles burst, chemicals combusted, ceilings crashed.

It took about three hours before the fires were put out. Mr. Ang slumped on the ground near the women, cradling a face black with soot. His clothes were singed in various spots and, where they were torn, were also stained with blood. He appeared to have lost his cap, revealing the smooth, shiny, fair skin on the crown of his head.

"Mr. Ang, we are so sorry!" Eleanor placed a consoling hand on the man's shoulder. "Might we help with your injuries?"

He glanced up, dazed, as though he didn't recognize her, and then shook his head and covered his face, looking utterly defeated.

El presidente approached to express his sympathies to the Angs, and Eleanor said, "Mayor Dizon, isn't there something you could do for them? Perhaps let them stay with you tonight?"

"O, lo siento, señorita. Or people attack me, too!" El presidente seemed to have finally learned to speak some English.

"But isn't your job helping and protecting your citizens, especially at a time like this?" Eleanor cried.

The mayor pressed his lips and hastily left to join another group exchanging accounts of the razing.

"It's all right, Miss Karsten," Mr. Ang said with a hoarse and weak voice. "The fire has luckily not reached our house." His head leaned in the direction behind the burned structures.

Eleanor had always assumed the merchant resided in the rooms above his store. "Don't you think you should sleep elsewhere tonight? Just in case the people who attacked you returned? I could offer you my house. We would be tight, but if you don't mind it, you and Mrs. Ang are welcome to go home with us."

"Thank you, but it's not necessary," he replied. "They have already exacted their pound of flesh. I don't expect them anymore tonight. Now, if you'll excuse us…" He stood and took his wife's hand and, together, they trudged toward their house.

Eleanor and Estrella were startled by Lieutenant Waterstone's voice. "Evenin,' Miss Karsten, Miss Santiago." Both women turned around, and he continued, "Are you ladies all right?" The officer's eyes were glued on Estrella, who lowered her gaze.

"We're fine, lieutenant," Eleanor replied. "I think we'll go home now."

"May I escort you both, then?" He briefly glanced at Eleanor but quickly returned his eyes to Estrella.

"Thank you, but there's no need for that," Eleanor said.

The officer turned to Eleanor and said, "Beg to differ, ma'am. The streets aren't safe. Especially not tonight. And for two lovely ladies like yourselves. Please, allow me."

Eleanor glanced at Estrella, who met her gaze and, to Eleanor's surprise, nodded. Eleanor glanced back at the officer. "If you promise to be good company, lieutenant."

His face lit up and he smiled. "Oh, come on, Miss Karsten! Don't I deserve credit for good behavior? What do you say, Miss Santiago?" He turned to Estrella, who, for the first time, smiled at him, though timorously.

From then on, Lieutenant Waterstone met the ladies after their shift at the hospital to walk them home. On weekend nights, he also visited Estrella at the house, where the now seemingly beguiled native teacher entertained him in the sala. During such times, Eleanor retreated to the bedroom to read or write, allowing the couple privacy.

On one of those nights, Yolanda frantically knocked on the bedroom door. Without even waiting for Eleanor's reply, she entered the room, saying, "Señorita, visitantes!"

"What? Who?" Eleanor languidly replied, glancing up from a book.

"Por favor, señorita—come!" Yolanda cried.

"Why? What's going on?" Eleanor followed Yolanda to the sala.

Standing by the open front door were a livid-looking Diego and Juan. Estrella stood, all flushed and frozen beside Lieutenant Waterstone, who sat, seemingly unperturbed, on the sofa, where the couple must have been sitting side by side when the unexpected guests arrived.

Juan stomped off, leaving Diego, who embarked on barking at his sister in their language.

Lieutenant Waterstone stood. "Hey, mister—that ain't no way to speak to a lady!"

Diego turned to him with a snorting glare, hands clenched into fists, knuckles white with rage. He seemed about to lunge at the officer, while the latter assumed a defensive stance, stepping back a leg and raising both fists.

Eleanor rushed between the men and extended her arms against them, crying, "Diego, no!" Turning to the officer, she exclaimed, "Lieutenant, please!" She glanced at Estrella, whose eyes were now full of tears. "Estrella, perhaps it's time to ask the lieutenant to go?"

"Now, wait there, just a minute, Miss Karsten!" the officer interjected. "Why should I have to be the one to leave when it's those muchachos who rudely barged in here?"

Estrella interjected, "James, I mean, lieutenant—Miss Karsten is right. Please, I need to speak with my brother. Alone."

The officer sighed heavily. "Well, okay, darlin.' I guess I'll see you next time."

"No!" yelled Diego, pulling his sister to his side. "No next time!"

"Now, that's the lady's decision, buddy!" retorted Lieutenant Waterstone.

Yolanda shrieked and slinked back to the kitchen as Diego lunged at the soldier, held back just in time by both Eleanor and Estrella.

"Lieutenant, I beg of you—please! Leave now!" cried Eleanor.

The officer smirked, straightened his uniform, and swaggered to the center table where he picked up his hat. He took his time putting it on, turned to Eleanor and Estrella, smiled at them both, and tapped the side of his cap, saying, "Well, goodnight then, ladies." He sneered at Diego on his way to the door and stepped down the stairs with a self-assured gait.

Diego wriggled out of the women's hold to go after the officer, but Eleanor and Estrella held onto him more tightly. After Lieutenant Waterstone's horse had trotted away, the ladies released Diego. Estrella turned to her brother, tears streaming down her cheeks. She screamed at him in Vicolano and ran to the bedroom, slamming the door shut.

Diego was about to chase after her when Eleanor blocked his path. "Diego, I understand you're angry. But please leave her alone, for now. You all need to calm down before you could even talk."

"You!" Diego hissed. "You are blame for this! Why you allow this?"

"Me? Let this happen?" Eleanor cried. "You forget you were the one who asked to bring your sister here to live with me. You must also remember that I graciously agreed, although I didn't have to. But I did not sign up to babysit a grown woman, which, if you haven't noticed, Diego, is what your sister is! She's not a child anymore and not as helpless as you think! When are you men going to stop patronizing us women and respect us to make our own choices?"

"¿Qué?" Diego looked as if he didn't comprehend what Eleanor said. "I think I take Estrella now!"

He tried to sidestep her to get to the door, but she blocked him again. "Take?" Eleanor echoed with a mocking tone. "Who gave you that right? Estrella is welcome to stay here for as long as she likes. And no one—not even you, could force her to leave, or take her away without her consent."

Diego finally succeeded in sidestepping her and went straight for the bedroom door. He tried turning the knob, but Estrella had locked it. Diego pounded on the door, yelling at his sister, who responded by wailing.

"Stop! Stop!" Eleanor cried, grabbing Diego's arm, pulling him away from the door. "Diego, please, stop! Or…"

"¿O que?" He turned to her abruptly, throwing her off him.

"Or… or I'll complain to the police! I mean, the soldiers!" Eleanor snapped back, crossing her arms. "I… I'll tell them that… that you broke into my home and kidnapped my roommate!"

"¿Qué?" Diego asked, tilting his head with a scowl.

"Diego, ¡vete ahora!" Eleanor demanded, glaring at him while pointing to the door. "Leave now, or I'll have to call for help."

He looked into her eyes, bit his lip, and looked away, shaking his head as he ran off.

Within three days, a wagon full of soldiers on their way to Hacienda Gonzaga was reportedly ambushed at almost the same spot where Eleanor had been attacked a few months ago. Half of the soldiers were killed, while the rest were seriously injured through bolo-inflicted wounds. A soldier reportedly lost an arm, while another lost an eye. In another instance, the insurrectos attacked two army wagons traveling from Legazpi to Magayon just past the border, causing the deaths of seven escort soldiers and the loss of a big cache of guns, ammunition, and canned food and water.

Lieutenant Waterstone retaliated by leading a troop of soldiers to the hacienda which resulted in about thirty alleged insurrectos being shot to death, including a few women and children who got in their way or tried to intervene. Altogether, the dead from among the native population amounted to almost thrice the number of American soldiers killed. It appeared that the soldiers had stopped taking prisoners and resorted to summary executions of anyone suspected of being an insurrecto or rebel collaborator.

Given the multitude of deaths from the epidemic and insurrection, the resourceful Mr. Ang returned to business in a new enterprise: making coffins. And he couldn't seem to keep up with the demand. The poorest of the poor, however, having no means to purchase coffins, simply wrapped their dead in banigs and buried them outside the walls of the campo santo.

Yolanda sadly shared with her mistress that, inside the parochial cemetery, an affluent family preparing to bury their dead found the corpse of the vagabond, Toto. They discovered, to their horror, the mendicant's rotting body inside their family mausoleum. People speculated that the mendicant must have continued to live inside the cemetery. Yet, how he fed himself was a mystery because he hadn't been seen since he was allegedly released by Lieutenant Waterstone before Christmas. Yolanda suggested one could live off the food and fruit offerings often left by well-to-do Chinese inside their family crypts or by foraging and hunting in the woods. Eleanor recalled the patch of her students' vegetable garden, which they'd assumed was plundered by a wild boar, rabbits, or mice, and wondered whether the culprit might have been Toto.

Eleanor was surprised by her grief over the dead stranger. To think he died alone and unknown in a town where nobody cared enough to look for him or learn what happened to him was unbearable to contemplate. She took on the burden of communal guilt. *Why didn't I look more into Toto's disappearance?*

She purchased Toto's coffin from Mr. Ang and paid for a burial plot. Padre Damián refused to perform the last rites, compelling Eleanor to turn, instead, to a young Episcopalian minister named Pastor Willoughby. She'd met the Protestant pastor at the hospital while he was saying prayers for some of the patients. Because of the sheer number of people dying every day, Padre Damián proved incapable of providing all the religious services requested by the grieving families. Pastor Willoughby appeared seemingly out of nowhere, ready to fill the vacuum, despite the padre's protestations, which fell on deaf and dead ears.

It was then that Eleanor witnessed the natives' disposition for practicality and pragmatism. Given the choice of having or not having prayers said by a man of the cloth over their dead and dying, most people proved surprisingly receptive to substituting the Protestant minister in place of the Catholic priest.

"Surely, Padre Damián, God would not condemn us for merely turning to a fellow Christian during an emergency?" some of them had reportedly declared. "And, surely, padre, if God does not judge us, neither should you." In this way, the Protestants gained a foothold in Magayon and became the proverbial thorn in Padre Damián's side.

Whatever the reason for Toto's grudge against the priest died with the vagabond, Eleanor thought. During Toto's burial, however, Mr. Ang handed Eleanor a locket he'd found hanging from a leather cord around the mendicant's neck. "I threw away the strap for sanitary reasons," Mr. Ang said. "But I thought you might like to have this since you seem to have become the poor fellow's padrona."

When Eleanor opened the locket, it revealed a miniature photograph of a Filipino lady bearing an uncanny resemblance to Padre Damián's niece, Maria Teresa.

Estrella responded to the hacienda executions in a simple, yet unequivocal manner: She stopped seeing Lieutenant Waterstone.

As Eleanor and Estrella were leaving the hospital one afternoon, the officer was waiting for them, as usual, outside the gate. The native teacher said to him, "I do not think we should see each other anymore, lieutenant."

"Why? What's this about?" His glance shifted between the two ladies. "Is it because of…? We didn't start it, remember?"

"No, lieutenant. You started it all by coming here! To our land! Uninvited!" Estrella exclaimed.

Lieutenant Waterstone stared in disbelief at Estrella. "Now, hold on, Miss Santiago…"

"Lieutenant," Eleanor interjected, "I suggest you respect Miss Santiago's wishes. Please understand—it's a difficult time for everyone. Especially for her."

The officer turned to Estrella and shrugged. "Suit yourself." But just as he turned around to leave, he swung back to face Estrella. "I'm curious, Miss Santiago, does that include Miss Karsten, too? Among the uninvited, I mean. Because, if that's the case, then she shouldn't be here either. Last time I checked, Miss Karsten was still an American." He turned to Eleanor, glaring. "Or have you changed loyalties now, la maestra Americana?"

Estrella covered her face and wept, and the officer left. Eleanor clenched her teeth and gripped her hands into fists. Waterstone may have returned to being a cad, yet what he said was a spade of truth that sliced into her core.

The insurrection's rekindling was not limited to Magayon. In late April, the town was grim with smuggled news of the massacre of U.S. troops by guerrillas on the island of Samar, followed by General Jacob Smith's order to kill every native over the age of ten on the island as a reprise. It was said that Samar's air was saturated with the smell of corpses. A dreadful vision pierced Eleanor. If General Smith's order had been applied to Magayon, more than half of her students would have been executed.

Recollections of macabre postcards of dead Filipinos piled in trenches, sent by Americans to family and friends back in the states as objects of amusement or blithe curiosity haunted her again. She suffered a repeating nightmare of the postcard come to life—this time, of trenches stacked with the corpses of her students intermingled with the bodies of her Magayon friends and neighbors. The horror of such a vision weighed upon her as a premonition. She drew upon her memory of that dim glow in the dark Pacific horizon, which had captivated her on that night she stood alone on the deck of the *Thomas*. *Just hold on long enough to reach the light*, it seemed to say.

It indeed appeared darkest before light. And the dark could seem so impenetrable and unfathomable, that it was easy to lose one's way. It began with Estrella, although as Estrella suggested from her statement to Lieutenant Waterstone, one had to go back further, to the true beginning: the American invasion.

One afternoon, the Filipina teacher told Eleanor she wasn't feeling well and asked to leave her shift early. "Should I accompany you home?" asked Eleanor. "There are four other nurses here who probably could cope by themselves today."

Estrella sighed. "No, thank you. I will be fine going home by myself. I just need to rest."

When Eleanor arrived at the house later that evening, she was alarmed to learn that Estrella hadn't come home yet. It had been five hours since her roommate had left the hospital. Eleanor panicked, unsure of what to do, whom to run to for help. *How do I reach Diego and Luis at the hacienda this time of the night? Should I ask for Lieutenant Waterstone's help?* Though she wasn't sure where to go, she asked Yolanda to fetch her a calesin. She started to worry that Yolanda was perhaps having difficulty hiring a carriage when the maid yelled, "Señorita! Señorita! Open door!"

Heavy footsteps ascended the creaking stairs just before Eleanor swung the door open. It was Senyong, carrying Estrella, or a simulacrum of Estrella—bloodied and broken. Behind them stood Yolanda and a small group of neighbors that included Nanay Auring. Most had their hands clamped over their mouths while their shocked, fearful eyes glistened with tears.

"Here! Right through here, Senyong!" Eleanor exclaimed as she led him to the bedroom.

Yolanda and Nanay Auring followed. After Senyong laid Estrella on her bed, Nanay Auring sent him away.

"What happened?" Eleanor turned to Yolanda. "How did Senyong…?"

"Senyong say he see Señorita Estrella walking on street, look like very sick," Yolanda tearfully replied. "He go to her, and she fall to the ground. So he carry her here."

"Oh, my dear, sweet friend! What happened to you?" Eleanor wailed as she knelt beside Estrella and held her hand.

Her roommate was breathing yet unconscious. Her clothes were muddy, blood-stained, and torn to the point of nudity in some sections. Her face was bruised red and black, cheeks and lips cut and swelling, nose bloody. Her hair hung in loose, rumpled strands as if yanked off from her pusod. Some of her fingernails were broken and, wedged beneath some of them, were whits of bloodied skin, as though she managed to scratch and gouge her attacker. She also seemed to have sustained some injury on her upper legs, for blood had trailed from there to her mud-crusted, bare feet.

Nanay Auring told Yolanda to fetch some things from the kitchen. As the old woman began examining Estrella's body, she whimpered.

Eleanor's heart dropped further. "What? What is it, Nanay Auring?"

Nanay Auring lifted part of Estrella's torn skirt to show what Eleanor had already feared. Eleanor was overcome with nausea. Her legs crumpled to the floor, where she vomited. Yolanda hastened to her side, but her mistress pushed her away and told her to focus back on Estrella. Eleanor covered her face, squirming in silence, suppressing the decibels of her sorrow. She wanted to scream to the high heavens, to shout out her condemnation of the sadistic attack on her friend. Yet, Nanay Auring reminded her that, when a woman's honor was involved, secrecy was key to protecting her. Their duty now to their fallen fellow woman was to help preserve her honor by concealing the fate she'd been dealt with—a fate most people considered worse than death. No one should speak about it or do anything without the victim's consent. And the victim was presently mute.

Eleanor lamented how society regarded women as either saints or sinners, a Mary or Magdalene, angels or witches. Women were good or bad, depending on how well they guarded their virginal chastity. There were no nuances, no grays between the blacks and whites, no ifs or whys. Men, on the other hand, seemed to serve the divine will by testing women's fealty to virtue. Hardly were they held as responsible actors in obtaining carnal knowledge of a woman, even when such knowledge was obtained without the woman's consent.

But shouldn't I inform Diego, at least? Having been witness to recent developments in certain personal aspects of Estrella's life, she had little doubt about who was probably responsible for the heinous act: Lieutenant Waterstone. Did he finally break and give in to his lecherous desire for the Filipina, to take what he couldn't win?

Bad as things were, however, informing Estrella's brother, who was likely the leader of the local insurrection, that the head of the occupying

American forces may have raped his sister, would surely spawn an evil in Magayon greater than what the epidemic and insurrection, put together, had already inflicted on everyone. It would mean more carnage between Filipinos and Americans, which not even the survivors of the Blue Death may survive. Could she bear to carry such lives on her conscience to gratify her impetus for personal justice?

Although Eleanor wasn't sure where the scales of morality lay heavier, she decided that she could, at the least, eliminate doubt. She would visit Lieutenant Waterstone in the morning—to see for herself where Estrella had marked him with his guilt.

At first light, Eleanor headed for the infantry station, intent on catching Lieutenant Waterstone likely nursing his wounds. She had just entered the plaza when savage caterwauls called her attention to masked men jumping out of the windows of the burning infantry station, chased by half-dressed soldiers. The insurrectos had attacked while their enemy was still asleep!

Gunshots blasted through the hissing haze. In the chaos, Eleanor failed to see someone hurtling toward her. She would have been thrown to the ground as they collided, were it not for the other person catching and grasping her hand in time. The deep, rough scars on the palm that pulled her up gripped Eleanor with such an alarming percipience, she pulled on the hand so she could see the face of its owner. Although taller and slimmer now and masked with a bandana, he was, unmistakably, Bayani. His eyes registered equal shock on seeing her, but before Eleanor could say anything, a whooping cry distracted them. An insurrecto holding a bolo dripping with blood, was frenziedly waving to the boy to hurry away with him on his horse. Bayani's ghost soon disappeared into the fog of smoke, along with the other masked man whom Eleanor indubitably recognized as Juan.

The soldiers pulled their compatriots' bodies out of the burning building. Eleanor set about helping them—checking pulses, examining injuries, stripping sections of her under-slip to bandage body parts and stem the loss of blood. One of the wounded was young Private Patton, who was writhing and moaning in pain, holding up his forearm.

"Let me see!" cried Eleanor. When he surrendered his arm to her, she saw bone under the cut and gaping flesh. "What's your name, private?"

"Patton," the boy replied weakly.

"No! The name your parents call you!" Eleanor said as she wrapped his arm with a band of her slip.

He whimpered. "Tom."

"All right, Tom. Listen to me: Survive this, and you'll get to see your parents again. The doctor will patch you up in no time. Hang in there—all right? Tom? Tom? You hear me?"

He winced but nodded.

Another soldier was laid alongside Private Patton. Eleanor was stunned to discover it was none other than Lieutenant Waterstone. His lifeless body had been hacked in several places and his throat was slit so deep his head was barely attached to his neck. There was no chance of verifying whether some of his wounds were the marks of Estrella's resistance. The man appeared to have carried his sin to the grave. But, perhaps, Juan already knew it and, thus, killed the officer in vengeance. However, Eleanor felt no satisfaction in seeing Waterstone dead even if he did rape Estrella. If this was vengeance, she drew no comfort from it.

Estrella wasn't getting well. She refused to eat and speak. The only sounds that could be heard from her were groans of pain and nightmare shrieks. She'd also been running a fever, despite Yolanda's guava tea washes and Nanay Auring's wound salve.

The native healer demonstrated how to make it from beeswax, coconut oil, crushed guava leaves, and, to Eleanor's surprise—mold scraped off days' old pan de sal, among other strange ingredients. Nanay Auring mixed, ground, and stirred everything until she produced an ointment she then applied on Estrella's wounds, particularly on the genitals. On the fourth day of the fever persisting, Eleanor was forced to call for Doctor Langford.

"Bloody hell, Eleanor!" Doctor Langford cried upon seeing Estrella's condition. "Why didn't you send for me right away?" It was the first time he'd raised his voice at Eleanor. He was thinner, grew half plums under his eyes, and the hair framing his face had turned silver. The cholera epidemic, although easing now, appeared to have exacted its due toll on him.

"I'm sorry, doctor," Eleanor said, sniffling and wiping her nose with her handkerchief. "I've no excuse. Except that because of the delicate nature of her injuries, we bet on being able to take care of her ourselves."

"Bloody hogwash!" Doctor Langford exclaimed. "I expected more from you! Now, she has a urinary tract infection in addition to all her serious injuries. Only a strong narcotic would help her with the pain and fever. And she has to eat or else… Could someone damn bring me some coconut juice this instant?" he yelled.

After Yolanda timorously brought in a cup of the juice, Doctor Langford commanded, "Eleanor, help me sit her up!"

Eleanor slid between Estrella and the headboard and slipped her arms under the young lady's armpits to pull her up. The doctor placed the cup near Estrella's lips, but the Filipina mestiza turned her face away from it. Doctor Langford grabbed Estrella by the mouth and forced it open to pour in some of the juice. Estrella gasped, hacked, coughed, and wheezed. Eleanor wept, and Yolanda left.

"Doctor, please, allow me," Eleanor pleaded. Doctor Langford appeared to hesitate but eventually surrendered the cup to her. In a gentle voice, Eleanor said, "Estrella, honey, you've got to drink. You've got to live! Don't you want to see your brother again?" Estrella whimpered, bursting into sobs. As Estrella calmed down, Eleanor massaged her jaw, coaxing her mouth to open. Eleanor lifted the cup to Estrella's lips, and the latter finally sipped some of the juice.

Doctor Langford gave Estrella a morphine shot. When she appeared to be sleeping, he turned to Eleanor, and in a grim voice stated, "My dear, you disappoint me. How could you keep this from me? Did you think I'd tell?"

Eleanor shook her head and burst into crying again.

The doctor sighed and sat beside her on the bed. "There, there." He placed a hand on her shoulder. "I… I'm sorry. I'm just shocked to learn of this only now." He sighed again. "I suppose you're right. I don't know what… what else I could have done if I'd been here when you found her. Frankly, I'm amazed by what you've achieved. Her sutures are amazing."

Eleanor wiped her eyes and blew her nose on her handkerchief. "That was all Nanay Auring," she said hoarsely. Through candlelight magnified by mirrors that Eleanor and Yolanda had held up for Nanay Auring on the night of the assault, the healer managed to stitch up the young woman's torn vagina. Eleanor glanced sideways at Doctor Langford. "Doctor, do you think the homemade salve might be a reason for the infection?"

"Hard to say," he replied. "It's probable the attack itself had caused it. I'll check on her again tomorrow. Meanwhile, keep up with the cold presses for her fever and keep making her drink that juice. She's dangerously dehydrated."

CHAPTER 22

Prelude to Love

The assassination of Lieutenant Waterstone and attack on the infantry station compelled Vicol military governor, General William Kobbé, to send a new station commander to Magayon. He also ordered the whole town placed under martial law. A Major Clarence Davis soon arrived, armed with an additional troop of two hundred soldiers. El presidente's civil authority was suspended and, due to the loss of the infantry headquarters to the blaze, Major Davis and his staff occupied the ayuntamiento building. The major also invited himself into the mayor's residence, claiming two bedrooms for himself and a staff assistant.

The soldiers' barracks behind the old station were saved from the fire, but weren't enough to house the new soldiers. Thus, the newcomers set up tents on the plaza grounds. The soldiers also barricaded the plaza perimeter and installed checkpoints on all roads leading to and from Magayon. The town was under lockdown again—this time, with containment measures more stringent than those imposed by Lieutenant Waterstone during the cholera seclusions. Only certain caciques, such as Luis, were granted passes to travel to and from the town proper, except during curfew hours.

It was in one of Luis's visits when Eleanor asked him what she'd been contemplating since the attack on Estrella. "Luis, could you please help me get in touch with Diego? His sister is… terribly ill. He has to know."

His eyes widened. "Don't tell me she has the cholera?" He was sitting in the sala and glanced toward the bedroom.

"No, no," Eleanor assured him. "It's... another kind of infection. But it's been a few days now, and I feel he has a right to know."

"I'll let him know, then."

"That's not enough," Eleanor said.

"Why not?" Luis looked her in the eye.

She flinched from his gaze. "Because... there are certain things I need to tell him that... that only *he* has the right to know since he's her brother. You know?"

He pressed his lips, stood, and walked to the window. He stayed there a while before he turned around to face her again, arms crossed. "Eleanor, what if I told you that... I... I'm her brother, too?"

"W-what?" exclaimed Eleanor.

He sat beside her. "Sí. A half-brother. Just like Diego."

Eleanor's mind reviewed all the scenes from when she'd first met Diego, Estrella, and Luis. She scrutinized Luis's face and indeed saw some of Estrella in him. Now, it was no longer a wonder why, although Diego and Estrella also shared some similar features, they were night and day: He was dark, while she was light—like Luis.

In a hushed voice, Luis continued, "Mi papá... he was the typical Spanish macho man. He was not a faithful husband." He smiled. "But I also cannot completely blame him. You know how Mamá is—exacting to the point of emasculation. Estrella's mother... she was the villa's housekeeper. She served Papá in ways he liked a woman to serve him. In the beginning, I suspect, this meant simply listening to him. Until... it was not just that." He turned grave and spoke almost in a whisper. "When Estrella was born, Diego's father, our housekeeper's husband, perhaps realizing the child was not his, hung himself in the woods."

Eleanor gasped. It all made sense now: how Estrella said her god-father had sponsored her education. "Does Diego know?"

"I will not be surprised if he does. These things... they are suspected but not talked about openly. Mamá—well, she knew, of course. But like most wives, she did not make a fuss to avoid an *escándalo*, as long as her husband returned home and maintained her position in society. Theirs was not a love match, you see. All she demanded was for Estrella's mother to be dismissed and sent away. Papá agreed, but when Estrella's mother died, he had the girl live in the foreman's hut with her brother. Maybe that was his way of making it up to them. He was quite fond of his daughter, and Mamá learned to live with it by pretending Estrella did not exist."

"Does Estrella know?"

"I suspect she does, and like everyone in this society, pretends not to know. But you and I, Eleanor, we need to get rid of all pretenses between us. These perilous times tell us that life is too short for secrets between people who care about each other. So, please, querida, tell me. What did you want Diego to know because you believed him to be Estrella's only family?"

Eleanor contemplated the question before she replied. "I will tell you what's going on with Estrella, Luis, after you tell me what's going on between you and Diego. And why you've condoned his and your men's acts of insurrection! Really, Luis, to the extent you allowed them to ambush me and torch your carriage? I understand I wasn't supposed to get hurt, that it was all for show. But you, a cacique, in league with campesinos? I can't understand it!"

He looked away abruptly before he turned to her again with a countenance that registered determination and defiance. "Can you ride?"

"What? You mean—a horse?"

"Sí."

Eleanor scoffed. "Don't you remember I was a farmer's daughter? So, of course—yes!"

"Muy bien," he said. "Tomorrow, I will send you a carriage. It will take you to a place where I will meet you with a horse for you to ride. And we will go see Diego together. Bring a bag for the night. You will have to sleep at the villa because of the curfew. Just tell everyone you're going to the hacienda because we've invited you to dinner. But you must not tell anyone—and, I mean, no one—that you are going to see Diego."

Luis sent his carriage to her in the afternoon, well before the six o'clock curfew. The roads, which used to be bustling scenes of farmers coming home at day's end carrying produce on their backs or pulling beasts of burden, were almost empty now. In the few instances where Eleanor saw people, they were soldiers accosting natives, holding them for inspection and interrogation.

At the checkpoint just outside of town, a group of campesinos held their hands clasped behind their heads as soldiers, armed with bayoneted rifles, examined their clothes and bodies—even the women's. One of the women wept uncontrollably—Eleanor was sure, from both fear and humiliation of being felt up by a man who was not her husband. The soldier running his hands all over her yelled, "Shut up, b**ch!" He slapped her with a force that threw her to the ground, prompting one of the native men to lunge at him. The soldier speared him with his bayonet.

Eleanor yawped and whimpered, stifling her cry with her hand. Just then, the checkpoint guard hailed the carruaje to stop, and the cochero handed him a pass. A couple of soldiers walked around the carriage, occasionally knocking on its walls as if inspecting for hidden compartments. One of them looked inside the carriage and, upon seeing Eleanor, tipped his hat to her. "Evenin,' ma'am."

"Good evening, corporal," she replied in as steady a voice she could muster.

"Goin' to the hacienda, are you?" His eyes surveyed her from head to shoes.

"Yes." Eleanor clasped her hands.

"What's your purpose going there?" He continued scanning the carriage interior.

Eleanor managed a smile and lighthearted tone. "Oh, just dinner. On invitation from Doña Ximena and Don Luis. It's been too long, they said, since we've all had the pleasure."

He narrowed his eyes. "I see. You mind if I check your bag, ma'am?" He smiled ruefully.

"Oh. Is that really necessary?" Eleanor asked. "It's just things for the night—considering the curfew, you know." The soldier arched his eyebrows, and she added, "Intimate women's things."

"Sorry, ma'am. Major Davis's orders. If you like, I could inspect it inside the carriage." He nodded at the seat opposite her, where her bag sat.

Eleanor sighed. "Well, all right," she said begrudgingly. "But please—be gentle with my things."

"Of course, ma'am." He opened the carriage door, sat opposite her, and proceeded to poke inside her portmanteau.

Eleanor cringed when she noticed the caked dirt under his fingernails. The new commander was clearly not taking any chances, not even with a fellow American.

As Luis had said, the carriage brought her to a part of the hacienda where he met her with another horse in tow. She was surprised to see him wearing peasant clothes—loose black trousers and a white, long-sleeved, cotton camisa. The carruaje departed for the villa with her bag, leaving her alone with Luis. She wore a skirt with deep pleats that hid a split in the middle, which had allowed her to comfortably ride a bicycle to school during the warm months in Iowa. The same skirt now served her well mounting the steed astride. She hadn't ridden a horse in a while, yet, like riding a bicycle, the skill lent itself readily to her.

They rode until the cerulean sky changed into a dome of reds, oranges, pinks, and purples, reminiscent of the sky over Manila Bay when the world stopped to hail the setting sun. Here, though, the same colors evoked, not the solemnity of a sacred moment but the turmoil of an all-consuming conflagration. On the horizon, Mayon Volcano streamed its ancient smoke signal telling everyone that, despite the tranquil surface of the earth, the planet was at war with itself, ablaze underneath. This was a land of fire—its children, a fiery people. How long before they singed the wings of the American eagle?

Eleanor recalled how U.S. Army generals had bragged they'd secure full control and occupation of the Philippine Islands in no time at all. Yet, here they were, almost four years after Dewey had declared victory and more than a year since General Frederick Funston had captured the commanding general of the insurrection, Emilio Aguinaldo—and, still, the native people were fighting them. It was a war that upended the classical rules of battle and gave the insurrecto a tactical edge over the American soldier who'd trained, instead, in traditional warfare. The natives called it guerrilla combat; its advantages: agility, unpredictability, and invisibility—the enemy hiding in plain sight, striking when least expected.

Eleanor galloped resolutely toward what she expected would be the secret den of the local insurrection. Who was the enemy hiding in plain sight—the insurrectos or she? It was the same question the late Lieutenant Waterstone had asked her. Whose side was she on? She didn't know the answer back then. Now, she knew it was because the question was wrong. It wasn't so much with whom she sided but for what.

She wasn't for or against anyone as she was for something: the ideas that formed the principles that created the world she agreed to live in. And persecuting and killing people for ideas wasn't one of them. It didn't matter if such concepts were of god, religion, political or economic systems, patriotism, nationalism, or even the very idea of America itself. She just couldn't abide slaying people for philosophy— for philosophy, she believed, existed to serve human beings, not the other way around. Thus, she supposed, she was the enemy of those who were willing to sacrifice humans to their so-called ideals.

She and Luis rode to the hills, then up to a forest of hardwood trees and coconut palms, and, higher still, to where boulders peeked from thick foliage. At the foot of a mountain that met with the crest of a hill, he dismounted, and she followed suit. A mosquito landed on her cheek and she swatted it, its demise certified by its spindly corpse and blood on her palm.

They secured their horses' reins to some branches. Luis unhooked a kerosene lamp from his saddle and lit it. He offered his hand to her as they descended to a depression in the earth and passed through a jungly screen of ferns, aerial plants, and hanging vines, which Luis parted like a curtain. The dense vegetation concealed a cave entrance that looked like the open jaw of a monster spiked with cuspated, jagged teeth. This could very well be Hellmouth—the gates to hell! She gripped Luis's hand as they wound their way around stalagmites and ducked below the pointed tips of stalactites. The cave was a veritable rock version of a medieval iron maiden. Its floor was slick with water dripping down from the cavern's canopy, which, throughout the ages, must have formed the monstrous canine teeth and fangs.

"Watch out for the guano!" Luis exclaimed as he pulled her away from nearly stepping on the mound of droppings.

He raised the lantern, allowing her to see, as she feared, the twitchy wings of a multitude of bats nesting on the cave's ceiling. The sun had set, and the nocturnal creatures stirred. The soft rustling of their wings became a plenitude of clicking that sounded the colony's exodus. A rich harvest of mosquitoes surely awaited them. Eleanor was imbued with gratitude for the chiropterans' service, ridding her of her aversion and fear of them.

Luis paused from walking and whispered, "Mi querida, we will soon reach another chamber. Just trust me. ¿Bien?"

She nodded, and he added, "You will see things that may appear strange, perhaps even scary. But if you keep still and quiet and remain where I tell you to stay, it will be fine, and you will be safe. ¿Entiendes?"

She nodded again, and they trudged on until the voices of men arguing echoed from farther inside the cave. Luis tucked her into a rocky niche.

Up ahead, by the light of several torches, about seventy-five to a hundred men were gathered, wearing hoods of black and green marked with strange symbols and script. Behind them, hanging horizontally across the rock wall, was a flag with a white triangle sewn against a red field. Within the triangle was a pyramid, and at the center of the pyramid was a red sun marked with the letter *K*. It recalled Juan's tattoo. Eleanor also now knew, from one of the newspaper articles about the Philippine-American war, that such letter was the symbol for the *Katipunan* movement—the Filipino revolution against Spain. Sam was right! This wasn't just an insurrection or rebellion; it was the continuation of the natives' revolt against their former colonial ruler, now directed against the Americans.

Luis placed a finger on his lips and astonished her when he produced a black hood like what the men were wearing and placed it on his head. After aligning the peepholes with his eyes, he squeezed her hand before he left her to join the group. When he reached the gathering, Eleanor's breath caught as one of the men addressed him in the hybrid language. Unlike everyone else, he wore a red eye mask instead of a hood, and was further distinguished by a red sash banded in green laid diagonally across his torso. From the sound of his voice, his hair and shape, the very kinesics of his body, all of which Eleanor knew too well, she knew he was Diego.

Her ears, which had become attuned to the sound and sense of the hybrid Vicolano-Spanish language, gleaned the gist of the discussion. The crux of contention seemed to be the recent attack on the infantry station that resulted in Waterstone's death. Diego challenged one of the men, whom Eleanor likewise recognized as Juan, to explain why the tattooed man led the raid without his permission. It wasn't authorized by Diego? She strained to hear Juan's reply, yet failed to follow the fusillade of his belligerent answer.

Diego bellowed, "Traidor!" Traitor. He stripped Juan of his hood and tore off a triangular medallion hanging from a ribbon band around Juan's neck. Diego ordered Juan's cabals to be similarly stripped of their hoods and insignias. Eleanor's heart sank at the sight of Bayani among the unmasked. Diego commanded Juan and his men removed, but the rogue group wrestled against their expulsion. A great majority of the men appeared to remain loyal to Diego and overpowered them. They bound the schismatics' hands with ropes behind their backs and led them away toward the cave's exit.

Eleanor curled behind a rock as the prisoners and their guards passed her hiding spot. Assuming they were gone, she raised her head to peek just as Bayani glanced her way. The boy's eyes widened and he yelled, "Espía! Espía!" Spy. One of the guards dragged her out from her hiding spot and shoved her on her knees before Diego. Juan's wicked cachinnation reverberated and echoed throughout the cavern as he and his band of rebels were whisked away. Eleanor gazed up to meet the shock and consternation in Diego's eyes.

"What this mean?" he growled.

"¡Esperar! I can explain!" Luis interjected, stepping forward. "But only to you, jefe!"

Diego dismissed all but one of his men who wore a green hood over his head. He then ordered Luis to explain Eleanor's presence in the secret society's lair. Eleanor was amazed that in this realm, which was almost an alternate world to the world outside the cave, the amo and katiwála' appeared to have switched roles: Diego now ruled while Luis obeyed.

Until now, Eleanor could not comprehend why a haciendero like Luis hadn't acted aggressively against the ambush and destruction of his carriage. Caciques and ilustrados like Luis had enjoyed every possible privilege under colonial rule—short of ultimate governing power. Perhaps, therein likewise laid the wellspring of their subversion. The elites couldn't rise to the topmost rung of Philippine society as long as they had a colonial master. Thus, they had allied themselves with the peasantry in a common cause to expel the foreigners.

Eleanor understood that Diego and Luis were motivated by grievances against their Spanish colonial rulers that similarly compelled American colonists to revolt against the British. Now, it appeared that the Americans themselves had supplied the same imperative to Filipinos. How the formerly oppressed became the new oppressors!

Addressing Luis, Diego said, "Katipon, you know this not allowed! Now, this Americana know who we are, where we meet. How can you trust she not tell soldados Americanos?"

"Jefe," replied Luis, taking off his hood, "please forgive me. But Señorita Karsten begged me to take her to you because she has something important to tell you about your sister. She refused to tell me what it is until I bring her to you." Turning to Eleanor, Luis added, "Now, señorita, please tell us what you have to say." He helped her to her feet.

Eleanor stood and turned to Diego. "I'm sorry for my intrusion, but it's a matter of life and death. It's also of a very delicate personal matter. So, I will tell you once that man leaves." She pointed to the green-hooded man.

"No!" Diego cried. "I trust my kawal. Now, speak!"

Eleanor blenched from the ferocity of his tone. It reminded her of the last time they saw each other, when they quarreled about Estrella and Lieutenant Waterstone. Now, she felt guilt come over her. If, as Diego had rightly accused her, she hadn't condoned the American officer's courtship of his sister, perhaps Estrella wouldn't have been raped.

The green-hooded man surprisingly spoke. "Está bien, señorita." He also shocked her when he took off his hood and revealed his identity. Senyong! "Tell them," he urged.

She nodded at him and turned to Diego. "It's about Estrella."

"Why? What happen?" Diego cried and pulled off his eye mask.

"She, uh… she's sick," Eleanor said, tears brimming in her eyes. "Not with cholera, but still serious."

"¿Qué?" Diego asked.

"She, she's very ill," Eleanor replied. "And she doesn't seem to be getting any better. She has a fever that won't go away. And she refuses to eat or even speak. It's… like she's… she has lost her will to live! You need to go see her, Diego!"

"Pero, señorita!" exclaimed Luis. "Why did you not tell me this while I was at your house? I could have brought the doctor!"

Eleanor summoned her teacherly tone and glanced at each of the half-brothers. "I assure you both that Doctor Langford has attended to her to the best of his ability."

"But what happen?" Diego demanded. "How she get sick?"

"Diego, I… I regret to tell you that… your sister was… was assaulted," Eleanor replied.

"As…What that mean?" Diego cried.

"Oh, Diego, I'm so sorry! Estrella was… was raped!" She burst into crying.

Luis slapped his forehead. "¡Dios mío!" He turned to Diego, who wore a puzzled expression, and said to him, "Violada."

Eleanor glanced up at them with tearful eyes. "It was fortunate that Senyong found her."

Diego glanced at Senyong and paced the cave floor—vehemently shaking his head as he cradled it with his hands, hyperventilating. He turned back to Senyong, yelling, blaming his deputy for not telling him sooner and pounced upon and wrestled him to the ground.

"Diego—stop!" Eleanor cried. She and Luis tried to separate them. Luis succeeded in pulling Diego away, and Eleanor helped Senyong to his feet. "Diego, it's not Senyong's fault!" as she exclaimed. "In fact, if it weren't for Senyong, Estrella might not be alive! He carried her home. And Nanay Auring, she told us not to say anything to anyone. To protect your sister's honor. Nanay Auring, Yolanda, and I—we did our best to take care of your sister. Doctor Langford also helped. B-but now… I'm truly afraid for her life!"

Diego, who was slumped on the ground with Luis, picked himself up and stood. Grabbing Eleanor up by the arms, he hissed, "Who… who do this? You know?"

Eleanor winced from the pinch of Diego's grip. "No. Not exactly. But I did suspect someone. I wasn't sure, so I went to see him. When I got there, your men had already killed him. Lieutenant Waterstone."

"¡Él era el mismo diablo!" Diego cursed, howled, and staggered back to the ground. He embraced his knees and rested his forehead on them.

Eleanor knelt beside him and placed a consoling hand on his shoulder. "Diego, I'm so sorry."

"You! This your fault!" He gripped her arms again and shook her. "You let Waterstone go near my sister!"

Eleanor trembled, yelped, and whimpered.

"Stop, Diego!" Luis cried, as he rushed to shove Diego away from Eleanor and pulled her up and away from him. "There is no use blaming everyone for no one's fault except Waterstone!"

Eleanor buried her face in Luis's chest, sobbing softly. The haciendero embraced her.

"Jefe," Luis said in a somber tone, "perhaps this is why Juan attacked the station—to kill Waterstone. Perhaps you should just forgive him and those who only obeyed him. It's no good fighting your own men. No es bueno para la moral de sus hombres."

"Sí, jefe," Senyong agreed, nodding.

"No!" Diego cried with clenched fists. "Juan no right to kill Waterstone! That—my right! Juan steal it from me!" He pounded on his chest.

Eleanor turned around to face Diego again, wiped her tears, and said, "Diego, I understand how angry and frustrated you are," Eleanor interjected. "But don't you think it's more important now that you see Estrella before… before it's too late?" She glanced up at Luis.

Luis responded, "I agree. But we have to think of a way for Diego to see her in secret. ¡Es muy peligroso!"

"Yes, it's dangerous—for all of you!" Eleanor said. "There are many checkpoints and the curfew to consider. We need to make a smart plan."

Luis and Eleanor left Diego and Senyong in the cave and rode away together to Villa Gonzaga. When they arrived at the mansion, Doña Ximena was reticent yet civil toward Eleanor. She had her servants serve them some dinner and sat with them while they ate. "So, Señorita Karsten," she said, "now you know about my son and this… this crazy thing he get in with insurrectos. What you think?"

"Mamá!" Luis protested, shaking his head.

"I think," Eleanor interjected, "he's incredibly brave."

Luis smiled at Eleanor.

"Brave?" Doña Ximena scoffed. "¡Está loco!"

"Mamá, if we don't fight to be our own masters, we will never truly possess our land," Luis stated in a softer tone. "We will always be under the capricho of the extranjero."

"And what about her?" Doña Ximena challenged, jerking her head toward Eleanor. "Is she not a foreigner? How you know she will not tell?"

"Because…" Luis said, glancing at Eleanor with affectionate eyes, "I trust her."

"O, hijo, do not take me for a fool like your papá!" Luis's mother exclaimed. "I know it is more than that!"

"¡Basta!" Luis cried, slamming the table so hard the cutlery jumped and jangled.

Doña Ximena flinched.

Eleanor interjected, "Doña Ximena, I understand why you don't trust me. But if you can't trust me, then trust this: If the army found out I met with the insurrectos tonight, I could be accused as a traitor and hanged for treason. I may be American, but I have a different reason for being here. I'm a teacher who only wants to help the children."

Doña Ximena glanced at Eleanor and stood. "Discúlpame. I think I will go to bed now. Luis will show you to your room later."

"Yes, of course," Eleanor replied. "Goodnight, and… thank you, Doña Ximena. For letting me stay."

Luis stood and kissed his mother on the forehead. "Buenas noches, Mamá. Dormir bien."

Doña Ximena nodded curtly. As she left, Eleanor glimpsed the iron lady misty-eyed.

After dinner, Luis walked Eleanor upstairs to the bedroom prepared for her. "I hope you will be comfortable here." He opened the door and stepped aside to make way for her to enter it, and, stunningly, remained outside the bedroom. "There is a bathroom in there for your personal use." He pointed to a smaller door in the room.

His seeming deference was a pleasant surprise. At an earlier time, he'd now be aggressively making advances on her. "Thank you," she said. "I'm sure I'd be more than comfortable here."

Lighted oil lamps on a bedside table and dresser illuminated a well-appointed bedroom. Her Gladstone was already sitting on a tapestry-covered bench at the foot of an ornately-carved four-poster feather bed. It had a lace canopy and panels tied to its posts, ready to be unfurled to serve as a mosquito net.

"Mi querida," Luis said with a tender tone, "thank you for... for what you said earlier to Mamá... about me."

"I meant it, Luis." She walked back to him. "I regret I may have underestimated you. I understand what you're trying to do for both your family and people."

He reached for her hand and cupped it with both of his. "Eleanor, I know this is not best time to ask again. But is it... would it be possible for you to consider... my feelings for you?"

Eleanor glanced down and just as soon looked up at him again. "Luis, I appreciate your regard for me, but my priority is my mission."

"Querida, por favor..." He smiled ruefully. "Just think about it?"

Eleanor sighed. "Luis, please... I'm quite tired. I'd like to go to bed now."

"Por supuesto. But I am not sorry I asked. For I will keep asking, you know!" He flashed his old, mischievous smile. "Pues, I bid you goodnight. Sweet dreams, mi querida." He kissed her hand.

Sleep again proved elusive for Eleanor in that unfamiliar bedroom, chased away further by the mating calls, it seemed, of hundreds, if not thousands of frogs. The full moon beckoned from behind the lace curtain over the glass door that led to a Juliet balcony. She didn't bother to grab a robe as she stepped out in her cotton nightdress, for summer's heat prevailed, preserved by the delay of the rains that should have ushered in the wet season.

Champagne moonlight shone silver on the canopies of mature acacias that looked like venerable sage giants hunched over the villa's gardens. The balmy air was soaked with the musky-saccharine scent of a mysterious flower that was no longer a mystery to her. Eleanor's nose followed the trail of the perfume of the night-blooming jasmine, *Dama de Noche*. Clusters of tubular, star-like, ivory florets peeked between the oblong, lanceolate leaves of a shrub that grew from a trellis below to the bottom of the balcony railing.

During a similar balmy evening a few weeks ago, she'd detected the mysterious scent and asked Estrella about it. "It is the Dama de Noche. Lady of the Night," her roommate replied, pointing to a shrub that grew against the fence in the back garden. She said its flowers appeared a few times a year, yet only bloomed between dusk and dawn. "They erase the smell of death, don't they?" Estrella added, smiling poignantly.

Eleanor expressed hope that the blooming of the Lady of the Night signaled the beginning of the epidemic's end. Little did they know then it was just the start of an ordeal more personal to them. Now, Eleanor associated the flower with something ominous.

She returned to the luxury of the feather mattress, determined to get the sleep she needed. There was much to do in Magayon, including helping to plan the clandestine reunion between Estrella and Diego. Her eyes misted again, recalling Diego's anger toward her. She was surprised to realize she felt no resentment toward him, but rather hoped to make amends by assisting him to meet with his sister. The man was understandably furious in addition to grieving over the tragedy that befell Estrella. As the leader of the Vicol revolution, he must be frustrated realizing he was ultimately powerless to protect his own family. Eleanor's heart ached for him.

Not long after she'd lain her head on the pillow, she heard a ticking on the glass of the balcony door. When she turned to it, a shadow moved behind the curtain covering the glass door, startling her. "Eleanor, por favor, abierta!" it whispered with a tone of urgency.

She recognized the voice and, for a second, wondered whether she should let him in. She hopped off the bed and drew the curtain aside. "Diego! What are you doing here?" He pointed to the door latch, and she shook her head. He rattled the doorknob, and she shushed him. He tapped on the glass again. Afraid the noise would wake her hosts, she was compelled to unlatch the door.

She stepped back as he stepped inside and closed the balcony door behind him. He glanced around the room and turned to her with glistening eyes ridden with seeming remorse. He approached her gingerly, and she crossed her arms over her chest, suddenly feeling naked without her robe. "Eleanor, I…." His voice cracked, and he knelt before her. "Por favor, perdóname. I very sorry. You right. Not your fault what… happen… to my sister. Thank you… for taking care of her." He produced sampaguitas from his shirt pocket and offered it to her.

She accepted it, this prelude to love. She buried her nose in the blossoms and inhaled their achingly-sweet perfume, erasing the memory of Dama de Noche's morbid scent.

He stood and pulled her into his arms. He pressed his lips on her mouth, and she surrendered the mendacity of resistance. It was no use. They had both been moving toward this moment for some time now. She grasped and grabbed at his body as he did hers, and they explored each other's mouths, drinking from each other to satisfy a long-unquenched thirst.

As though he couldn't bear for anything to separate them any longer, he pulled off her nightdress, shed his clothes, and carried her to bed—where he made long, slow love to her, until they reached the pinnacle of their union and collapsed together in euphoric exhaustion. Just before she drifted off to sleep, she heard him whisper in her ear, "Te amo, Eleanor. Te amo."

When a ray of sunlight hit Eleanor's eyelids and woke her, he was already gone. But before she thought it was all a dream, the now browning petals of the sampaguita flowers on the pillow next to hers told her it wasn't. She breathed in the redolent though fading scent of the blossoms and realized she was still naked under the sheets. She tittered as she sat up to look for her nightdress and found it draped on the bench at the foot of the bed. How thoughtful of him!

Pushing off the covers, she reached for it and noticed a brownish-red spot on the bedsheet. Her ruptured maidenhead had left a telltale sign. Running her fingers over the stain, she thought of how rupture and rapture sounded similar—differentiated only by one letter. Yet, one was sacrifice, the other, gift. She decided this was Diego's gift to her. Oh, how to describe the pleasures to the uninitiated? Before this, Eleanor believed that the pleasures of the mind were enough. Now, her body had toppled her from such hubris through Diego.

Eleanor stripped the bedsheet and brought it to the bathroom where she washed off the mark of her womanhood. She squeezed the sheet dry and tossed it back on the mattress and made the bed, hoping the maid who would service the room later would not notice the subtle outline of the blot stain that remained.

Estrella still refused to speak. During the rare times she opened her eyes, she stared blankly, rarely blinked, and was seemingly unconscious of her surroundings. Yolanda prepared a porridge she called *lúgaw*, betting it would entice their patient out of her stupor and reinvigorate her. She simmered rice in chicken broth and seasoned it with ginger, garlic, salt, and the all-important ingredient that seemed to give life to every Vicolano: sili pepper. The scent alone was so enticing, Eleanor had some for herself. It seemed to do the trick. Yolanda and Eleanor were both overjoyed when, finally, Estrella accepted some of the pottage.

Nanay Auring suggested a plan aimed at helping Estrella's wounds heal faster while also allowing Diego to secretly meet with his sister. Estrella's fever had, fortunately, diminished enough to allow her to travel to the curative hot springs at the foothills of Mayon Volcano. Nanay Auring swore that soaking in the thermal mineral waters would heal any festering wounds.

Luis fetched Eleanor, Estrella, and Nanay Auring in one of Hacienda Gonzaga's covered carriages. They left at daybreak so that Luis could carry his half-sister—dressed only in her nightdress and wrapped in a blanket—into the carruaje with minimal risk of nosey neighbors gawking at them. Luis sat Estrella between himself and Eleanor.

They rode for almost two hours, which must have been a tortuous journey for the broken body of their patient, yet Estrella never complained and sat quietly with her head resting on Eleanor's shoulder, asleep. As they traveled, Luis occasionally held his half-sister's hand and stroked it. Eleanor smiled. She'd never before seen such tenderness in him for his half-sister. Perhaps the tragedy drew out his brotherly love for his father's love child.

In Naples, Eleanor had once read, there was a real place that inspired Dante's Inferno. The land of the hot springs was how she imagined it would look like, if the poet's hell were located in Vicol. In the foothills of Mayon Volcano, the earth hissed steam from its bowels and clouded the atmosphere with the fog of condensation, while the smell of rotten eggs, the Devil's scent, laced the air. And, there, Eleanor's heart lurched again at the sight of Diego. Her Pluto.

He and Senyong were already waiting, equipped with a hammock with which to carry Estrella. Luis handed Diego their half-sister, and Diego carried Estrella to lay her on the litter that Senyong had spread on the ground. Diego wept on seeing his sister's fragile, battered body. Estrella's lips and cheeks were still slightly swollen, her cuts now scabbed, and the bruises on her face and arms had faded from black to blue and greenish-yellow.

"¡O, mi querida hermana!" Diego cried tearfully. "¿Qué te ha pasado?"

Estrella, for the first time since the night of her attack, burst into sobbing. She held onto Diego and buried her cries in his chest.

Diego and Senyong lifted the litter that held Estrella and carried it to the steaming waters of what appeared to be a natural pool. Luis said it was fed by both hot and cold spring waters. A cool mountain spring merged through natural channels in the earth with the groundwater boiled by hot, igneous rocks and poured into the pool where the water was quite warm but not scalding.

Diego waded into the pool with Estrella in his arms. He held his sister's body aloft to soak, everyone hoped, into healing. Yet, mending the body did not always cure the wounds of the mind and spirit that, Eleanor was sure, afflicted Estrella most.

After about half an hour, Luis relieved Diego and took his turn in soaking their half-sister in the pool. Nanay Auring and Yolanda set off to procure some magma-heated water as a base to make a fresh batch of their wound balm.

Diego sat poolside, staring at the catatonic figure of his sister carried by Luis in the water.

Eleanor approached him. "Diego, would you like to walk?"

He glanced at her blankly, yet nodded.

Eleanor felt Luis's eyes on their backs as they walked away, but she no longer cared for what he or anyone else might think about her and Diego.

CHAPTER 23

Choice and Consequence

They walked until they reached a woodland prefaced by granite pillars that stood like monuments to some prehistoric god. Eleanor pulled Diego behind the rocks and embraced him—something she'd yearned for since witnessing his devastation on seeing his sister's condition.

He fell into sobbing and pulled her down to the ground with him. He cried like a boy who soon turned into a man—a man broken and needful of a woman's consolation. He pushed her onto the soft bed of grass and poured out his rage, sorrow, and passion inside her—her power as a vessel to contain him, limitless. They heaved and choked at the hysteria of love and hatred that engulfed their world and carried them away with its tide. They clung to each other, as if allowing nothing to come between them, until a flood of delirium washed away their pain, albeit briefly.

As Diego lay spent beside her, Eleanor's heart lurched as she heard leaves rustling and twigs snapping in the woodland nearby. She raised her head to check. Standing at the edge of the woods appeared to be a figure of a young lady dressed in a vermillion sari and crowned with a tiara of flaming rubies. The gems' fire didn't seem to hurt her, nor burn her straight, glossy ebony hair that reached her bare feet. And what Eleanor first thought as red dye on her dress now appeared to be blood spreading from her heart. Eleanor gasped, and the lady smiled at her before she turned around and disappeared into the woods. Daragang Magayon?

Diego stirred and asked, "¿Qué?"

"Nothing," she replied. "Go back to rest."

When they rejoined the group, Luis appeared piqued and asked with an irate tone, "Where have you two been?"

Diego retorted something in Vicolano, which silenced Luis, who nonetheless seemed to seethe with jealousy. Eleanor sat beside Yolanda, who stared her down with a knowing look, discreetly picking off leaves and debris from her mistress's hair and clothes. As if to quell the tension that arose from the now apparent contest between the half-brothers for la maestra Americana, the maid announced that it was lunchtime. She served a simple picnic of pork adobo pan de sal sandwiches, fruits, and camotes and eggs that were boiled in the shallow hot spring where she and Nanay Auring had likewise prepared Estrella's unguent.

The native healer whispered to Eleanor that she and Yolanda had already applied the balm to the wounds of their patient, who was now dressed in a dry set of clothes. Nanay Auring was about to feed Estrella with mashed bananas and camotes when Diego volunteered for the task. He thanked the old woman and urged her to go have her lunch.

Senyong helped smoothen the ruffled notes of the afternoon by playing a soft ballad on his guitar—something he hadn't done since Tomasa's illness and death.

The hot mineral waters appeared to have achieved their miracle. Estrella's fever vanished, and her wounds dried up. She also started speaking, although she kept to mundane, quotidian subjects. She never mentioned who'd assaulted her and, yet, flinched when Eleanor informed her that Lieutenant Waterstone had been killed during an attack on the station. Eleanor wondered at the tears that streamed from her roommate's eyes. Were they tears of relief or regret?

The town, too, seemed to be on a path toward healing and normalcy. The atang ritual, though slow in bestowing its blessings, appeared to be finally delivering results. Doctor Langford announced a significant decrease in Magayon's cholera deaths—to the applause of his nurse brigade. Doña Beatriz hugged her husband and planted a kiss on his lips before everyone—inciting another round of clapping.

On the 2nd of July, Secretary of War Elihu Root declared the end of the Philippine-American War, followed by President Roosevelt's July 4th announcement of the amnesty program for insurrectos. The official termination of the war abolished the office of the military governor. Outgoing Military Governor Kobbé announced, pending elections, an interim civilian governor through the appointment of Don Luis Gonzaga. The Philippine Constabulary replaced the U.S. Army and assumed police powers over Magayon under the leadership of Major Davis, until a police chief could be trained and appointed in the officer's place. During the transition toward civilian governance, none appeared more ecstatic than el presidente, who'd expected to resume his mayoral duties.

The epidemic's end coincided with the arrival of the rainy season. The first rain poured on the parched earth and seeped into the sleeping chambers of the land. It became the catalyst that initiated a chain reaction that released the planet's elixir, reviving terra firma and its inhabitants. Daily mortalities decreased to a number that allowed Eleanor to reopen the school. The problem, though, as she feared, was that the school buildings were far from ready to be evacuated of the sick and dying.

Major Davis, who, like most men of his generation, sported a handlebar mustache, one that had gone cygnet gray, cut a strict yet supportive father figure image that reminded Eleanor of her own father. He offered her the use of the whole second floor of the ayuntamiento, while he and his staff occupied the first floor. He also promised her access to the entire town hall as soon as the old infantry station, which was being rebuilt, was ready for the constabulary to move into. This suited Eleanor since she didn't need much classroom space now. She had lost half of her students to cholera and the war. The major volunteered his men to transfer the school furniture from the church to the new school premises.

Sam and his family also survived the epidemic, allowing the former soldier to return to teaching. But not Estrella. It soon became evident that the young lady was stricken with a new condition that, while also marked by nausea and vomiting, had nothing to do with cholera.

Yolanda shared her suspicions with Eleanor, who called for Nanay Auring, instead of Doctor Langford, to examine Estrella again. The partéra confirmed Yolanda's suspicion, whispering to Eleanor, "Ella está embarazada."

"Embarrassed about what?" Eleanor asked.

Nanay Auring pressed a finger to her lips to shush her as the three women huddled in the sala, away from Estrella's hearing.

"Not embarrass, señorita," Yolanda said under her breath. "She going to have baby."

Strange, Eleanor thought, how the Spanish term for pregnancy sounded like the English word associated with shame. Why was pregnancy an embarrassment? Eleanor pondered on how Spanish culture was so influenced by Catholicism that even its language reflected the religious repugnance for anything related to sex. In a society where procreation was strictly restricted to the bounds of matrimony, a word like embarazada was, understandably, albeit unjustly, considered appropriate for someone like Estrella, who was pregnant yet unwed. It didn't matter that she never consented to the act that made her pregnant. Pregnancy out of wedlock expelled her from decent society as it likewise disqualified her from teaching. Eleanor contemplated how to discuss the matter with Estrella, and decided to wait until the young woman was stronger.

Eleanor began fearing Estrella's situation for herself. It was possible that she could also be embarazada like Estrella without knowing it yet. She spent the next few weeks waiting for her period to come, fretting and stressing over the possibility, so that she failed to notice the little jade-green, heart-shaped fruits that began to appear and grow on the mango tree in the backyard. The season of mangoes had arrived—just in time, it seemed, for Estrella's craving for the unripe version of the fruit. She loved to snack on the sour, crunchy slices, especially when dipped in the salty, malodorous shrimp paste that Yolanda—thrilled over the young lady showing interest in food again—now brought home daily from the fish market.

That crucial time of the month came for Eleanor, and Yolanda rejoiced as much as her mistress did when the latter asked her to prepare a new set of rags for her. Yet, Eleanor vowed she'd never forget the terror of waiting for her menses to come and the relief she felt when they arrived—as though it was a reprieve from a death sentence. She took it as a warning that, unless she controlled the uncontrollable passion between Diego and herself, she would fail to fulfill her mission in Magayon. Thus, although it was almost unbearable for her to stay away from Diego, she had to avoid him, if only to stave off the inevitable, until she could have a serious talk with him about whatever was going on between them. She would tell him they could no longer leave matters to chance unless she was also willing to suffer Estrella's fate and be deprived of the vocation she loved.

She considered her options, and found none, aghast to realize she was shamefully ignorant about contraception. She wondered whether Nanay Auring could suggest a preventive remedy. Of course, there was another solution. To get married. But get married to Diego? How could that work? They had barely exchanged words. Their longest conversation, so far, consisted of fighting over the late Lieutenant Waterstone's courtship of his sister. Diego may be an ideal lover, but was he good enough to be her life partner? Besides, he hadn't asked—to marry her.

Oh, what a floosie she'd become—falling for mere flowers—and, all right, a python reticule! And, oh, by the way, how, exactly, did he attain the knowledge—nay, expertise!—he clearly possessed in pleasuring a woman? She imagined him surrounded by a harem of camp followers, ready and willing to serve any and all needs of their hero and jefe. A sharp pang of jealousy shot through her heart, making her blood boil.

Where was he, anyway? And why hadn't he come to see her yet? She was overcome with fear she may have committed the biggest mistake of her life. *See what happens, Eleanor, when you don't think of the logical consequences of your actions?* Poor Luis, who was so willing to share his good name and good life with her! Yet, she rejected him—and for what? For some passing fancy of her lustful body?

How the haughty had fallen, indeed! She resolved to reclaim control over her life—and body!—to prevent Diego from running amok with them again.

If anyone doubted that the insurrection had not died down with the cholera despite the official declaration of the end of the war, such doubt was squashed by news of the bodies of four Thomasites, Louis A. Thomas, John E. Wells, Ernest Heger, and Clyde O. France, who all had earlier disappeared from Cebu Island, had been discovered. On the 23rd of July, their remains were returned to Cebu amid reports that the American teachers had been attacked and murdered by a lawless band of criminals, whose leader had also been killed. Yet, Eleanor knew better. One man's criminal was another's freedom fighter.

And, as often happened in tragedies of epidemic magnitude, the beast did not go down quietly. It screamed, kicked, thrashed about, and dragged, tooth and nail—one last prize with it. Eleanor agonized over letters from Maude and Ida sadly sharing they'd lost their sweet, beautiful Arabella to cholera. To think that Arabella had died of a cruel disease—alone in a foreign country and a strange city—was almost too much to bear. Ida had tried unsuccessfully to have her body transferred to Manila. And because Arabella had died of a contagious disease, the authorities reportedly buried her body hurriedly with those of many others, in a lime-powdered mass grave somewhere in Zamboanga, the site of continued violent clashes between Americans and Filipino Muslims. It appeared that Moro country had stolen their sweet, beautiful friend, after all. Maude wrote that Arabella's death forced her to cut her teaching term and return to the states. Not only could she not believe that her best friend was gone; she had, moreover, no body to bury, nor a grave to grieve over, to help her accept it.

What struck Eleanor as miraculous amid the misery of all the uncertainty that continued to bedevil them was the serendipitous certainty of Estrella's baby. Conceived in violence, cocooned in illness, it nevertheless dared to aspire to life. The child was already a survivor; the very idea of it—hope. The mother, on the other hand, was another matter.

One day, as Eleanor supervised the transfer of the book crates from the crawl space under her house onto the wagon that would take them to the new school premises, Estrella stunned her by running out of the house. "Why, hello, Estrella!" she greeted her roommate. "Are you going to get yourself more green mangoes?"

Estrella shook her head. With a timid smile, she spoke softly, with an almost forgotten light now gleaming in her eyes again. "Eleanor, when do you plan to start classes? Perhaps we can talk about lesson plans and schedules?"

It squeezed Eleanor's heart. She had delayed discussing the problem of her assistant's return to teaching for far too long. "Estrella, let's talk about this later. I just have to finish this one last task. All right?"

"If you wait a minute," Estrella interjected, "I could change into proper clothes and accompany you to help with the books. Like I did before?" Estrella banished Eleanor's silence with a nervous grin. "Gracias a Dios, Major Davis gave us the ayuntamiento, sí? I am so excited to see our new classrooms. They will surely be a luxury compared with the old ones, right?"

Estrella's cheerful smile proved even more heartbreaking to Eleanor. "Oh, thank you, dear," Eleanor said, "but the cochero is already waiting. Why don't you just rest again today? I mean, just to make sure you're all healthy and ready for… um—sorry, got to go, my dear!"

Estrella's smile faded, yet she nodded, waving listlessly at Eleanor as the latter rode away in the carretela.

Later that night, Eleanor sat through a strained and quiet dinner with Estrella and Yolanda. It prevented her from enjoying the first ripe, golden mangoes harvested from their tree. She remembered what Mr. Ang had said about the Philippine variety. It was indeed much sweeter than the one she'd had in Honolulu.

After the maid had cleared the dishes away to the kitchen, Eleanor said, "Estrella, I know you want to return to teaching, but I'm afraid you may not be ready."

The Filipino mestiza, who'd held her head down during most of the meal, glanced up with a resentful expression. "Who says I am not ready?"

Eleanor sighed. "My dear, you've suffered through so much. And you fought so well to get well. We are very proud of you, and so should you be! Why not take it slow? Don't you think it's wiser to focus on preparing for the baby?"

The younger lady's eyes widened in horror, and her face crumpled into anguished confusion before she finally managed to reply, "W-what b-baby?"

It was only then that Eleanor grasped the extent of Estrella's innocence, including her incredible ignorance about her pregnancy. But how was this possible? How could the young woman, despite being a teacher, not know—unless she, having been orphaned of a mother so young and then convent-bred—was never taught about such things? Either this, or Estrella was in denial. Eleanor also just now realized she'd wrongly assumed that Nanay Auring had informed Estrella of her condition. How could no one, not even Yolanda, nor even herself—for goodness' sake!—have said a single, darned thing about it until now?

Tears welled up in Estrella's eyes. "Por favor, Eleanor. What—what baby are you talking about? Whose baby?" The mestiza glanced behind her at Yolanda, who stood between the dining room and the kitchen, wearing a sympathetic expression, and she pleaded, "¡Yolanda, por favor, explícame! ¿Que bebe?"

Yolanda approached and hugged Estrella. "Señorita, you going to have baby. No worry, we help you everything."

"No!" Estrella screamed, shoving Yolanda off her, standing so abruptly that her chair fell over backward. "I am not having a baby! That is impossible! You two do not know what you are talking about! You are mistaken! How could anyone have a baby when it is a mistake? How can a baby grow from a mistake? That is wrong! God will not allow it! God does not put souls into babies made from mistakes!" She ran to the bedroom, slamming the door closed.

Eleanor and Yolanda chased after her but found the door locked. Estrella was crying and wailing on the other side of it.

"¡Señorita, por favor! ¡Abre la puerta!" Yolanda cried and hammered upon the door with her fist, sobbing.

Eleanor stayed Yolanda's hand and put an arm on the muchacha's shoulder. "Yolanda, she needs to be alone, for now. Just let her have her rest."

Yolanda nodded and walked back to the kitchen, sniffling, wiping her eyes and nose on the sleeves of her camisa.

In the days that followed, Estrella grew increasingly lachrymose. She kept to the house and refused to go outside, not even to pick green mangoes—for which she'd developed a sudden distaste. She spent her days in bed and stopped speaking again.

Eleanor thought to give her time to get used to the idea she was going to be a mother. She was sure Estrella only needed more rest to fully recover her health, which she hoped would also improve her state of mind.

Meanwhile, Eleanor's days were consumed with preparing the new premises for school re-opening and making new lesson plans. Whenever Eleanor returned home, Estrella appeared to be asleep. Eleanor was secretly relieved by it, for it was easier to stay silent than talk about difficult things.

Since the expedition to the thermal springs, Luis likewise appeared to have kept away. Eleanor assumed he was busy as acting civilian governor, whose office was located in Legazpi. Yet, it was also possible he was angry, aware now perhaps about her relationship with Diego.

With the war's ending, criminal laws went into effect, replacing military law. Insurrectos who hadn't surrendered to Major Davis under the amnesty proclamation were now considered brigands and outlaws, subject to incarceration as common criminals. Eleanor concluded this was why she hadn't seen Diego.

In the meantime, Estrella's half-brothers thus remained ignorant of their sister's new condition, compounded by the young woman's renewed melancholia. If her roommate's mood failed to improve soon, Eleanor knew she had to find a way to meet Diego and Luis again. She needed their help to cheer up their sister and make plans for the baby's arrival, which must include, she'd advise them, sending Estrella to a friendly place to have her baby—where no one knew her, which would allow her to pretend, perhaps, that she was a pregnant widow—to save her from the humiliation of Magayon gossip.

Eleanor had read about a school of Eastern philosophy, which taught that one did not change the world by fighting it, but by surrendering. If that were true, she thought then, Americans would still be ruled by British tyranny. The principle was the very antipode of American mentality. But her journey through the Philippine Islands and its people taught her something else about surrender: It was far from passive. There were ways to resist an unjust system that didn't require killing one's enemy, although due to the intransigence of the unjust, the principled sometimes did have to surrender their lives to witness to their convictions.

She believed that most people were good, and they just wanted to live their lives with the least interference and trouble from anyone, to be simply human and enjoy some measure of peace and dignity to live out some humble dream without pressure to be heroes or martyrs for some ideal. This, it seemed to her, was the practical significance of Roosevelt's offer of amnesty to the insurrectos. And it didn't go unnoticed by the masses, despite all the rhetoric against it in the name of nationalism, sovereignty, and independence, which were beautiful words, moving words—the luring language of the learned, the ilustrado.

Yet, for every ilustrado who'd sacrificed his life for his people, like Jose Rizal, it seemed to Eleanor there was a great number among them, like Luis, who changed loyalties as fast as the winds changed because their personal and family interests remained unchanged. And there was an even greater number of the masses, like Diego, whose ichor was what soaked and fertilized the planting and fighting fields of humanity.

History was loaded with the wars of kings—carried upon serfs' shoulders. And Eleanor was weary of it. She decided that no philosophy remained pure, once stained with blood. She viewed any belief system that required life—any life—to be sacrificed in its name as no different from a religion that required human sacrifice to an invented god.

One morning, as she and Sam began the day's classes, an unusual commotion seemed to be developing outside the ayuntamiento building, as suggested by the rush of soldier's boots, the cocking of rifles, Major Davis shouting orders, followed by the slow trotting of horses, and the tapping of a multitude of sandaled feet on the flagstoned plaza floor. Many of her students stirred and glanced anxiously at the windows behind them.

"Now, class, stay calm," warned Eleanor. "Remain in your seats, please."

From his classroom across the hallway, Sam ran to her, exclaiming, "Miss Karsten, ya may want to see this!"

"What is it?" she asked, although she feared the answer.

"I think Kumander Diego and his men are finally surrendering!"

She didn't expect that! She could no longer restrain her students from rushing to the windows to watch the event unfolding outside, for she, too, couldn't wait to see it. When she peered out, her eyes were greeted by a sea of campesino straw hats characterized by their upturned front brims. Diego, mounted on his horse, glanced at her with a subtle smile on his lips and that old sparkle in his eyes. She grasped what he was doing. He was surrendering one fight for another. And he was doing so not only to preserve what remained of his men and their families who'd already been greatly decimated by war and disease, but also for their sake, so they could finally be together without fear or shame.

Her eyes filled with tears. The fullness of his love enveloped her heart, urging her to restrain her love no longer. There—there was her answer to all her doubts and questions! She loved him. It was as simple as that. And it was all she needed to build a life with him. Her compassion for the nobleness of his struggle, her pride in the essential courage of his act—all flowed out of the wellspring of her core toward him. And she felt one with him, despite all the souls standing between them.

Likewise mounted on a horse beside him was his deputy, Senyong. Behind them, on foot, were about two hundred other insurrectos. Notably absent were Juan and Bayani. Diego and Senyong dismounted and surrendered their rifles and revolvers to Major Davis, who accepted them and shook their hands. The rest of the insurrectos followed. They retreated to the back flanks as they finished their turn, sitting on their haunches as they waited for all their comrades to complete their turn.

A blanket of solemnity, interwoven with grief and hope, seemed to fall upon everyone. The civilian populace, who probably learned from the grapevine about what was happening at the ayuntamiento, arrived in hordes to watch the ceremony. They either smiled with happy tears or wept bitterly. A historic day it was of mixed joy and sorrow!

Eleanor dismissed the students early, urging them to go home to their families and ponder upon the profound significance of what they'd just witnessed. When she exited the ayuntamiento later, the plaza grounds were already almost empty—except for Diego, who was waiting for her, along with two horses.

"Want go ride with me?" He smiled that usual impish smile of his.

She grinned and grabbed the reins of one of the steeds and mounted it. "Lead on, jefe!"

He led her back to the Cagsawa ruins. After they hitched their horses, Diego grabbed her hand and, together, they clambered up the mossy stone steps to the top of the ancient bell tower. From the belfry, the view of the perfectly cone-shaped volcano towering over the countryside was sublime, just as Eleanor had imagined it. The fields, checkered in patches of verdigris, ochre, and sienna, were now free of the smoke of the burning chaos and conflict that blew across the land for most of the recent months. And, as though in like celebration of the moment, a murmuration of glossy starlings wove joyous ribbons of flight across the luminous blue sky. Except for the birds, dragonflies, and butterflies that flitted around them, Eleanor and Diego were alone.

And, as often happened when they were alone, Diego pulled Eleanor toward him, kissed her on the lips, and began making love to her. She gently pushed him away.

He looked stunned. "What the problem, mi amor?"

She looked him in the eye and replied, "Diego, I love you. It's insane, but I do love you!"

"O, Eleanor, that mean very much to me!" he cried in delight before grabbing her again.

"Wait, wait!" Eleanor grinned, pressing her hands against him. "Not so fast, mister. Now, we have to talk."

"Talk about what?" He looked bemused and befuddled.

"Talk about us—what happens to us now and in the future." She held his hands and swung his arms as a little girl might do with a playmate. "Diego, darling, we can't keep doing this. I mean, what if we have a baby? I'm a teacher—remember? It would risk my job!"

"Is all right! You not need to work. I work and feed you and baby!" he said, smiling brightly.

"Oh, but you don't understand, sweetheart," she interjected, "I love being a teacher too much to give it up! It's not work to me—it's a vocación. My calling!"

He observed her countenance as he listened. And then he laughed.

"Hey—that's not funny!" Eleanor protested.

"No worry, mi amor!" He pulled her to him again. "¡Es simple! ¡Cásate conmigo!"

"Ca… casa… ?" Eleanor tried to recall what the word meant.

"¡Sí!" he exclaimed, smiling brightly. "Marry me!"

Eleanor giggled. "Me, marry you? ¿Tú?" She pointed from her bosom to his chest.

Diego glanced around and shrugged. "Sí. I see nobody else here but me!"

"Oh, Diego, mi amor! Could we… really? You don't mind marrying an American?" She twisted her lips and raised her eyebrows.

"Sí. ¡Mañana, si quieres!" He nodded vigorously. "Tomorrow, we go see padre!"

"Oh, my sweet, darling insurrecto!" She attempted to kiss him, but he surprised her when he was the one who pulled back. He took out something from his trouser pocket wrapped in a wad of cloth. "I make this for you." He unwrapped it and presented it to her.

It appeared to be a silver ring inlaid with mother-of-pearl. He had cut out and sliced the iridescent white shell into veneers shaped into the star-like petals of a sampaguita blossom. Flanking the flower was a pair of green abalone shell inlays cut into ovate leaves. *He'd exceeded his craftsmanship of the python reticule!* She glanced up at him, and just before she could utter a response, he said, "Look." He pointed to the inside curve of the ring where he'd etched the first letters of their names with a heart connecting them. "Can I?""

"Please!" she cried, her voice faltering; breath trembling.

He took her right hand and slipped the ring on her fourth finger, which reminded her that this was where the natives wore their engagement and wedding rings. Only a tad loose of a glove's fit, it was thick and solid on her finger.

"Oh, Diego, this is the most precious ring! ¡Muchas gracias, mi amor!" She hugged and kissed him on the mouth.

He took off his shirt and laid her gently on the soft, mossy stone floor. There, she allowed him to make exquisite love to her again. This time, they indulged in the luxury of reacquainting themselves with each other's bodies—as though they had eternity at their fingertips. When their bodies were spent, they continued to hold and caress each other.

"Promise me," Eleanor said as she lay her head on his shoulder.

He glanced down at her face. "¿Que promesa?" he asked.

She looked up at him. "Promise me we would breathe our last breath together."

He smiled and kissed her forehead. "Prometo."

They returned to Magayon just as the sun was painting a fiery palette across the firmament. They spotted Senyong at the corner sari-sari store, which was recently reopened by Tomasa's niece. Diego's former deputy appeared to be celebrating the new regime of peace with neighbors and former insurrectos over plentiful glasses of lambanog. Senyong saluted Diego and Eleanor as the couple rode by. "¡Viva la jefe! ¡Viva la maestra Americana!" The rest joined in with rowdy cheers and applause. Diego returned their salute, and Eleanor waved back, grinning. It was their first public appearance and acknowledgment as a couple.

After hitching their horses on the fence of Eleanor's yard, they ran up the steps to the house, holding hands, eager to share their good news with Estrella. But as they entered the house, weeping and wailing reverberated from the bedroom. They scuttled to the room and, there, found Yolanda and Nanay Auring holding Estrella, who was lying on a bed of blood and other bloody matter.

"Señorita!" cried Yolanda, standing. "She try to get baby out! Now she…" The maid burst into sobbing again. She and Nanay Auring surrendered their spots on both sides of Estrella to Diego and Eleanor.

Eleanor held one of Estrella's hands. It was deathly cold.

"Hermana, what you do?" Diego cried as he gathered his sister in his arms. "¿Por qué?"

Estrella turned her pale face toward her brother. Her eyelids fluttered open and her fingers curled signaling him to lower his ear to her lips. When he did, she expended her last breath, whispering her terrible secret to him. The erstwhile leader of the local insurrection howled like a wounded animal as he cradled his sister's lifeless body. His angst soon appeared to turn into wrath, and he bolted out of the room.

Eleanor chased after him, crying, "Diego! Where are you going? Come back!"

Without looking back at her, he hurled himself into the viscous night—where ravenous shadows seemed to swallow him whole.

Nanay Auring tearfully shared how Estrella had pleaded with her to concoct an herbal potion to induce miscarriage. The old woman declined, telling Diego's sister that abortifacients were outside her expertise, and she didn't trust herself to brew a safe solution. But Nanay Auring had underestimated the young woman's resolve. Estrella employed, as her tool of last resort, the metal gaff used for hooking and pulling down fruits out of hand's reach—the same one she'd used to pick off green mangoes from the backyard tree. By the time Yolanda and Nanay Auring found her, Estrella had already lost much blood.

As Diego's sister hemorrhaged to death, her last word to him was a name—the name of her true rapist. Juan. They all heard it. Now, Diego had surely gone hunting him down. Eleanor was never more affrighted than she was now for her beloved, for she knew well the savagery and villainy of which the tattooed man was capable. She had to find both men if she were to prevent another tragedy from happening. Thus, she asked Yolanda to bring Senyong to her.

She recalled and reviewed the instances that should have dissuaded her from jumping to conclusion that Waterstone was Estrella's attacker. She should have seen the signs pointing to the equal possibility that Estrella's other ardent suitor was to blame. Now, it was clear why Juan had murdered the American officer. He must have been crazed on seeing Estrella not only entertaining but also appearing to enjoy the attentions of his sworn enemy.

But it was not only out of mad jealousy that Juan had killed Waterstone, Eleanor believed. It was surely aimed at distracting everyone from considering him as a suspect for the bestial deed. Whatever abrasions Estrella's fingernails had marked him with were thus conveniently disguised as injuries sustained in the carnage of his unsanctioned attack against the infantry station.

Juan turned out to be the tiger who couldn't change stripes that Eleanor had warned Estrella about. Yet, at that time, she was thinking of Waterstone. Now it appeared it may have been the American who truly was in love with the native teacher. From the cad the officer was in the beginning, he'd reformed his courtship of Estrella almost in the manner of a gentleman. In hindsight, Eleanor realized the officer's attitude toward her had also changed. He'd given increased support to her school and, upon her plea, freed Toto over Padre Damián's objections.

Now, Eleanor knew that love had the power to change people. Otherwise, only the circumstances of life changed while human beings remained prisoners of their own natures. Ultimately, however, the soldier chose loyalty to his country, which, inevitably, set him at odds with the woman he loved. To be torn between one's nation and one's beloved was a treacherous bog in a time of war. How could she and Diego reconcile such opposing forces in their lives? How could one build a life with someone that one's people believed was their enemy?

Juan must likewise be partly to blame for Bayani's radicalization. He must have stoked the hatred already incipient in the boy due to the deaths of his family and the burning of their bodies and home by the American soldiers. The tattooed thug's bad influence over Eleanor's favorite student must also be partially responsible for Bayani quitting school and joining Juan's mutinous gang. How she detested Juan even more!

Now, she wished she'd given up Juan to Waterstone when she had the chance. If only she did, none of the tragedies that befell Bayani and Estrella might have happened, including what was currently happening. Now, Diego was also paying for her mistake. She would beg Senyong to help her change what she still could. She'd ask him to take her to Juan.

When Yolanda returned with Senyong, Eleanor told him about Estrella's demise and her death-bed revelation. Senyong staggered and slumped onto a chair, weeping and covering his face. He then shared with Eleanor, through the help of Yolanda's translation, what he knew about Juan, who, he said, was another deputy of Diego.

Juan's unsanctioned attack on the infantry station would have been punishable by execution: the penalty for gross insubordination under their Katipunan rules. However, in exchange for Juan and his men surrendering under the amnesty program, Diego spared them. But the infantry station attack wasn't the first time Juan had defied the Katipunan leader's authority. The ambush against Eleanor was another unsanctioned initiative of the tattooed thug. Diego only learned about it when the attack was already underway and rushed to the ambush site. Eleanor remembered a horse arriving, just as Juan straddled her to the ground.

Diego was furious about the unauthorized ambush, yet, for the sake of unity, didn't want his fellow Katipuneros to know he'd lost control over one of his deputies. Thus, he ordered the carriage's torching to make the ambush look as though it was planned, all along. Since then, Diego kept Juan close to keep him in line. It helped when Juan turned docile while he was courting Estrella. Unfortunately, Lieutenant Waterstone stirred that pot again.

When Juan and his men failed to surrender themselves under the amnesty earlier that day, it became clear that Juan had only feigned agreement to the amnesty to escape execution under their Katipunan rules. Since Diego had surrendered under the program, Juan announced himself the new leader who vowed to continue fighting the Americans. He accused Diego and his followers of being traitors to the revolution. Senyong had just gotten wind of the schismatic group's plan to kill all former revolutionaries who'd surrendered when Yolanda reached him.

Eleanor was filled with greater dread. Diego and Juan's drive for mutual vengeance could mean a fight to the death.

CHAPTER 24

Mountain of a Lesser God

Eleanor mounted the same horse that she rode home with Diego earlier. He'd left it hitched to the bamboo fence in her yard and rode away with the other. Seeing the animal there without its mate struck her with the pain of her lover's absence. She had to find him before fate snatched him away from her. Sometimes, it took more effort to persuade life to do her bidding, yet her persistence often won it over. Except with death. Death took away the people she loved, like her parents—whittling her down to everyone's size. Truly, the equalizer of all.

She and Senyong galloped at breakneck speed toward Mount Malinao. Recalling how the natives believed Malinao was the mythical home of the evil god, Aswáng, Eleanor prayed that Gugurang would keep the fire in her heart burning to sustain her determination to save Diego. A distant thunder rumbled, seeming to herald another battle of mythic proportions.

As they approached Mount Malinao, Eleanor grasped why the natives believed it to be the home of an evil and lesser god. It seemed to have aspired to Mayon's majesty until some prehistoric geological havoc had thwarted its rise, fractured and knocked it down—consigning it to a low and ragged peak. The source of Gugurang's power was said to reside in the sacred fire he kept inside a coconut shell hidden in the bowels of the Mayon. Envious, Aswáng schemed to steal it. A cataclysmic battle for supremacy ensued between the brother deities that ended when Gugurang threw a thunderbolt at Mount Malinao, thus cutting Aswáng's bulwark in half and creating Malinao's grotesque, bisected form. Gugurang had foiled his evil brother's attempt to grab power, but now Aswáng seemed to be up to his old evil tricks again.

Eleanor and Senyong slowed down and dismounted where a sharp incline made it risky for the horses to take them higher. Senyong explained they had to hike up the mountain to avail of the shortest route to where he believed Juan's camp was located. There was an easier way to get there, but it took longer.

Eleanor considered Senyong's suggestions. They had the benefit of a full moon that dispensed with the need for lamps, freeing their hands to climb the steep outer crater wall. She assured him not to worry about her and proceed with the faster route. The sooner they got to Juan, the sooner they'd find Diego and, hopefully, prevent what she was sure her lover was planning to do: avenge his sister by killing Juan. She would persuade him to surrender the tattooed thug to the constabulary. Let the law deal with the criminal, she'd tell him. And then she would remind him of what was more important: their love and building a new life together.

Aided by her boots and leather riding gloves, Eleanor began her climb toward the crater's peak. She clutched on exposed tree roots and vines to help her with the ascent. As her clothes entangled with brambly brushwoods, she simply tore herself away from the thorns and this- tles. When they finally reached the peak, she realized the ordeal hadn't ended, for, now, they had to descend into the crater without falling or sliding. And, this time, there appeared hardly any tree roots and vines to hold onto. The loose, sandy soil and rocks made slipping and falling straight to the crater's pit more likely. This, to her mind, made Mount Malinao a superior hideout compared to Hellmouth cave.

Senyong grunted as he slipped and fell. Eleanor stifled a cry, afraid of alerting anyone of their presence. Since she heard no thud from wherever Senyong had landed, she hoped the slope of the ravine was more gradual than she feared. On the other hand, his silent fall also meant the descent was much deeper than she imagined. Blindly, she kept climbing downward. When she reached the bottom, she spotted Senyong's motionless body among some bushes. She rushed to him, relieved to see him breathing, although he appeared to have sustained some gashes and scrapes. "Senyong! Senyong!" She nudged and shook him. He groaned but didn't open his eyes.

She decided to leave him where he was and set out on her own. Already, the outlines of a few rambling huts were visible among the foliage. The camp wasn't far ahead. She crept toward the huddled huts where she saw not only men but women—the camp followers?—watching what sounded like two men fighting. Her ears tuned in to her lover's voice. Diego!

"I'm only after you, Juan!" Diego yelled in the native language. "Fight me like a man, and I'll let your men go free!"

Juan cackled, and many of the spectators sniggered. "Your sister deserved what she got!" Juan hissed. "She defiled herself when she became the p*ta of that Cano! Just like the w**re your mother was and the traitor you are!"

The crowd growled in agreement.

Eleanor wanted to scream, *no, Diego! Don't get baited!* But she soon heard Diego's war cry, followed by the swift clash of metal. When she came close enough to see them, Diego and Juan were dueling with their bolos around the campfire. She crawled and hid under one of the huts, unnoticed by the spectators absorbed in the fight. Many cheered for Juan, while a few seemed to remain on the hedge, waiting to see who'd finally come out the victor. The dins and rackets recalled the pandemonium of a cockfight. She could smell the blood lust between the combatants. Neither man would be satisfied until one of them was dead. It was too late for her to do anything except to avoid distracting Diego from the fight.

Both fighters wielded their bolos fiercely and skillfully. The campfire flames reflected in the dull gleam of their blades that swung in brisk arcs and nimble loops, thrusting and parrying, swiping and shielding. Eleanor gasped as the fighters' bolos struck and pushed against each other in an even parry. Juan kicked Diego, causing the latter to fall within inches of the flames. Fortunately, only the tip of Diego's bolo fell into the fire.

Eleanor's hand flew to her mouth as Juan rushed toward Diego with his bolo aimed at decapitating her beloved. The memory of Waterstone's almost severed head chilled her. Yet, Diego used his sword to scoop up and flick some of the embers at Juan, who yawped, blenched, and paused to brush off the sting from his face, thus halting his momentum.

Diego rolled away, jumped to his feet, and, with one fluid swing, smote the bolo away from Juan's grip. The force with which he achieved this likewise threw Juan to the ground. Diego scuttled toward his defenseless opponent, raised his bolo, and poised it at cutting Juan in half. A collective gasp slashed through the air thick with tension before everyone and everything stilled in anticipation of the inevitable conclusion.

But in a move that shocked everyone, including Juan, as seen from the stunned look on his face, Diego unbelievably chucked his advantage by tossing his bolo away. Instead, he lunged at Juan, pulled him up by the shirt, and punched his sister's rapist so that Juan's nose bent to the right side of his face. Diego pummeled blow after blow upon Juan's torso and hurled the thug back to the ground. Juan's face was cut and bleeding in multiple spots, swollen, and bruised black and blue — looking eerily like Estrella's face after he'd raped her.

Diego stooped to pick him up again, and Eleanor shrieked as Juan pulled out a blade hidden in his boot and stabbed Diego in the belly. Diego staggered and fell backward, the knife sticking out of his stomach. Time seemed to slow as Juan stood and wiped his bloody nose and eyelids with his backhand, picked up one of the bolos from the ground, and marched to where Diego lay helpless. Juan sneered as he pressed his foot on Diego's chest and raised the bolo over his former jefe's neck, poised to decapitate him.

Eleanor shrieked, "No!" Juan's head jerked toward where she was hiding. At that moment, a dagger flew from the forest and lodged itself in Juan's heart. For a second, the villain appeared frozen in mid-action with an astonished expression on his face before collapsing. Eleanor glanced at where the dagger came from and saw Senyong emerging from the woods.

She scrambled over to Diego and knelt beside him, crying, "No, no — don't touch it!" But he had already pulled out the knife from his belly and blood was oozing out of the wound. She tore off one of her sleeves and crumpled and pressed it against Diego's bleeding side. Relief surged through Eleanor when she saw the blade wasn't long enough to have inflicted a mortal wound. She hugged Diego. "Oh, my love, I think you'll live!"

She told him to continue pressing on his wound as she tore off a section of her slip into a band that she then tied around Diego's stomach to keep the gauze pressed on his wound. She had just helped him to his feet when she heard a scuttling from behind them and a gunshot, followed by a ringing in Eleanor's ears. Diego's legs buckled, pulling Eleanor back to the ground with him. She glanced up and saw Bayani standing no more than three feet away from them, clutching a smoking revolver.

"No, no, no, please, no..." Eleanor repeated like a mantra as she examined Diego's now bloody torso, frantically searching for where the bullet had hit.

The boy approached and stood over the couple, declaring with contempt, "That what a traitor get!" He smirked and spat on Diego.

As he turned around to leave, Eleanor wailed, "Bayani Burgos, where has all the goodness in you gone? How have you become this monster?"

Bayani swung around and rushed toward her, bending from the waist to plant his face in front of hers. He sniggered and growled. "How? How, Miss Karsten? You! You made this aswáng—you and all Americanos who burned all the good in my life!" His voice had deepened, though it still cracked like the voice of pubescent boys. How young he still was; yet, how ancient his hatred!

He pointed the warm muzzle of his revolver between Eleanor's eyes. "And you will be next if you don't leave my country!" He straightened up and likewise spat on her before he walked away, followed by some of the men and women.

Eleanor returned her tearful attention to Diego to look for his gunshot wound again, hoping to stem the bleeding. Yet, his blood-soaked shirt made her search impossible. Diego rasped and gasped for air. When she held up his head, he coughed out blood. His eyes stayed on hers briefly before they fluttered close and his head hung limp.

"No, no, no! Don't you dare die on me, Diego Santiago!" she cried. "Please, mi amor! Diego, wake up! Help! Somebody—please help!"

Senyong ran to her side. Soon, complete chaos descended on the camp as constabulary soldiers arrived, firing rifles and chasing after the fleeing rebels. Their rescue had thankfully arrived! Before Eleanor had left her house, she instructed Yolanda to run to Major Davis and tell him where she was headed and to urge him to follow after her if he wanted to capture Juan and his band of outlaws. The soldiers now surrounded the camp, rounding up what remained of Juan's gang.

With the help of Senyong and a couple of soldiers, Eleanor transported Diego's unconscious body back to Magayon. As soon as they reached the town's outskirts, she sent Senyong away to get Doctor Langford. When she and the soldiers arrived at her house, she was surprised to find many of her neighbors standing in her front yard, holding lighted candles, praying. The crowd burst into grim gasps and murmurs on seeing Diego's bloody body being carried by the soldiers. They parted to make way for them and Eleanor. There were also several women in the sala, kneeling and praying the rosary, who stood when they saw who had come.

In the bedroom, Eleanor was amazed to see Pastor Willoughby with Nanay Auring and Yolanda. The young, tall, lanky minister was wearing a stole and holding a Bible, saying prayers over Estrella's body. The blood-soaked sheets and mattress on Estrella's bed were gone. In their stead was a clean sheet over the caned bed surface on which the now washed and dressed remains of Diego's sister lay. The three glanced up in alarm as Eleanor and the soldiers barged into the room and laid Diego on Eleanor's bed.

"Nanay Auring, we need you!" Eleanor cried. "Yolanda, boil water! Bring towels!"

The old healer scampered over to Diego as the maid and soldiers left the room. Nanay Auring whimpered upon seeing Diego's bloody torso. She caressed his hair away from his face and whispered lamentations.

Pastor Willoughby approached. His voice was soft and earnest when he said, "Miss Karsten, how may I help?"

Eleanor glanced up at him, dazed. "Just… just do whatever you do best."

Although Eleanor had questioned religion most of her life, she now found it strangely comforting to have a man of faith in the same room with her. The minister closed his eyes and folded his hands in prayer as she skittered to her desk drawer for a pair of scissors to cut away Diego's shirt.

Eleanor and Nanay Auring had already washed off most of the blood and grime from Diego's body when Senyong arrived with Doctor Langford. The doctor looked stumped upon seeing Estrella dead and Diego dying in Eleanor's bedroom. After examining Diego's stab and gunshot wounds, he glanced at Eleanor with the same expression on his face whenever a cholera patient had turned terminal. He sighed, shaking his head. "I'm afraid the bullet is too deeply lodged into his chest. I can't simply pull it out. Even if I could, it would only hasten... It may have a punctured his lung. That explains why he's wheezing."

Eleanor quivered and felt her extremities go cold. "William, how long?"

The doctor met her gaze grimly. "Not going to lie, my dear. It may happen before sunrise."

Eleanor looked at the fading shadows behind the capiz shell windows. She held Diego's hand and buried her face in the mattress, squirming in agony.

Diego stirred and squeezed her hand. "Mi amor, cas... cásate con... conmigo...," he said.

"What?" She glanced up at him and wiped her face with her hands and drew her ear near his lips. "What's that, my love?"

"Cásate c-conmigo," he repeated softly. "Ahora."

She glanced up at Pastor Willoughby. "Pastor, could you do it?"

The minister appeared confounded and overwhelmed. "Do what, Miss Karsten?"

"Marry us!" she cried.

"What?" Pastor Willoughby exclaimed. "You mean... you and this... this indio?"

"He's not an indio!" Eleanor yelled. "He's a man, and a hero, and his name is Diego Santiago! Who happened to have just expressed a dying wish!"

The pastor flinched and flushed. "I'm sorry, Miss Karsten. I only meant that... this is rather an unusual... request. B-but n-not impossible! We just need to have... a witness."

"You have three here, pastor!" Doctor Langford volunteered. "What are you waiting for?"

Eleanor sent the doctor a grateful glance.

Pastor Willoughby made up for his obtuseness by proving efficient in paring down the marriage ceremony to its basics. Diego wheezed and whispered his replies to the ritual questions. During the exchange of rings, Eleanor pulled off the silver and mother-of-pearl ring she was already wearing and placed it in Diego's hand. The mother of pearl, now soaked with Diego's blood, had turned rufescent. She helped him push it on her finger. Nanay Auring pulled out her widow's ring and handed it to Eleanor. Though small for a man, Eleanor was able to put it on Diego's right fifth finger.

"The groom may now kiss the bride," Pastor Willoughby announced.

A feeble smile lit up Diego's face. Eleanor pressed her lips to his, and when she lifted them from him, she watched for the sign. When he gripped her hand, she knew. She pressed her mouth on his again and inhaled his last breath, fulfilling the promise they made to each other.

"Sweet dreams, mi amor, my husband," she whispered in his ear. Only after she'd caressed his eyelids closed did she break down into wailing and sobbing—gripping her heart, which felt as if it had been stabbed and was now being cut out and wrenched from her chest. This was what Daragang Magayon must have felt. And the grieving Mother of God as Our Lady of the Harvest—of sorrows.

Eleanor bought a double plot at the cemetery to bury Diego and Estrella beside each other. At an earlier time, Padre Damián wouldn't have permitted the remains of someone like Estrella whom he condemned as a baby killer to be buried there. Yet, the land where the cemetery was built was owned by the municipality, not the church, although it was called the parochial cemetery. American governance had curtailed the scope of the priest's power over the municipal bureaucracy, which might have yet allowed his influence to hold sway.

Yolanda had informed Eleanor that, on the night of Estrella's passing, the maid went to Padre Damián to ask him to perform the last rites on the young woman's body. The priest had arrived at their house, only to refuse to bless the deceased upon learning the cause of her death. It was then that Nanay Auring sent for Pastor Willoughby.

Thus, it was to the Protestant pastor that Eleanor likewise turned for the burial service of her husband and sister-in-law.

Eleanor was grateful to have Doctor Langford, Doña Beatriz, Sam, and Cristina by her side at the burial, along with Yolanda and Nanay Auring. She was delightfully surprised that Mayor Dizon and Doña Hermosa likewise attended. The presence of Pedro, Senyong, and many other former insurrectos and their families also consoled her. Most of the campesinos who showed up were Diego's fellow workers at Hacienda Gonzaga, which highlighted the absence of Luis and Doña Ximena.

Two months after Eleanor had buried Diego and Estrella, she knew she was with child. It was September again, almost exactly a year after she first arrived in Magayon. Her term's end. Although she had the option to renew it, she announced she was leaving, declaring her desire to write a book about her experience as a Thomasite in honor of her parents' memory. No one questioned her reason. But the truth was—she couldn't bear to continue living in Magayon, surrounded by memories of Diego, yet achingly bereft of him.

The fickle elite didn't wait for Eleanor's departure to withdraw their children from her school, reportedly scandalized by la maestra Americana stooping so low as to have married an "indio." She had allegedly shown herself of questionable character by choosing Diego over Don Luis, who was secretly, yet widely known to have pursued her. "Who would reject the finest bachelor gentleman in all of Vicol if not a woman who was beneath us and, thus, definitely not of our kind?" some had been heard to say.

Aggravating the situation was the launching of a private Catholic school for boys and girls in the same church school building that Eleanor had rejected. Doctor Langford apologetically confessed to her that the upper-class parents had long been collaborating with Padre Damián to establish the new school. When it opened, some of the less affluent parents likewise pulled out their children from the public school and transferred them to the private school—although it was a mystery how they could continue paying the steep tuition. They bought into what the rich parents were bragging about: that attendance in the private school meant automatic prestige and academic excellence for their children. Padre Damián bolstered their confidence by preaching that enrolling their children in the Catholic school signified their family's fealty to the true faith.

Eleanor shuddered to think what other problems would confront her when the people also learned she was pregnant. It didn't take much calculation after the baby's birth for them to know her child was conceived before marriage. Yolanda also alerted her of ugly rumors about la maestra Americana's sullied chastity leaking from Villa Gonzaga. This validated her decision to leave. She had to go before she further compromised the Thomasite mission in Magayon.

She entrusted the school to Sam, promising to secure a new set of teachers to assist him when she reached Manila. He and Cristina invited her back to their home for a farewell lunch. Although they expressed sadness over her departure, they were happy to tell her they were expecting their second child.

Yolanda, though despondent over her mistress leaving, confided that her life had taken a happy turn. Pedro had asked her to marry him and, despite their eleven-year difference, she accepted. "He a good man, and good man hard to find," the girl declared. Eleanor was surprised by her cluelessness about the romance that had developed between her muchacha and Sam's muchacho. She congratulated Yolanda and gifted her with the velo she'd worn during that fateful Thanksgiving, expressing hope it could serve as the maid's wedding veil. Yolanda tearfully accepted it and hugged her mistress.

Nanay Auring wept like a mother losing a daughter as Eleanor performed the custom of touching an elder's hand with her forehead to express love and respect. The healer and midwife placed her hand upon Eleanor's head and blessed her with the sign of the cross. She cupped her mouth to Eleanor's ear as she whispered in the hybrid language, "Send for me, señora, when time for your baby to come." Eleanor nodded, smiled, and tearfully hugged the old woman.

"Words aren't enough to thank you, Mr. Ang," she said to her Chinese friend. "I couldn't have started the school without you." She informed him she'd written both Major Davis and el presidente to confirm their agreements about the former school buildings to facilitate their turnover, including the return of the land on which they stood, to him. She hoped this compensated him for what he'd lost, she told him. The man smiled serenely as he solemnly bowed to her.

Doña Beatriz and Doctor Langford feted her with a despedida party at their villa—attended, surprisingly, by many of the town's luminaries, including the Three Musketeers, who appeared especially jovial. One thing the elite were indeed good at, Eleanor mused, was not forsaking good manners, despite their true thoughts and feelings. Keeping up appearances was everything. This was why she was shocked that Luis also failed to attend her farewell fete. Doña Ximena extended his regrets, citing his commitments as governor. Eleanor wasn't convinced. The haciendero must not have taken kindly to her choosing Diego over him, which may have likewise caused him to lose face before his own social class.

Before the party, Eleanor made time to provide the mayor's wife a friendly tutorial on makeup under the guise of sharing the latest American beauty trends she'd learned from her Radcliffe friends. During the despedida, Doña Hermosa, looking almost beautiful, unabashedly wept, declaring how heartbroken she was at her American friend's departure.

Eleanor said a sad goodbye to her students, who gifted her with handmade cards and dyed sinamay flowers. She was sadder, still, about Bayani. She didn't know what became of her erstwhile favorite student after that tragic night on Mount Malinao, unless rumors about a boy general pursuing the insurrection from the wooded highlands of Vicol could be believed.

She left Magayon via Legazpi Port, where she was to board the new, stately *Heneral Blanco*. There, she was surprised to find Luis, surrounded by bodyguards, sitting in an open carriage. He appeared likewise startled on seeing her and volunteered, without her asking, that he was waiting for Maria Teresa's vapor to arrive—the same boat on which Eleanor was to travel to Manila.

She gleaned from this that Maria Teresa may not have returned to Spain, after all, but bided her time in Manila until her intended fiancé got over his infatuation with la maestra Americana. *A shrewd young woman she proved to be*, Eleanor thought, smiling. Far from the naïve, innocent, convent-bred young lady everyone thought she was.

Because of this, Eleanor was sure Maria Teresa would make a perfect wife for Luis.

Perhaps out of courtesy more than a desire to speak with Eleanor, Luis stepped down from his carriage. His once flirtatious, easy-going manner seemed to be gone, replaced by a strained formality. "I regret I was not able to attend your despedida, Miss Karsten. But I wish you good fortune in your future endeavors." He took her hand and performed a proper gesture of a kiss.

"Thank you, Luis… I mean, Governor Gonzaga. And, by the way, it's Mrs. Santiago now." He blenched subtly. To dispel the awkward silence, she added, "Congratulations on your new political career! I hear you plan to run in the elections after your temporary term?" He nodded, and she smiled. "I sincerely hope you'll achieve as governor of your people what you had hoped to gain through the revolution."

"Ah, well… that… sí, gracias," He glanced around before turning back to her with apprehension in his eyes. "Pero, señora—I would greatly appreciate that you do not mention my involvement in… well, you know…. especially to your friends in Manila. That is, as you Americans say, water under the bridge." He grinned somewhat nervously.

"Oh. Yes. Of course," Eleanor replied, disappointed by his changed politics, yet subdued into concession by the tension between them. She glanced toward the vessel where passengers were now stepping down the gangplank. "I guess it's time for me to go. Goodbye, again, Luis." She offered her hand in a handshake, which he accepted.

Halfway through turning away, she faced him again and grabbed his hand, stunning him. "Luis I… I just want you to know I truly appreciated all you did for my school and… for me. Thank you… for everything. You'll make a fine husband for Maria Teresa, and she deserves you more than anyone. I wish you both a happy life."

He averted his gaze, but before he did, she caught him misty-eyed. She released his hand and hurried toward the vessel. She was about to pass Maria Teresa, who appeared oblivious to her. She held back the young lady's arm, greeting her with, "Señorita Vasquez! How lovely to see you again!"

"Oh. It is you," the young lady said, looking disconcerted, until a smug smile took over her countenance. "Leaving?"

"Yes. Returning to Manila," Eleanor replied. "But what luck seeing you! I take it as a sign for me to give you this."

"¿Qué?" the Spanish mestiza asked, appearing perplexed.

"Oh, just something I believe was meant more for you than me," Eleanor said as she pulled out the object from her python reticule and deposited it on Maria Teresa's lace-gloved hand: Toto's locket that held the photograph of the native Filipina who, apart from being dark, was almost the spitting image of its current recipient. Eleanor said no more nor waited to witness the Spanish mestiza's reaction, but rather hurried up the gangplank—smiling.

On the deck of the *Heneral Blanco*, Eleanor's eyes stayed on the Mayon until it blurred away from view.

She sought sanctuary with Ida, who had just returned from the mainland after her appointment as the new Superintendent of Public Instruction for the Philippine Islands. Eleanor confided her dilemma to her friend. With no family to go home to and with a child coming, she confessed she was at a loss on what to do, where to go.

"And why do you think you are without family?" Ida retorted, sounding slighted. "Who am I, my dear, if I am not family to you now? Rest, write your book, birth your baby, after which, you could help me by returning to teaching. At the Women's Normal School, perhaps? I'm sure our future maestras could learn much from your experiences."

Together, they rented a house in Intramuros. It was one of those charming *bahay na bato* or "house of stone."

"A sturdy home to raise a sturdy child!" Ida declared.

And a hardy one to hold herself when she fell apart again in grief, which still happened—often, when she least expected.

Melancholia had a canny habit of attacking her during the most innocuous of moments, such as when a sampaguita lei vendor called out from the street below, or when she caught a certain twinkle in someone's eye, or the way another inclined his head, or from the scents of coconuts and lime. Coconuts and lime were everywhere. And so was Diego.

Leaving Magayon did not make it easier for her to forget. The nights proved most difficult—when she yearned for his touch and smell, the fevered timbre of his voice in her ear, the warmth of his breath on her skin, the understanding between them undeterred by a lack of words.

As the child in her belly grew, Eleanor wrote the memoir of her first year as a Thomasite. What did it all mean? She came to the Philippine Islands to teach, but became the student, instead. Perhaps, this was the point. She wrote what came to her, not in the order in which it occurred, but what insight, born of memory and reflection, determined. And her fingers complied on her father's Remington.

Are my memories the sum of my life, or is it the life in me that chooses what to remember? The book was not just a map of her experience but of chosen memory—a testament to the inherent subjectivity of personal and public history. It was her *obra maestra*, her masterpiece, her baby: the figurative and the literal, gestating along with each other.

She glanced at the wall where she'd hung Luis's portrait of her. Diego was right. It was nice, but Luis only saw what he wanted to see—not all of her, which Diego had recognized from the beginning. The glorious beauty and majesty of Mayon Volcano, however—that, Luis had captured. She would have been happier if he had gifted her the Mayon landscape painting that hung at his late aunt's house. The one with the bell tower. Where her child was conceived.

Her baby quickened, and Eleanor caressed the knee, foot, elbow, or fist that pushed against her womb. The child tucked itself in, tumble-turned, and swam inside her like some thalassic serpent, reminding her that all was not just memory. What was past was still present in palpable form: unseen but not hidden, mysterious but not secret. The serpent of knowledge of the past, present, and future—existing and happening simultaneously, changing only skin. Like that fearsome python transformed into a gift of love and the child, who was love incarnate.

She considered the ring on her finger. The gleam and strength of silver. The luster and iridescence of mother-of-pearl—infused with the blood of her beloved. Transmuted. Alive. What was ivory was now a rosy shade of pink, still beaming its fiery opaline whites: the ghost of all colors burning in the soul of the mother-of-pearl. She decided her child would be the same: strong and filled with the sanguine life force created by the melding of its parents' blood. Perhaps this was what humanity needed—the blending of all races, ending the illusion of division by skin color.

Her one regret was Bayani. She failed her own first rule in the classroom: to pay attention. She failed to pay attention to her pupil's blossoming intellect, because she'd underestimated his intelligence in the first place. Just like she'd underestimated Diego. Bayani had already shown more than once that he was troubled by the Pilgrim-American Indian story. Yet she ignored it. What suffering could have been avoided, if only she'd been a better shepherd of the boy's education? On the other hand, how much shepherding could she have done, if she were, after all, the ignorant one?

She was incredibly cavalier in exposing the boy to potentially controversial material, obtusely naïve about the power of books to provoke a sleeping innocent into rude awakening. Yet, how might have she instructed the boy through history books and novels, and expect to control the path of his independently evolving consciousness? Oh, the fallacy and hubris of control! History was controversial, depending on who wrote it. The very existence of books themselves was controversial. This was why first on a tyrant's agenda was the consolidation of power by banning and burning books. She should have understood this from church history alone.

And she failed to consider that, to the pure of mind and heart like Bayani, her presence in Magayon presented an anathema to principle and philosophy. She presumed she could separate herself from the likes of Waterstone, believing herself different, better. She pretended she had nothing to do with the American occupation of the islands and assumed she could make her own way—detached from it all. Yet, Bayani rightly saw through her. Her complicity was clear as the first shot fired from the gun of the American soldier who arrived with the army of invasion. No amount of softening that blow with beautiful words like "benevolent assimilation" erased the ugly truth for the Filipino.

Now, she understood there were always unintended consequences from trying to do good in the name of saving someone. Often, good intentions weren't good enough. Now, she grasped the arrogance of believing anyone could save another. It presumed someone needed saving to begin with.

Yet, she still believed in the value of a pure intention—that despite the brokenness of its outcome, there remained the unassailable truth of its goodness. Good and bad co-existed in the world, after all. They did not cancel out each other. One could not exist without the other, though they possessed the power to diminish each other.

In the late afternoons, Eleanor enjoyed promenading with Ida at the Luneta. It was a good exercise for both of them, especially for Eleanor, whose ankles were swollen from carrying her body's precious cargo and all the sitting required by writing. They hired a calesin to bring them there, walked by the water, and watched the sun famously set over Manila Bay. They talked about their day and reminisced about Arabella and Maude, happy to have received a letter from the latter informing them she was now attending MIT's architecture program, intent on pursuing her dream of designing and building her own school.

Many of their fellow promenaders appeared delighted to see a pregnant Americana. They often stopped to congratulate her, asking when the stork was due to arrive. Whether they were Filipinos, Spaniards, Americans, mestizos, or mestizas, it didn't matter—they always assumed Eleanor's husband was an American whenever they inquired about him. This happened so frequently, it compelled her to compose a ready reply. She first corrected their error and matter-of-factly stated that her spouse was a Filipino who was a casualty of the war. Her inquisitors' faces sometimes twitched, but their smiles always faded as they grasped what she said and grappled for an excuse to be on their way. In time, no one stopped to greet her anymore.

It was the quiet moments at home with Ida she loved best, for it was during such a moment that she realized it was possible to live a happy, contented family life with a friend and companion. One evening when, as usual, Ida sat reading across from where Eleanor was writing,

Eleanor glanced up to observe her friend. Ida's forehead furrowed into deep grooves, and her eyes narrowed as she adjusted the spectacles on her nose for a better look at the book she was perusing. Her hair was almost all silver now, and her frame shorter, slimmer.

Eleanor stood and walked over to Ida. She cupped her friend's face and gazed into her startled, faded gray eyes. "Thank you, dearest Ida, for sharing this voyage with me," she said, kissing her friend's forehead.

Ida, eyes glistening, pressed Eleanor's palm to her cheek.

May 30, 1903

Dear Maude,

I hope you are well and that you are enjoying good prospects for an apprenticeship with an atelier of your choice. It seems only yesterday when you dared to imagine this dream at the Bishop Museum, spurred on by Eleanor and Arabella. I'm proud of you.

I regret to bring you bad news, albeit tempered by the good. I will start with the latter, for life is hard enough without celebrating the positive. The good news is little Señorita Laura Santiago y Karsten was born on the 8th of May. She is a beautiful, winsome, and vigorous child. A perfect blend of east and west!

The tragic news is that her mother, our dear Eleanor, chose to forfeit her life to give life to her daughter. I prefer not to dwell on all the grim details. Suffice to state I laid our beloved friend to rest where other Thomasites are here likewise interred. I have also arranged for a tombstone to be laid beside Eleanor's that bears Arabella's name, so that we may remember them together when you visit.

On a side note, I had proposed to buy more land in the Manila North Cemetery to integrate with the current burial plots of our departed fellow Thomasites and dedicate it all as the American Teachers Memorial. I hope for this to be one of my legacies as superintendent.

Regarding baby Laura's care, I am fortunate to have more than enough wet nurses and nannies, for now that the war is over, this society seems determined to make more babies and money. The first explains the almost unlimited supply of wet nurses, and the latter, the wave of peasants seeking employment in the city via domestic or factory work.

I dare say that the amassment of more wealth by those who are already some of the wealthiest families in Philippine society is the real motive behind all their talk of nation-building, nationalism, and independence. I doubt real social change could happen here without disemboweling it of its feudal underbelly.

The ilustrados, who well understand this because of their education, have nonetheless been too easily seduced by their new political and legal careers, which, not surprisingly, also serve to entrench their families' economic and political interests. Everyone has unbearably become an orator or demagogue. Candidates for public office recall the Pied Piper of Hamelin—no different, I suppose, from what is happening on the mainland. The colony mirrors its colonizer. It is clear for whom this assimilation is proving benevolent.

Thus, I have come around to Eleanor's view of disabusing ourselves of the illusion that we have any power to effect change beyond what we may achieve in the lives of the people we could directly affect by our presence, such as our family and friends, or through our work, such as our students and colleagues. Whatever positive difference we might be so lucky to create beyond that would simply be the progression of what we had already begun in our little circles of life. Ripples of change, Eleanor liked to call them.

In this connection, dear Maude, I have the honor, grave though it is, to inform you that you and I have a child to raise together. Eleanor's will designated us as her daughter's guardians, naming us "ninangs," or what Filipinos call godmothers, asking us to consider ourselves second mothers to her daughter. She left a substantial trust for little Laura and expressed the hope it could give her daughter the same freedom her parents had bequeathed her.

She particularly requested that we guide Laura's education—first, by enrolling her in your school when she comes of age. I foresee this happening at about the time I am ready to retire and return to the mainland. Eleanor also asked that we help her daughter secure a spot, if the girl is minded, in an excellent coeducational university that treats its female students equally with the males. I told her, in this regard, we had better make sure we win suffrage. You can imagine how she laughed with me about that.

Finally, I send herewith Eleanor's memoir manuscript and request your kind assistance in procuring a publisher in New York. I do declare it to be much better than most impressions of the Philippine Islands I have read. Perhaps this is because it is written not from the perspective of a conquering hero, nor that of a passing traveler, but one who truly fell in love with this land and its people. I would be glad to write a foreword should the publisher ask. I hope it is not too presumptuous to think that the endorsement of the first female

Superintendent of Public Instruction in the Philippine Islands does not make for an insignificant statement.

I wish you continued good health and success, my dear. And hearty congratulations on your impending graduation from architecture college! May your work, and mine, pay worthy homage to our fallen colleagues, especially those dearest to our hearts: Eleanor and Arabella.

Your friend,
Ida

EPiLOGUE

On the centenary of the Thomasites' arrival in the Philippines, a young American lady wearing a sampaguita lei enters the Manila North Cemetery. She stops by the office; asks for directions. A security guard offers to accompany her. She agrees, and he leads her toward the special section.

When they reach it, she pulls out a camera from her bag and asks him to take a picture of her with the memorial in the background. He obliges, and she thanks him, tipping him with a five-dollar bill. His earnest, brown face breaks into a huge smile as he leaves her to the privacy of her mission.

She surveys the monument before her. A roseate cement pathway at the center of the plot leads to an obelisk bearing the carved, black-painted text, *American Teachers Memorial*. A pair of gigantic neoclassical urns flank the centerpiece sculpture, connected by a built-in bench that forms a continuous low apron arching behind the obelisk. The memorial appears to be rendered in concrete, painted white; its decorative details highlighted in mustard gold. In the foreground, arranged in neat, straight, broadly-spaced rows, are about two dozen rectangular, white-painted grave markers lying flat on the baked, fawn earth.

The young lady meanders among them, searching for a name. When she finds it, she kneels and sweeps off the dust and debris from the tombstone's surface with her bare hand. She smiles. It feels real now. She's finally found her. She's no longer just a name in a book.

Tracing the letters with her index finger, she says, "Nice to meet you, great-great-granny Eleanor!" She takes off her lei, kisses the name on the grave, and lays the flowers upon it.

ACKNOWLEDGMENTS

Profound thanks from the author to the following who helped make this book a reality:

Her children—Francesca and Travis—in whom she sees the best of both the American and Filipino, who thus greatly inspired the writing of this book;

Jose, her father, her Bicolano, who sowed a curious mind in her and shared stories of his youth with his children, amid the beautiful landscape of his hometown that inspired the novel's setting;

Her aunt and high school history teacher, Anicia A. Gueco, and all her other history teachers in the Philippines, who introduced her to the wonderful world of history, including the Thomasites;

Arielle Haughee of Orange Blossom Publishing, who immediately "got" was this book is about and why it's important to share it with the world;

Her writing critique partners—Nupur Maskara, Mary Eicher, Janelle Scheffelmaier, and Julia Suderman—who patiently read through rough first drafts, offered suggestions that improved the manuscript, and provided the necessary reality check;

Her first readers—Steven Smith, Francesca Smith, Henry Grageda, Bona S. McKinney, Jane Gregg, Ashley Colletti, Toni Stinnett, and Deb Filer—who generously invested their time reading an early draft of this novel, were kind not to dismiss it as the work of a madwoman, provided feedback on how various readers may react to the story and characters, and cheered her on her publication journey;

Kaitlyn Katsoupis of Belcastro agency, who kindly read, and suggested edits to the final draft of the manuscript, including insights on translating history for contemporary readers;

Antone Granada, for his prompt and precious help with the Bicolano language;

Some members of the following Facebook history groups, who offered helpful historical information and supported this book: Philippine-American War, Filipino American National Historical Society, Pamagaral King Kultura at Literaturang Kapampangan, Filipiniana, La Cultura e Historia de Filipinas/Ang Kultura at Historya ng Filipinas, and Authors for Heritage Preservation;

And last, but not least, Ian and Carmel, who laid themselves faithfully at her feet, kept her company as she wrote this book, and dogged her to rise, now and then, from her writing chair.

To view the **HISTORICAL NOTES**,
please scan the QR code or visit
www.OrangeBlossomBooks.com/thomasitenote

To view the **BOOK CLUB DISCUSSION QUESTIONS**,
please scan the QR code or visit
www.OrangeBlossomBooks.com/thomasitequestions

ABOUT THE AUTHOR

Victoria Grageda-Smith is a lawyer turned writer and award-winning Filipino American author published in the creative writing genres of fiction, nonfiction, and poetry. *The Thomasite* (Orange Blossom Publishing, 2023) is her debut novel, a literary historical fiction book inspired by a history class when she was a high school student in the Philippines.

She is likewise the author of the Driftless Unsolicited Novella Award-winning *Faith Healer* (Brain Mill Press, 2016). Her short story, *Portrait of the Other Lady,* won first place in the Fifth Annual Ventura County-Ventura County Star national short story contest, which marked the first time she entered a writing contest. The Ventura County Star published the short story on November 28, 2004. Her story collection manuscript, *Faith Healer and Other Stories,* was a semi-finalist in the 2015 Elixir Press' Fiction Award contest. The manuscript developed into the story collection, *Daughters of the Bamboo*, which is on the publishing track for 2024.

She is the author of the Kirkus-acclaimed poetry collection, *Warrior Heart, Pilgrim Soul: An Immigrant's Journey* (Amazon, 2013). Her poetry appears in various literary journals, including the *Slippery Elm Journal, Crosswinds Poetry Journal, New Millennium Writings, Reed Magazine, Lyrical Iowa*, and *Dicta* (The University of Michigan School of Law literary journal). Her poems were recognized with distinction in the 2016 Crosswinds Poetry Journal International Contest, 42nd New Millennium Poetry Awards, 2016 Knightville Poetry Contest, and 2016 Edwin Markham Poetry Award. She has a new poetry collection manuscript, *Mother of Exiles*, which furthers her exploration of the Filipino diaspora and immigrant experience that she began in her first poetry collection.

The anthology, *Others Will Enter The Gates: Immigrant Poets on Poetry, Influences, and Writing in America* (Black Lawrence Press, 2015), features her essay, "Gatekeepers and Gatecrashers in Contemporary American Poetry: Reflections of a Filipino Immigrant Poet in the United States."

She and her husband have two children and two dogs and live on an enchanted island in the Puget Sound.

Readers may follow her on VictoriaGSmith.com; Facebook, Author Victoria G. Smith; Twitter, @AuthorVGSmith; and Instagram, victoriagsmithauthor.

ABBREVIATED BIBLIOGRAPHY

The The following is a partial, non-exhaustive bibliography of the research materials that informed the writing of *The Thomasite*, in addition to the author's personal knowledge and experience of Philippine and U.S. culture and history:

Thomasites Centennial Project. *To Islands Far Away: The Story of the Thomasites and Their Journey to the Philippines*. Manila, Philippines: Public Affairs Section, U.S. Embassy, Manila, 2001.

Fee, Mary Helen. *A Woman's Impression of the Philippines*. Chicago: A. C. McClurg & Co, 1912.

Racelis, Mary, and Ick, Judy Celine (eds.). *Bearers of Benevolence: The Thomasites and Public Education in the Philippines*. Pasig City, Philippines: Anvil Publishing Inc., 2001.

Shay, Michael E. (ed.). *A Civilian in Lawton's 1899 Philippine Campaign: The Letters of Robert E. Carter*. Missouri: University of Missouri Press, 2013.

Worcester, Dean C. *The Philippine Islands and Their People*. New York, U.S.A.: The Macmillan Company, 1901.

de Quesada, Alejandro, and Walsh, Stephen (illustrator). *The Spanish-American War and Philippine Insurrection*. Oxford, U.K.: Osprey Publishing, 2007.

Guerrero, Milagros Camayon. *Luzon at War: Contradictions in Philippine Society 1898-1902*. Mandaluyong City, Philippines: Anvil Publishing Inc., 2015.

Best, Jonathan. *A Philippine Album: American Era Photographs 1900-1930*. Makati, Philippines: Bookmark Inc., 1998.

Sta. Maria, Felice Prudente. *The Governor-General's Kitchen Philippine Culinary Vignettes and Period Recipes: 1521-1935*. Mandaluyong City, Philippines: Anvil Publishing Inc., 2006.

Parco de Castro, María Eloisá G. *Carlos L. Quirino's Old Manila*. Quezon City, Philippines: Vibal Foundation, Inc., 2016.

Souza, George Bryan, and Turley, Jeffrey S. *The Boxer Codex: Transcription and Translation of an Illustrated Late Sixteenth-Century Spanish Manuscript Concerning the Geography, Ethnography and History of the Pacific, South-East Asia and East Asia*. Leiden, The Netherlands: Koninklijke Brill NV, 2016.

Capistrano-Baker, Florina H. *Multiple Originals, Original Multiples*. Makati City, Philippines: Ayala Foundation, Inc., 2004.

Liliuokalani, Queen of Hawaii. *Hawaii's Story by Hawaii's Queen*. Boston, U.S.A.: Lee and Shepard Publishers, 1898. https://digital.library.upenn.edu/women/liliuokalani/hawaii/hawaii.html

Mintz, Malcolm W. *Bikol Dictionary*. Honolulu, Hawaii: University of Hawaii Press, 1971. https://scholar-space.manoa.hawaii.edu/server/api/core/bitstreams/e8cd63fb-3acc-4c23-a197-66be6865ffbd/content

Javier, Niccolo. *The Rigodon de Honor*. 2008. http://kulang-sa-tulog.blogspot.com/2008/03/rigodon-de-honor.html

Eugenio, Damiana L. "Asuang Steals Fire From Gugurang," in Philippine Folk Literature. http://bicolanomythsofgodsandmonsters.blogspot.com/2016/11/asuang-deity-of-evil-and-chaos.html

SNAC (Social Networks and Archival Context). *Kobbe, William A. (William August), 1840-1931*. https://snaccooperative.org/ark:/99166/w65c64x6

Rydell, Robert W. Soundtracks of Empire: "The White Man's Burden," the war in the Philippines, the "Ideals of America," and tin pan alley. *European Journal of American Studies*, 2012. https://journals.openedition.org/ejas/9712

Harris, Charles Kassel. *Chas. K. Harris' Complete Songster*. Harvard University, Cambridge: F. J. Drake, 1903. https://www.google.com/books/edition/Chas_K_Harris_Complete_Songster

Willard Lossinger's Music Channel, Chas. K. Harris' "Ma Filipino Babe" Baritone Ukulele 2015 07 10, https://www.youtube.com/@willardlosingersmusicchann569

"I'll Take You Home Again Kathleen" History & Lyrics. https://www.liveabout.com/ill-take-you-home-again-kathleen-3552918

College Physicians of Philadelphia. *The History of Vaccines*. https://www.historyofvaccines.org/timeline#EVT_85

www.ingramcontent.com/pod-product-compliance
Lightning Source LLC
Chambersburg PA
CBHW061610210726
48287CB00001B/73